Mike,

May God bl—
as you show His lov—
to others through your
genuine caring heart.

In Christ Jesus,

Jay

THE CURRENT AND THE OUTCAST

JAY ALLEN

WestBow Press books may be ordered through booksellers or by contacting:

WestBow Press
A Division of Thomas Nelson & Zondervan
1663 Liberty Drive
Bloomington, IN 47403
www.westbowpress.com
1 (866) 928-1240

ISBN: 978-1-5127-0035-0 (sc)
ISBN: 978-1-5127-0037-4 (hc)
ISBN: 978-1-5127-0036-7 (e)

Print information available on the last page.

WestBow Press rev. date: 01/30/2016

There are two equal and opposite errors into which our race can fall about the devils. One is to disbelieve in their existence. The other is to believe, and to feel an excessive and unhealthy interest in them. They themselves are equally pleased by both errors, and hail a materialist or magician with the same delight.

—C. S. Lewis, *The Screwtape Letters*

AUTHOR'S NOTE

The purpose of this work is to encourage readers in their relationships with the Lord Jesus Christ in an engaging way. I hope to pull back the veil on a few worldly things that evil forces use to keep people from a life in Christ. I do not believe that there is a demon behind every tree! But I do believe that many of us are blind to the evil forces constantly assaulting us. I am not an expert on Satan and demons and am portraying them in a way to make a point via dramatic effect. Please permit me this liberty and forgive me any exaggerations, knowing that I absolutely do not want to glorify evil in any way. All glory is only for God in Christ Jesus.

INTRODUCTION: THE CURRENT

There once was created a being so brilliant and dazzling that he stood at the top of all God's created beings. And like other created beings, this one had the gift of free will from God. In His perfect love, God did not force His creation to love Him; rather, He allowed him to choose to reflect love back to his author.

This being was called Lucifer. When Lucifer observed the glory of God, he coveted it and used the gift of free will to steal the glory for his own. But a created being cannot steal from its Creator, and the once high being was evicted from heaven and was conquered at the cross by Christ Jesus the Lord. Evicted, that ancient Serpent, called the Devil and Satan, injected God's created mankind with the venom of his own sin. Conquered, that furious Dragon now wages war against them. He has set up his evil kingdom in the realms of mankind and established a government for the purpose of evil calling to evil for destruction. The evil forces entice the sin nature within men. Where the evil flesh of men ends and the evil influence of a demon begins is invisible to man's eye. But like vipers hidden in crevices and camouflaged in grass, the threat of this danger is not diminished by its invisibility. It's heightened by it.

Satan and his demonic government stealthily sway the tides in the functioning of worldly things. Ordering his demons to sabotage the good that God intended for man, they appeal to man's existing sin nature and sweep him obliviously along in a treacherous current that carries him farther away from God. Those who resist this current that buoys the masses who hate loving and love hating find themselves outcasts in their own world.

PROLOGUE:
A HISTORIC GRUDGE

Two sat in the truck that late spring afternoon, and yet three were present. The driver was a seventeen-year-old, fair-haired boy known for his uprightness and innocence. It was ironic that these admirable characteristics prevented the inclusion he wanted from others into the lifestyle he did not.

His Achilles's heel, like that of so many other teenage boys, was a pretty face that could launch a thousand ships. This time his juvenile crush was on a small, brown-eyed brunette—Kate Castle—who was as wild as ragweed. She was lost and looked to whispering tigers to scratch the itch she found impossible to reach. One of her attempts last month—not that it was her most recent—had resulted in a small but life-shattering problem. When her faithful monthly visitor, which assured her with its nagging demands that life was still okay, stopped coming, she knew that another more demanding person was about to enter the picture. Hopeless, she now turned to an assassin of a doctor to make her whole again.

The third person in the truck was an uninvited and ambitious demon. He sat between the two kids, massaging the girl's neck with his filthy, clawed hands and blowing puffs of smoke into her mind. With his tail, he covered the boy's eyes to distort his vision and prevent any unnecessary involvement.

"Are you sure you don't want me to come in with you?"

"No, I'll be fine. Just come back in about an hour or so."

"I think I'll just sit here and wait. You know, just in case you finish up early."

"Thanks. You're so sweet."

The girl got out of the truck and moved nervously down the cracked walkway, neglected like the intentionally low-profile building it led to. Everything about the place told the casual observer that there was nothing to see here. She paused but didn't look back. She stared at the heavy steel door in front of her. It seemed to come to life and accuse her: "Murderer!"

An explosion of tears welled up from within, but she turned stone-faced. Kate seized the handle of her accuser, heaved the door behind her, and moved determinedly through the threshold.

The boy watched the girl's mechanical steps and saw her hesitate at the door, doubtful of her decision. He furrowed his brow in confused frustration. What else could he do to help? With his eyes opened—he would be too embarrassed if someone noticed him sitting there alone with his eyes closed—he prayed. He prayed for the girl, for safety of the procedure, and for the little spirit within her, which, woven with flesh for only a couple of months, would now be separated from its chance at life on earth.

Just fifteen minutes had passed when the small girl pushed the giant, steel-hinged accuser open again. It accused her again: "Coward!" She jogged back to the truck, hopped in, and said, "Drive! Just go!"

"What happened?" the boy asked as he hurriedly started the truck and threw it into reverse, thinking someone may come after her.

"I'm keeping my baby," she resolutely replied. "I don't know what happened. I had my mind made up when I went in, but then, all of a sudden, I just felt like everything would be okay. I felt like this baby has a purpose ... like I have a purpose." Tears—a mix of sorrow, fear, shame, relief, and love—broke through the windows of that beautiful facade and washed down her cheeks.

"What can I do to help?"

"Just promise me you'll always be my friend."

The boy smiled and nodded. He could do that.

The demon was left behind at the clinic, still stunned by the burst of light that had struck him. All the effort and time he had spent on this one girl was lost. He had been tremendously successful in the past thousands of years. This one girl was to be the starting point of his ingenious plan to set in motion a domino effect of evil that would echo across eternity and position himself for an even higher appointment. He had spent decades watching, waiting, crafting, manipulating, and fighting. Now, in one sudden, unexplained burst of light, *it was all gone.*

Gathering himself, he flew toward the truck and took up his position between the two. He sniffed the boy and smelled a horrible fragrance; it was the incense of prayer. The demon writhed in fury like a tornado. Had he been tangible, he would've destroyed the entire truck. He uttered a vow: "You will pay for this, little praying boy. I will crush you, Jay." This written in his stone, Spaw returned to exact his vengeance on other demons, stealing what he could to make up for years of lost climbing.

1

A Current Discovery

Thirty years later

Jack Allen was a typical fifteen-year-old boy. Fair-haired and blue-eyed with pale skin that refused to tan, he was average in his lanky five-foot-two-inch stature and developing coordination, but what he lacked physically he made up for in mental aptitude. Schoolwork kept him occupied, but his mind had plenty of time to meander, observe, and think over the course of the day. He wasn't naturally charming, but his kindness was obvious to all. He seemed to have been born with the desire to help others. He was tagged as a nice boy, which didn't always attract the attractive girls, nor did it get him in the in crowd.

As he lay back in his bed, ready for sleep, his mind picked up the demonic horror movie he had just finished watching. Jack examined it well beyond the director's intent, contemplating a theological question rare to most teens: How did Satan, an invisible demon, exert his power in the physical world? His eyes closed heavily, sleep washed over him, and he dreamed.

—◦◦◦◦—

The brightness in Jack's eyes dimmed. He looked up, the darkness around him lightening into dawn. He found himself standing in a wooded area under the deep shadow of a canopy consisting mostly of oaks and pines, which filtered the angled rays, progressively revealing more shades of green and brown. The air was as cool and dense as the earth beneath his feet, which was covered in a variety of decaying leaves. They filled the air with a stagnant, moldy odor that seemed to be consistent with the picture developing before his eyes.

It must be fall, he thought. The trees seemed to be in the midst of exchanging their summer coats for the barren nakedness of a winter soon to come. Jack wondered at the oddness of it—they take off their coats for the cold winter and put them back on again for the hot summer. He didn't linger much on this trivial observation, for a movement caught his eye—a little red bird flitting past. As it passed, Jack was sure he heard the bird whisper something that sounded like "Here it comes." Standing in mild disbelief, Jack heard a swelling of noise rustling through the branches. Before he could blink, several hundred more red birds flitted past him, all whispering the same words: "Here it comes. Here it comes. Here it comes."

Here what comes? he thought—or maybe he said it out loud. One bird suddenly hovered by his head and stuck its beak so close to Jack's ear that he actually felt its breath when it whispered, "The Current." Its words delivered, the bird vanished into the woods to rejoin the streaking red cloud.

The shadows of the woods seemed to be growing deeper and darker. The remaining leaves on the trees seemed to be trembling, and the air became noticeably cooler. Just as he was about to be gripped by fear, he saw what appeared to be a beautiful white bird floating toward him. It landed silently and delicately upon a thick branch of a nearby oak tree bearded in moss. The tree shuddered and, as if bowing in reverence for the majestic aura radiating from its new guest, shed its leaves completely. As the leaves drifted downward, adding to the existing collage on the floor, both the tree and the boy drew a lengthy inhale and held it. He supposed the tree, like him, was awestruck.

To describe this creature fully would extend beyond the capability of words, but it mostly resembled an elegant and graceful swan. Its feathers were so pure and clean that if it were to snow, the two would be perfectly matched. While its body and neck were long and smooth, its head was like that of a hawk, with a beak hooked and sharply pointed. Its legs too were akin to those of a hawk in that the feet had powerful talons. The eyes were a mesmerizing ruby red, and when Jack stared into them, he could see the light of a flame flickering in its spirit. The combination made this creature seem like it might be a mistake of nature, but somehow, the combination of features seemed in perfect harmony. With its blend of beauty and strength, much like ancient civilizations' depiction of the Greek goddess Athena, Jack found that both were captivating to his eyes.

Who are you? he wondered, a sense of complete acceptance gently washing over his mind. At that moment, nothing else mattered, and he completely let himself go. His whole body relaxed and seemed to be caressed and carried up into the heights on a warm breeze. "You have found me," he heard the soft whisper of a girl as he drifted farther and farther up.

3

2

A VIOLENT EDDY

Jack's eyelids popped open as the shrill *gritos* of Mexican music blared through his clock radio. *Anna Claire has been jacking with my stuff again,* he thought, *or Avery!* He remembered a small but insulting jab he'd given Avery yesterday. He had stayed up well past midnight pumping beats of music into his ears and was tired, but the burst of the same angry adrenaline from the tunes that had pushed back sleep came rushing back at the thought of his sister's meddling and pushed back sleep again. He launched his body into his daily school routine. *I know, I know, the bus will be here in thirty minutes,* he thought, mentally practicing his reply to his dad's everyday, well-intended prodding of "Jack, you'd better hurry or you're gonna miss the bus!" Jay was a good dad, but his insistence on routine and punctuality could get annoying, especially after a bad night of sleep.

Jack stumbled to the bathroom, lifted the lid on the commode, commended himself, "I'm such a good brother to always put the seat down for the girls," and relieved himself from the night. "What kind of a weird dream was that?" he mused. He tried to recall the specifics: the woods, the whispers of "Here it comes," and then the

4

white bird. He glanced sideways into the mirror of the medicine cabinet and replayed the encounter in his mind. "You have found me"—but whom had he found? Who was it that he'd been looking for? And had he lost her now that he was awake? Question after question whirled through his mind. "Rachel" was the soft reply whispered to him.

Jack became aggravated when his deep and pleasant thoughts were interrupted by his dad's call. "*¡Sí! ¡Ya voy!*" he yelled to his dad in the kitchen, knowing that for some reason his dad thought learning another language was good for him. Jay replied in Spanish, "*Que something-o!*" but Jack, not caring to understand, called back, "*¡Sí, sí!*"

As Jack passed by the girls' doors, he gently knocked, opened them both, and announced from the hallway, "It's time to wake up!" The girls both buried their heads under their pillows and simultaneously yelled, "Get out of here!" The revenge for messing with his alarm had been exacted; they didn't have to wake up for another forty-five minutes. Jack laughed loud enough for the girls to hear him and started down the hall. Pausing midstep, he felt as if he was being watched. He looked back to the girls' rooms, but no one was there. He looked toward the laundry room— no one there, either. Frozen in the moment, the wonderful feeling of his dream washed over him again. He felt happy, free at last. For once, he felt like he was his own person.

"What's for breakfast?" Jack asked when he got to the kitchen.

Jay replied, "Whatever you fix!" Jack wondered what had happened to the days when his dad would trip all over himself to make sure he had a healthy start to the day.

"What do you have after school today?"

"Nothing special, just going to Bobby's house. And yes, we will be playing video games."

"I think one day you'll be sorry for putting that stuff in your mind. You can't even imagine how all of that killing, violence, and filthy stuff impacts your spirit."

"Don't start, Dad. I can handle it. I know the difference between fiction and reality—it's not like we're gonna go live it out or any stupid thing like that!"

"Son, at this age you're your own person, and ultimately you're accountable to God, not me. You know that."

"Yes, sir," Jack muttered, but he thought, *Yeah, yeah!* accompanied by a secretive eye roll indicating his real feelings on the topic. The sound of a loud airbrake pumped outside, and Jack started out the door.

"Bye, have a good day!" yelled Jay.

Jack jogged across the living room, slammed the door behind him, and headed out without a returned word or gesture. It felt good for Jack to ignore his dad sometimes—it made him feel like less of a kid and more of his own person. Jack heard a voice and turned his head toward their neighbor's house.

"You haven't lost me, Jack. I'll always be here with you."

He focused his eyes below the car next door to see if feet were on the other side. He saw no one and wondered, *Am I hearing things?* To this thought, there was surprisingly a reply: "I'm not your imagination, Jack. I'm here."

Okay, okay, this is weird! he thought as he sped up his steps and turned his focus toward catching the bus without looking like a complete nerd as he did it.

When Jack arrived at school, he saw his friend Bobby Glenn already there, his head bowed to his iPad. "What's up?" Jack asked as he took his usual seat next to him on the floor.

Bobby, without looking up, answered, "*Nada*, just trying to snipe this dude from Tallahassee. He's the dude that made that beast video on YouTube where he shot those cats with an AK-47. And now I'm gonna snipe—dang it!"

"What happened?" Jack asked.

Finally looking up, Bobby replied, discouraged, "He called in a drone. Now I'm dead."

Changing to a happier subject, Jack said, "Dude, I hear Jake's parents are leaving town this Friday, and he's going to get some guys over for an all-nighter of *MW7*. You going?"

Looking hopeful, Bobby said, "Not sure. First I'll need to think up some good reason for going there so my parents won't get suspicious or anything."

Jack nodded. "Yeah, me too. My dad knows his parents really well, and it'd be very easy for him to text them to check up on me. He doesn't get it. I'm fifteen now. I know how to live my life, and I don't need his *wisdom*," he said, sarcasm etched into the last word. "I mean, what wisdom? He did this same stuff when he was young. He even tells us about it."

Looking amused, Bobby responded, "He tells you what he did when he was our age? That's pretty cool."

To ensure it was clear that his dad was not cool, Jack added, "Well, it's not like he's bragging or anything. He actually tells us to show that he's been there, done that, and wouldn't do it again."

"Well, that's kind of cool too."

"Yeah, I guess so," Jack admitted.

"Heck, my parents act like they were so perfect when they were young. I know that's not the truth, because I talked to my aunt once after she got drunk, and she told me some things my mom did. Let's just say I'm a saint compared to her! Do you know she has a tattoo of a swan on her butt? Oh, wait, I've got to stop. I'm completely grossed out!"

The bell rang, interrupting Bobby's story, and Jack was relieved because he really didn't want to hear any more about Bobby's mom's crazy childhood life.

The sound of excited voices swelled across the school commons. Jack looked at Bobby with eager surprise, and both started running toward the upheaval.

A mob of kids was huddled around four guys. Evidently, one guy had a new girlfriend, and one had a new ex-girlfriend and two friends to help him take out his anger at being alone again. The new ex-boyfriend finished a verbal tirade and started pushing the new boyfriend, who quickly realized that he was outnumbered. Seeing him glance backward for an escape or a friend to help, the two friends of the new ex slid behind him, grabbing his arms to prevent any retreat.

All this in place, the new ex started swinging. The first punch was a haymaker, landing on the new boyfriend's left ear. The victim staggered backward and turned to run, but the two friends gripped his arms tighter. Already at the point of wanting mercy, the victim looked at the attacker and started a plea. The response was punch number two, connecting with his nose and sending his head jolting backward and then wobbling a bit to the right. A third blow was delivered to the victim's unprotected gut, causing him to hunch forward.

The victim's full weight pulling toward the floor, the two friends released his arms to let him fall to his shame. But before his fall was complete, the attacker delivered one last uppercut to his cheek. The victim lay helplessly on the ground, his hands covering his bleeding face. Like sharks whipped into a blood frenzy, a few others, who may or may not have known the victim, continued the assault with several kicks, accompanied by some loud cusswords and laughter.

The mob of less aggressive bystanders weren't doing anything to help the kid on the ground, which would have spoiled the entertainment— they just stood there, laughing and yelling, "Fight! Fight! Fight!" It was as if they were being swept away in the enjoyment of seeing this guy getting pummeled, just like being in the front row at a UFC fight. Without much thought, Jack and Bobby joined the mob, yelling, "Fight! Fight! Fight!" They were part of something big and exciting, and it felt good. Jack looked around to take in the moment. He saw forty other laughing and scowling faces, all united in a common, violent bond. They all understood one another and all accepted one another.

"Go with it, Jack," a voice whispered in his mind. And he did. The three attackers had their fill of admiration from the mob and, now worried about any consequences from the school cops, put on a normal appearance and disappeared into the horde. The mob, however, wasn't quite ready to let the mouse out of the trap. Three new attackers approached the victim and delivered a few kicks apiece, some to the legs, some to the back, and a couple to the back of the head. Their mission accomplished, they too blended back into the mob. The victim, who was now in a growing puddle of blood, tried to let the pain settle before he attempted to stand. Two others persisted with verbal attacks, taunting and ridiculing him as he lay there. Jack compulsively joined in the fun, yelling, "They kicked your butt! You better watch out, or I'll kick it too!"

At this point, the victim didn't seem to hear much of anything. Jack felt a twinge of guilt turn in his gut, but the feeling of physical domination was way too strong for him to even consider dwelling on something as insignificant as guilt. Bobby and Jack walked to class, both reveling in the excitement of the beating and talking about how one day they ought to give an annoying kid named Johari a beat down like that.

A kid named Tom, whom Jack recognized from church, passed through the dispersing mob that still crowded the hallway. Tom had a grimace on his face, and his head moved from side to side as if he disapproved of the morning's action, which everyone else had so elatedly met. Noticing this, Jack nudged Bobby and pointed at Tom, saying, "Tom is so weird. That's why he's such an outcast."

3

A NEW CHANNEL OPENS

Faith Sparks was only fourteen going on fifteen, but between her appearance and the sophistication of her character, she seemed more comparable to a young woman of eighteen. She was naturally striking in every way: beauty, brains, and athleticism. Her hair was a deep shade of brown, just one shade removed from black. Her eyes sometimes appeared gray, sometimes blue, but always had a deep glistening in them that caused others to pause in their passing glances. Standing five foot ten, she was among the taller crowd in her class, including the boys, but she was not the thinnest. She was dense with a feminine muscularity, but had it not been for her regimented workouts, she could very easily tip the scales quite a few more pounds than most would be happy with. But she was comfortable with herself. Needless to say, Faith was gorgeous. When out shopping, it wasn't uncommon for her to hear comments like "Have you ever thought about modeling?" If others' view of her had been a mirror, Faith would've seen a princess, but she used a different mirror and saw an ordinary girl.

If beauty was one strike, Faith's second strike was her intelligence. Her grades reflected this and indicated that she'd only be spending a few years in high school before going straight on to Harvard, Yale, or perhaps Oxford. While many kids of above-average intelligence become too arrogant to mine the knowledge of studying, Faith never considered herself too smart to grasp every bit of it she could. The result was that she permanently retained every piece. Rarely, if ever, did she utter the words "I don't remember" or "I don't know," because she did remember and she did know. And once she grasped and held the pieces, she could easily assemble them into the frames of logic, reasoning, creativity, and intellect to put them to their best use.

Faith's third strike was her athleticism. In elementary school, she had played every sport she could—soccer, volleyball, basketball, and tennis—and she even did a little karate. It became evident to the various league officials, with the support of parents who wanted to see their own daughters actually have a chance at the spotlight, that she had more talent than the other girls in her age group, so they would force her to "play up" a couple of levels with kids older than herself. This brought her a lot of attention from coaches and a lot of snubbing from parents and, correspondingly, their daughters.

By the time she had reached high school, she had dedicated herself to one sport, soccer, and as a freshman, she had already proven herself the best varsity soccer player in the district. This caused the all-too-familiar social pattern to continue. Attention and letters promising a full-ride from college coaches were already pouring in, and along with them came the ignoring and snubbing of her teammates, who felt it unfair that such a young girl should be blessed with such skill.

These three strikes of beauty, brains, and athleticism may seem like every kid's dream, but the reality was that it caused Faith to be left out—out of the sacred social game that all kids played to figure out where they fit in and what role they could call their own, whether good or bad. Girls didn't want to hang out with her because she was too pretty and presented too much competition for the attention of boys they secretly—or, more likely, openly—liked. Classmates didn't want to hang out with her because she was too smart and presented too much competition for the praise of teachers. Teammates didn't want to hang out with her because she was too good and presented too much competition for their individual glory.

Nonetheless, Faith refused to tone down her giftedness just to appease others. She wasn't arrogant—she was as humble as they came—she just wanted to be accepted for who she was. While almost all her relationships were more of a friendly acquaintance type, she did hang out from time to time with Nicki and Amber Tingle, the twin girls who lived across the street. Faith had been their neighbor most of her life, so Nicki and Amber knew her well enough to know that she was "just Faith" and wasn't out to take anything away from them.

On an ordinary Friday evening, Faith was in the front drive sitting on the tailgate of her dad's truck talking to her brother, Matt. The conversation was around who Matt should ask to the homecoming dance. He had a dilemma and trusted Faith's intuition to help him solve it. On one hand, Ashlyn was crazy about him and would be excited to go with him. She was cute but could sometimes be a bit bossy. Keira, on the other hand, was both pretty and kindhearted; not to mention Matt had a crush on her since his sophomore year.

"I hear what you're saying, Faith, but I'm just scared that she will say no. Then what?" Matt asked, showing his underlying frailty.

Faith put her hand on Matt's leg and looked tenderly into his eyes to reinforce the sincerity of her answer. "Look, Matt, who cares if she says no? Your pride may be stung for a day or so, but you'll get through it. If you like Keira, then ask her. Regardless of what happens you can always take me! I'd be proud to go with you!"

Matt smiled at the reassurance. "Yeah, yeah! Okay, I'm gonna go text her."

"No … You are going to go *call* her."

Matt's big smile widened even more. "Okay, okay! I'm going to go *call* her!"

Matt jumped off of the tailgate and patted Faith lovingly on the head like a nice little sister on his way inside. Faith was swinging her legs back and forth and wondering what Keira's answer would be when she saw the girls across the street come out of the house.

"Hey, Faith!" they called.

"Hey," she replied.

"Wanna come over? This is our cousin, Clara," they continued.

Faith slid off of the truck, slipped on her flip-flops, walked the twenty steps across the warm but cooling pavement, and introduced herself. As this evolved into a conversation, a discussion about the latest zombie movie arose. Faith had heard of it but hadn't seen it yet; she didn't have any friends to go with.

"I thought it was pretty scary," Nicki said. "I mean, think about all of those dead people trying to bite you. That's just gross! And even though everyone knows that dead people can't come back to life, it still creeps me out."

Just then, Faith's dad slammed shut the tailgate on his truck across the street. Faith jumped with a gasp and turned her head, seeking out the source of the noise. The girls laughed, and Faith smiled to try to cover her racing heart. Faith wasn't sure why, but all her life, she was as easily spooked as a newborn fawn in a wolf-infested forest. It was just embarrassing.

Clara continued the conversation. "Dead people can come back to life. I've seen it."

"What do you mean?" asked Amber.

"Once I was staying over at this girl's house. I didn't really know her that well, because she was new to town and then moved a few months later—I think her dad was in the army or something. But anyway, her mom could talk to people who'd died. She said she was a medium or channel or something. I didn't believe her at first, but then some people came over, and they all got around a table and held hands, and her mom started calling out to the spirit of some Greek god, like in the movies. Then, after about five minutes, her voice changed, and she started talking like she was the daughter the people used to have who had died of a drug overdose."

"No way!" said Amber.

"It's true!" retorted Clara.

"Let's try it!" said Nicki.

They all looked at Faith for her response. "Uh, okay" were the words that came from her mouth, but in her heart she was saying, *Please don't!* During the discussion, the sun had set, casting darkness across the neighborhood and prompting the mosquitoes to wake up and start finding people to pester. The girls moved single file into the house and then into Nicki's bedroom.

"Okay, turn the lights off," said Clara.

"No way," replied Amber. "This is creepy enough. I want to see if some zombie or something is charging at me from out of the closet."

"Okay, just turn on that little lamp, then," said Clara, pointing to a reading light in the corner by the dresser. The girls assembled themselves in a circle and held hands. "Okay, who do you know who's dead?" asked Clara.

The girls drew a blank. None of them really knew anyone who had died—just a distant aunt or grandparent who had died when they were babies.

"Okay, I'll just ask for anyone who is out there," said Clara. She started in a haunting voice, "Oh mighty powers from beyond, we come before you to summon Zeus, Athena, or Justin Bieber—if he happens to be around, we'll take him!" All the girls gave a laugh. Faith thought that the little experiment would turn back into just harmless conversation, but Clara continued, "Okay, let's concentrate. Oh mighty gods of the ancient days, bring down your power and prove to us that you are real!"

Nicki's phone bleeped with a text. "Sorry!" she said.

"You're too popular for your own good!" said Amber.

"Hey, I can't help it if I've got it," Nicki replied. The phone silenced, the girls again focused their attention on Clara, and the mood became serious. There was a knock at the bedroom door, all the girls glanced up, and Faith noticeably shook and instinctively pulled back her hands to cover her mouth.

"Y'all want some ice cream?" asked Nicki and Amber's mom.

"Not right now!" Nicki and Amber replied together.

"You'd think somebody doesn't want us doing this," commented Faith. The twins each reached for Faith's hands again, and she reluctantly took theirs. As they moved their eyes back to Clara, they noticed a strange look had come over her face, and her eyes had a strange stare to them. Faith thought that she was a very good actress—until she started to speak. Clara's voice had indeed changed. It wasn't intentionally haunting; it was pleasant yet powerful—which was haunting.

"Who is it that calls out to the spirits?" Clara spoke.

"Um, it's four witches who seek enlightenment," replied Nicki. She'd seen something like this in a wizard movie on TV.

Scared to trembling, Faith loosened her grip on Nicki and Amber's hands, but they held fast to hers.

"I am a spirit guide and will help you as long as you are willing," the voice said.

"Okay, tell us who you are so we can see if we want to take this journey," said Nicki.

A slight scowl came over Clara's face, and then it returned to a peaceful expression. "My name is Rachel. I'm from Greece and used to serve in the temple of Athena, the beautiful and powerful goddess who is worshipped around the world and helps many armies defeat their enemies," said the voice.

"How old are you?" asked Nicki.

"I was only sixteen years old when I died from illness. My spirit is now twenty-five hundred years old."

17

Faith was petrified. If this was a joke, she was buying it completely. She wanted to go home but was too scared to move.

Nicki continued the interview. "That's a long time. What do you do now that you don't serve in Athena's temple?"

"When I left my mortal body and entered the paradise of spirits, I began to serve Athena herself," Rachel said.

"You mean Athena is real and still alive?" inquired Nicki.

"Most certainly. The mortal world you live in is only a womb. Real life begins once you are set free. Everyone will take the journey and come here eventually. Here you can do nothing wrong. Everyone is accepted. Everyone is love."

Faith's wits arose enough to utter a prayer in the quietest whisper. "Jesus, help me get out of this!"

As soon as the air carried the words past her lips, Clara slumped forward into the circle of hands, and her head bumped against the soft carpet. Nicki grabbed her, one hand on her arm and the other gripping at her back, to help her back to a sitting position. Clara looked disoriented, and her eyes seemed foggy.

"Okay, not doing that again," mumbled Clara.

"What do you mean?" asked Nicki.

"I heard the whole thing," Clara remarked. "It's like I was sitting next to you, watching my own body with someone else's voice. I was trying to stop, but it's like I was tied up and gagged."

"Why did she go away?" asked Nicki.

"I don't know. All I know was that I felt the ropes and gag disappear, and I jumped up as quickly as I could. I'll never ever do that again," Clara concluded.

Nicki, on the other hand, had her curiosity piqued. The girls stared around at each other and decided that it'd be better if they kept this little secret to themselves. Faith used the dinner excuse and left the girls to eat ice cream on their own. As she walked back to her house, she whispered one more prayer: "Thank You, Jesus. I'm so sorry I let that happen. Thank You, Jesus."

4

A Current Crafter

The sudden shock of hearing the name of Jesus caused Spaw to flee upward, leaving his naive peasants abruptly. Trying to get His name out of his thoughts, he quickly looked around his wide-ranging territory and found Intrigued, one of his subjects. Summoning him, Spaw slashed him across the face with his talon, causing a small cloud of ash to puff in the air. Intrigued bowed low in submission to his superior demon.

"Four peasants entered my territory tonight and opened themselves up. Three of them have hidden, but one named Nicki has left a channel of curiosity open. Find her, charm her, and drag her deeper down," commanded Spaw as he shook off the last shivers caused by the name of Jesus. With his face radiating in pain, Intrigued immediately and obediently moved in the direction from where Spaw had come. Within the hour, he had found Nicki and, finding no light, imperceptibly fastened himself as a leech under her armpit. Once there, he began to inject his toxic whispers into her mind.

Spaw moved about in the upper realm of the territory, ensuring that his deceptive strategies were being implemented without error in any part. From his vantage point, he could see the millions of peasants who hosted his subjects. A good peasant could host several hundred subjects, but most of the time, only one or two could do the task. Weaker subjects were limited in their charms, but stronger ones could manifest multiple snares. As for Spaw, his ambition taught him to weave several hundred types of binding cords.

Rebellion approached low to Spaw as he returned from roaming his region. "Forever power, mighty Spaw," he said submissively. Spaw made no reply, indicating that Rebellion could speak. "I've found an open peasant named Jack, and—"

"Leave him alone!" Spaw interrupted. "I've already met him and am taking him as my own. His dad is a praying man who has boldly defied me, and his service to the Enemy has begged my wrath. We'll see how long he stands firm once I've finished with his son."

Rebellion pressed his gaze downward, expecting a blow, but when one did not come, he carefully lifted it up again to find that Spaw had vanished.

5

BEHIND THE SURFACE

It was a Sunday night, and based on the social media traffic, everyone was getting into "Sunday night rest before Monday morning test" mode. Jack had just finished the last geometry problem of his homework and was letting his mind go numb to recuperate. Lying back on his bed in the twisted sheets, he stared up at the ceiling fan, which was turning on low speed. He tried to follow a single blade as it turned round and round, but his eyes were too tired to have much success. He let them relax and stare blurredly at the hypnotic fan. They were getting heavy, closing for a second and then jerking open again. His thoughts were starting to get weird as some thoughts do in those moments between wake and sleep when the mind starts to slide into dream mode. With eyes shut and breathing at an even rhythm, he entered a dream—or at least what felt like one.

-oooo-

There he was again, continuing his upward float toward the beautiful white bird. As he drifted closer and closer to her, she gently glided off of the branch toward the ground. His upward motion was checked, and he started descending, magnetically drawn to her movement. His eyes became his guide, and wherever they looked, his body seemed to drift that direction. In his descent with the bird, he saw a full-length mirror standing on a bare spot of ground.

The bird, almost in a hover, entered into the mirror as if slipping into a pool of the most serene water. As she passed through the reflective liquid, her aura erupted into a brilliant illumination, and he could no longer see her. As he narrowed his eyes to see through the fountain of light, he smelled an aroma as fresh as a honeysuckle vine and heard a rhythmic humming sound that caused him to shiver. He inhaled the illuminating vapors and felt his lungs burn, tingle, and then take on a sense of refreshment that he'd never known before. Fear—perhaps of something new or of losing this bliss—shot through his being and almost brought him to tears.

As he recovered his senses ("Real men don't cry, do they?"), the brilliance dissipated, and he could make out the image of a girl in the mirror. Her appearance was so captivating that it made her age difficult to guess, but he estimated that she was still in her teens. Her hair was black and flowed about her shoulders with the strength of a galloping horse's mane. Her eyes were as deep, dark, and mysteriously frightening as a lake on a moonless night. Had it not been for several speckles of red, he couldn't have seen any outline of pupil at all. Her complexion resembled the fairness of a half-moon, which perfectly displayed the deep red of her lips and nails. She was arrayed in a wispy white dress that seemed to ebb and flow in the currents of the air. She was a model of perfected beauty.

Feeling his feet grounded again, he briefly cast a glance downward and moved one of them to make sure he was completely down. Looking back up at the mirror, he could see his reflection, only all his features seemed exaggerated. His eyes were a deeper blue, his hair a lighter blond, his skin a golden tan, his body taller and more muscular. He reminded himself of a Greek demigod. Just as he began to wonder if this was really his reflection or someone else was looking out at him, he saw the girl behind the mirror. Her right hand was extended to him, and with her left she motioned him to come closer. She needn't motion to him at all—her whole appearance invited him in, and he longed to go in.

He approached the mirror and touched it. He was expecting to feel glass, water, metal, or something, but there was nothing there. It was just an illusion of a mirror. Then he did feel something. He felt a cool and tender grasp of his hand as the girl drew him into the illusion. The moment he passed the portal, the girl slipped her arm around him and gave him the hug of a grateful friend. She laid her head against his shoulder, and he glanced back at the mirror and saw what appeared to be his normal-looking body standing on the other side, frozen in a blank stare.

"You have found me," she said. "It's been so long, but at last you have found me."

"Who are you?" he asked.

Her eyes started to tear up. "Have you forgotten? It's me, Rachel," she said as a tear slid down her cheek.

"What a beautiful name," he marveled.

"Sit here, and I will bring you a drink," she said and floated away through the trees. Her response and tears confused him.

"I need to remember. I can't lose her again. She is so beautiful." Amid his desperation, he looked around, hoping that something would prompt his memory. Like his new image, everything seemed so exaggerated, so unreal. Much unlike the outside, all the trees were perfectly straight and had every leaf in its proper place. A few yards away from where he was now sitting down, there were patches of perfect flowers. The colors were so amazingly coordinated and the scents so well harmonized that he thought this had to be a dream. He listened and could hear a high-pitched chorus of birds chirping above a low-pitched rhythmic hum. The floor of the woods where he sat was like a velvet rug that penetrated his skin with its touch. He lay down to get the full effect and thought that if he fell asleep, he might never wake up.

This thought gave him a start, and almost instinctively, he cast another glance at the mirror and saw his statuelike, not-so-beautiful body in a now embarrassingly awkward gaze. He closed his eyes and buried his head in the plush carpet at this flash of reality. He turned, lifted his head in the opposite direction, and opened his eyes, and Rachel was once again in front of him, staring into his eyes as if she was reading his mind or trying to enter it.

"Jack," she whispered, "here is your drink. You must be so tired." She handed him a cup, and he placed it to his lips and sipped. The cup was made of a rough, ironlike metal, which made it difficult to tell what the drink was, especially since he was more accustomed to plastic. His tongue shrunk back at first contact with the liquid, and he almost gagged. Rachel firmly grasped the cup, and pressing it to his lips, she lifted the bottom to allow the liquid to pour out down his throat.

"You are so thirsty it is hard for you to drink. Relax. Let go, Jack. This will help you get better." She smiled a bit as she said these words, and another tear slipped down her cheek. He could see hope behind her eyes. His head felt light, and his eyes became heavy. His vision blurred, but he felt as if for the first time in his life he was starting to see clearly.

MUSICAL IMMERSION

Several days had passed, and Jack had been working on his legitimate excuse to spend the night at Jake's that weekend. He opted just to tell his dad that it had been a long time since he had hung out with Jake and that he had invited him and Bobby over.

Jay probed a bit and asked, "So y'all are just going to hang out?"

Jack, with his best poker face, replied, "Yep, believe it or not, Dad, a late night of video games and lots of junk food is actually really fun."

"And his parents?"

"I don't know," he said. This was true—he didn't know. "We'll be in the game room."

Jay gave a doubtful look, but since he wanted to let this be an opportunity for Jack to build trust, he approved. Jay had always told Jack that by the time he was a senior, if he'd earned enough trust, he wouldn't put a curfew on him, because if he went off to college, it'd be good to have had at least one year of making responsible, independent decisions while still at home. So periodically, when reasonable teaching moments came up, Jay gave more leeway than the kids might typically have had so that they could learn responsibility and build trust. In this case, for Jack, the timing couldn't have been better.

It was just around dinnertime when Jay dropped Jack and Bobby off at the corner gas station to make the eight-block trek to Jake's house. Neither Jack nor Bobby wanted to be seen getting dropped off like a toddler for a play date. This also worked well because it prevented Jay from trying to visit with Jake's dad and then, finding him not home, blowing the whole deal. Jack was pleased with how well his dad's naïveté worked for him.

Bobby and Jack knocked and pushed the unlocked door open. Jake was already in the midst of *MW7* artillery battle and was working on his second bag of chips.

"What up, dude?" Jack said, plopping down on the couch.

"What up?" Jake replied, extending his fist to bump a greeting to both boys. "Dude!" exclaimed Jake. "Paul just called and said he has three extra tickets to the TrashMouth concert tonight at the Rocker! Y'all wanna go?"

"But how?" asked Bobby. "We don't have a car."

"Not a problem!" Jake replied as he pulled a set of keys from his pocket and dangled them proudly in their faces.

"No way!" Jack said.

"Yes way! We play some games, eat some chow, and then, yes, we hit the town!" said Jake. So that was exactly what they did. Jake was only fifteen, but he'd been driving on the ranch since he was a kid. Motorcycles, tractors, four-wheelers, trucks—he could drive almost anything, and he'd only had a few wrecks, none of them major. With this credible record, Jack and Bobby figured the chances of something going wrong were small enough to take the risk.

The day had passed into night, indicating that it was time to head out. All three feeling like bundles of nerves (though none of them showed it), they got into the truck. Jake scored up some TrashMouth on his phone to play on the stereo—a warm-up for the real thing. Between the music and the thrill of the ride, Jack felt the adrenaline pulsing through his veins. He felt alive. He felt as if all his problems with school, his sisters, his mom and stepfather, his dad, and everything else evaporated in the current of the moment. "Let go, Jack," he felt a voice whisper in his mind, so that is exactly what he did. The volume was cranked so loud that for a moment he thought his convulsing ears were going to bleed. Jack, although familiar with the song, couldn't exactly make out the words, but he didn't need to. He could feel the flow of the music. It was lifting him up and carrying him along. To where, he didn't know or care. The floating sensation reminded him of the dream he'd had when Rachel appeared as a white bird. *Wow, this is life, and life is good!* he thought.

In what only seemed a like a split second, the truck pulled to a stop in a dimly lit parking lot. Jake shifted to park and removed the keys, and the earsplitting music instantly stopped. Every ear in the truck was ringing with pain but was overrun by the adrenaline rush of their arrival. Bobby, partly from excitement and partly because he couldn't hear the volume of his voice, screamed, "Let's rock!" The doors flung open, letting all the energy escape from the truck. The three of them slowly got down, trying to look cool and hide the boyishly excited grins hiding behind their lips.

With a smug facade, they took their place at the end of a line outside of the club. The kept quiet, not having much to say and fearing they would be judged young if overheard. They looked up and down the line for Paul and Victor. Jack began to notice the other teens, college students, and even adults in the line. It seemed as if everyone had the same eager thirst for a deep drink of the musical nectar of the gods. Their messed-up hair seemed to reflect a neglect of their person. Their pierced and tattooed bodies seemed to serve as a tribute to their preferred idols; some worshipped beauty, some love, some rebellion, some anger, some hatred, some other people, and some the Devil. Their pale faces made them look like vampires consumed by their passion for consuming. But it was their eyes that were so haunting. Their eyes, each and every one, seemed glazed, as if these people were already under a deep sedation.

"Look at these people," Jack whispered to Bobby. "I think they're all on meth."

"Nah," Bobby said, "they're just ready to ride the current of music! This is gonna be awesome!"

It's weird that Bobby would put it that way, Jack thought. He heard that voice again: "Let go, Jack. Let go." So he did.

With the line moving fairly quickly, Jake texted Paul and Victor to find out where they were. They had just pulled into the parking lot, and with a quick exchange of some cash, each had a ticket. The boys entered the club and pushed as close to the stage as they could. The stench of beer, whiskey, and even pot was so strong Jack wanted to gag, but he kept a straight face as if it wasn't his first time in such a nasty place. Pushing into the herd, they finally came to a stop where all the bodies were tightly packed. They literally couldn't move anymore. Whether it was good or bad, their final place was right in front of a speaker that towered over them. The boys exchanged glances in appreciation of their good fortune and continued pressing forward, backward, and from side to side to defend their territory from the masses pressing into their bodies.

There was a nervous excitement in the room. The dinner bell was lifted to ring, and the feast was about to start. The ravenous pack was about to be fed and fed well. The lights went completely black, and a hush briefly came over the pack before an eruption of yells broke out. Jack couldn't understand exactly what the words were, but it sounded like a united voice shrieking, "Blood! Blood! Blood!" A bright flash like lightning filled the room, accompanied by a bone-shattering boom. Illuminated by the brief burst of light was the lead singer, called Blood, who had earned the nickname by once biting off the head of a rat and letting the blood spew from his mouth onto the front row of his worshipping fans. He stood alone on the stage with his head bowed, his arms raised, and his hands making a shape as close to a goat's head as he could. Everyone knew this was his sign for the Devil, and they imitated his position. For a split second, fear gripped Jack, but then the music erupted, and all the adrenaline in his body charged to life.

He recognized the song; it was "Playing with the Devil." Although he was very familiar with the words, it all sounded new. "Ain't got no worries, no frets, and no tears. Playing with the Devil, I ain't got no fears. Playing with the Devil, I ain't got no fears. Playing with the Devil, I ain't got no fears." Over and over, these words pulsated through his mind, driven deeper and deeper into his spirit, and it felt good. No worries, no frets, no tears, no fears—that was what he wanted. That was what he needed. Numerous events flashed into his mind with the yelling of each line. Worries—he could have no more pressure to do well in school, at sports, or in life. Frets—he could have no more concerns about fitting in or being liked. Tears—he could have no more tears at remembering his parents' arguments.

Fear—I won't fear anything ever again! Jack thought. "Let go, Jack! Feel the power. Feel the freedom." Jack was starting to like that little voice in his head. The image of Rachel flashed into his mind, and Jack let himself go up on the swell of music.

7

STARTING TO SEEP IN

"Let's go, boy. We gotta leave in thirty minutes for church." Jack heard Jay's voice, accompanied by a passing knock on his door. First feeling relief and then hit with intense thought, Jack contemplated the nightmare that had just been interrupted. For several months now, he'd had a dream that recurred every few weeks. The dream was so lifelike, with vivid colors, smells, touches, and feelings.

He would find himself in an inner tube like the ones he'd once used when his family floated down the river in the Texas hill country. There was a group of around a hundred other people all drifting down a slow but steady river about as wide as a basketball court. Although he didn't recognize any particular faces, he knew that they were all his friends. They were all laughing, listening to music, telling jokes, eating junk food, drinking Cokes, and having a great time. But then he saw a large alligator about one hundred yards ahead absolutely destroying people.

The gator swam to a boy, grabbed him, shook him, and then left him shredded in the water. He swam to a woman, grabbed her, shook her, and bit off her arm. He swam to an old man, grabbed him, and plunged him under the water in one big upturned roll. Jack was the only one who seemed to notice the alligator; all the others were too busy enjoying themselves. Jack started to yell at the others, trying to warn them about the alligator.

He jumped off his tube and swam to the boy next to him. "Turn around!" he shouted as he shook his arm. "There's an alligator up there, and he's gonna eat us!"

The boy rolled his face toward him, and Jack saw his glazed eyes as he pulled back his lips in a smile. "Let go, man," he told him as he nodded his head to the pulse coming through his earbuds.

Next, Jack turned next to a girl and pled, "Look! There's an alligator! You need to get out of the water!"

She glanced up from her iPad nonchalantly and asked, "What? The Destroyer?" She pointed a finger toward it. "Oh, don't mind him. He's harmless." She returned to her game.

He looked downstream and saw that the Destroyer was on to him and was now swimming his direction. He tossed his tube at him and started trying to swim upstream, but the massive number of people in the current blocked his way. He swam sideways, trying to make it to the bank. The alligator was getting closer and closer, but Jack managed to push his way to the muddy shore. It was a fairly steep bank, and his feet were slipping in the mud. He clawed his way to the higher ground and started running. He looked behind him, and the alligator was still there. This was where his dream would change from time to time—sometimes he chased him through town, sometimes across an open field, sometimes up a tree, or sometimes through the air.

Jack slid out of bed a little bit warmer than usual but not quite in a sweat. He combed through the dream in his mind, trying to remember all the details in hopes of finding some kind of clue as to what it all meant. Unsuccessful, Jack threw on a pair of athletic shorts, a nice T-shirt, and some flip-flops. He ran his hand over his hair a few times to smooth out the bedhead look and headed to the kitchen for breakfast. Before he turned the corner, the smell of chocolate chip pancakes wafted past his nose. *Just what the doctor ordered,* he thought.

Jack sat down at the bar to find three plates lined up, each with an oversize pancake ready to be covered with syrup and scarfed down. A squabble came from the hallway. "Anna Claire! Take off my shirt!" Avery demanded. Avery was two years older than Anna Claire and was extremely particular about her clothes, especially when it came to letting someone else wear them. She joined Jack at the bar with an exasperated look on her face. "I wish some people would ask before they just go digging through my drawers!" she loudly exclaimed.

"Oh, relax," said Jack. "She's just trying to be like you." Avery scowled at Jack and then looked back toward the hallway to immediately jump on Anna Claire if she turned the corner still wearing her shirt. Jack continued, "Besides, if you just give her some attention and let her wear some of your clothes, she'd probably quit bothering you so much. The whole reason she does that is just to be with you. You should be flattered. Just go with it!"

Avery turned her head to Jack and, with a face looking as if she'd just had a great revelation, paused just long enough for Jack to believe that he actually helped her. Then she blurted out, "Mind your own business!" Jack shrugged; he knew it was a stretch.

Like Jack, Avery skipped the syrup, tore at her pancake with a fork, and yelled toward Jay's room for him to get her some milk. There was no reply. Jay had learned to wisely ignore some requests where the obvious answer was "Get it yourself!" Avery slipped off of her stool and walked to the fridge.

"Do we have any chocolate syrup?" she asked.

The typhoon over, Anna Claire turned the corner, wearing one of her own shirts, and answered the question. "Yes, look behind the barbecue sauce. Can you fix me a cup too?"

Avery, perhaps realizing her earlier reaction was a bit over the top, didn't answer but did grab two cups instead of one. Anna Claire took a seat at the bar, smothered her pancake with syrup, and started nibbling at it. "Dad said he might let you drive to church, Jack. Are you going to do it?" she asked.

"Maybe," he said.

"I bet he'll have a wreck!" added Avery as she put a cup of chocolate milk in front of Jack.

"Don't be dumb," he answered. "I'm a good driver."

"And when have you ever driven anything other than a bike or a golf cart?" asked Avery.

"I've driven lots of times—at the deer lease, the last time we visited Grandpa, and once me and Mason took Leah's car and drove around the block two times," he defended.

"Um, I'm telling Dad!" chimed in Anna Claire. At ten years old, Anna Claire was her dad's best informant regarding sibling secrets, so Jack knew she wasn't bluffing.

"Be quiet!" he said. "You tell, and I'll never take you anywhere when I get my own car."

Anna Claire paused to let that sink in. "I don't care. I'm still gonna tell." But Jack knew that she wouldn't.

Avery, already halfway through her pancake, looked up at Jack and said, "So I heard you went to the TrashMouth concert the other night. Was it fun?"

"Shut up!" Jack urgently whispered looking around toward Jay's room. "I didn't go anywhere the other night!" he insisted.

"Well, Kacey's little brother said he saw you, Bobby, and Jake driving in Jake's dad's truck with the music so loud it made the windows on their house shake," she said.

"So? We just went to the gas station and back. And Jake's dad let him do that," he insisted.

"Well, Jill is Facebook friends with Bobby's little sister, and Jill said that his sister posted a picture of a TrashMouth shirt that Bobby got at the concert! So you are lying!"

"Okay, okay, just keep it down!" Jack said with anger mounting in his tone.

"Well, was it fun? I can't wait until I can go to my first real concert," she whispered.

Jay walked in the room, and a brief hush fell over the trio. He broke the silence. "Glad to see y'all up and moving. We've got to be leaving here in—"

"We know, twenty minutes!" they all replied at once.

"Yep. Hey, chocolate milk? Really? What, you don't think there is already enough chocolate in the pancakes?"

Jack forced a smile to ward off any attitude monitoring from Jay. Jay regularly tried to read their attitudes in case one of them needed cheering up. Jack's forced smile was too plastic, and Jay picked up on the cover-up.

"What's wrong, Jack?" he asked.

"Nothing," Jack answered.

"Then why the face?" he probed.

"What face? Can't a guy have a face that's not perfectly pleasant? It is eight thirty on a Sunday morning, after all!" Jack defended.

Jay allowed the implied request for space. Silence had no time to settle in. Jay and the girls launched into a discussion about a YouTube video from a Christian comedian that Avery had played for them last night.

"Dad, wasn't that Tim Hawkins video hilarious?" She changed her voice to a country twang and continued, "I'll take you for a ride on my pretty pink tractor ..."

Jay joined in, quoting a different part. "If Barbie was a farmer she would drive it ..."

Then Anna Claire had her turn. "It drives real loud, so you can't hear the laughter ..."

Avery added one more. "It's like a redneck Sesame Street!" All three started laughing, and Jack cracked a smile; he'd seen the video before. It was conversations like these that gave Jay a deep joy.

His life centered on Jesus, and he was glad that his kids could see that humor didn't have to be filthy or worldly. After all, God created humor; evil didn't. Evil just took humor and twisted it into something it was never intended to be—just like everything else evil snatched. Jay constantly taught these types of lessons to the kids, helping them to understand the truth of life.

Every night as he tucked the kids in, even Jack at fifteen, he prayed with them and said that Jesus was the only purpose of life. Every day in interacting with the kids, Jay would regularly show them how an event, a thing, a relationship, or an experience could be used to help them know God more. He'd point out, for example, that both pleasure and pain have the exact same reason for existing: the pleasure so that we'd get on our knees and discuss the benefit with God, the pain so that we'd get on our knees and discuss how it can produce a benefit with God. His philosophy was that everything in existence had the purpose of knowing God more through Jesus! Sometimes his observations caused the kids to be a bit embarrassed in front of friends, but when they saw the respect their friends had for him, the embarrassment usually disappeared.

Once at church, with the praise music over and everyone sitting back down for the sermon, Jack's lack of sleep washed over him. He pressed the button on his phone, and his heavy eyes looked at the time. *Only thirty more minutes. I can do this,* he thought to himself. He was tempted to leave the phone on and act as if he was looking at the Bible app to covertly send off a text message to Bobby, but he figured that the required amount of key strokes for any halfway-decent conversation would give him away. He saw the Angry Birds app, which he hardly ever played anymore but had never taken the time to delete, and opened it.

"*Chiiirp!*" The shrill sound pierced the now silent and attentive air in the worship center. Jack immediately turned the volume down before his rooster crowed a second time, giving him away. Jay glanced down the row but knew that Jack would already be remedying the situation, so he turned his attention immediately back to the pastor. Avery and Anna Claire each looked over at his screen to see what game he was playing. Before either of them could whisper to him to ask for a turn, he shut it down. Disappointed, they each returned to their drawings on that day's bulletin. Jack slid the phone back into his pocket and made a few glances around the congregation, looking for friends. Not seeing any, he glanced around again to see if anyone—or any girl, rather—of significance was in direct view of his eyes, which were now getting heavy again. This check done, Jack closed his eyes but kept his head as attentive-looking as possible.

Avery nudged Jack. "What?" he asked as his eyes slowly opened.

"Let's go!" she replied. "It's over."

Jack, stunned at the fact he had slept through the entire sermon, started to feel some pride at having done it without being noticed, but then he looked down at his shirt and saw it wet with some drool.

Anna Claire saw him looking down and smiled. "Good thing you didn't snore!" she remarked.

In confidence, Jack asked, "Could anyone tell I was asleep?"

Anna Claire's smile widened. "Only the people sitting next to you."

Jack looked over his shoulder to see a college-aged girl talking to her parents, all of them smiling. She met Jack's eyes and her mouth seemed to intentionally close. At this clue, a flush of embarrassment washed over Jack's face, and he urged Anna Claire, Avery, and Jay to hurry down the aisle away from his audience.

Separating from the family, Jack headed upstairs for high school Bible study. On the way, he met Tom, the outcast loner who'd had that weird look on his face when that kid got beat up at school. Ordinarily, Jack wouldn't go out of his way to talk to him, but now he wanted to find out why the goody-goody had had such a problem with the fight.

"Hey," Jack said, "I saw you watching that fight the other day at school."

Tom corrected him. "I wasn't watching it. I just passed by it."

"Yeah, whatever—anyway, I saw you shake your head, and it kind of came across as a bit judgmental."

Tom stopped. "Yeah, so?"

Jack, taking on a more holy air, rebuked, "Well, if you're going to be a Christian, you shouldn't walk around judging people." Jack expected a revelation and a response of gratitude.

"Oh, you're right!" said Tom, sarcasm dripping in his tone. "Violence is certainly not something we should be judgmental about!"

Jack wasn't about to be out-spiritualized; he'd been in Sunday school since he was a kid. "Hey, even Jesus made a whip and turned over the tables at the temple!" he retorted.

Tom's jaw dropped slightly but unintentionally. "So you're saying that those boys who attacked the other kid were somehow doing it to protect the reputation of God?"

The question, which shined the spotlight squarely on Jack's ungrounded logic, made Jack wince, but his pride wouldn't let him admit defeat. "Anyway," he said, exasperated, "I'm just saying that if you ever want to fit in, you need to pay more attention to how you act."

Tom rolled his eyes and continued his tone of sarcasm. "Oh, gosh, thanks! Fitting in with the world is just what I wanted!" Tom turned and continued to class.

"You're welcome!" Jack called out and shook his head. Jack couldn't believe that someone who was such an outcast would so blatantly reject his Christian social advice.

Arriving home from church, Jack scurried to his room, shut the door, and got online to play some *MW7* with his friends. Typically, he would mute the other players because they used about every bad word in the book, but with his pride still stinging from its own reflection, he left the microphones open and justified it to himself by thinking, *I'm fifteen years old, for crying out loud!* However, to avoid any blue streaks the profanity might cause in the house, Jack put his headphones on to keep it a private matter. Almost immediately, the realistic images of war were accompanied by the realistic expletives of war.

For the next hour, Jack had a constant stream of words pouring into his mind. Before he was conscious of it, those same words were now pouring through his mind and out of his mouth. Sin always has a way of escaping its barriers. But to Jack, these little words weren't as nasty a thing as sin; they were just sound bites thrown into the empty air, meaningless. Nonetheless, they felt good to him, ironically proving that they weren't completely void of significance. With each word, a shot of excitement hit his formerly wounded pride, and his growing ego rejuvenated to a bigger and stronger level. "This is what it means to be free. The more you let go, the more you grow," Jack felt a voice whisper.

Fortunately—or, for Jack's fellow soldiers, unfortunately—Jack remembered the report he had to finish on Homer's the *Iliad*. His teacher was very impressed at his selection of the ancient text, which Jack had made only because it had to do with warfare and mythology. After about fifteen minutes into the story, reading names like Agamemnon, Kalkhas, Patroklos, and Akhilleus and words like *quell, respites,* and *smote,* Jack realized he should've just selected Twain's *Huckleberry Finn* or Dickens's *Oliver Twist*. Even upon this realization and with plenty of time to change horses, Jack's desire to live up to the teacher's admiration overrode his desire for an easier route. So Jack persevered and now lacked only a couple of hours of focused writing before his objective would be met.

With his laptop awaiting its massage of keystrokes, Jack mustered up his most intense concentration for this final push. In the next room, the girls were watching a singing show and had the volume of the TV above its usual level. The varying quality of voices squealing, screeching, and squawking were all successful in their unanimous attempt to distract Jack from his monumental labor. "Turn it down!" he shouted with his eyes intently focused on his masterpiece. The volume didn't go down. "Turn it down!" he shouted again more emphatically. The volume still didn't go down. Now red in the face, he yelled, "I said, turn it the *freak* down!"—only he didn't say *freak*.

To this, the volume instantly turned down. *I fixed that!* Jack thought proudly. Two sets of feet came pattering across the carpet, then the tile floor, and finally the carpet of the hallway to his door. Jack looked up and saw Anna Claire and Avery standing at the door, both with a look of shock, one in tears and the other in anger. "What do you want?" he sarcastically asked, but they both just stood there, staring at him with hurt feelings from such a hateful word. "Shut the door!" he slowly but emphatically said so that neither could mistake his command.

As if of the same mind, they both turned on their heels and retraced their steps back to the TV. The volume arose some, but not very much. Jack's pride swelled at having forced his demand so effectively, and now his attention turned back to his artistic endeavor. There was that invigorating feeling again—and there was that voice again encouraging, "Go!"

8

NICKI FINDS A FRIEND IN SPITE

It was only nine o'clock in the morning, but Faith had already played the early Saturday soccer game across town and was just getting out of the car when she saw Amber picking up toilet paper from her front shrubs.

"Y'all got wrapped last night?" called Faith.

"Yep," replied Amber. "I've been picking this stuff up for over an hour now. It's embarrassing!"

"Any idea who did it?"

"No, but I'm pretty sure it has to do with Nicki and some jealous girl getting revenge."

"Humph. What are you doing today?" Faith inquired.

"Nothing planned. Wanna hang out?"

"Sure, let me get changed, and I'll come over."

In a few moments, Faith was changed out of her uniform and into some normal clothes. She arrived just in time to help Amber pull the last few streamers of cheap toilet paper out of the trees. "Where's Nicki?" asked Faith.

"She's too embarrassed to help," said Amber.

"Image must be a hard thing to protect sometimes," Faith sarcastically remarked.

"I wouldn't know. But she's agreed to fold my clothes for the whole month, and I'll take that trade any day." Amber looked up and smiled, and Faith chuckled.

The chore complete, the girls headed inside, where Nicki was eating breakfast.

"Hey, Faith," Nicki greeted.

"Hey," Faith replied.

"I guess you saw the mess in the yard. Did you see anything last night?" Nicki asked.

"Nope. I went to bed early because I had an early game today."

"I'll bet it was Jana," Nicki smirked. "She's never liked me, although I hardly even know her and have never done anything to make her not like me."

"I'm sure it'll be on Twitter pretty soon," said Amber.

At this idea, Nicki jumped up, dashed out, and returned with her iPhone. "Aha! It looks like it was Shawna! It was a joke! Here's a picture of her and Stephanie and Carrie right on our front porch. Those tramps!" Nicki was now smiling from the act of camaraderie from older girls.

"So you're not mad?" asked Amber.

"Heck no! These are my *amigas!*" Nicki replied happily. "I just need to figure out a way to return the favor. That'll be fun! Clara said to tell you hi," said Nicki, not even looking up from her phone.

"Who, me?" asked Amber.

"No, Faith."

"Oh," Faith remarked, surprised. "Tell her I said hi back."

In three finger taps Nicki delivered the message.

"She said she hasn't tried talking to that Rachel girl anymore," said Nicki.

"What are you talking about?" asked Amber. Faith's heart shuddered. She remembered what Nicki was talking about.

"You know, when she did that spirit thing last time."

"That was scary," said Amber.

Faith nodded and added, "You know, that stuff is real. I'll never do that again."

"Oh, grow up!" remarked Nicki. "Maybe it's real for a reason! Maybe it's real because that's who we really are supposed to be following. I saw this lady on a talk show once, and she was telling all about her near-death experience and how she now had, like, her own personal spirit guide. Now she's rich and has a husband who adores her. What more could a girl want?"

Faith's intelligence wouldn't let her be silent. "There's more to life than just money and men! That occult stuff, from what I've read, always ends up bad."

"Define 'bad!'" challenged Nicki.

"Well, like drugs, diseases, poverty, mental disorders, even suicide!"

"That's stupid!" said Nicki. "So you're going to sit there and say that scary little devils are behind all of that?"

"Well, now that you put it that way, I guess so," Faith retorted proudly.

Nicki shook her head in disbelief and, as she stormed off to her room, threw one last comment at Faith: "I think Oprah knows a little bit more about life than you do!"

Amber touched Faith's arm. "Come on, let's get out of here." As they started for the front door, they heard Nicki's door slam in an attempt at giving one more jab at their ignorance. Amber, not to be outdone, slammed the front door upon their exit as if to reply, "No, you are the ignorant one!"

With their adrenaline still at a fairly high level—neither of them was very comfortable with arguments—the two without much thought began walking down the sidewalk away from the cul-de-sac. Amber, although less involved in the discussion, was the one who needed to vent the most. "I can't believe Nicki. She's so stupid! First of all, to really think that some celebrity has some special knowledge of life just because they're on TV is just plain ignorant!"

Faith nodded in agreement.

"Then to get that stupid look on her face like she's so high and mighty and say"—here Amber took on a mocking tone—"'So you're going to sit there and say that scary little devils are behind all of that?' I mean, who else is behind evil if it's not the Devil? Right?"

Faith nodded again, and Amber continued, "I mean, we don't even go to church much, well, except for Christmas and Easter, and even I know that!"

Faith's adrenaline had already returned to normal; now she was just helping Amber's to do the same by listening. As Amber continued pouring out her frustration with her sister, she felt the bond of friendship strengthening between her and Faith. It wasn't just that Faith listened; it was how she listened, with a compassion that Amber had never really seen before. Amber could tell that Faith truly cared about her, as a person, as a friend.

As the girls continued down whatever street their feet directed them, Amber saw a little blonde girl in the next driveway with a water hose, a giant tub, and a dog that looked like an oversize stuffed animal. "Look at that dog! It looks like a sheep or something."

Faith looked over. "I think it's a Labradoodle. How cute!"

"Isn't that Jack's sister?" asked Amber.

"Jack from school?" replied Faith with a twinge of excitement in her tone.

Amber noticed it but didn't bring it up. "Yeah, he has two sisters, Avery and Anna Claire."

"How do you know these things?" asked Faith.

"You gotta remember who my sister is. She knows everyone and everything. Popularity has its price, you know."

They approached the girl and her dog. "What kind of dog is that?" Faith asked.

"A Labradoodle. Her name is Harley." The dog began to wag its tail and approach the two strangers, who had already knelt down with their hands extended to pet the curly blonde locks.

"Does Jack live here?" asked Amber.

"Yep. He's inside."

Faith gave a nervous glance at Amber. Amber was amused and continued, "Are you Avery or Anna Claire?"

"I'm Anna Claire. Do you know Jack? I can go get him if you want."

"No, that's okay," Faith quickly replied, standing and taking a step back in the direction they'd come from.

Amber, a bit more cool, replied, "No, just tell him his friends from the math club said hi."

"Okay" was Anna Claire's reply as she grabbed Harley by the collar to keep her from walking away with her new friends.

As the two girls moseyed away, Faith a little bit more quickly than Amber, Anna Claire admired them. They were friendly, had cute outfits, and were so grown-up, and she'd gotten the impression that they liked her brother. Her thought was quickly broken by a burst of cold water spraying from the nozzle of the water hose filling a tub. Harley, seeing Anna Claire's distraction, made the most of the moment to escape the bath. Anna Claire let out an involuntary shiver and shrieked, "Harley!"

The two girls looked over their shoulders, and Anna Claire heard one of them say, "How cute!"—which made her smile and wish they'd stayed longer.

Amber looked amusedly at Faith and said, "I take it you know Jack?"

Faith, trying to camouflage her emotions, admitted, "Sure, who doesn't?"

"What do you mean 'who doesn't'? It's not like he's Sam Sweeney or anything. Lots of people don't know him," pursued Amber.

Knowing that she had to give a more thorough explanation, Faith continued sheepishly, "Well, I don't really know him that well. We both go to the same church, so I know a little bit about him."

Amber pressed, "The same church? You should know him pretty well, then."

Faith replied, "Well, it's a really big church. We have, like, over a hundred kids just in our grade alone, so unless you reach out to someone or they reach out to you, you never really get to know them very well."

"Well, what do you know about him?" asked Amber.

"I know that he's one of the nice kids. He's at church with his family every Sunday. His dad used to teach in our groups, and I've seen Jack help him in different church activities," replied Faith.

Amber countered, "Yeah, but there are a lot of kids who go to church every Sunday and then Monday through Saturday live like something else. Remember that girl named Kipper who died from an overdose on meth? She was in church every Sunday. Her dad was the preacher!"

"Yeah, but with Jack you can tell it's different. You can tell he really is a good guy."

Amber relented because she could see that too. Jack had some friends who were a bit reckless, but you could tell his heart was in a different place. "So you like him?" Amber asked, turning up the intensity of the conversation and putting her arm around Faith's shoulders.

Turning red from embarrassment, Faith quickly smirked. "No!" But the look on her face told the story of a tiny hidden crush that had lain buried for quite a few years. Both of the girls laughed, each hearing the unsaid words. A loud backfire echoed from a car a couple of blocks away. Faith jumped as if someone shot at her.

"Are you all right?" Amber asked with a sudden look of concern.

Faith's heart was pounding, but her face took on an artificially calm look. "I'm okay. I just get startled real easy," she replied, intentionally slowing her heartbeat to normal. "I've always done that."

Faith just considered herself a jumpy person in general. Since as far back as second grade, she would startle at even the smallest of unexpected noises. A sound suddenly fired off and her body would shudder, a rush of adrenaline would shoot to her stomach, her heartbeat would accelerate, her face would show a microexpression of fear, and sometimes her hands would shake. Over the years, she'd perfected the recovery but hadn't yet been able to quite get at the heart of the matter for a cure. Amber accepted the halfhearted answer, and Faith's smile gave her the reassurance she needed to continue the walk home, talking about this and that.

-⊙⊙⊙⊙-

Nicki slammed her door, frustrated with her stupid sister and the smart girl. The thought of them thinking that they were better and more intelligent than she was made her adrenaline shoot through the roof. She thought about punching the wall but opted for a pillow on the bed instead. Starting to vent her rage with a few cuss words, she threw herself on her floor with her back against the bed, jammed in her earbuds, and turned up the volume as loud as her ears could stand it. Taylor Swift's voice, accompanied by a chorus of harmonizing guitars and fiddles, came screaming into her ears with the latest and most popular country/pop love song. Even more enraged, Nicki quickly browsed through her music library and tapped on a section labeled "Hard Core."

Like the changing of a calm to the actual storm, the beat shifted from one of lighthearted puppy love to a driving rage that more appropriately matched her mood. TrashMouth's newest song, "Viper Lust," burst into her head. The words were angry and sensual at the same time. To Nicki, this song understood her. In the pain of her anger, she somehow found pleasure, and she wanted to increase that with a different kind of pleasure. It was a roller coaster—anticipation going up the hill and then the exhilarating fear coming down the hill. The combination of the two increased the overall sensation. The understanding of the song soothed her fuming rage, and after an hour or so, her heartbeat slowed to normal.

With her brain successfully numbed, she craved more excitement. The music still blaring its angry messages, her mind slammed back to her conversation with Amber and Faith. An idea struck her. She cursed her two opponents, crossed her legs, and held out her arms. She recalled what instruction she could from the afternoon talk shows and let herself relax into a lifeless state of mind. She recalled Clara's words and repeated them as she focused on clearing her mind.

"Oh mighty gods of the ancient days, bring down your power. Here is a servant who seeks the wisdom of Rachel."

Nothing happened. Nicki shook out her hands, relaxed all her muscles, and bowed her head as her breath intentionally deepened and slowed. "Oh mighty gods of the ancient days, bring down your power. Here is a servant who seeks the wisdom of Rachel." Nicki felt herself roll over from her sitting position onto her side.

A dreamy state washed over her vegetated mind, and she found herself lying in a wooded area with her face in a carpet of plush grass. The aroma that filled the air exhilarated her as she inhaled deeply. A soft touch came upon her shoulder, and she turned around.

"I'm Rachel."

Nicki took an involuntary step back as her eyes drew in the presence of this person. Rachel was about the same height and slenderness as herself. She had the lightest strawberry-blonde hair and sparkling crystal-green eyes. Taking another involuntary step back, Nicki could see a beautiful tapestry of colors behind her. Rachel had the wings of a large and beautiful butterfly. The wings fluttered as she smiled at Nicki.

"You have found me!" said Rachel.

Nicki still stood in disbelief, her mouth open in awe. Rachel, seeing this, waited for the moment to pass. "Is this a dream?" asked Nicki.

"No," chuckled Rachel as her smile spread wider across her alabaster face. "I'm the one you asked for. I'm the one who has been appointed to you by Ohm."

Nicki always made friends fast, but this bond was instantaneous. "Who is Ohm?" she asked.

Appearing pleasantly surprised, Rachel replied, "Ohm is the primary force of the universe—or at least that's what those in my clander call it because that most resembles the pulsating life force you feel when you connect with it. Other clanders have different names for it, like God, the force, God consciousness, universal love, self-actualization, Brahman, or nirvana."

Nicki had heard some of those names before, so it felt like that part was making sense, but she had a hint of confusion on her face.

"I can tell you have a question," Rachel said. "Always feel free to ask me anything. That's the only way you'll learn."

"I understand the idea of a force and all the names and stuff, but what is a clander?"

Rachel put her hand on Nicki's shoulder. "Oh, you do have so much to learn!" Nicki gave a faint smile. Rachel continued, "I'm sorry—a clander is just a group of spirits that have been interwoven together in the supreme fabric. In more earthly terms, think of your existence as one huge, beautiful, cosmic quilt." Rachel held her palms down in front and spread them to emphasize the vastness. "A clander is one of the squares of fabric. You see, you and I will be interwoven together like this." She interlaced her fingers with Nicki's, who noticed that her touch was tender and cool. "Now hold your other hand out that way," she said, pointing to the side. "Someone else will be interwoven with you on that side."

"Do we get to choose who is next to us?" asked Nicki.

Rachel smiled sympathetically again. "Yes and no. You for sure will have your soul mate connected to you—that's what most people are worried about—but you will also have others joined to you that the Ohm directs. You see, the Ohm is the creator force, the weaver of the quilt; it keeps all beauty perfectly in balance and harmoniously connected."

Nicki's heart warmed at this idea. "So I'll be connected to you and to another person?" probed Nicki.

"Well, that's where the quilt analogy breaks down. Now think of the quilt, if you can, as a three-dimensional quilt. I know it's hard to imagine, but try to relax your mind so that it can expand and take in more possibilities—because, actually, the quilt is infinitely dimensional!" Rachel delightfully answered, her face gleaming with excitement.

Nicki's eyes dazzled in a flash of amazement and said, "Wow, that sounds, well, awesome."

"Oh, it is, but I don't want to overload you. Sometimes beauty can be so overwhelming on its surface that we miss the deeper beauty within," said Rachel.

"But how can we? I mean ..." started Nicki.

"For now, let's just say that the closer to the Ohm you get, the more people you can connect with," concluded Rachel.

"Wow! This is just too fantastic! Can I tell people about this?" asked Nicki, thinking of a few others she'd like to spend eternity connected to.

"Well, that's where we have to be careful. You see, most people won't even make it to the level you've already made it to. I'm sure you've always had a feeling that you were special and different from others, right?" asked Rachel.

Surprised, Nicki exclaimed, "Yes! I always knew I was different."

"Better!" said Rachel.

"Better?" asked Nicki.

"Yes, better! The lesser souls—or, rather, the less beautiful, normal souls—won't be able to join into the cosmic union. Only those of a better, purer spirit will," replied Rachel.

"Well, what happens to the others?" asked Nicki.

"Look at you! You are already expanding your mind so much in just one talk," remarked Rachel. "Well, those who aren't chosen will simply be banished."

"Banished?" gasped Nicki.

Rachel smiled comfortingly. "Yes, but don't worry. I use that term, but it's not really like you think. They're not locked out of paradise or any other miserable thing like that. And by the way, all those stories and worries about the Devil, hell, angels, and heaven—all fake! But that's a different lesson. Those lesser, average souls are cast down to be part of Pergyss, a type of sea—an ocean of souls." Rachel spread her palms again to emphasize the vastness. Nicki thought that sounded more appealing. Rachel continued, "Once they get there, they find themselves satisfied in being exactly what they were created for, which is nothing. In their present life, they are tormented by trying to discover who they really are. In the next life, they will find their place in this sea and be perfectly content in being absorbed into it."

Nicki nodded her head at these profound revelations. It all made perfect sense to her now. She made up her mind that she, now knowing that she was special and different, would pursue this new path with all her heart.

"I can tell you're in deep meditation of all that I've revealed to you. That's good, but it's time for me to return to my clander. Whenever I'm away from them for even just a moment, I miss the feeling of the true love being exchanged in the union of the Ohm."

Nicki would've been sad at this good-bye, but her mind was filled to capacity. She focused her gaze on Rachel's eyes. She wanted to take in every bit of beauty she could before her return to her present life. As she did, she felt as if her whole soul was diving into those crystal-green eyes, like diving smoothly into a green spring of water on a hot summer day. She was relishing the experience as, stroke after stroke, she swam deeper and deeper into the pool. The cool water around her was like oxygen that she deeply inhaled. Lost in a floating sensation of peace, happiness, excitement, and love, she felt a twinge of fear spring from within her own spirit. It was like an unseen bump had knocked her off of her bike as she glided down a long hill-country path. She couldn't explain exactly what it was or why it happened, but the experience was ruined.

Nicki opened her eyes and found that she was still lying on her bedroom floor, even more agitated than before. As she was forcing her mind to recount every detail of her experience with Rachel and the feelings it had produced, she was immediately swept away by the raging current of the song blaring into her ear. The song was "Vengeance Is Mine," and she could feel the driving beat inflating her appetite for destruction. The words tasted as raw meat might to a ravenous wolf: "Bite me once, shame on me. But you've bit me once, and justice I'll see. You went to him with your sweet perfume. Little did he know that it would be his doom. Vengeance is mine! You're gonna pay! Vengeance is mine! You'll rue the day. Vengeance is mine! Vengeance is mine! Vengeance is mine!"

The song resonated with Nicki, and it felt good, but realizing her feelings were quite the opposite of those peaceful ones she'd felt with Rachel, she pulled the buds out of her ears. Exhausted, Nicki fell asleep.

9

SIPS OF INTOXICATION

Finally, another Friday night had arrived. It had been another long week of school, and Jack, despite learning, told himself that he was bored all week long. On top of the boredom were a couple of arguments with Bobby, whose friendship usually helped the time pass more lightly. Like most arguments, they were over debatable things and prideful opinions like who had had the farthest hit in Little League, which college football team was the best, and whether people could go to heaven if they committed suicide. Although Bobby and Jack were each other's automatic plans for weekends, Jack decided to ground Bobby by not texting him for a couple of days.

It was in this dull frame of mind that Jack plopped down on the couch and decided to channel surf, but because his dad didn't have cable, his surf was limited to the dozen local stations, and half of these were in Spanish. *Now I see why dad wants us to learn Spanish,* Jack thought. He scrolled through the guide and saw *Iron Man 2.* "Sweet," he mused to himself in surprise and hit the enter button.

The picture disappeared and then reappeared. The camera zoomed in on the hero, whose lips began to utter words, but the sound wasn't exactly in sync. "*Si, soy Iron Man … dinero, burrito, taco, por favor*" was what it sounded like to Jack. It was a bit less "sweet" but still better than a Friday-night sitcom. He continued watching the movie while the tape of the English translation played in his mind from the ten times he had seen it before. After *Iron Man 2* was over, Jack rolled through the guide again in hopes of finding an English-language action movie, but by this time, lame late-night talk shows had asserted their postnews presence. His choices were limited to a Batman movie, again in Spanish, or an old psycho killer movie that needed to crawl back to the 1970s. He opted to call it an early Friday night and head into his room.

Stretching himself out across his bed, Jack stared blankly at the lifeless TV screen on the desk. This week had gotten the best of him, and his energy was spent. With his mind begging to be recharged by sleep, he protested by forcing his heavy eyes to remain open. He began to imagine a movie playing on the blank slate screen. His mind revisited his dream of Rachel. He imagined her walking to him and touching him and them walking hand in hand through that surreal wonderland. His emotions bathed him in the peaceful sensation of love. Taking advantage of this relaxation, his exhausted body finally pulled him into sleep to watch the latest episode of an old dream.

Jack found himself back in the river with the same group of friends. All on their inner tubes, they were heading downstream having a wonderful time. He spied the alligator he now knew as the Destroyer in the distance, attacking and chomping on others. But this time he wasn't worried or fearful. He felt stronger and more powerful now. The gator was but a pest in his eyes, and Jack felt like he could easily be the beast's destroyer if it attacked. As he continued to drift down the river, he engaged the friends around him in conversation. They were talking about music, sports, and how other people just didn't understand what was really important in life. He had a feeling of complete happiness.

When his tube finally arrived in the Destroyer's area, the beast made its way through the debris-filled water and opened its mouth. Jack began to laugh hysterically, pointing his finger at it and mocking, "What are you going to do, eat me?" He waved his hands in the air as if he were frightened.

The Destroyer, however, did not respond to this in jest. It opened its jaws, grabbed his arm, and pulled him off of his tube, plunging him under the water and beginning its death roll. One instant Jack's body was below the water, and the next he was being turned across the surface. He sucked in a bit of air and was able to scream for help to the others nearby. But by the third or fourth roll, he could make out that they were actually making fun of him and laughing at him.

"Oh, it got that boy good!" he heard one man say.

"He won't be coming back!" a small boy exclaimed.

"Look at that gator bait!" said a lady. Amid his terror at being eaten alive, he actually could feel a deep pain in his heart at the careless remarks he was hearing from the people who he had thought were on his side. The pain of their rejection tore at him just as much as the alligator's clenching teeth.

⌐◦◦◦◦⌐

The next morning, Jack awoke as if he had never gone to sleep at all. His bed was wet from sweat, and the sheets were in a swirl. Although he could only recall his one brief alligator dream, he figured that the entire night must have been just as bad, given the condition of his bed. With that kind of night, he was starting to be concerned for how the day was going to be. He lay still for a moment longer, listening to see if anyone else might already be up. He heard some voices speaking with an intentionally muffled tone in the kitchen. A plate clinked as it was laid gently in the sink and was immediately followed by "Shhhh! Jack is still asleep."

"Sorry!" was the whispered reply.

Jack rolled over and looked at the clock within arm's reach. "Yikes, it's eleven forty-eight! Almost noon! I've missed the whole morning." A new rush of energy pushed him out of bed. He rolled over the edge and, with his legs betraying him, landed on his knees. Being in a kneeling position, he thought about praying but chose instead to consider his health. He was noticeably weak and exhausted. Thinking he might be getting sick, he touched his forehead to feel for fever, but it was cool and clammy. Attributing his state to a general lack of sleep, he raised himself on his elbows and then to his feet, where he ordered his legs to toughen up. Although not yet confident that he wasn't coming down with some type of illness, he pressed on and changed into more appropriate Saturday attire to start what he hoped would be a normal day.

As he turned the corner into the living room, Jack saw his dad and the girls watching some episodes of a TV show from when his dad was young. Jay liked it when the kids actually showed an interest in some of the nostalgic things from his past. Although the show was dated and goofy by modern standards, at least there was the comfort of knowing that a curse word wouldn't appear out of left field for no other purpose than to get a more mature rating, which equated to a larger target audience, which equated to more money for the Hollywood liberal elite. How sad it was for the cinema that instead of a profitable story, it was profanity, gore, and sex that seemed to drive profit, or at least a significant portion of it.

"Good morning, sleepyhead," Jay said as Jack, still looking half-baked, staggered into the living room.

"You mean 'lazy bum'!" added Avery.

"Shut up," Jack retorted as Jay's eyes automatically scowled at him in disapproval.

Message sent, Jay turned his glance to Avery and scolded, "Avery!"

"Well, I'm just saying ..." She raised her brows to add emphasis and innocence.

"I thought you went to bed early?" asked Jay.

"Yeah, somewhat. I guess I was just really tired."

"You want something to eat? Breakfast? Or, I guess, lunch?" Jay inquired.

"I'll find something," Jack said. He went to the fridge, pulled out the milk, and poured the last bit over a bowl of some kind of healthy cereal. As he sat and ate with his family, Jack replayed in his mind the first dream he'd had of Rachel. Then he replayed last night's dream of the alligator. Were they connected? He wasn't sure. A feeling of worry started to sprout in his mind as he thought about the common vividness of the dreams. Compared to all the dreams he had had over his fifteen years, the ones about the alligator and now Rachel were so real that it was scary. Just then, he felt that voice in his mind whisper, "Relax, Jack. Don't overthink this. Don't get tangled in your thoughts. That's what crazy people do." Less than comforted, he still couldn't tell if this was his voice, some type of a conscience, like Jiminy Cricket was for Pinocchio, or something completely different. Regardless of the source, Jack heeded the advice and distracted himself with the old TV show.

While rinsing his bowl in the sink, Jack announced, "I'm going out!" to whomever could hear him.

A voice hidden by the couch protested, "Where are you going? I wanted you to play basketball with me." It was Anna Claire.

"None of your business, and I don't want to play basketball," Jack said with more than a hint of rudeness, which jabbed at her feelings.

"Whatever. I bet you're going to some girl's house—probably one of the ones who walked by here this morning. Does Dad know what you're doing?"

Jack ignored her and started for the door, but as he digested her words, his curiosity got the best of him. "Who came by here?" he asked doubtfully, trying to disguise his interest. If there was a girl who liked him, Jack wanted to know about it.

"Oh, I don't remember …" she said, playing difficult now.

"Okay, whatever!" Jack turned to snub her and then turned back to face her. "What color hair did she have?" he asked, still trying to cover his now piqued interest.

"I just can't remember …" Anna Claire continued to play, recalling his earlier rude comments.

"Okay, I get it. I'll give you two dollars if you can remember."

"I don't want your money!"

Finally catching on that what she wanted was for him to repair the damage, Jack said, "Okay, I'm sorry for being rude … and I'll still let you have the two dollars to prove it." Jack could see her face light up a bit.

"Aha!" she exclaimed, her hurt feelings completely mended. "You really do want a girlfriend!"

"Oh, yeah, you're really funny! I'm not giving you anything!" he said, embarrassed at having his interest taunted.

"One was real pretty, with dark brown hair, big brown eyes, and a really big smile; she wore shorts that weren't too short but not quite to her knees. The other one had lighter brown hair and a cool T-shirt with a peace sign on front, and they were both really friendly. Oh, and they both had their hair pulled back in a ponytail. There, you happy?"

Jack's heart started getting excited at her words, but his cool exterior didn't show it. "What'd they say? What happened? Did they ask for me?"

Anna Claire started to smile, realizing that she had captured her brother's attention even more than she could have imagined. "Well, I was hanging out in front with Harley, wondering if I should wash her or Dad's truck, and they came walking down the sidewalk. They were glancing at the house and whispering to each other. The shorter one in the cool T-shirt said, 'Does Jack live here?' I said, 'Yes, he's my brother.' Then she said, 'Are you Avery or Anna Claire?' I said, 'I'm Anna Claire. Do you know Jack?' The girl in the T-shirt did all the talking. She said, 'Yes, we're friends of his from math club!' and they looked at each other and kind of giggled."

"I'm not in any math club! Why didn't you ask them their names?"

"How was I supposed to know you weren't in math club? You are a nerd!" Anna Claire couldn't miss an easy opportunity for a poke.

"Yeah, yeah, what'd they do then?" Jack was unashamedly interrogating her now, and Anna Claire wanted him to solve the mystery.

"Well, then they just kept on walking and said bye, so I said bye and kept on playing with Harley. Harley liked them. They seemed nice."

"That was it? No names at all? Which way did they go?" Jack pressed, somewhat bothered by her lack of useful information.

"Well, the one who was real pretty was pretty tall too, even taller than you." She paused and grinned. "But that's not hard!" Bam, two pokes!

Pressing his lips and rolling his eyes, Jack asked his last question again. "Which way did they go?"

"Toward Audrey's house."

"And that would be …?"

Anna Claire looked at him with a *Hello?* expression and pointed her finger in the direction of their exit. Jack's mind started to take a quick mental jog down the block to see if he could deduce who the mystery guests might have been. Coming up short, he asked one last question. "Was that all?"

Anna Claire tilted her head and moved her bright blue eyes upward, showing that she was trying to sweep together every fragment. "Yep, that's about it!"

The inquisition over, Jack turned back toward the door to leave, and as he started to close it behind him, he heard Anna Claire call out, "What about my two dollars?" Jack, not satisfied with the quality of information she had given him, ignored her and kept moving. As the door slammed behind him, he could hear her last "Hey!" His rude departure caused Anna Claire's feathers to ruffle again.

Jack pulled his bike out of the garage and onto the driveway. It was a Sledgehammer with shocks and pegs made for tricks, although he had never taken it off of any sweet jumps. His mom had bought it for him when he was in elementary, thinking that it would last him all the way through high school. She was right—it had lasted—but Jack had been too embarrassed to ride it for the past two years. He didn't, however, have much of a choice for convenient local transportation. He considered going back on his weekend vow and heading for Bobby's, but his pride discarded that option. He finally concluded to just start riding and see where he ended up.

He rode along with one eye on the road and the other in search of the mystery girls from earlier that day. Finally he reached the end of his neighborhood and pulled into the corner gas station. He felt in his pocket and found a few coins and the wadded-up two dollars that he had promised Anna Claire in exchange for her information. Now, it seemed, there was a change of plans, and Jack decided the money would be more satisfactorily spent on a drink. Jack examined all the drinks trying to figure out just what exactly he was craving: chocolate milk, Coke, Gatorade, Dr Pepper, beer …

Beer! He wondered what beer really tasted like. He figured that it couldn't be too bad if companies spent billions of dollars each year making it and selling it and millions of people kept buying it and gulping it. Surely it had to have something good about its flavor. After all, his reasoning continued, it was made all around the world and had been around even since the days of kings and knights and stuff. Jack glanced at the gas station guy behind the counter, who was busy with a customer. The thought crossed his mind that since he couldn't actually buy a bottle, he could shove it in his pocket or something. While the thought of this gave him a nervous adrenaline rush, he wasn't prepared to do something so obviously stupid.

"Come on Jack, just go with it," said that all-too-familiar voice of encouragement. He examined his pockets, imagining what a bottle or a can might look like shoved in. Accepting the fact that they weren't nearly big enough, he figured the next time he'd bring a backpack and "go with it." Getting back to reality, he opened the glass door and felt a chill of air rush over his feet. He pulled a bottle of Dr Pepper from the rack, and the next one immediately slid forward, making it impossible to reverse the transaction. The price of a buck seventy-nine was going to leave him just short of being able to buy a candy bar or pack of gum too.

An angry word involuntarily leaked from his mind and spewed out of his mouth: "Shoot!" Only it wasn't *shoot*. A little girl standing spitting distance away was wrapped up in the difficult candy dilemma of chocolate or no chocolate and was violated by the hateful word. Even though she couldn't have possibly comprehended its ugliness—she was too young—its impact firmly slapped her little ear. Her head spun from the blow, and she scowled at Jack for the offense and ran back to the safety of her dad in the next aisle.

She'll hear it one day, Jack justified to himself, and he returned to his mathematical calculations. Reworking the problem and finding that he was still the same amount short, he reexamined his pockets to see how a candy bar or pack of gum might look. He figured that even if he did get caught he could always say he had bought it earlier at the other gas station only a few hundred yards away. Jack hesitated at the resurrected idea.

"Stronger. Freer. Go," emphasized the voice. Pleased at the encouragement, Jack took the place of the little girl examining the candy. He didn't want to look too suspicious, so he kept his eyes on the candy boxes and his attention on the people around him. His adrenaline surged to a height he had never felt before. His heart was racing like a hunted rabbit and was beating as loud as the TrashMouth bass drum. He reached out his hand as steadily as he could toward the candy, but on seeing it tremble, he returned it empty to his pocket. "You can do this," the voice assured him. Steadying his breath and his nerves, Jack took his hand from the pocket, grabbed two Twix bars, and held them closely together as if they were only one. He let both of his hands ease down next to his pockets and let one of the Twix bars fall in.

A quick glance up revealed that the gas station guy had been watching him. Jack tried with all his strength to disconnect his face from his emotions. He then tried with all his strength to believe his own lie that he wasn't doing anything that bad; it was only a piece of candy. He took two steps down the aisle as he raised both the drink and the candy. He examined the candy, put on a facade that showed anyone watching that he changed his mind, and placed the one Twix bar back in the box. He glanced down at his pocket to see the shape of the second candy bulging in his shorts. It seemed as if he had stuffed a baby coyote in there, and it was howling for the whole world to hear. Still not convinced that he was in the clear, he threw a glance at the gas station guy, who was still sizing him up.

As Jack walked, the candy bar—or, rather, the baby coyote—started howling as if its life depended on it. "Wooooooo, woo, woo, wooooooo! Help! Stop, thief!" The volume of his pulse cranked higher with every step: "*Boom, boom, boom!*" Turning the end of the aisle, Jack half-expected to see a police car screeching to a stop in the parking lot with sirens announcing to everyone within a mile, "Jack's a thief! Jack's a thief!" This imagery checked Jack in his step, and the relieving thought of putting it back flashed across his heart. But then there was that voice: "Go with it! What a rush! What a story!" Jack mustered his cowardly courage— for any thief is truly a coward at heart—and set the drink on the counter.

The gas station guy looked at him and asked, "Will this be all?"

No, that's not all! I have a candy bar in my pocket! I'm sorry. I'm so, so sorry! thought Jack, but instead he replied, "Uh, yeah." The question then occurred to Jack of why the guy would even ask that question. *He knows! He has to know! He probably sees this stuff every day. He probably saw me on some camera. Oh, man, I messed up big time. God, please help me. I'm so, so sorry! Just let me get out, and I'll bring back the money next time.* All these cries whirled through Jack's mind in a fraction of a second.

The gas station guy looked intently at Jack and narrowed his eyes at him. "Are you Jack?" he asked. Time froze, and what seemed like an hour was compressed into a moment.

With twisted thoughts, Jack's voice creaked as he replied, "Yes, sir."

The man smiled. "I thought so! You look just like your dad! I'm Phil. I'm in your dad's Bible study at church."

Jack swallowed hard. What had he done? What had he done? Jack gave Phil the pleasantly surprised look he was waiting for, nodded, and said, "Oh, yeah."

Phil gave Jack back some change and then reached over to the candy bars next to the register. "Here, let me throw in a little something extra," and he handed Jack a Twix bar.

Jack's spirit sank, but he put on a smile of excitement and said, "You don't have to do that!"

Phil nodded. "I know, but it's the least I can do after all that your family has done for me!" Jack thanked Phil and started out the door.

"See you Sunday!" Phil called out.

Jack mounted his bike and immediately rode out of the parking lot and around the corner where Phil couldn't see him anymore. Jack pulled up to the first park bench he could find to gather himself. "Holy cow! Holy cow! Holy cow!" he repeated to himself until his adrenaline, which was still pulsing through his hands, arms, and legs, died down to a manageable level. Jack ran through his self-diagnosis of body, spirit, and mind. His body was still trembling, and his legs felt like wet noodles. His spirit felt—well, his spirit didn't feel at all. His mind felt on fire.

What a rush! Next time, I'll get the beer! he boasted to himself.

"You go!" the voice affirmed.

"I will!" replied Jack out loud.

Jack remounted his bike, still enjoying the shivers of adrenaline that rippled through his mind like aftershocks of an earthquake. In his distracted excitement, he unintentionally left the Twix bar that Phil had given him on the bench to melt in the sun. He continued his aimless journey to nowhere in particular, turning into a neighborhood and passing through the closing security gate as a car exited.

The entrance had a familiarity to it, and Jack recalled that he had been to it once before. When he was a fifth grader, his dad had been invited to meet with a couple who was struggling in their marriage. They had a boy Jack's age, so Jay took him along to entertain the kid while the adults talked in private. He and that boy sat upstairs in the fancy media room playing Nintendo Wii for two hours with a smorgasbord of the best snacks and drinks money could buy. The family ended up staying together, but her company relocated them to California a year later. Jack recalled the scared smile and laughter of the boy. He couldn't recall his name, but his face was etched deeply in Jack's memory. Jack had almost invited the boy to pray—both of them knew what the visit was about—but was worried that the boy might think he was a geek.

The houses in the neighborhood were oversize, as were the lots they sat on. In the driveways of families with kids of driving age, there were usually extra sports or luxury cars that wouldn't fit into the three-car garages: Porsche, Mercedes, BMW. In the driveways of families with younger kids, there were usually luxury SUVs: Lexus, Infiniti, Cadillac. These wouldn't fit in the three-car garages either, because the spaces were overstuffed with sports equipment, bikes, and other oversize toys. "Oversize and excessive" seemed to be the mantra of this neighborhood, just like all the other ones in the suburbs of a wealthy oil city.

Jack followed his meandering course and turned his scrutiny away from the stuff and toward the people. Kids were playing in streets, yards, and driveways. Women were taking dogs for walks, visiting with other women, or loading up uniformed kids into SUVs. Men were supervising crews doing yard work; in the garage playing with one of their own toys, usually a boat or motorcycle; or sitting in the SUV, waiting on the women to finish loading the uniformed kids. Perfect kids, perfect women, perfect men, perfect pets, perfect houses, perfect everything—"Perfect," Jack muttered enviously.

A sense of anger fell over him and burned his mind. He pedaled on, looking, watching, and hating. He saw a kid about his own age riding a bike toward him on his same side of the street. Their paths were on a collision course. A stubborn thought struck Jack, and he made up his mind that he wasn't going to move over for some kid with a silver spoon shoved down his throat. The game of chicken was on, and Jack maintained his course and speed. He imagined the conclusion of this game if his newly discovered foe didn't redirect his path. He would jump off of his bike, grab the kid by his high-dollar athletic shirt, pull him to the ground, and then launch a series of blows before the kid knew what happened.

The two continued the game, and the distance between them was shrinking—thirty yards, twenty yards, ten yards. Jack's fists clenched around his handlebars, his jaw tightened, his glare intensified on its target, his feet lightened in preparation to jump, and adrenaline returned to power his body. Jack's hands squeezed on the brakes, and he pulled his bike to a sudden stop and dismounted like a gymnast from a pommel horse.

"Hey, Caden!" he exclaimed as if he was expecting to see the boy all along. Upon recognition, all the adrenaline and anger drained out of Jack as if someone had broken off the bottom of a Coke bottle, letting gravity swallow it up in one gulp. Caden Granger was a boy he superficially knew from school. They'd had a couple of classes together in junior high, and he knew that he sometimes played *MW7* online but was more into the sword- and assassin-type games, which was a totally different group of gamers than the *MW7* circle Jack ran in.

"Hey, Jack. What are you doing?"

"Just out killing time. Being bored. Nothing else to do."

"Yeah, same here. My sister had a volleyball game today, but I figured I could be just as bored here as I could there, so I stayed home. My parents are always trying to get me to go with them, but her games are so stupid and boring."

"Yeah," Jack agreed in sympathy.

"You wanna come to my house?" Caden asked. "We can play some Dare Dragon."

"Sure, that'd be cool," Jack replied.

The two rode the short few blocks to Caden's house and dropped their bikes in the front yard. Jack saw that there was little room in the oversize, overstuffed garage for bikes. It didn't matter, because the front yard was perfectly groomed and had the appearance of artificial turf. Every blade of grass was combed into place like a preacher's hair on Sunday morning. There were no weeds in the flowerbeds, and all the shrubs and trees looked like they had just had a fresh haircut from a fancy salon. They walked into the house, and the first thing Jack noticed was the smell. The air was fresh with the artificial scent of Hawaiian fruit. It smelled so good it actually made him hungry for a coconut or pineapple. Caden didn't seem to even take a noticing whiff. If you live in a place long enough, you soon become so used to the roses that you forget to smell them.

The interior of the house resembled more closely a museum or a pristine luxury hotel lobby than a house where people actually lived. There were high vaulted ceilings and highly polished dark cherrywood floors covered by burgundy oriental rugs. A grand piano, harpsichord, and harp were artistically positioned in a large parlor area with plush couches that could comfortably seat an audience of a dozen or more.

Noticing Jack's stare, Caden remarked, "My mom is the musician. She used to play for the Houston symphony but quit when my sister got into elementary and our nanny went back to Argentina. At one point, when I was in, like, first grade, the symphony begged her to come back. She tried but couldn't balance being both a mom and a concert musician at the same time. That's when she went solo—or, rather, 'so low' she started drinking. She plays society functions, political fundraisers, and stuff like that." Jack was amazed. It sounded like a character from some afternoon soap opera. Caden's tone was matter-of-fact, even cold, as he told it. To him, her music was just another continual reminder that he was in the way of the real love of her life.

When they arrived upstairs in the deep-red, windowless media room, Caden dimmed the lights to a candle glow, which brought out the high-def on the HDTV that covered over half of the front wall. "You want something to drink?" offered Caden.

"Sure, I'll take a martini—shaken, not stirred," Jack said, trying for a nice James Bond witticism.

Caden laughed, and Jack told him of his little plan to try to smuggle a beer from the gas station. Upon the story's conclusion, Caden stood up, walked over to a built-in bar that lined the back wall of the cavernous room, and extracted two brown bottles. "Is that root beer?" Jack asked.

"Nope. You don't have to steal anything from the gas station—I've got it right here!"

Jack's throat tightened at the appearance of the two oversize brown bottles covered with labels in a language he didn't recognize and two straws. It was one thing to have a little plan crafted in his mind but a totally different thing to have the treasure so effortlessly appear right in front of him. Jack's gut reactively clenched as if he had boasted of some great ability like jumping off of a cliff and had now, in front of witnesses, been given a dare to carry it out.

His gut knew this was not good and replayed the tape of his dad's lifetime of counsel about the danger of alcohol and drugs posed by their ability to make you more vulnerable to demons, who could use it to poison your whole person: body, mind, and spirit. Jay called them a sweet/bitter escape that people used to hide from the pains of life because they didn't rely on Jesus for who He really was. The sweetness of the sin always spoiled into bitterness eventually; that was just how sin worked. It was Jay's belief that if people knew how good Jesus really was, no one would want the dangerous escapes that drugs or alcohol provided. But understanding that they were all still flawed humans in a fallen world, he would remind the kids that the best way never to get addicted to anything, whether it be drugs, alcohol, lying, gambling, etc., was to never try it the first time. This was the wisdom he applied to his own life, at least as an adult, and it seemed to complement his growth in Christ quite well.

"Dude!" Jack exclaimed. "Won't your parents know?"

"My parents let me drink beer," Caden replied. "They think that if they let me and my sister drink alcohol here we'll be more responsible when we have the chance to drink it somewhere else."

"That sounds logical. Dude, your parents are so cool."

"Not really." Caden handed Jack a bottle and a straw. Jack looked at the straw with confusion and asked, "Why the straw?"

"I saw online where drinking beer through a straw makes you get drunker." The boys, with the tips of the straws barely visible above the twenty-ounce foreign bottles, clinked them together and said,

"Cheers!" Jack took a long, deep sip. The chilled liquid filled his mouth and assaulted his tongue. The taste was nasty, and Jack's face showed it.

"You get used to the taste," Caden said as he read the expression and spoke from his own experience. By about the tenth sip, Jack's taste buds were finally numb enough not to send the display-a-nasty-look message to his brain. He was still a long way, though, from appreciating the flavor that was praised by millions—but he was only a short way from appreciating the impact that was praised by them.

The boys continued to play the game and sip from their little glass friends. Jack could tell that their conversation was getting goofier and goofier. Everything seemed so funny, and the game seemed to require so much more concentration. Jack felt like he was giving the best performance of his life, but he kept getting killed; it didn't make sense. After about twenty minutes he felt himself getting dizzy. The beer didn't have quite as strong an effect on Caden—he had a higher tolerance built up—and he was laughing at Jack. Jack was laughing back, but he wasn't sure exactly why. Still repulsed by the taste, he finally gave up on finishing the whole bottle and left it in the chair's cup holder. He turned his full attention to their game. Another hour passed, and there was a door chime from downstairs. Jack heard the voices of Caden's parents and grabbed the bottle in a panic.

"Should we hide the beer?" he asked and looked to Caden's expression to shape his own. Caden didn't even look up from the game.

"Nah, they don't care. Besides, they never come up here."

Jack, unconvinced and excessively paranoid from the mild intoxication, said, "What if they want us to come down to talk or something?"

"They won't. They hardly ever talk to me. To them, I'm just a kid who lives upstairs, eats their food, and spends their money. As long as I stay out of their way, they leave me alone. It works just fine for me." Perhaps it was the beer, but Jack's heart sank at Caden's description of his parents. A feeling tingled inside Jack's gut, and he wanted to go home to his dad. But before this feeling could grow into a plan, a voice interrupted. "Whatever!" Jack felt his heart regain its strength and independence and resumed play.

Jack looked at his phone to see that two more hours had passed. His mind sufficiently numbed by the alcohol and the game, he wondered if playing a video game could be considered a sweet/bitter escape. Rationalizing that it couldn't be and congratulating himself on his deep intellectual consideration of the matter, he told Caden that he'd better start heading home. Caden escorted Jack downstairs in the event that his mom or dad would see him and want an introduction. As they exited the room, though, everything was quiet downstairs; his parents had left again. Jack's head still had a spin to it. Holding the handrail so as not to stumble and give an indication of his inferior drinking skills, Jack descended the staircase one focused step at a time and eventually made it outside.

Lifting his bike from the smooth grass, Jack turned to Caden, who was still standing at the door. "Hey, thanks, man. See you Monday."

Caden gave an upward nod. "Sure. See ya." He closed the door.

Mounting his bike, Jack found that his body was still a bit numb like his head, and his arms and legs weren't responding very well either. He initially selected the sidewalk as his best route for avoiding cars, either parked or moving, but after swerving into the grass a few times, he opted for the wider street. He was buzzed, but he wasn't completely unaware of his condition. Jack glanced around to see if anyone was watching him ride, but everyone he saw seemed to be preoccupied enough with their own stuff that they didn't notice him. When Jack occasionally swerved to a noticeable extent, he would try to cover it by making it look like he was intentionally meandering carelessly down the street.

Eventually, he made it back to his house, which took him longer than it should have due to a few wrong turns trying to get out of Caden's neighborhood. Jack put his bike in his usual parking spot against some steel shelving. Knowing that his dad usually kept a pack of gum in his console for the kids, Jack quietly opened the truck door and pulled out two pieces to help hide any beer smell that might still be on his breath. The spearmint flavor the gum released in his mouth with every chew brought refreshment to his dulled taste buds—if only the gum would do the same for his similarly dulled head.

He started to announce his return as he usually did when he came back into the house from being away so long, but he stopped himself short, not wanting the attention. Instead, he walked quietly into his room and closed the door. Privacy was what he needed right now; privacy was the blanket he'd pull over himself to hide from the threatening fear of discovery. As he lay there in self-imposed isolation, his darkened mind slid into the still waters and stroke by steady stroke paddled its way into that darkness just before the dawn of a dream.

-ᴏ-ᴏ-ᴏ-ᴏ-

He could hear the same rhythmic humming sound as before vibrating softly in the air. Its call invited him in.

"Jack, wake up."

He opened his eyes to darkness, as if he were blind, and then a dim face became clearer and clearer with each blink. It was Rachel. Her beautiful dark eyes were only a few inches from his own. He could feel her cool exhales on his cheeks, and the sweetness of her breath was as refreshing to him as the scent of mint, pine, camphor, and honey all placidly infused in eucalyptus. With the intake of each breath, his mind increased its sharpness, helping him realize just how dull of a state it had been in previously. She was lying next to him, her long, black hair draped in front of her neck, perfectly displaying the enchantment of her face, much like a diamond on black velvet.

As he sat up, her eyes held his gaze, and she said, "You're awake! I was waiting for you." Her tone was one of excitement and longing, and it made him feel masculine. That was a strange descriptor of his feeling, but that was the only one that accurately captured it. At the same time, he felt confused. She seemed to know him and to have known him for quite some time, but he still didn't know her. He felt like he had amnesia, and based on their first encounter, he accepted this as fact.

He spoke her name, "Rachel," and it felt so deeply significant that he spoke it again. He inhaled to speak it a third time but held it in his lungs to let the first two utterances have their full effect in soothing his soul. Rachel sat in the silence without judgment or rush. Her eyes told him that he was experiencing something good. "Rachel, help me understand …"

It was difficult to think and speak because he felt so incredibly intoxicated by this beautiful person who was now stroking his arm as he lay there. He pulled his eyes away from her gaze and let his own gaze drift down her arm to her hand on the ground. Only then could he speak. "Rachel … you have to help me. I don't remember anything in my mind, but in my spirit I remember everything."

Rachel looked tenderly at Jack, although he still averted his eyes from hers so that he could speak plainly.

"Patience, Jack. We have a long time for this."

"But I want to know now."

"Oh, my precious." Rachel lay back down beside him and gave him a half hug. "I don't want to rush you. I don't want you to get frustrated in remembering."

Her tender treatment rubbed poorly against Jack's masculinity. With an influx of strength, he cast a glance directly into her eyes and said, "No, I need to know now."

As the words came so emphatically across his tongue, his first instinct was to immediately apologize for offending such a beautiful girl, but her voice came before an apology could. "As you wish, but please stop me if you start to feel angry with me."

Jack chastised himself for even the idea of ever being angry at her and said, "I'll never get angry at you. I know you are trying to help me."

Rachel smiled understandingly and appreciatively. "Just promise me that you won't go into shock or be upset. I can't lose you to the world again."

Jack didn't fully understand this but trustingly nodded and braced himself mentally. Rachel took a deep breath and spoke. "Jack, in the year 490 BC, you were taken from me at the Battle of Marathon, where you fought for Athena to destroy the Persian dogs." Rachel's expression became severe at her last words, and his jaw dropped slightly in shock. He had braced himself for the unexpected, but this was beyond that. However, he liked the sound of it; he'd always felt a connection to ancient Greece and its mythology.

Rachel pressed her lips together and pushed back tears to continue. "We had had such peace under the democracy of Athena for so many years, until that evil Persian dog Darius got the idea that he could pick us as one of his Eastern lotus blossoms. But you"—Rachel intensified her gaze and petted the side of his face—"fought bravely for us."

At her words, a chill recoiled his body, and his mind raised to life the images of war from the *Iliad*. "I can still see you as you left our prayers in the temple." Her eyes became filled with pride, and she shook her black locks slightly from side to side, emphasizing her sincerity. "Your helmet pushed back on your head, your cuirass rippled like the muscles it protected, and your greaves showing the strength of your legs." He was glued to her every word and dared not interrupt her magnificent tale of himself. "We prayed to Athena that we would always be together and knew right there that she allowed our request. After two weeks, your brother, Aristides, brought back word that your eyes had filled with darkness after an arrow pierced your throat. I was running to the temple to curse Athena and enter darkness with you when she gave me an omen of her word. I saw a small boy with a sling and a stone. He swung the stone and hit a dove, knocking it from its perch. The boy ran to retrieve it, but when he got there, the dove was recalled to life and flew into the heavens. Then I noticed the boy looking closely at something where the dove had been lying. I went over to see what it was, and a butterfly had just come free from its cocoon. As I watched, the butterfly followed the exact path of the dove into the sky. With that sign, I knew that we would be together again in the next life."

His mind was whirling from this detailed account of his past. Rachel paused to let him digest it, and then they both sat up. "How do you feel?" she asked.

"I'm fine. It just seems so surreal."

"Let me ask you this. Have you ever really felt like the life you have now is really where you are supposed to be? Have you ever felt accepted by it?"

Realizing the unbelievable truth revealed by her questions, he answered, "No, not really."

"It's because you're more than that!"

"So how did I get separated from you in the afterlife?"

"When you were struck by the arrow in battle, you turned your heart away from Athena, not understanding her plan to reunite us. In her anger, she cast you into Pergyss, but I pleaded on your behalf. I told her that you had been loyal to her and that if I couldn't be with you in the afterlife, I wanted to go into Pergyss too. Out of her love for me, she agreed to let you walk the earth again. And she agreed that if you found me, I could help you. So at last you have found me!"

Rachel stood to her feet, helped Jack to his, and hugged him as if it was the first time she'd ever seen him. He felt as if everything made sense now, and in his relief, he hugged her back with equal fervor. Rachel pulled back and looked steadfastly into his eyes. He wasn't lost in them as he was before. He felt more in control of himself now—like his real self.

"Jack, just because you know a little of your past, that doesn't mean that this will be easy for us," Rachel sheepishly stated and cast her eyes down.

"It doesn't?" he asked.

"No. The earthen world is a mean and cruel place. It doesn't understand truth, and it molds you to believe its lies. So you have to focus on listening to me and not the things that other people tell you—even people you think are good and loving."

"What is the truth?"

"You'll know it when it comes to you. You'll hear it in your mind like a whisper. The key is to go with it. Just go with it."

"What will happen if I do something else or mess up?" he asked in doubt of himself.

Rachel's lip started to quiver, and tears started to stream down her cheeks as she buried her face in his shoulder. Holding her firmly against him, he apologized for asking that. Her reaction and silence answered his question; he would be eternally separated from her. The thought of this angered him, and he vowed to himself to do anything he could to be with her—forever.

"It's time for you to go," Rachel said gloomily.

"Why can't I stay longer?" he protested.

"Our meetings are limited because you have to finish your journey."

He nodded, pretending to understand all that that meant. Rachel produced the iron cup, and they lay back down on the plush grass. He sipped from the cup as before, and the bitterness was again overwhelming. This time, however, he pressed the cup to his lips without her help and forced his throat to gulp it down. He released the cup into her grasp and rested his head on the ground. He looked directly up beyond the treetops above; there was a dimness to the expanse that made it feel empty. He closed his eyes and felt his body lift off the ground. It was as if he had become one with the air of the new truth, which now was as transparent as the gust that blew his mind.

❖❖❖❖

It was now eight o'clock, and the girls were waking up and getting ready for church. Noticing Jack was still asleep, Avery snuck up to him with the idea of waking him with a gentle scream.

"Wake up, little sleepyhead! It's time for church!" But as she approached him, she noticed that his sheets were soaked with sweat and twisted off of the mattress. "Jack, are you okay?" she asked, her tone turning to concern. "Are you sick or something? Did you pee in your bed?"

Jack came out of his sleep and looked around wearily. "What?"

"You're soaking wet. Do you feel okay?" she asked.

Seeing what Avery saw, Jack was embarrassed. His eyes squinted with each thump of his aching head. "Yeah, yeah. I'm fine. Just leave me alone and get out."

With a perplexed look on her face, Avery turned and walked out to finish her preparations before breakfast.

"Don't tell Dad!" Jack called behind her. Jack felt his head for fever but realized that, more than likely, this was just a hint of what a hangover felt like. He could sense the wetness all over his sheets with his back. *Gross! Stupid beer,* he thought as he rolled out of bed and surveyed the navy sheets twisted into a pile. With renewed anxiety, he quickly pulled the sweat-drenched sheets into a ball, walked to the laundry room, and jammed them into the washing machine. He grabbed an armful of dark clothes from a pile of dirty clothes

85

and crammed them in to cover the sheets. If asked about his doing laundry at such an odd a time as Sunday morning, he decided he would say that he wanted to wear a certain pair of shorts this afternoon. That may not be completely believable, but it was close enough, and it was the only excuse he had outside of wetting his bed, which was not really an option at all.

The washing machine stopped filling with water, and Jack measured out the detergent. He closed the lid, and the agitator began to turn. *Mmm, mmm, mmm.* Jack froze for an instant, listening to its call. *Mmm, mmm, mmm.* It resembled the rhythmic humming of his visits with Rachel—that subtle pulse hidden beneath the surface that somehow moved energy through the veins of life. He turned his attention to his heart and felt his pulse—*buh-bum, buh-bum, buh-bum.* He moved back to his room and through the stillness of the morning listened to the rhythmic pulse of the clock—*ticktock, ticktock, ticktock.*

He had never realized how the rhythms of this world pointed to those of the next one with Rachel. He mused arrogantly at his new revelation, feeling that he drank from the purer spring water three hundred feet below, while those less fortunate intellects contented themselves with sips from someone else's bottle. So, weary from the remnants of alcohol but peaceful from his new enlightenment, he continued his Sunday routine of getting polished up for church.

10

RISING ON THE FLOOD

A group of four older boys was hovering in a hallway where every inch of wall was lined by lockers. The hallway provided the excessive storage required to accommodate the excessive storage needs of the students, whose parents paid excessive taxes to support their children's excessive education. The group of boys was composed of two seniors and two juniors, each wearing a varsity athletic jacket with his name or nickname proudly stitched across the back. On the sleeves and pockets their cloth trophies were on constant public display. The sports varied some, but the one they all had in common was football.

They were warriors of the gridiron, fighting valiantly each week on behalf of the students of their high school tribe. They were the forces that established and maintained the battleship of pride on which every other student could let their local identity ride. They were in-house celebrities celebrated by all. Younger kids went to games to watch the battles, believing that these athletes must come from some mighty and mystical place that had to be in a faraway land. Freshmen and sophomores worked their bodies to look like grown men in hopes of getting their turn one day at fighting the enemy as so many had done before them. On this day, the conversation of the small band of heroes was not about football, it was not about school, and it was not about girls. The conversation on this day was about an entertaining pastime: online gaming. One of the boys turned his head out of the circle, and looking down the hall, he lifted his arm, extended his finger, and exclaimed in a somewhat clandestine voice to the others, "That's him. That's CMD101." The others in the group paused their conversation, their eyes following his finger to the kid coming down the hall.

Jack's thoughts had been vacillating between the lesson in Bible study the other day and his dream of Rachel's incredible yet seemingly credible story of his past. A reconciliation was in order, and this would take time, thought, effort, and focus. He meandered steadily down the hallway, his walk taking the path of least resistance through the congested river of students. He glimpsed a finger and four faces pointing at him. He turned his head to the back left, looking for the object of attention, and then he turned it to the back right toward that same end. Finding no obvious answer, he returned to the mysterious finger and faces. They were still there. He examined the faces. He examined the jackets. He examined the owners of both: Sam Sweeney, Jordan Summers, Moose Moak, and Jerome Brett. It was an intimidating crew for a freshman like him to behold.

Jack's stomach filled with butterflies when he realized that they were standing right next to his locker. He would have to somehow politely, very politely, ask them to move so he could get his book for his next class. Or maybe, the next thought quickly flashed into Jack's mind, he was somehow at odds with them. His mind very quickly played through all his sarcastic and scathing social media posts over the past two weeks. Sure, he'd made many insulting remarks and offensive jabs, but none that could be linked to any of them—or so he hoped.

Putting on his most innocent face, Jack approached the group.

"Are you CMD101?" asked Jerome, taking the lead.

Jack considered a witty remark like "That depends on who's asking," but with intimidation comes humility, so he answered, "Yeah … why?"

Jerome took the question. "We've been playing *MW7* as a team, and we can't get past the Seventeenth Campaign." He needn't continue, because Jack knew that campaign inside and out, but he continued anyway. "It's the one where you have to infiltrate Molina's nuclear hideout and dismantle the warhead while millions of stupid zombies attack you relentlessly."

Jack listened attentively to show that he had the utmost respect for them. Jerome paused from his narrative and looked at Jack, who looked back at him. Jerome asked, "Do you know how to get past this one?"

The group waited for the answer to what seemed to be an impossible question. Without hesitation, Jack nodded and said, "You just have to inject yourself with the zombie toxins. That way, they won't attack you, and you can disarm the warhead."

In a poor imitation of a Mexican accent, Jordan comically mimicked an old movie line: "Zombie toxins? We don't need no stinking zombie toxins!"

Jack took advantage of this comic relief to alter his expression from innocent curiosity to a disarming but brief smile. "When you first enter the fortress and all of the computer troops head down the stairs to the right toward the warhead, you have to turn to the left, squat down, and look up. You'll see a grating that looks like it's covering a window high on the wall. Grab some of the barrels, climb up to the grating, and then hold down the X and Z buttons to jump through it." After Jack finished outlining the first step of the seemingly simple solution, he looked at the boys to see if they were tracking. They were nodding as if they were playing the game in their minds. As he spoke, they tossed question after question at him. The second bell rang out, indicating that they were all tardy to fifth period, so Sam finally proposed that they continue the conversation later. Jack watched them stroll away in lockstep as one united team. Then he quickly opened his locker and replayed the conversation in his mind. His pride swelled, and he wondered if anyone else had seen him talking with them, hoping they had seen him strutting smugly and carelessly tardy to his class.

The next day, Jack entered the cafeteria and was on his way to his usual spot with Bobby, and now Caden, when he heard his name. Turning, he saw Sam, Jordan, Moose, and Jerome sitting at the lunch table they frequented when they didn't go off-campus to eat. Jerome slid a chair back, indicating that this was where Jack should sit. As Jack reached for the chair, he cast a glance at Bobby and Caden. Jack had not told them of his gaming conversation with the group, so they both stopped their lunch, trying to figure out what was going on. Seeing them watching, Jack gave an upward nod and sat down next to Jerome. Jack's heart—or rather his head—began to swell, and his eyes darted around to see who else might be watching him running with the big dogs. The group picked up the prior day's conversation, and Jack walked them through campaigns seventeen and eighteen. To his pleasant surprise, Moose had the idea to just let Jack join their battalion online and lead them through the campaigns. All the boys looked around and nodded in agreement that this was the best solution.

Jordan realized their campaign problem was solved and turned the discussion in a different direction. "Have you ever heard of *Mithras?*"

"Like, a game called *Mithras?*" asked Sam.

Jordan nodded. "Yeah. My mom's second cousin is an actress in LA, and I was texting her son, Dalton, about the Texans whipping the Chargers. He started telling me about it—said that it's gonna be globally epic. He's been a big gamer for a long time now, and he said that there's never been a game as popular as this one is gonna be."

All the boys looked at Jack, their new resident expert in games. He shrugged his shoulders and nodded. "Hmm, that sounds really cool. I'll have to keep an eye out." Jack took a mental note of the game's name, *Mithras*, so he could research everything about it. He wanted to further secure his place in the popular group.

Not to completely disappoint his new students, the new self-considered master added, "I'm sure it's like most games and you *just go with it!*" "Just go with it!"—this sounded like a motto of success to Jack's enlarged ears on his newly enlarged head.

"Hey, y'all!" a voice called out as a girl walked by dressed in half of the fabric most other girls were wearing. The conversation came to an abrupt halt, and each head turned to watch the little sheep pass by the wolfish pack.

In true packlike unison, they responded, "Hey, Nicki!"

Nicki turned her back to continue her stroll, and though the boys turned back to their conversation, their eyes continued to watch her instead. Jack, not yet part of the pack, watched this scene take place. He saw the cool facade of each cool boy. He saw the hot undergirding of each hot boy. He saw the sheep pretending to be wolves. He saw the wolf pretending to be a sheep. At the conclusion of the drama, his mind stood to its feet and cheered, "Bravo! Bravo!" This was the play he longed to act in: *Popularity*—act one, scene one.

11

A SEDUCTIVE SWIRL

Nicki was always bummed out the Saturday morning after her school lost a Friday-night football game. The hours of relentless cheering to encourage the packed stadium to dial up the volume and give their team a competitive edge sapped her physically and mentally. Then there were the elite after-parties for only the popular clique, which usually kept her out until as late as two o'clock in the morning. Who knew that being a school celebrity was so exhausting? Her self-reminder of her popularity helped draw her tired self out of bed.

Scared of the silence, which always made her feel so alone, Nicki reached for her iPad mini and touched up some vintage Britney, whom she still appreciated despite the Vegas act. The song was "Overprotected," and the words resonated so much with her that feelings of frustration with her life flooded her mind, and she tapped over to TrashMouth. The screech of the guitar reflected the scream going off in her head.

The burden of life was heavy, too heavy for her to bear, and she was angry deep within. She didn't know where exactly her anger was smoldering; she just knew it was there somewhere, burning. She screamed at it from behind a pretty little smiley-faced mask. She despised this mask and the one who wore it. With all this contorting her mind, tears filled her eyes. She stared into the full-length mirror on the back of her door, watching the tears streak down her unmade and tired face. This wasn't her. This was a pathetic loner isolated in her flesh.

"Rachel, I need you …" she muttered, watching the girl's mouth move in the mirror. She dropped to the ground on her hands and knees and put her face to the ground. If she looked at the girl again, she would scratch out the eyes that told those lies. "Rachel, I need you. Rachel, I need you. Rachel, I need you—where are you?" Nicki crawled under her bed. Although chastised and threatened, the eyes still mourned for their wearer. "Rachel, Rachel, Rachel …" Nicki repeated this distress call over and over until she finally blacked out.

◀━○○○━▶

Nicki blinked off the darkness on her eyelids and drew in a breath. The pleasant earthen scent cleansed her senses, and the soft foliage beneath her comforted her body. She felt at home. She sat up and looked around. Just like at home, the silence scared her. She called for Rachel, but there was no reply. An adrenaline rush stood her to her feet. Her eyes were darting around the woods, and her ears were on point. She heard a gust of wind disturbing the leaves in a nearby tree.

Her eyes and ears immediately directed their attention upward. Something was swirling the treetop. Panic seized her by the throat, and she couldn't scream. The gust of something swooped down from the treetop and stroked her face. Chills shook her whole body, and she started running. The gust easily caught her and stroked her again, blowing her hair forward. She stopped and turned to run in the opposite direction. The gust of wind blew again, this time directly into her face. As it did, she closed her eyes as tight as she could, and the image of a clawed hand caressing her jawline flashed through her mind.

With nowhere to run, she fell down sobbing. An even louder rush of wind sounded above her head. Expecting some type of whirlwind, she looked up to determine which way she should run, but she saw a light like a camera flash instead. Panicked like a rabbit cornered by a wolf, she dove to the base of a tree and clung to it, her face pressed against the bark and her tears soaking her cheeks.

"Nicki," a voice called, and she felt a cool touch on her shoulder. Recognizing the voice, Nicki turned, sprang to her feet, and reached out both of her arms to firmly grasp her savior.

"Rachel, what was that thing?"

Rachel looked confused and shook her head. "What are you talking about, Nicki?"

"Something like a gust of wind was chasing me and touching me." At the recollection of it, Nicki shivered.

"There's no one here but me," Rachel replied innocently. "The Ohm only allows you and me to meet here."

Nicki wasn't convinced; she knew what she had seen and what she had felt. She was insistent. "No, Rachel, I'm telling you—something was here. It chased me, and when I shut my eyes, I saw this hideous claw thing touch me right here." Nicki pointed to her jaw.

Rachel shook her head again and with the most sympathetic look and tone said, "Nicki, Nicki, you brought some fear with you. I'll bet before you came you were in a not-so-good place, and you brought that feeling with you. Evidently you brought fear."

Nicki tried to remember but couldn't. Her mind felt restricted, but this certainly was a credible explanation. Nicki wondered to herself who was more likely to be right, her or Rachel. Deciding it was Rachel, Nicki let out an exhale of relief and smiled.

Rachel warmly reflected her smile and said, "Now there, we can put that negativity away. This is certainly no place for that!"

Nicki chastised herself for letting her naïveté disrupt her peaceful place, and this caused a spark of anger to flare up within her. She instinctively wanted to drown her anger in music, and this sprouted a point of contention in her mind.

"Rachel, I'm a little bit ashamed to admit this, but when I get angry about something, I listen to this one band called TrashMouth. Their music is loud and angry, but it's like I can feel it connect with my soul or something. It's the opposite of what I feel when I talk to you, so is that something I need to stop?"

Rachel gave her an encouraging look, which seemed to be becoming her responsive look to most of Nicki's questions, and said, "I know this may sound strange—I guess it all sounds a bit strange to you still—but there are no bad feelings. What's bad and will keep you from getting closer to the Ohm is restraining your feelings. Most people are taught not to feel extreme things. Extreme anger will cause you to hurt others or yourself. Extreme happiness will cause you to live in an unrealistic fantasy. All of these lies prevent people from the truth of who they really are. For example, you've been taught that drugs are bad, right?"

Nicki nodded hesitantly, because she had seen this firsthand when a friend of a friend had died from an overdose of meth.

"Well, drugs can be used to expand your mind and take you into a closer union with the Ohm. Let me put it this way. Would you rather overdose on meth and have your mind expanded to its maximum extent, which will take you to the highest level in the Ohm, or would you rather spend your time here resisting it and then only attain a low level of union in the Ohm?"

Still a bit doubtful, Nicki replied, "I guess the highest level."

Rachel could see that Nicki was still unconvinced. She twisted her face in concerned thought, appearing to come up with a different way to explain it.

"I knew someone who died from an overdose of meth," Nicki interjected, thinking it was a coincidence that Rachel used this example, "and they didn't seem to have their mind expanded or experience any good thing. In fact, it was very, very bad."

Rachel smirked. "I know. It was Kipper, who was Stephanie's friend."

Nicki's brow furrowed in surprised confusion. "How did you know?"

"You have to remember: the Ohm has assigned you and me to be connected. I've been keeping tabs on you since you were very small," replied Rachel. Nicki felt comforted and then discomforted by this thought. Rachel continued, "In Kipper's situation, she was a lesser soul. Her destiny was for Pergyss. While the drugs seemed bad, they only helped her attain her destiny quicker. So to her, they were helpful in that they killed her body. Now, to those of us who are better, like you, the drugs help us to get to a higher level, and *if* they diminish your body, it just moves you quicker to your destiny."

Like another crystal of ice melted, Nicki's mind grasped the idea, and her face lit up.

Rachel noticed her reaction and clapped. "You got it!"

Nicki sighed in relief, nodded, and grinned in a small amount of embarrassment from being so slow to grasp this truth. Rachel reinforced her progress. "Nicki, don't ever get discouraged in your journey. You've been conditioned to think and feel in a physical body, so you're going to find many things are hard to learn or relearn. There is really no right and wrong like you've been taught. And a rainbow isn't light, but rather life. Another one we'll leave for later. For now, just know that there is a reason that the TrashMouth music appeals to you so much, and that is because your beautiful soul craves the expansion of feelings it produces. So just go with it!"

These last words had a familiarity to them that served to reinforce their validity. Nicki repeated the words as they soaked in. "Just go with it." She moved her gaze back up to Rachel and observed, "You know, Rachel, a friend of mine has been using that motto a lot lately. His name is—"

Rachel interrupted to demonstrate her depth of knowledge. "Jack!"

Nicki's eyes widened in surprise. "How did you ... oh yeah, you can see a lot, being a free spirit!"

"Yep!" Rachel replied. "I've been watching Jack for some time. I think he might be your soul mate, but the Ohm hasn't proven this yet. If he's not, he's definitely one that you would want to connect to."

Nicki conjured up the image of Jack's face in her mind. She smiled to herself. "He is kinda cute. And nice. I bet his soul is deep."

Rachel watched Nicki turning this idea over in her mind, and involuntarily, one of her eyes turned from crystal green to deep red as she herself contemplated the image of Jack.

Nicki glanced up with another question but was checked by the one red eye. "How do—Rachel, your eye!"

Rachel, realizing her mistake, quickly recovered her full mask by concentrating solely on Nicki. As if nothing had happened, Rachel replied in urgent concern, "What is it, Nicki?"

"Your eye was red!" Nicki reported.

Rachel laughed and in an almost mocking tone replied, "What? My eyes turned colors? Wouldn't that be fun!"

Nicki's confusion between her eyes' testimony and Rachel's mocking response made her feel ashamed of just how flawed she was.

To completely smother the lapse, Rachel added, "I think that was just your human imagination!"

Nicki nodded in agreement and let out a laugh of relief, joining Rachel's continuing laughter. Nicki turned around, took a deliberately deep breath, and looked away into the woods.

Nicki's back now facing her, Rachel pulled off her mask completely. Her eyes, two orbs of deep red, burned with fury at this peasant. She drew in a deep breath and clasped the mask quickly back on her person.

Nicki returned to the conversation. "I'm sorry, Rachel. I must've been overwhelmed by everything being so new."

Rachel peered lovingly into Nicki's eyes and said, "No, I'm sorry for laughing. I should be more patient with you. Our love for each other is deep, and I want it to grow even more."

Nicki held out her arms and hugged Rachel, saying, "I can tell that the Ohm was right in joining us together. Your soul has such a unique beauty about it." At the warmth of her own words, Nicki tightened her embrace.

From a hiding spot atop a nearby tree, Spaw peered down, watching Nicki embrace the air in front of her. Nicki's heartfelt embrace was like a hairball in the throat of a cat, and he involuntarily gagged. Clearing his throat, he quickly returned to the master illusion, which only a handful of demons could conjure.

The sensation on Nicki's arms was cool and empty, just like the air. This struck Nicki as strange, but she decided she didn't know what a spirit would feel like, anyway, without a real body. She felt a cool breeze cross her back and supposed it to be Rachel's arms. Nicki broke the embrace and stepped back. She looked longingly into Rachel's deep-green eyes. "Rachel, why can't I go with you now?"

Rachel mirrored her look of longing and said, "You have so much to learn, and the only way you can learn it, unfortunately, is to return to the school of life." Nicki nodded and Rachel continued, "Go back. Get to know Jack." They both smiled at the unintentional rhyme. "And keep coming back for our talks. Forever will be here before you know it."

With that, Nicki knew the time had come to end the session. She dove into Rachel's beautiful crystal-green eyes and began to glide through their depths. She inhaled deeply as she went, her feelings again intoxicated by peace, happiness, excitement, and love. Then, just like before, her euphoric state was interrupted. She felt a turning sensation in her stomach as if she was about to throw up. She stopped herself in midstroke to cover her mouth just as the bitterness in her stomach erupted in the transparent green pool around her. It was as if an octopus had spewed black ink around her face. She couldn't breathe. She frantically waved her hands back and forth to move the darkness away from her eyes and to get a breath, but it wouldn't move. She felt her body go limp from suffocation and was wondering if she was dying. Just as she was surrendering the battle for a life-giving gasp, she awoke in a feverish sweat under her bed.

Exhausted, her body wanted to go to sleep, but she fought the plea and stood up. Relieved to find that she hadn't really thrown up, she glanced again at the girl in the mirror, this time more numb than angry. She involuntarily lost a breath when she saw the girl. It wasn't her, but who else could it be? She moved closer to the mirror, reaching out with her hand, as if touching her would somehow make her, Nicki, prettier. The first thing she noticed was the dark circles under her eyes. Then, moving her finger up the glass, she examined her bloodshot eyes. She moved her finger back and forth in an attempt to erase these things she had never seen before, and she saw a streak of sweat on the mirror from her fingertip. She altered her stare from the reflection to the fingertip and rubbed it against her thumb and then across her other hand. The finger glided easily, as she was drenched in sweat.

She looked back at the girl and saw her crying again, this time from her horrid appearance. Without being fully aware of her motions, she opened the door, went into the bathroom, and locked the door behind her. She turned on the water in the sink. The noise gave her a sensation of normalcy. She grabbed a hand towel from the rack and began to wipe up the sweat. Once she had wiped her forehead, then her entire face, and her neck, the towel was close to saturation. She drooped the towel over the bathtub to dry and then again caught the image of that girl in the mirror. Mesmerized, she again reached out her hand to touch it. The bathroom lights clicked off, separating the two girls. She took in a breath, coming fully back to herself, and felt for the light switch. She flicked the light back on, washed her face, and coated it with makeup.

Now dressed in full battle array—makeup bronzing her face, eyeliner framing her eyes, her dark hair pressed straight and free to move with the breeze, a low-cut shirt to pull down to overexposure on command, and denim shorts that looked painted on—Nicki yelled to her mom that she was going outside as she closed the front door. Passing from darkness into the light of the sun, she slipped on her designer sunglasses, which helped spark to life the perk in her step, announcing to everyone that she was someone they should want to know.

Nicki marched to the end of the block and paused. "Now which way does Jack live?" she asked herself. Remembering that her friend Chloe caught the bus at the same stop, she turned left and proceeded to Chloe's part of the neighborhood, which was only about six blocks away. As Nicki walked along confidently, she thought back to her conversations with Rachel, the idea of a soul mate, and the possibility of it being Jack, who, in all honesty, she hardly knew. Just the thought of having someone to love and to love her to the degree that Rachel described made her giddy with excitement.

She smiled and even let forth a giggle as she skipped down the sidewalk. Her anticipation was high as she turned the final corner to Chloe's—and, more importantly, Jack's—street. She was in luck! A car had just pulled up in Chloe's driveway, and she could tell that the passenger was Chloe. Nicki quickened her pace so as to catch her before she went into the house. This would look more casual and wouldn't obligate her to stay as long once she got the information she needed. After closing the car door, Chloe looked down the street to see if she might know the girl who was walking a couple of houses away. She recognized the girl as Nicki, lifted her hand in a wave, and shouted, "Hey, Nicki!"

Nicki continued her accelerated pace and replied, "Hey, Chloe!" Thinking to stall Chloe in case she had obligations inside, like putting away groceries, Nicki continued, "What are you doing?"

Still being a bit far off, Chloe couldn't exactly make it out and called back, "What?"

Nicki, taking on a playful air, yelled again but with pronounced words, "What are you doing?"

"Oh, nothing," Chloe replied, knowing that she couldn't explain exactly what she'd been doing until Nicki came closer. She began to move down the driveway toward the sidewalk, which was just how Nicki had planned it. In a few brief moments, Nicki was face-to-face with Chloe.

"Where've you been?" Nicki asked, glancing around at the surrounding houses, wondering which one was Jack's and how she was going to talk to him.

Chloe instinctively followed Nicki's glance, as she supposed something had caught her attention, but seeing nothing out of the ordinary, she replied, "My mom and I just came from getting my iPhone screen fixed. My little brother, who is only four, got it off of my dresser and spiked it against the tile floor imitating a football player he saw after a touchdown. At first I was furious, but then, after my mom said it could be repaired, I thought it was kind of cute."

"You're such a nice sister!" Nicki affirmed with a smile.

"Thanks!" Chloe replied with a deeply sincere expression on her face.

"So what are you doing now?" inquired Nicki.

"Well, unfortunately, my mom and dad have to go to my older brother's game, and I have to babysit my little brother and little sister," answered Chloe. "What are you doing?"

"Oh, just killing time. I was supposed to go shopping with my sister, but sometimes I just want to get away," replied Nicki.

"Well, you can hang with me if you want," Chloe invited. This was just what Nicki was hoping for.

"Sure, that'd be great!" Nicki replied enthusiastically. She knew the art of making other people feel special.

Chloe's parents came out of the house and climbed back into the car. "We'll be back in a few hours," said Chloe's dad.

"Okay, we'll be here," she replied.

The car backed slowly down the driveway and then sped off toward the ball fields. With the car safely out of sight, a four-year-old boy and an eight-year-old girl bounced out of the front door. "We're going next door!" they announced to the entire neighborhood.

"Stop!" cried Chloe, much like a quarterback changing the play at the line of scrimmage. They both looked at her in disgruntled disbelief. "Make sure you're back in two hours, and don't go get hit by a car or kidnapped or anything stupid like that!" Chloe said in a firm tone.

Both the kids agreed and headed off in separate directions. Chloe again stopped them. "Wait a minute! Whose house are you going to anyway?"

"I'm going to Jimmy's house," the little boy remarked.

"And I'm going to Anna Claire's house," said the little sister.

Hearing this, Nicki recognized the somewhat unique name as being Jack's sister. She began to work her angle.

"Who are Anna Claire and Avery?" Nicki asked the girl, who looked back with some confusion because she hadn't said anything about Avery.

"She's my best friend. Avery is her older sister, and most of the time she won't play with us."

Nicki, annoyed that she had tipped her hand but delighted that the little girl hadn't called her out on it, followed the girl's pointing finger directly across the street. *That's the house!* she thought to herself, and she plotted the next step of going to it.

Chloe jumped into the conversation. "Yeah, that's Jack's house. You know, he's friends with Bobby, who I dated last year."

As if unsure of herself, Nicki replied, "Oh, yeah, I think I know who he is. Red hair, lots of freckles?" She pretended to be mistaken to further cover her intentions.

"No," Chloe remarked with a hint of perplexity, "that's John … I think. Jack is about this tall"—she held up her hand about two inches above Nicki's head—"and has kind of blondish hair. He usually sits toward the front of the bus."

Nicki assumed a contemplative expression and then sparked her face as if she'd had an aha moment. "Yeah, yeah, he's been hanging out with Sam Sweeney before school—you know, the quarterback. He's a junior." Nicki knew that she had found her leverage. Chloe had

had a crush on Sam since he'd broken up with his old girlfriend after the New Year's Eve party. Nicki threw out the bait. "Does Jack ever talk about Sam?" she asked Chloe.

With her interest heightened Chloe replied, "I don't know. I haven't talked to him much since we've been back in school." Nicki could read Chloe's thoughts: she'd love to know more about Sam Sweeney.

Nicki suggested, "Why don't we take your sister over to Anna Claire's house—you know, just to make sure that it's okay if she plays there? You are the babysitter, right?"

Chloe took the bait, and her eyes glinted with excited agreement. *This is why Nicki is so popular—she really knows people,* Chloe thought and said, "You're right! I need to make sure that she's not messing up their day or anything like that!"

The little girl, already walking across the street, had an aggravated look on her face when she heard Chloe call out, "Wait a second, Lucy! I need to go with you to make sure it's okay for you to play over there first!"

Chloe and Nicki scurried up to Lucy, whose brow furrowed in disapproval. "Whatever!" she exclaimed and turned to continue the short trip to Anna Claire's door, intentionally ignoring her two new tagalongs. The little boy, seeing what had happened, quickened his walk to a run, making sure that Chloe wouldn't stop him too.

Lucy reached the door first and rang the doorbell. Chloe looked excitedly at Nicki, who had her gaze set through the glass door, watching for any activity that looked like a teenage boy. Instead, a younger, brown-haired girl answered the door. It was Avery. Opening the door, her eyes quickly moved above the little girl's head to the two older girls.

"Hi, Chloe!" she greeted.

"Can Anna Claire play?" asked Lucy from below.

Before Avery could get the reply out, Chloe interrupted. "I wanted to make sure it was okay with your dad if Lucy played over here."

Avery was a bit confused since Lucy always came over and played but was too polite to show it—and she didn't want to do something that might give them a bad opinion of her. "Oh, it's fine," she said to Chloe. Then, casting a downward glance at Lucy, she said, "She's in her room."

On hearing this, Lucy took the usual liberty to push right by Avery and head toward Anna Claire's room, where they usually played online together working to build up virtual lands of dragons, castles, and monsters—and then to tear them down with epic battles against online enemies. Avery, who enjoyed hanging out with the slightly older Chloe, took advantage of the opportunity. "Y'all want to come in?"

"Sure!" replied Chloe. "This is Nicki."

Avery, knowing who she was and being aware of her popularity status at school, said, "Oh, yeah, I know you. I was in a cheer camp one summer with you." Thinking she might have to prompt Nicki's memory more, she started to continue, "It was the—"

"Yeah, I remember." Nicki interrupted. "You have a little sister named Anna Claire and a brother who is a freshman named Jack." Avery, very pleasantly surprised and honored that Nicki remembered her, excitedly replied, "Yeah!" To reinforce the desire to be casual friends instead of just acquaintances, she added, "How has cheer team been going?"

Nicki replied proudly, "I'm not on that team anymore. I'm a cheerleader for the high school now!"

"Oh that's great! That's ..." Avery hesitated, as she was just about to use the word *great* again, which would've sounded awkward. "I bet that's a lot of fun!"

Nicki gave a few quick nods. "Yeah!" She started to direct the conversation toward herself and her cheerleading experience, but then she recalled that she was there for a bigger purpose (and it was rare for Nicki to have a purpose bigger than her own image) and turned the conversation back to Avery with a pause.

"Oh, come on in," Avery said as she stepped back from the door, letting the girls pass by. As they did, Nicki's eyes inspected the entryway and critiqued it in her mind. She had seen a show on the Psychic Network about feng shui, some Chinese philosophy of harmonizing your surroundings with the forces of the universe, and believed that you could tell a lot about a person just from seeing how they decorated his or her room. The décor was overly simple. It lacked the froufrou feel provided by little knickknacks that nobody really noticed but somehow added to the ambiance. Chloe, having lived across the street for the past five years, had fairly tight friendship with Avery and could ask more casual questions without raising any suspicions of motive.

"What's Jack doing today?" she asked in a carefree tone.

"He's in his room, probably playing his Xbox with his online friends," Avery replied.

As the girls migrated through the entryway toward the kitchen bar, Nicki joined in again. "Who are some of the people he plays with? Are they from around here or, like, around the world?"

Avery replied, "I think most of them are from around here, because he says they talk about it at school. What's funny is that he makes fun of some people because 'All they do is play this video game and then talk about it constantly at school,' but then he does the same thing."

Nicki and Chloe nodded and give a chuckle. Chloe probed, "So who are some of the people he plays with?"

Avery, realizing she hadn't answered the question, continued, "I don't know all of them, but some I've heard him mention are Bobby, Jake, Caden, Sam, Brad, Brian ..." Avery paused and turned her eyes up in an attempt to supply more information to the two inquisitors. "That's all I know of."

Being the good hostess, Avery moved to the refrigerator and pulled out three cans of Dr Pepper and placed them before each of them. She didn't even need to ask if that was the drink they wanted, because she knew it was the popular drink. The girls without any thought popped the tabs on the cans and took a sip.

Nicki, knowing of Chloe's interest in Sam, picked up the trail. "Sam? Like Sam Sweeney from the football team?"

"Yep," Avery replied.

"I saw them hanging out the other day at school," Nicki said.

"He's cute," Chloe added, hoping to find out everything Avery knew about him.

Avery agreed, "Yeah, I know, right?" Nicki smiled and nodded her agreement, and the girls let loose a bonding giggle as they glanced at each other, looking for acceptance, which they all happily affirmed.

The sound of company coming into the house had caught Jack's ear, the sound of three Dr Peppers being opened made him curious as to who it was, and when he heard the rounds of girl giggles, his interest was piqued enough to investigate. Stopping by the bathroom first, he examined himself and made a few alterations to ensure that his hair, face, breath, and odor were all good, just in case one of the girls was cute. His walk was carefully casual, and as he approached, he listened to the voices in an attempt to recognize them. There was Avery, Chloe, and one other girl who he couldn't quite place.

It sounds like Nicki, but what would she be doing here on a Saturday at this time ... or anytime? Jack wondered as the thought of her caused his adrenaline to surge. His walk involuntarily became a bit more rigid, and he could tell. He tried to convince himself that he could care less if it was Nicki, in an effort to avoid an awkward appearance, but his nerves continued to stand on end. Nonetheless, he persevered and turned the corner into the kitchen area, heading for the refrigerator.

He acknowledged the girls with a slight lifting of his head and a cool hey as he pulled the door open and reached in for a drink. His plan was just a quick flyby to snag a Dr Pepper of his own and return to his room for his next move, but seeing that the girls had grabbed the last one, he had to pause longer to decide between a can of pear nectar, which would look uncool to drink, or a glass of tea, which would require him to pour a cup in front of the girls, which might reveal his nerves or, even worse, lead to an embarrassing spill.

After some quick contemplation, he opted not to take either risk. He pushed the door shut, grabbed a cup from the cabinet, and jammed it under the water dispenser in the door. He focused his attention on the water spraying into the plastic cup and then a horrifying sight reached his eyes. He had grabbed a Strawberry Shortcake cup that Avery had gotten at a birthday party when she was only six years old!

Jack chastised himself for the mistake, but he was forced to continue. Maybe he could hide the cup from the girls as he walked quickly back to his room. But just then, Chloe, being a longtime friend of Jack's too, called out, "Hey, Jack! Do you know Sam Sweeney?"

Jack's mind abandoned his cute cup in light of this new topic of interest. As if Sam was his best friend, he replied, "Sure."

Avery, knowing her brother well, could see his nerves showing through his appearance, but she had enough appreciation for him not to try to add to his predicament. She knew when she could get away with embarrassing him in fun and when it might just be mean, and now, in front of a girl as cute and popular as Nicki, was definitely not the time. However, Avery still had to grin at Jack's little pink cup until he met her grin with his pleading microfrown.

Thanks to some enjoyable conversation primarily instigated by Chloe about Sam Sweeney, Jack's nerves settled down, and he thought himself to be in quite a zone with his quick wit and humor. Nicki, continuously watching Jack watching her, couldn't help but take the helm of the conversation. "So, Jack, how long have you been hanging out with Sam and friends?" Nicki asked, referring to the popular jocks. Jack wanted to embellish a bit but knew that Nicki had had friendship connections into that group for quite some time. "Oh, just a couple of months," he only slightly exaggerated.

"Oh, wow. What's the connection? You are a freshman, and they're juniors and seniors. Do you play a sport too?" Nicki inquired.

Answering the last question first, Jack replied, "I play football." He didn't pursue this topic because he wasn't exactly the fastest receiver on the team—actually, he was the freshman team second string. In fact, he had already decided that this would probably be his last year and that he'd narrow his sports endeavors to tennis, where he was a bit more competitive.

"We mainly talk about gaming. They're into *MW7*—you know, the war game—and I'm pretty good at it. So we talk about different strategies and tips that you don't find in any of the books." Jack, hearing his own words coming out of his mouth and seeing how Nicki might think he was one of those weirdos who ate, slept, and breathed for the controller, reached for more elaboration. "It's not just one of those little mindless games where you go around digging and building stuff or scoring points; you have to actually use your mind, know your weapons, and develop team strategies."

Jack, again hearing how nerdy this defense was, stumbled for a subtle adjustment in the topic. "Summers was telling us about a new beast game he's going to start playing called *Mithras*," he said, referring to one of the guys by his last name to give the impression that he was tight with him. "He said this game is supposed to be like some epic breakthrough in online connection, graphics, maneuverability, and realism." After a third time hearing that his words were screaming "Nerd alert! Nerd alert!" Jack decided it was time to let Nicki talk and closed his mouth, wondering if he needed to do any damage control.

Nicki actually was a little bit interested, so playing the part of the interested girl wasn't quite so challenging as in other conversations with boys. She knew exactly how to transition from interested to flirtatious. She looked Jack straight in the eyes, held the gaze about two seconds longer than usual (which communicated a deeper interest but didn't come across as creepy), and threw back a probing question to set Jack up for a profound answer that would showcase his talent.

"Wow, I bet you actually have to spend a lot of time practicing that stuff to be as good as you are, don't you?" she baited.

Jack, relieved that her reaction wasn't "Well, Chloe, I need to be getting home," took the breeze into his sails and replied, "Not really. Sure, I play around ten hours a week, but some of the real extreme dudes play like six hours a day and nonstop on weekends. What a waste of a life!"

Nicki nodded and, extending eye contact again with an added look of disdain to affirm Jack's last remark, said, "Totally! I couldn't imagine being holed up in my room for that long. Could you imagine if you pulled back their curtains and let the sunshine in? They'd probably hiss and bury their heads in their pillows!" She raised her arm as if to block imaginary sunlight for dramatic effect.

It wasn't so much what she said that was funny; it was how she said it. Nicki could really charm an audience. They all laughed. Chloe and Avery glanced around the circle to check for acceptance, but Nicki and Jack just exchanged glances, checking for a romantic interest. From Jack's point of view, he was sending the message "I really, really like you!" and receiving the message "I think I like you too!" From Nicki's point of view, she was sending the message "Here I am. You want me?" and receiving the message "I'll do anything to know you more!" Nicki had the upper hand, and she knew it. But had she ever doubted it would be like this?

Chloe and Avery could sense that a little love connection was forming between Jack and Nicki and exchanged their own nonverbal communication. Avery's facial expression sent the message "Chloe, this is weird. He's my brother! Ew!" Chloe's facial expression said, "Yeah, this is weird. Let's go somewhere and leave these two lovebirds alone."

Avery, looking at Chloe with urging eyes, said, "Chloe, have I showed you the new shoes I got for volleyball? They're really cool."

Chloe, seizing the opportunity to make a fast exit, replied, "No. Let's see them." She glanced over at Nicki to see if she was going to come with her, but Jack, seeing the opportunity for Nicki to make a polite exit, answered her look instead with another question to Nicki.

"So do you play any games, Nicki?" asked Jack. He heard a voice inside his head encouraging him to "just go with it." He recognized the voice as Rachel's.

"No way," Nicki replied. "It's not that I don't want to, but all those buttons and stuff—I could never use one of those controller things." She sensed inside her head that her flirtatious actions were exactly what Rachel was talking about.

"If you really wanted to learn, I could teach you," offered Jack.

"You'd do that for poor little old me?" Nicki dramatically said in a southern accent, moving her hand in a waving motion and bringing it to rest on Jack's arm. Then she replied with sweet smile and the real answer as she pulled her hand back. "Nah, that's okay. I'm more into movies than video games when it comes to TV." Nicki was again working her angle.

Jack, not too disheartened by the rejected offer because of the physical touch, picked up his turn to move and said, "What's your favorite movie?"

"Oh, how can anyone have just one favorite movie? I'm like a movie freak! I like everything from Twilight to James Bond to anything with Adam Sandler to—yes, don't tell anyone, or I'll kill you." She made a threatening face and gesture at Jack. "Even Harry Potter."

Jack raised his hands to show his surrender and replied laughingly, "Harry Potter! Oh, that's sweet!"

Nicki grabbed him by both wrists and playfully threatened again, "You tell anyone and you're dead! I mean it!"

Jack relented, "Okay, okay! I promise." Nicki released his wrists but still maintained a cautiously suspecting glare. Jack enjoyed the closer look into her eyes. They were so pretty. Nicki pulled back onto her stool, and Jack said, "Okay, since you were honest with me, I have a confession myself."

"Yeah, what is it?" Nicki asked with skepticism in her tone.

"You can't tell anyone," he cautioned.

Nicki held up her hand and said, "Scout's honor!"

"I like Harry Potter too!" He hung his head in shame.

"I knew it! I knew it!" Nicki shouted.

Jack picked up his head to see her playful smirk. He wondered where the conversation would turn next. He knew where he would like it to turn—to a date—but he wasn't sure how to get there.

But Nicki, being on the same path, was more experienced at directing conversations her way. "Hey, I had planned on just chilling tonight and watching a movie at home alone with a big bowl of popcorn. You want to come with?"

A bit stunned on how easily that had gone, Jack jumped at the offer. "Sure, I was going to hang with Bobby tonight, but we didn't, like, have any definite plans," he said.

"Great! Let me text you my address. What's your cell number?" Nicki asked artfully, managing the exchange without any note of awkwardness from either of them.

Although Jack knew exactly where Nicki lived, he played along and gave her the number. Nicki put it into her phone and immediately texted him with the address. Jack's phone vibrated and came to life in his pocket with a sound bite of a TrashMouth tune: "Ferocious is as ferocious does …" Jack swiped the screen to end the tone and examined Nicki's reaction to this new evidence of who he was.

Nicki's eyes lit up as she exclaimed, "That's TrashMouth! How'd you get that?"

Jack replied with an uncertain tone, since he was still evaluating Nicki's reaction, "I used my computer to split it off of the song."

"That's sweet! Can you send it to me?" she enthusiastically requested.

"Sure," Jack replied. In less than five seconds of finger taps, he looked back up at her and proudly announced, "Done!"

Nicki's phone illuminated to a woman's voice amid a background of bass bumps and remixed club music stating that she wanted something: "I wanna, I wanna, I wanna, ooh, ooh, ooh. You wanna, you wanna, you wanna, me, me, me?" Nicki let the tone play on a bit so that Jack could evaluate her through it.

"That's a cool one," he said and bobbed his head in acceptance.

"Not as cool as yours. I'm gonna change it right now!" Nicki remarked and started tapping to make it happen. Jack's pride swelled, and his mind was a bit intoxicated with the knowledge that he and Nicki now shared the same text tone.

Avery and Chloe talked intentionally loudly as they left Avery's room and returned to the kitchen area. Nicki and Jack hurried to exchange one last extended look before the girls reappeared. The look started with shared aggravation from the ending of the private moment but quickly morphed into eager anticipation to continue it later that evening.

Chloe did the final breaking of the moment. "Nicki, look at these shoes." She handed the natural leather shoes to Nicki as if presenting a sacred relic.

Nicki received the shoes and let her face take on a look of wonder and excitement, as she was well practiced at doing. "These are precious!" she exclaimed.

Avery's face brightened, and her heart swelled with pride. Chloe added, "She found them at a little store in the middle of nowhere in Oklahoma."

Nicki's face turned to disappointment, and she inquired, "You mean we can't get a pair like them?" She looked up from the shoes to Avery.

Avery smiled and said, "Nope, but if you wear a size six, I'll let you borrow them whenever you want."

Nicki was touched by the offer and replied, "Aww. I wear a seven. But you have to promise me that the next time you go there, you'll get me a pair just like them!"

"Me too! You need to go into fashion design. You're a natural!" added Chloe.

Avery was ecstatic about such outstanding approval of her fashion sense. She smiled even bigger and nodded excitedly, indicating that the next time she was remotely close to Oklahoma she would complete her mission to retrieve the two pairs of shoes.

The sound of a bedroom door swooshing open was heard around the way, and Lucy's voice cried out, "They do too!"

Almost immediately afterward was Anna Claire's voice: "No, they don't!"

The girls were having a rather emotional debate as to whether a dolphin breathes underwater or in the air. Lucy came around the corner and was heading for the pantry for the snacks that she knew were kept there in full stock.

Chloe, however, seeing that it was a natural break for her and Nicki to exit and debrief about the informational tidbits they had gotten about Sam, grabbed Lucy by the arm and announced, "Well, I think it's time for us to go!"

Lucy, in complete shock, instinctively jerked her arm free and wheeled her head around with her tongue extended as far as it would go. Chloe, unsure of how to react, bent down slightly and gave Lucy a big hug, saying, "Oh, you've just gotta love little sisters!"

However, the hidden firmness of her grip and the hidden firmness of her tone was a very apparent threat to Lucy of what would happen if she didn't fall into compliance. Lucy weighed her options and wisely decided to give in. Chloe could feel the decision in the loosening of Lucy's muscle tension and reciprocated by loosening her hug. Without a word, Lucy marched toward the front door. As if not wanting her prisoner to get too far ahead, Chloe followed in polite pursuit. Avery followed her steps, but Nicki and Jack lagged behind a bit.

"My parents are leaving around six thirty to go see a play downtown. So how about seven o'clock? I'll order some pizza, so don't eat dinner," Nicki commanded.

Jack wondered if he needed to keep this off his dad's radar and embarrassingly asked, "Are your parents okay with me coming over when they're not there?"

Nicki took delight in his wanting to respect her parents and replied with a smile, "Sure! They go out all the time, and Amber and I always have friends over."

Jack thought to himself, *Oh, yeah, Amber. So I guess we won't be quite so alone after all.* The thought was a small rain shower on the parade he was having for himself. Nicki passed through the open door, and Jack stopped at the portal. Just before Nicki passed Avery, who was standing at the elbow of the front walk, still talking to Chloe, she turned to give Jack a flirting smile, knowing that he'd be watching her full departure. As Jack stood in silent observance of Nicki's walk, he couldn't help but notice the same kind of feelings he felt when he thought of Rachel.

12

THE WATER GETS HOTTER

Jay was coming in from the back porch grill with full hands. One hand held a large, oblong platter on which rested an oversize slab of smoking salmon. In the other hand was a large, round plate on which several pieces of browned corn on the cob were rolling around. Struggling to balance the two plates, fend off the dog, and close the door, he saw Jack entering the kitchen and yelped for help. "Hey, can you grab this door for me?"

Jack increased his speed to close the door before any mosquitoes could follow his dad inside.

"Thanks," Jay said. "There's a ton of fish here, I hope you're hungry."

"I'm not eating," Jack replied. "I'm going over to Nicki's, and they ordered pizza."

Jay, always in support of his kids' friendships, wasn't disappointed in the reply but did need to know more about this new name. "Who is Nicki?" he asked.

Jack knew this inquiry would be coming, and he had planned his reply all afternoon. Plus, he was more than a little bit excited to talk about it, because he was proud of the fact that a hot and popular girl seemed to like him. With a casual tone, he answered, "Oh, it's just this girl."

Jay smirked. "Yeah, I gathered that! Who is she? Where does she live? Who is going with you? Etc., etc."

Jack wanted to smile like he was on the inside, but he maintained a cool and collected face and replied, "She's from school. She lives about six blocks away, so I'm just going to walk."

"Who else is going to be there?" pressed Jay.

Jack, flattered that his dad would press this point, indicating the question had more to do about romantic responsibility than anything else, replied, "She said that her parents were going to a show or something, but she has a twin sister who is going to be there. *We* are going to eat pizza and watch a movie."

Hearing the plates clink on the bar, Avery and Anna Claire came into the kitchen. Jay started to pull four cups from the cabinet and then put one back.

Hesitating, he looked at Jack. "You want something to drink before you go?"

Jack looked at the clock on the microwave and ran the calculations of how long it would take to walk six blocks in his mind. "No, I'm fine," he replied.

"Where are you going?" asked Avery. She examined him from head to toe in an attempt to find a clue.

"Nicki's," he replied. His pride swelled at hearing himself say her name.

"What?" Avery exclaimed more than asked with a raised voice.

Jay, listening to the conversation now, stopped his pouring and looked inquisitively at the two. Avery moved her glance to Jay and continued with every detail she knew. "Dad, Nicki is one of Chloe's friends. In fact, both of them came by today when Lucy came over. She is a cheerleader and is real popular and is really pretty! And she likes my new shoes." Avery paused for a breath.

Jack lifted his hand gesturing for her to stop, but he checked his opposition there. The fact was that he liked to hear her give such a spectacular report. Avery, undeterred by the stop sign, continued, "She has a really nice twin sister named Amber, but she doesn't get near the attention from the boys as Nicki does. Nicki hangs out mostly with juniors and even seniors. Her parents let her go out on dates and—"

Avery's report had started to crash and burn, so Jack quickly interrupted. "Uh, Avery, you can shut up now!" he rudely remarked.

Jay's expression went from one of amusement, to concern, and, with Jack's last remark, to disapproval. "Jack! Don't talk to your sister like that!" Jay exclaimed.

Jack was still glaring at Avery, but quickly realizing that any further progress down a less-than-polite path might ruin his going anywhere tonight, he quickly changed his countenance. "I'm sorry," Jack immediately, almost automatically, told Avery.

Avery didn't believe it for one bit, but realizing that she had violated an unspoken teenage social code that held true even between siblings, she quickly retorted, "Okay," and then backpedaled. "Yeah, I'm not sure about that last stuff. I'm just going by what I heard."

Jack grinned at her, indicating his approval of her move, and Avery felt a twinge of satisfaction at their return to neutral ground. Jay, however, still didn't look convinced. He asked, "So what time do you plan on being home?"

"It's just pizza and a movie!" Jack thought out loud.

Jay pressed, "So what time do you plan on being home?"

Jack knew he'd better play ball the old man's way. He answered, "Pizza at seven, start the movie about eight, the movie lasts a couple of hours, and then we'll probably hangout for a bit. I'll be back around midnight."

Jay was doing the math in his head too and continued the interrogation. "So what time are her parents supposed to be back from the movies?"

"They're not going to the movies. They're going to some play downtown. So I guess it'll be after midnight."

Jay appreciated Jack's honest answer. "Okay. I want you to text me when you get there. And if I text you and I don't get a reply in less than five minutes, you're losing your phone. Got it?" asked Jay.

"Wow! Lighten up, chief! It's just pizza and a movie," remarked Jack.

Jay asked again with emphasis, "Got it?"

"Yes, sir," replied Jack, not willing to mess up this opportunity. Jack looked at his watch arm, without his watch, and announced, "Okay, I'm going!"

Anna Claire looked at the microwave clock and observed, "But you still have twenty minutes!"

Jack's glare let her know that she, like Avery, had violated a sibling protocol, and she continued chewing her food. Jack walked toward the door and gave Jay a look of mature assurance as if to say, "I've got this!"

Jay, still wondering what the rest of the story was, trustingly said, "Okay, be careful, and if you need anything, just give us a call. We're going to have a movie night of our own."

Upon hearing this, Anna Claire's face lit up, and Avery faked a smile and halfheartedly exclaimed, "Family movie night! Yippee!"— although inside she really still enjoyed watching movies with her dad and sister.

It's strange how you can do something ninety-nine times, but with an alteration of circumstances, the hundredth is completely different. Jack had walked out of his garage and down the street more times than he could count, but walking out this time to cover the six blocks to Nicki's house was somehow different. He felt older, more confident, more intelligent. His head was lifted, and there was a noticeable swagger to his walk. Any passerby could have seen that he was amid the throes of love.

Jack, feeling all the emotions churning within, tried his best to maintain a cool outward appearance. He meticulously examined every aspect of his person as if he were a dog being presented at show. He mechanically ran his hand through his hair to tame any rogue strands and then scrutinized his fingernails. Then, holding his palm to his mouth, he exhaled and sniffed in an attempt to detect any malicious odor. Instead of dropping the hand, he lifted it even higher in the air, turned his head in the direction of his exposed armpit, and gave another attempt to detect any malicious odor that might be lurking there as well. Smelling only the sweet scent of body spray, which extracted a tear from his eye with the excessive concentration, he finally returned the happy hand to its proper place and swung it in deliberate counterbalance with its neglected counterpart.

Snapping out of his trance of self-examination, he glanced nervously at his phone for the time. Seeing that he still had ten minutes until his official arrival time and only one block of ground left to cover, he changed his plan. Instead of the left to head to Nicki's house in the cul-de-sac, he nonchalantly turned to the right. He guessed that the distance he'd need to walk was to the park and back. However, because he was paranoid that someone might think that he was up to no good or just find his reversing direction curious, he determined to circle the entire block area. He estimated that this whole walk would take about fifteen minutes, but he'd just pick up his pace a bit and make up the time.

As he walked the shorter distance between himself and the park, he felt a bead of sweat stream down his face. It was still almost ninety degrees, despite officially being fall. He gritted his teeth in frustration for not including the heat in his calculations. He imagined himself soaked in sweat in front of Nicki's door. He imagined the look on her face as she looked at his shirt glued to his skin and then the transformation of her expression as she caught the scent of what a teenage boy's perspiration really smells like. At this powerful imagery, he stopped in his tracks to assess the likelihood of a stealthy turnaround. He subtly slid his eyes from left to right and then from right to left, surveying the area for onlookers. To his right, he found only a couple of small kids on the park swings with their sportswear-clad moms splitting their attention between ensuring the kids' kind behavior and their own kind gossip. To his right, there was only a yard crew finishing up a hard day's work, blowing the remnants of grass back into the yard from whence they'd come.

Confident that his abrupt one-eighty wouldn't be noticed, he executed it with expedience. "Hey, Jack!" Bobby yelled out as he approached from the blindside Jack was now facing. Jack rolled his eyes and let out a sigh of frustration with himself for being caught. As Bobby drew close enough to see the whites of his eyes, Jack looked at his phone to check the time and held the look to ensure Bobby understood that time mattered right now.

"Hey," Jack replied with a tone communicating his urgency. Bobby squeezed the brakes on his bike, bringing it to a slow stop.

"What's up?" Bobby asked.

"Nothing. I'm just walking around," Jack lied.

"Cool," Bobby said, which meant, "Good, I'll hang out with you then."

Jack looked at his phone time for real this time—five more minutes. Jack began to walk around Bobby's bike, which was between him and the path to Nicki's. "Hey, I've got to go right now, but I'll give you a call tomorrow."

Bobby's head swiveled as Jack worked his way by him. "Where are you going?" Bobby asked.

Jack started to pick up his pace and didn't even look back to make eye contact as he replied, "I've got plans!"

Bobby's curiosity was piqued. "Uh, okay!" he said, wondering why Jack had so spontaneously changed his direction for no apparent reason.

Jack's pace was quickening, as he didn't want Bobby to follow him with more questions. Another drop of sweat rolled down his neck and was absorbed by his dampening shirt. He slowed his pace and took a couple of deep breaths to slow his heartbeat. A small group of butterflies fluttered in his stomach. Coupled with the rush of adrenaline at the realization that he was finally at the front door, this returned the now suppressed sweat back to his brow. He wiped his forehead with his sleeve and rang the doorbell. The door opened to present Amber with a handful of cash for the pizza guy.

"Oh, hey, Jack!" Amber said as if she knew him fairly well. "Come on in."

Jack was a bit surprised by her casual welcome but followed her into the entryway.

"So you and Nicki are going to watch a movie?" asked Amber.

"Yeah, that's the plan," Jack replied. Jack was touched by the natural warmth of Amber's personality and the contrast to that of her twin's, which seemed intentionally dialed up a notch.

"Nicki! Jack's here!" Amber yelled in the direction of her sister's room.

A door opened, and Nicki's voice yelled back, "Tell him to come back here!"

Amber turned and with pursed lips and rolled eyes motioned Jack back. Jack picked up his chin in a gesture of acknowledgement and passed through the unlit hallway toward Nicki's closed door. Light was shining from beneath the door, which gave him enough illumination not to trip over the pile of folded laundry apparently awaiting placement in a closet. Jack tapped on the bedroom door, the butterflies still in his stomach. "Nicki?" he called as he turned the doorknob and slightly pushed on the door.

"Hey!" she exclaimed as she jerked the door open and pulled it from Jack's ginger grip.

"Have a seat," Nicki said as she plopped back down in a chair with her iPad.

Jack looked around and saw that the only place to sit was on a half-made bed. He decided to stand. Nicki glanced up to see him still standing and repeated her initial invitation. "Oh, have a seat. I just want to finish downloading this new tune. Have you ever heard of TrashMouth's basement albums?"

Jack, still feeling it was just wrong for him to be sitting on a girl's bed, much less one he didn't really know that well, forced himself to sit down on the edge. Nicki looked up again and pursued, "Have you?"

Jack, recovering from his seating dilemma and recalling the question, responded, "Oh, yeah." He nodded to support his answer. "I've had those downloaded for years."

"You have?" asked Nicki with a confused, skeptical expression. "They were only released last month."

Jack noticed her expression, tone, and words and continued his explanation. "I met a guy online a couple of years back who claimed to have these old tape rolls of TrashMouth's first songs. He said that he was a cousin of Gypsy, the drummer, and they used to practice in his basement because he was into mixing sound and stuff."

Nicki's eyes bulged in surprised disbelief.

Jack continued, "Anyway, I called him out on it, and he sent me a file with all of them on it. He told me not to sell it or put it on the web or anything like that, because it might cause problems with their record company. So I just listen to them in my room. I don't want to mess them up or anything."

Nicki's mouth was open, and she sprang to her feet. Pushing him, she excitedly exclaimed, "Get out of here!" Jack fell back on the bed, and sitting back up, he smiled. "You're lying!" Nicki insisted.

"No, I promise!" Jack countered.

Nicki examined his eyes, for what better place to detect a lie than in the eyes? Jack sat through the interrogative stare with a smile on his face. "You aren't lying!" she concluded. "How cool is that!" Jack noticed that all his butterflies had evidently flown away, and he felt very much at home. Nicki glanced at the download progress on her iPad.

"Okay, it's done. I would say let's listen to it, but you've already heard them all!" Nicki said.

She stepped toward the door, and Jack stood to follow. Nicki observed the clothes lying on the hallway floor and said, "How embarrassing! Don't mind the mess. Amber must have just put these there while I was in my room."

Her tone showed that she really wasn't too embarrassed, but Jack commented anyway. "No worries."

As the two turned the corner toward the living room, Amber turned from the front door with a pizza. All meeting at the coffee table, they seated themselves on an L-shaped couch, each within an arm's reach of the pizza and their drinks. Nicki grabbed the remote control and dialed up the movie menu. She scrolled through the available movies and paused on one. "How about *Switchblade?*" she asked the other two.

Amber replied, "No, I think that's one of those movies that tries so hard to be scary that it ends up being stupid."

Jack nodded in agreement but then looked at Nicki for her reaction. Nicki was already scrolling to the next option.

She paused on another. "Okay, how about *For the Love of Jell-O?*"

Amber again replied, "No, Courtney saw that one at the movies and said it was almost the same story as *Hi, Honey Nut.*"

Jack didn't respond and looked again at Nicki, who was already scrolling again.

"Oh, how about *I Sense You?*"

Amber looked at Jack for his thoughts, and Nicki followed her gaze.

"Is there a trailer?" Jack asked.

"Let's see," said Nicki. She tapped the remote a few more times, and the movie's trailer appeared on the HDTV screen. Jack was impressed: the sharpness of the picture was outstanding. Nicki pressed another button, and the surround sound kicked in with the full bass of the movie's music. Jack was even more impressed: it felt like a chimp was jumping on his chest and another was boxing his ears.

"Turn it down!" yelled Amber as loud as she could.

With her complete focus on the remote, Nicki was already pressing desperately to subdue the volume. The voice of the narrator spoke up as the music faded slightly into the background. "Polly was a boring housewife who lived in a boring suburb and had boring friends." Several scenes of ordinary-looking stay-at-home moms flashed across the screen. The first was a woman, presumably Polly, trying to feed several unruly kids breakfast; the second was a group of women having crustless PB&J sandwiches in a messy kitchen; and the third was Polly sitting in a line of minivans and SUVs at a school.

"But then, everything changed when she met Billy Jean ..." continued the narrator. The music intensified, and the scene shifted to showing an overweight, middle-aged lady dressed in a muumuu smoking an oversize cigar. Her face was comically covered in makeup with extreme rouge, extreme lipstick, and extreme baby-blue eye shadow. Her hair was so teased up it looked as if she had put her finger in a light socket. As she stood there puffing her cigar, she got a crazy look on her face to give the appearance of being wild, bold, and daring.

Then the music became eerie, and the scene shifted to a dark room with illuminated suns, moons, stars, and planets suspended from the ceiling. On the table was a glowing crystal ball around which the pair were holding hands. Polly convulsed with a fright, almost knocking the ball off of its stand, when a burst of light flashed from above them. Billy Jean didn't flinch, but her eyes circled in their sockets, and a voice much deeper than hers came from her mouth, saying, "I sense you."

The scene shifted to the two running wildly through a department store being chased by a security guard. The narrator's voice boomed again: "Life is a whole lot more fun when you know what is going to happen next!" The scene changed one final time to Polly climbing fully clothed out of a street fountain with the help of a man who looked like an underwear model but didn't appear to be her husband. As they peered romantically into each other's eyes, a loud voice whispered, "I sense you!" The scene faded to black.

"Sure!" Amber stated and looked at Jack.

"Okay," Jack said with a shrug of his shoulders.

"Great!" Nicki exclaimed in her typical cheerleader voice. She punched in the code to start the movie and positioned herself on the couch in the small space between Amber and Jack. Both scooted apart to maintain a comfortable distance. There was a knock at the door. Amber, seated on the outside, was the most logical person to get up, so she did. Opening the door, she saw Faith.

"Hey," Amber said.

"I was just seeing if you wanted to go get some fro-yo," said Faith.

"We just ordered pizza and started a movie," Amber replied and motioned to the living room.

Faith's eyes followed her finger, and she saw Nicki and Jack sitting side by side on the couch. Nicki waved. A flushed look came over Amber as she saw how this looked and remembered that Faith might like Jack. Amber quickly stepped in front of Faith to block her view.

"Uh, you want to come in?" she hesitantly asked. Faith usually would've turned down the offer, but she didn't have anything better to do, and she wasn't going to let a little crush drive her to bitter feelings. She was too mature and realistic for that type of trap.

"Sure," she said as Amber stepped back and examined her face for hurt feelings.

Amber took her place next to Nicki, and Faith sat next to Amber. Nicki looked over at Faith and said, "This is Jack."

Jack leaned forward to look at Faith around Nicki. Jack hadn't noticed Faith in quite some time, but in seeing her now, his immediate reaction was *Wow!* Wanting to reach out to her but realizing it was too awkward to shake her hand across two others, he extended a polite smile and courteous wave.

"Oh, hi, Faith," he said. "Faith and I go to the same church."

Nicki and Amber saw the twinkle in Jack's eye as he noticed Faith. Faith, in her humility, couldn't see it.

She politely reciprocated the gesture and said, "Yeah." Her introversion was kicking in.

The plug to purchase the film's soundtrack finished, the rating for the movie appeared on the screen as a large white "R" highlighted against a solid blue background. The side notes indicated that the show contained brief nudity, mild violence, and adult language. Nicki and Amber didn't seem to pay any attention to the rating, but Jack heard his dad's voice in his head: "Only you can control the kind of stuff you let in your head. There's some stuff that seems harmless, but whether you know it or not, it affects your spirit. It's kind of like smoking spiritual cigarettes."

Jack, still leaning forward, glanced at Nicki, then Amber, and then Faith to see if anyone else was reacting to the rating. Faith glanced down, and her expression showed that she was thinking about how to get out of a predicament without being rude. Jay's voice started playing again in Jack's mind: "Only you can—" Jack cut him off in midsentence. *Shut up, I got this!* At this pronouncement, Jack immediately heard another voice in his head: "Good, Jack. It's your life, and you're in control of it. Just go with it!" Jack liked this voice better, and he settled back with a warm piece of pizza, a cold Coke, and a hot girl next to him.

It only took about seven minutes for the movie to prove its R rating. Profanity and brief nudity was so widespread that even Jack was feeling a bit uncomfortable. Eventually Faith couldn't take it anymore.

She nudged Amber and said, "I'm going to head out."

Amber, thinking that it might be about Jack, said, "I'll go with you. Did you still want to get some fro-yo?"

"Sure," Faith replied.

Without an excuse, the two stood up and walked out the door. Jack felt as if he should say bye or something, but when he leaned forward, they had already made it out of the living room. Nicki glanced to her right at the distraction and then quickly returned to the movie. The plot continued to predictably and painfully roll out one nonhumorous scene after another.

Jack's mind shifted from the tearfully boring movie to the temptation of Nicki, who, at that moment, turned to him and said, "This movie is horrible!"

Jack nodded in agreement. "Yeah, it's pretty bad."

"Uh, then why'd you pick it out?" Nicki said in a lighthearted tone as she pushed him sideways.

Rebounding, Jack retorted, "I didn't pick it out—you did!" and he raised his arms to return the shove.

Nicki grabbed him by the wrists and said, "No I didn't!"

Unsure of what exactly was happening, Jack felt Nicki's lips press against his. She pulled back as if it was not the huge deal that it was to Jack.

They both glanced at the TV. Another scene of Polly and Billy Jean at the psychic table was playing. Polly appeared as if she hadn't slept for days and was looking desperately at Billy Jean.

"I *have* to know the truth!" she said. "I have to know if Pierce is my soul mate and if I made a cosmic mistake in marrying Craig ten years ago!"

Billy Jean sympathetically replied, "I know, sweetie, but Rachel said that she wouldn't be able to talk to you anymore since you went to church and doubted her. You know how these ancient spirits are— very temperamental!"

The camera zoomed in on Polly. She was sobbing, tears streaming down her pale and tormented face. "Please! I want a divorce, but I need to know the truth!"

Her pleading seemed to do the trick, like everyone knew it would, and Billy Jean relented. "Okay. Dry your eyes and take my hands. You're gonna get me kicked out of the spirit world for good!"

Polly dried her eyes and slowed her sniveling to a final snort into a crumpled up tissue. "Oh, thank you! Thank you!" Polly exclaimed as if she'd just been given a brownie after forty days of dieting.

The eerie background music started to rise as the overhead lights faded to gray and the dangling cosmic crescents, stars, and orbs began to glow. The light from the crystal ball lit up Billy Jean's face from below, adding to the drama. Billy Jean began to plead with the spirit called Rachel in an undeterminable language. Polly, at her wits' end, looked hopefully at her. The camera flashed back and forth between the two as Billy Jean apparently wrestled with a spirit.

Her language switched to English, and she said, "This lady needs to know the truth. Now get out of my way and let me see Rachel!"

The camera flashed on Polly, who gripped Billy Jean's hands tighter and closed her eyes as if to add her energy to the struggle. The music hit a crescendo and then stopped suddenly for dramatic effect. Billy Jean slumped back in her chair as if dead. Polly was in a tearful panic. She cried out, "Billy Jean! Billy Jean!" Polly sprang to her feet and went to Billy Jean. She repeated her cry. "Billy Jean! Billy Jean!" Polly, not getting any response, gave Billy Jean what appeared to be one last, tearful hug and said, "Billy Jean, I sense you."

Polly released the hug, and the camera slowly zoomed out. A burst of triumphant music erupted as Billy Jean's eyes popped open. Polly was blasted with amazement and called out, "Billy Jean!"

The answering voice was the deep baritone of a woman. "It's Rachel." Delighted as if seeing an old friend, Polly exclaimed, "Oh, Rachel! Thank you! Thank you! Thank you!"

Rachel answered, "I was being held captive by an evil angel, but Billy Jean set me free. Billy Jean says to tell you that she's okay."

Polly knew that time was brief and presented her dilemma. She said, "Rachel, I can't take my life anymore. My kids are annoying, my husband is too perfect, and I feel like my affair with Pierce just completes me. I need to know if he is my soul mate."

The music turned suspenseful again, and the camera zoomed in on Billy Jean slightly shaking her head. All indication was that Pierce was not her soul mate and that Polly would be locked into her suffocating life forever. But then, Billy Jean's mouth opened, and with deliberate dramatic slowness, she pronounced, "He certainly is, sweetie! He certainly is!"

Polly jumped up in the air in a fantastic frenzy as if she'd won the lottery. She hugged Billy Jean, who, apparently back in her own body now, began jumping up and down with Polly. The music began to play a romantic medley, and the scene shifted to a law officer serving divorce papers to an average-looking man who evidently had a small hardware business followed by a scene of a scantily clad Polly and Pierce kissing on a tropical beach at sunset.

"Aw! That turned out pretty good after all!" said Nicki.

Jack, being a pragmatist, replied, "Well, at least for Polly. What about the kids?"

"Oh, you!" Nicki said as she pushed Jack against the back of the couch, followed by another kiss and then another. "You know," Nicki said, pulling her face back, her brow furrowed in thought, "it's weird how that spirit's name was Rachel."

That fact had hit Jack during the movie like a lightning bolt. "Why?" he asked innocently.

Nicki had to test the waters, so she twisted the facts and said, "Well, my cousin who is into all that psychotic stuff"—Jack chuckled in his mind at the irony of her words—"told me about a spirit she talks to all the time called Rachel."

Jack tried to maintain a calm demeanor, but his face flushed with shock. "Huh?" he uttered.

Nicki continued, "I just think it's like a big coincidence that they used the same name. I wonder if it's the same spirit thingy?" Nicki looked at Jack to see if there was any resonation. She saw a glint of something, so she continued, saying, "Do you believe in that kind of stuff?"

Jack was sometimes guilty of too much transparency too soon and, without thinking through how it might land on Nicki, replied, "Well, actually, I've had like this really weird dream, and there's a girl in it named Rachel too."

Overcome by the coincidence, Nicki confessed, "Me too!"

Jack thought she was joking at first but quickly saw from her astonished expression that she was telling the truth. "Really?" he asked.

"For real. In fact, she even told me that she knew you."

At the realization that this was turning into something bigger than their casual realities, both of the kids felt as if they were in a cone of silence and shook visibly with chill. They stared into each other's eyes for answers to the questions whirling through their minds.

"This is kinda weird," offered Jack to break the stillness.

Nicki nodded. "What's she like in your dreams?" asked Nicki.

Trying to think of a way to say "She's hot!" without offending Nicki, Jack described, "She has black hair, deep dark eyes, and very light skin. Is that what she looks like in yours?"

Nicki shook her head. "No, she has strawberry blonde hair, green eyes, and—get this—butterfly wings."

Jack's expression became amazed. "Why the butterfly wings?"

"I don't know. I guess that's how she gets around."

Jack recalled the omen that Rachel had seen from Athena—the butterfly flying after the dove. It clicked with him as the answer to his question, but he didn't share this with Nicki. He didn't want to tell Nicki that he and Rachel had been lovers back in ancient Greece. How crazy would that sound? But then again, how crazy was this conversation?

"We can't tell anyone," Nicki warned, thinking of her reputation. "They wouldn't understand. They'd think we were crazy or something."

Jack nodded in agreement and said, "I'm not telling anyone." Nicki reached out and hugged him firmly. In that moment, a strong bond was growing between them that pulled them into each other. Jack returned the hug, and they locked into a youthfully passionate series of kisses.

⫟⫟⫟⫟

Sitting on the sidewalk tables in front of the yogurt shop, Faith and Amber raced the warm night steadily melting their frozen yogurt before it became just yogurt.

"I just can't do R-rated movies," said Faith.

"Why not? I know you've always been a 'good girl,' and I respect you for that, but what's so bad about it? We're not kids anymore," said Amber with an air of curiosity.

Faith put her spoon into her bowl, and in her mind she prayed to Jesus for the strength to be vulnerable with her friend. "Amber, why do you think I'm a 'good girl'?"

"Because you have good morals. You don't enjoy the bad stuff, so you stay away from it."

"There's more to it than that. When I was young, I would go to church with my parents and hear Sunday school stories about Jesus. Every Sunday, it was Jesus, Jesus, Jesus. In fact, I remember once when the teacher held up a picture of a squirrel and asked us all what it was. The class hesitated, and one boy said, 'It looks like a squirrel, but I think the real answer is Jesus!'"

Both the girls laughed, and Faith continued, "Anyway, when I was eleven, I went to a Christian camp. I didn't want to go, but I went because my parents had already paid and reassured me that I'd end up having fun. Well, during that week, I got to interact a lot with the camp counselors. I could tell that they had a happiness that was more than just happiness. It was deeper than that, and it was more solid than that. I didn't know what it was, but I knew I wanted it. The theme of the camp was the living water—uh, that's what Jesus offers. Anyway, the speaker talked about how all people were created with a spiritual thirst for the supernatural. She said that the world offers a lot of different drinks—like popularity, knowledge, pleasure, attention, beauty, fame, wealth, power, and acceptance—in many different cups, like music, sex, alcohol, work, drugs, violence, movies, and fake religions. But all of these drinks are really poisonous and end up killing our spirits. It'd be like if all I drank were Cokes. It'd taste good, but pretty soon I'd be sick and eventually die. She went on to say that because God created us, only He can quench our spiritual thirst. He did this by sending Jesus to live a perfect life, where we mess it up, and then to die on the cross to take our consequences so that we don't have to. Believing Jesus is taking God's living water, which quenches our thirst and leads us to live forever with Him."

Faith paused to check in, and Amber, feeling Faith's words resonate in her spirit, asked, "But what makes Christianity real and all other religions fake? Doesn't everyone in every religion think that their way is the right way?"

Faith was relieved with the question, because what she had feared was that Amber would start distancing herself, feeling awkward with a religious discussion. Faith replied, "There are a whole lot of reasons, but the one that really speaks to me is history."

"History? Like Christopher Columbus and stuff like that?"

"Yep. If you look at the historical facts around Jesus, who He said He is and what He did, you find that the facts support His claims. You do this on any other religion, and it falls apart. Look at Mormonism. The book they add to the Bible, the Book of Mormon, talks of great civilizations here in the Americas, but there isn't any archeological evidence to support it."

"Wow, I never thought that religion had so much to do with the other stuff in life. It sounds really complicated."

"Well, religion can get complicated. But what is simple is what's important. I don't have religion. I have a relationship. And that relationship is with my Lord and Savior Jesus Christ. He is the reason that I'm a 'good girl.' It has nothing to do with morals and everything to do with Him."

Amber's head was spinning. She could see that same happiness in Faith that was more than just happiness, and she was starting to feel her own thirst.

A horn honked, and a car pulled up into the lot, shining its headlights right into the girls' eyes.

"Hey, baby!" a voice called from the car as the headlights dimmed and two teenage boys jumped out. The girls didn't recognize them and looked into each other's eyes for a plan. The boys approached with a cocky attitude. "Hey, what's your name?"

The girls ignored the question and stood up.

The second boy, thinking his input would help, chimed in, "Hey, c'mon, we just want to know your name." The girls, with creeped-out expressions, sidestepped the two offenders and started walking briskly toward home. Insulted, the boys yelled out bad names, uttered some vulgarities, and moved into the yogurt shop to cool their hot tongues for more enjoyable obscenities.

"That's the kind of trash I'm talking about," Faith pointed out as the girls, now a couple of blocks away, slowed their pace to a casual walk.

"What do you mean?" asked Amber.

"Well, cussing and that vulgar talk like that. When you have Jesus at the center of your life, you just don't need any of that trash."

Amber took this in and thought about it. Mixing it with her own reaction to the boys' words, she understood what Faith was saying. The two continued the quarter mile or so walk and found themselves back at Amber's house.

"You want to come in?" Amber asked.

Faith looked at her iPhone to check the time. "Sure."

"I wonder if Jack is still here," Amber said. "If the movie is still on we can just go in my room and hang out there."

Faith nodded, touched at Amber's consideration for her. Amber pushed the door to the garage open, and the two stepped inside. Both of their eyes widened and their mouths dropped. Embarrassed, they made a quick one-eighty to head back out the door. Amber cleared her throat intentionally loudly so that Nicki could know what they'd seen. Nicki and Jack broke off their kissing and turned their heads to see Amber and Faith scurrying off. Jack was ashamed, then embarrassed, and then proud that they had been caught kissing. Nicki sat up, wiped her mouth, straightened her hair, and had no feeling about it at all—she was used to being interrupted during sessions like these.

"I'm sorry you had to see that," Amber said to Faith.

Faith put on an expression of indifference. "Oh, that's no big deal. I may be a 'good girl,' but I'm a 'big girl' too." Quickly changing the topic and emboldened by Amber's earlier curiosity, Faith asked, "Hey, do you want to come to church with me tomorrow?"

Amber paused. Her parents claimed to be Christian, so they certainly wouldn't have a problem with it; they might even be pleased. "Sure. What time?"

"I'll come get you around nine o'clock. And it's laid-back, so don't dress up or anything."

"Then what should I wear?"

"Whatever you want. I usually wear a decent pair of shorts and a cute top."

"That's cool! Whatever happened to Sunday dresses?"

"Oh, some people still wear them. I just like shorts better. God doesn't care!" Faith smiled.

Amber smiled back and said, "Okay, see you tomorrow!"

Faith walked the short distance to her house and whispered a prayer, thanking Jesus that Amber was becoming such a good friend. And she whispered a prayer for Jack. She prayed that Jesus would give him discernment in his relationship with Nicki and the evil things that might try and use it.

Amber turned and knocked loudly on her own front door to warn Nicki of her entrance. Passing through the doorway, she saw Nicki and Jack sitting on the couch without their faces pressed together.

Nicki felt a spiritual unity with Jack starting to form. "Have you ever thought about trying pot?"

Jack's gut came on full alert, and a feeling of panic erupted. "Just go with it," a voice encouraged. The panic was washed away. "No, not seriously at least."

"I was talking to Rachel just this morning." Jack was astonished that her knowing Rachel had moved from her cousin to a dream to someone like her best friend. "And she mentioned that drugs can actually help you expand your mind and take in more things. I guess the hippies really did know what they were talking about after all."

Seeing Jack's hesitated reaction, Nicki knew she had pressed one step further than he was comfortable with. Knowing that she was spiritually special, she thought to herself that she needed to be slow and caring with Jack, just like Rachel was with her. Nicki leaned in and gave Jack a peck on the lips to remove the topic from his mind. "Hey, what are you doing tomorrow?" asked Nicki.

"Well, I have church in the morning. Then I'm supposed to go with Caden and Bobby to work out. Then I have to finish some homework. Then I'm going to research that new game *Mithras* to help Jordan." Hearing his own answer, he realized that he was telling Nicki he was busy all day. "Oh, but I can change that around," he scrambled in case she wanted to hang out.

"No, that's fine," she said, flattered by his recovery. "I'll text you."

Recognizing this dialogue was the stopping point for the night, Jack stood up and walked to the door. Nicki escorted him outside to the front drive. She put her arms around him, and he reciprocated. After one last kiss good night, the two headed their separate ways. Jack looked at the house across the street and saw curtains in the window slightly sway back and forth. Somebody had been watching their good-bye.

Once home, Jack had a superficial debriefing with Jay and then went to sleep, where his mind drifted back to a dream on the river.

❦❦❦❦

Jack's friends became a bit annoyed at his lack of cordiality. It was obvious that he was distracted, and his eye contact caused the casual conversations to sputter, jerk, and shake along. *I can beat this thing,* he thought to himself as he mapped out his strategy to kill the Destroyer. He envisioned himself standing triumphantly over the alligator corpse and all his friends applauding his heroic victory. *Yeah! I got this!* he reassured himself, feeling stronger and stronger.

"Oh, excuse me for a second," Jack said to break off a conversation about the latest pop scandal.

"How rude!" he heard behind his back as he made eye contact with the Destroyer and started swimming to the bank, using himself as bait. Jack altered the pace of his swim to ensure that he made it to the shore before the gator. Climbing onto the muddy bank, he pushed his feet down to more solid footing and then reached to his hip and slid out a long sword. The gator continued its steady drift toward him and soon reached the bank.

Its claws pulled back on the mud, leaving scratches as it elevated its body. Jack lifted the sword and plunged it point first just behind the gator's head. The gator went limp, and its eyes closed. Jack pulled the sword out, waved it in the air, and announced, "I've destroyed the Destroyer!"

His expectation of cheers and applause was shattered when he examined the crowd of friends and found looks of skepticism and annoyance. Jack stepped knee-deep into the water, closer to the crowd, and announced his victory again. "I've killed the mighty gator! Now we can float along in peace!"

Cheers erupted, and Jack waved his sword in the air once more. He gave a bow to his admiring friends and then felt his hip shatter. The Destroyer had somehow returned to life and was again thrashing him about in the water. The death roll brought both of them back onto the muddy embankment, where Jack lay, inhaling mud and gasping for any breath he could get amid the roaring applause and excited chants of his friends: "Destroyer! Destroyer! Destroyer!"

At this, Jack's spirit was as confused and wrenched as his mutilated body. A small voice croaked in his ear from the muck, "What are you doing? This isn't your river. Get out. Get out now!"

INTERLUDE:
THE POWER OF PRAYER

God created prayer, just like everything else, to bring mankind into a closer relationship with Him. The Creator developed a divine instrument for the creature's use so that the creature could be transitioned more closely to His own image, to be more like Jesus. This divine instrument in a fallen world is mostly misunderstood and misused. God hears no prayers of those who are not in Jesus, apart from the spiritually doomed receiving His saving grace for the first time. And for those who are in Jesus, unacknowledged sin and self-reigning hearts still work to smother prayer's transforming effectiveness. The full power of this divine instrument, which is the most powerful thing in existence to man, is reserved for those who abandon all else to abide in Jesus Christ more deeply. Be it in praise, thanksgiving, or request, the purpose of all prayer is to make us more like Him for His glory.

So Faith prayed for Jack's discernment.

13

A NEW FLOW DRAWS DOWN

Like every other school day, the mass of people standing throughout the common area began to move like a herd of cattle at the sound of the first bell. The weekend now seemed to be just an echo of the past, and the reality of Monday morning was again pestering their dreams. Thoughts of homework, sports, grades, popularity, acceptance, exams, and college again washed across their growing minds.

For Jack, it was still the thought of acceptance that burdened his mind. As he started to move with his friends, he examined their clothes and then looked at his own to make sure his were close to their style. On the outside, all of them seemed to be confidently independent and went to great lengths to prove it. But on the inside, they were sweating profusely, trying to ensure they were just like the others around them. While popularity is the ultimate victory and normal is the consolation prize, not being accepted is the ultimate defeat that a teen can't survive. Life is safer in the herd, and those on the outside are despised into isolation and eventually starve.

Caden saw Jack ahead of him in the hall and yelled, "Dude, Jack, what's up?"

Jack looked back and waited as Caden caught up. "You had any more beer lately?" asked Caden.

Jack suddenly felt the pressure of acceptance bear down on him. "Yeah, a few," he lied. "You?"

"Sure, almost every weekend. I think I'm an alcoholic now," Caden boasted. "You want to come over tonight and have a few?"

"Sure, what time?" asked Jack.

"How about right after school? My dad got this awesome new online game. He tried to hide it from me, but I know how to get around his tricks. It's called *Mithras*."

Jack's excitement became obvious, and he exclaimed, "Dude! That's the game I was talking to Summers about the other day—the one he said was globally epic. I looked online for some stuff, and it looks like it's going to rock the world!"

Caden, joining the excitement, continued, "Yeah, you are actually a first-person demon fighting for Satan against angels. It's kinda backward, but that's what makes it fun. Lots of violence, gore, and bad language!"

Jack sensed something inside warning him of danger, but then he felt the pressure of acceptance rise to a higher level. Then, almost instantly, a voice intruded on his thoughts: "Relax, Jack. Just go with it. You don't want people to think you're a good boy, do you?" Jack recognized the voice—it sounded like Rachel. Yes, it was Rachel. A peaceful feeling misted Jack's mind, and the sense of alert was gone. "That's cool. I'll meet you by the gym after last period."

"Cool," said Caden. "See you then."

Jack continued his walk down the hall toward his class and heard Caden cry out, "Help! Can someone help me?"

Jack wheeled around, expecting to see Caden being attacked by someone, but instead he just saw him walking like normal toward his class.

"What?" Jack asked himself. "I think I really am going crazy."

-oOOo-

Caden opened the door, and he and Jack entered the house. "Go on up and turn on the TV. I'll get a couple of beers and *Mithras*," said Caden.

"You got any chips?" asked Jack.

"Lots of them. What kind do you want?"

"How about some spicy Cheetos?"

"Spicy Cheetos, brews, and *Mithras*, coming right up!" replied Caden.

As Jack climbed the stairs, he looked at the family pictures on the wall: one of a ski trip, one of a vacation to some tropical beach, and one in front of the Eiffel Tower.

"Wow, they've been everywhere. I wish I were that lucky," he said to himself, envious and sulky. Jack studied the last picture before the top of the stairs—one of Caden's mom and dad on some kind of yacht called *Sweet Stokes. Stokes is Caden's last name. Is that their yacht?* Jack wondered. He looked intently at the mom's face in the picture, focusing in tightly on her eyes, and her face faded away. Jack was startled. He looked away down the stairs and then back at the picture. Yep, her face was still gone—no eyes, no nose, no lips, nothing. It was as if someone had taken an eraser and removed it. Not fully letting this hit him, Jack turned his focus to the dad's face. He looked at his eyes; they were sunk deeply into his head and were dark brown. As he took in these details, he noticed the face starting to blur, just like the mom's had done. Jack tightened his attention on the face, and just like the many times he had erased the wrong answers on his math homework, the face was simply erased.

"Oooh," he heard a moan coming from the picture. "Oooh, help me," cried the voice of a woman.

"Oooh, get them off of me!" pleaded the voice of a man. Jack felt a sick feeling start in his stomach—he really was going crazy. He wondered if this was how people who ended up in psych wards started out.

But before he could get too deep into his fear, Caden appeared at the bottom of the stairs. "That's my mom and dad on our boat," he said.

"You call that a boat?" asked Jack, trying to forget his moment of cuckoo. "Y'all are rich."

"Yeah, but who cares? All the money in the world can't fix dysfunctional," Caden replied.

"What do you mean?" probed Jack.

"Well, my mom and dad may look perfect, but they are far from it. My mom really is an alcoholic, and all she does is hang out with her girlfriends all day at the country club. My dad is a workaholic and is constantly traveling. I think he stays on the road so much just to avoid my mom, because if they're not smiling for a camera or a social event, they give each other these stupid I-hate-you looks. They don't think that I see it, but I do. I'm not sure they even really know what love is." Caden caught himself, as he could feel sadness seeping to the surface. "So—check this game out!"

Caden inserted the game into the Xbox, which whirled to life, reading the disc and connecting with the other online players. Jack and Caden opened the chips and beer. A deep, evil-sounding voice boomed over the surround sound speakers.

"Who beckons Mithras?" This question begged a response before the game could continue.

Caden said, "All hail Mithras, the mightiest god of the underworld!"

Jack knew video games were advanced, but this kind of two-way audio technology was something he'd never seen before. "It can tell when you talk to it?" asked Jack.

Caden gave him a look to lower his voice and then whispered, "It's an online master who has made it to the level of Mithras. You have to interact with him to get into the game."

"Bow before the mighty Mithras," the speaker continued.

Caden replied, "We bow before the mighty Mithras and give our lives to his service."

Jack's sense of danger was going wild inside his heart. He didn't know if he should bow down with Caden or get up and run as fast as he could away from this place. Then, just like before, he heard Rachel's voice: "Jack, relax and just go with it. It's just a game."

While Rachel's voice was again soothing to the burning fear inside, he couldn't bring himself to bow to some video game; it just felt silly. So instead he reached for a beer and opened it as if he drank them all the time.

Caden got up off the floor and said, "Cool, we're in."

The screen faded to black, and then the image of a dimly lit staircase leading upward could be made out. They continued up the staircase past the exit. Turning around, they read a sign that hung above the entrance they had just left that read "Abandon all hope, ye who enter here." Jack wasn't sure what that was supposed to mean, but it sounded familiar, as though from some old story his dad had told him.

"That is the entrance to the underworld," explained Caden. "Now we have to go find the humans. We get more power by latching onto them and sucking their life out. But that's when the angels come in. They try to protect the humans, and we have to fight them off. The more humans we get, the more powerful we get. We have to start off at the Follower level, which means we can't fly, but once we get to the Worshipper level, then we get some cool bat wings."

Jack was disappointed that Caden knew so much about the game and he had only just found out about it the other day. He figured he'd better learn as much as he could so that he could report back to Jordan and the group at lunch.

"Did you get this stuff from the web?" Jack asked, knowing the answer.

"Yeah, there's like a million people all over the world that play this game. The map of players in Europe lights up even more than *MW7*. It's kinda like it has its own cult following. A lot of the older band kids at school are into it. I heard a bunch talking in the hall the other day, and they said they were going to have a *Mithras* party and dress up and do all kinds of crazy stuff," Caden said.

With this, Jack got the idea that if he could get to a high level, he'd have his new group plus a lot of other people thinking he was pretty cool, so he turned his attention to the game. Being a great gamer— he didn't earn GOAT (greatest of all time) status in *MW7* by being average—Jack began to rack up power. He wasn't just playing for fun; this was an opportunity to advance from accepted to popular. While these certainly weren't his conscious thoughts, this was what was driving him on.

After a few hours of intense concentration with no time to take a drink of the lukewarm beer that he really didn't want anyway, Jack's phone buzzed in his pocket with a text message. Hardly taking his eyes off of the screen, he pulled it out and readjusted his sight. It was from Avery: "Where are you?"

Jack set down his controller and texted back, "At friends."

The reply came back almost instantly. "Dad back."

Jack knew it was time to go home but texted back, "w/e," which meant "whatever."

Jack figured he had another hour or so since he let them know at least he was alive, but in order to make the most of the time, he intensified his attention. As he blazed around the city latching on to one human and then another, he saw a beautiful girl with black hair, red sparkling eyes, and a flowing white dress. It was Rachel.

"Don't get her!" Caden exclaimed. "She's a demon in disguise called Spaw!"

"How can you tell?" asked Jack.

"See her eyes? They're red. That's how you can tell she doesn't have the life of a human in her. She's pretty hot, huh?" answered Caden.

"What happens if you latch on to or attack her?" asked Jack.

"She'll whip out these big butterfly wings and then kill you. She's one of the highest-level demons and doesn't need to attack humans like we're doing. She mesmerizes them, and they come to her. She doesn't just suck the life out of the humans either; she actually consumes them. That's a lot more powerful."

Jack looked at her video image, and his head spun from the sensation that there was so much more to this than he could possibly comprehend. The beautiful Spaw character looked directly at Jack's first-person character. It felt as if she was looking directly at him through the screen.

Spaw said, "Well done, demon warrior! A reward in a kiss."

Caden shouted, "Move back! Get away! She's going to kill you!"

But it was too late. The beautiful Spaw grabbed Jack's face and gave him a kiss on the cheek. Spaw then vanished from sight. Jack's character view began to change from one of the ground to one floating in the air.

"I can fly!" said Jack excitedly.

"How did that happen?" asked Caden. "Usually it takes weeks to get to that level."

"Dude! I am the GOAT!" replied Jack, referring to being the greatest of all time. He bumped fists with Caden. Just then, a beeping sound was heard, indicating that someone had come into the house.

"My mom's home," said Caden.

"Should I go?" asked Jack.

"You don't have to. She'll just get on her phone and start texting all of the friends she just left."

Even with this little bit, Jack could sense the pain in Caden. "I just want her to love me," Jack heard.

"What's that?" Jack asked.

"What's what?" asked Caden.

"What you just said," Jack replied.

"You mean about my mom texting friends?" asked Caden.

"No, after that," said Jack.

"I didn't say anything after that," Caden responded.

"Oh, okay," Jack remarked as the thought of going crazy again hit his mind. "Yeah, I'd better get going. My dad would kill me if I was too late for dinner," Jack said.

"I wish my mom cared that much about me," Jack heard.

"What's that?" asked Jack.

"Huh?" replied Caden, confused again.

"Nothing," said Jack. "Well, I'll see you tomorrow." Jack turned and headed down the stairs. As he passed the picture of Caden's mom and dad, their faces were back, with two of the most perfect smiles he'd ever seen. Just as Jack reached for the door, he could hear—or thought he could hear—Caden crying upstairs. Jack opened the door, walked outside, and started jogging to his own house.

Getting home, Jack found his dad and the girls just sitting down at the table for dinner.

"Hey!" Jack greeted.

"Hey!" was the simultaneous reply from all.

"Where you been?" Jay asked.

"Nowhere," Jack answered.

"Were you at Bobby's?" Jay pressed.

"No, at Caden's," Jack responded.

"Who is Caden?" asked Jay.

"This boy from school. He lives in Tanglewood," replied Jack.

"Bring him over here next time so I can meet him," Jay said.

"Why? That's stupid! It's not like I'm some girl and you have to check out my boyfriend or something!" smarted Jack.

"No, I understand that, but I need to know who you're hanging out with. That's important to me. Plus, if you don't, you won't be able to go over to his house anymore," Jay replied.

Jack knew his dad's threat didn't really matter, because his dad couldn't keep that good of track of him after school. But he figured he'd go ahead and bring Caden over here once so his dad could see that he was just some upstanding, nice, rich kid who was okay to hang out with. Once this had passed, he could get even more game time on *Mithras*.

After finishing her homework, Anna Claire was up for a chat before bed. Avery was busy texting her friends about the latest app she had downloaded and didn't want to be bothered. Anna Claire walked down the hall and tapped on Jack's door. No response. She listened for a second and didn't hear anything, but she knew he was in there. She tapped again and then opened the door. Jack was writing something in a notebook with his earphones on, the music seeping out from beneath them. She went on in the room and tapped him on the shoulder.

Jack jumped a bit at the unexpected interruption. He looked up with an annoyed look on his face, slid down the volume, and took his earphones off. "What is it?" he asked with some firmness.

"I just want to hang out," Anna Claire replied.

"Why? Is something wrong?" asked Jack.

"No, I'm just bored … well, maybe even lonely," she answered.

Jack's first instinct was to tell her to go watch TV or talk to Dad, but he remembered a few nights when they were little and both Avery and Anna Claire would come into his room and want to snuggle with him. At the recollection of this, his heart softened, and he turned his chair around to face her.

"Well, what do you want to talk about?" Jack asked.

"I don't know—how about what you did today?" she replied.

"Well, I went to school and then went to a friend's to play video games," Jack answered.

"What game was it?" she asked.

Jack couldn't give her the real answer, because *Mithras* was way too mature for Anna Claire, and if she told Dad, Jack would be grounded for a year. So he told her about playing *MW7*, and even though he was telling lies, he justified it by pretending he was just telling her some type of bedtime story to make her feel better—and this made him feel better.

After a while, Anna Claire did feel better and left to go to bed. It was getting late, and Jack figured he'd better get to sleep too. There was another tap on the door as it opened; it was Jay.

"You ready for bed?" Jay asked.

"Yeah," replied Jack.

Jay walked in and sat down on the bed next to Jack. He leaned down, giving him a hug, and began to say a short prayer for Jack. It was basically the same prayer Jack had heard his whole life: Jay praised God for who He was, thanked Him for Jack being his son, said he was so proud of Jack and what God was doing in his life, said that God was the only purpose in life, and then ended the prayer in the name of Jesus. While this seemed to irritate Jack more and more as he grew older—he was, he thought, too old for his dad to say bedtime prayers with him—somewhere inside, Jack could tell that love was being poured into his spirit. After a reluctant "I love you too," the lights were out, and Jack dozed gradually off to sleep, hoping to dream of Rachel—and this was exactly what happened.

—◦○◦○◦—

Jack was pleased with himself for making it back, although he had no idea how he'd done it. He seemed to just allow it, and it happened. Looking around, he was oblivious to the beauty that encircled him. All he cared about was Rachel. Stepping out from behind a tree, he saw her. He jogged over to her, and they embraced, happy to see each other.

"I see that you've met Nicki," she exclaimed.

At this, his heart dropped as if he'd been caught cheating. No response came to his lips, but before the guilt lingered too long, she said, "That's a good thing!"

Still sensing some type of trap, he replied, "It is?"

"Sure. The more you broaden your experiences on earth, the stronger your spirit will become. Didn't Nicki tell you?"

"Tell me what?"

"Didn't she tell you that you and she will be joined together forever?"

At this, his countenance dropped—he'd thought he was to be joined with Rachel. "But I thought—"

Rachel had anticipated the question and cut in. "Yes, you and I are joined, and we will always be joined, but that doesn't mean that Nicki isn't joined with us. She didn't tell you about the clanders and the Ohm?"

Jack shook his head.

"I guess I forgot to tell her that she can tell you everything we talk about."

This made him feel like he was part of an elite spiritual group. They sat down on a patch of clover that seemed to hum a melody that massaged his body and enlightened his spirit. Rachel recounted what she'd taught Nicki about Pergyss, clanders, and the Ohm, all of which she had already mentioned to him but he hadn't fully understood.

"The pulsating sound you hear"—she paused to let him listen—"is the Ohm."

He heard the sound and combed over his memory from the previous visits. "Are we close to it or him?" he asked.

"'It' is more accurate. No, we are quite far and will have a long journey ahead of us when you get back."

"How does Athena play into this if the Ohm is the true god?" he asked, seeking to be enlightened as quickly as he could.

"Hmm, let me see. How I can explain this?" Spaw bought himself a moment to concoct a consistent and believable lie, and Rachel continued, "Okay, you know how I said that there are different clanders and levels of union?"

Jack nodded.

"Well, Athena—or the higher spirit I call Athena—is the thread that binds our specific clander together. The Ohm is like the weaver, but it uses these higher spirits to hold parts together. I say 'spirits' like they're separate—really, they are all one in the Ohm just like us. But I don't want to confuse you and make you regress."

Jack, more confused than ever, shook his head. "No, I understand."

Rachel smiled at his false comprehension.

"So is that you in the new video game *Mithras*? The character named Spaw looks just like you," he observed.

Rachel's brow furrowed seriously, and she said innocently, "What are you talking about?"

"There's a new video game about spiritual warfare. There is a senior demon character who looks exactly like you." Hearing that he'd just basically called Rachel a demon, he shrank back but figured that he'd wait for her reaction before launching a profuse apology.

Rachel blew it off like a Hollywood celebrity blows off tabloid trash. "Really? Oh, the world just doesn't understand the truth."

Very relieved that she wasn't offended, he tried to move on. "So how do we—"

Rachel interrupted. "The world, especially those outcasts called Christians, thinks everything spiritual is black or white. That's why they will end up in Pergyss and we'll end up in a clander."

He wasn't sure why but Rachel's face had become worried. Then he replayed her words in his head and thought about his dad and sisters.

Rachel read his mind and stammered, "Well, that doesn't mean that Christians will end up in a bad place, remember. It's just that we will end up in a better one. The good thing is that to them, Pergyss will be exactly where they've always wanted to be."

He listened to her explanation, and philosophically he understood it, but there was a nagging in his gut that hated the idea of being separated from his family.

Rachel brought out the cup and said, "Here, take a drink. I think we've had enough for today. I don't want you regressing." Her hand had a slight tremble to it as she passed the cup to him.

Trusting her determination that it was a good stopping point, he took the cup and pressed it to his lips. As the bittersweet drink poured into his mouth, a sensation came over him that convinced him his family would be just fine after all.

As before, the drink laid him down. This time he was still on the soft clover that was still humming its melody. All his cells seemed to melt into a living liquid that was lapped up by the clover and sprayed forth in a beautiful ode to the Ohm.

14

An Emotional Channel

Spaw knew he was good at this game, and he found enjoyment in it. Jack had always had an affinity for Greek mythology, and Spaw was successfully exploiting his inherent fascination with the supernatural—using what was intended to help draw him back to God to move him in the opposite direction.

Spaw swooped down to find Nicki. She was heeding his advice and buying some pot from one of her cheerleader friends. The girl offered to smoke with her, but Nicki declined because she had special plans. Spaw, whose pride was already swollen from his skillful session with Jack, pounded his chest to assert his power across the territory. "Romance!" he shouted.

Before the echo of his cry could die off, a handsome demon called Romance appeared and bowed his head. Even Spaw seemed to have an attraction to this beautiful and seductive creature. He reached out his clawed hand, and Romance pulled his face back. Spaw stood like a statue and stared at Romance. Romance, concerned that

Spaw's obsession would turn into consumption, said, "All power, great Spaw!"

Spaw heard his name and broke off his obsessive glare. "The peasant Nicki is buying drugs. When she takes it, she'll open a new channel. Go into her and shred her emotions."

Wanting to complete Spaw's orders, Romance didn't linger. His dovelike wings raised high and then pressed down to the ground, catapulting him into the air, and in a blur, he was gone. Spaw wanted to call him back—he had left too soon—but his pride was stronger than his lust.

15

SHATTERED, SHAKEN, STRENGTHENED, AND SAVED

It was seven thirty on Thursday evening, and Jack hadn't seen Nicki all day. He hadn't texted her either, because he had expected to see her each break, but now it was evening and he was already home. He was eager to tell Nicki about Rachel's good report of her and about seeing Rachel in *Mithras*. This was too much for a text, but he thought they could talk quietly by phone.

Jack tapped in a text message: "Where are you? Call me." He hit the send button and saw the little symbol that indicated she was writing back.

"Meet at park at 9."

"Kk!" was his reply. Jack was ecstatic that his relationship with Nicki was so comfortable that they were making plans to meet by text. Plus, knowing that they would be together forever made it even more thrilling. He jumped on his homework and started plotting his excuse to leave by nine.

At 8:50, Anna Claire was already in bed for the night, and Jay was helping Avery finish some math homework at the kitchen bar. Jack walked by them and nonchalantly announced that he was going to Bobby's to help him with a computer project he was having problems with.

Jay and Avery looked at each other curiously. "Hold on," Jay said. "It's almost nine o'clock."

Jack anticipated his next few sentences and said in a matter-of-fact tone, "It's due tomorrow."

"Can't you just help him virtually?" asked Avery.

Jack's responding look told her to butt out. Jay waited for his answer. It was a good question.

Jack thought quickly and answered as if there were an obvious reason why that wasn't an option. "It's computer work. We can't chat virtually and program at the same time."

"How long will it take?" Jay probed.

"I don't know. I think I could be back in an hour," Jack surmised, as he didn't think that he and Nicki would be hanging out at the park that long.

"Okay, but text me at ten," Jay said.

Jack nodded and went out the door. Avery looked at Jay and commented, "He's lying. Want me to follow him?"

Jay smiled and shook his head. "No."

The humidity had already started to convert itself to an early dew. The dampness in the air made the illumination of the streetlights look like large coned lampshades restricting their lights to the ten-yard radius directly beneath them, which made the shadows of the park even deeper. Behind every well-groomed shrub was a cubbyhole of darkness. The fort area was in an even larger hole of darkness, big enough for a serial killer to hide inside. Jack's imagination started to flail around, and he wondered where Nicki was. Jack heard a giggle from the dark fort.

"Nicki?"

"You can't even tell I'm here, can you?" she said in a giggly voice.

Jack glanced around for any witnesses and walked quickly to the fort. Jack ducked his head and squirmed into the hole with her. He could just make out her face in the dim light. She immediately grabbed his face and started kissing him passionately. He tried to pull back and speak—he had so much to tell her—but she kept a firm grip on his head and continued to press her lips against his. As firm as her grip was, her movements seemed to lack coordination.

Jack took a breath, and it smelled as if Nicki had spilled perfume on herself. He sniffed again, and beneath the strong perfume was another pungent aroma. Jack pulled back and with a flattered smile—it felt great to be loved—said, "Hold on a second."

He pulled Nicki into a close hug so she couldn't regain her grip on his head. "Hey, hey," he said. "Are you okay?" He held the hug but pulled back to look into her eyes.

Her eyes were damp with tears. "I love you. I love you so, so much." With this, she started to kiss him again, but Jack held his ground.

"Are you high?" Jack asked, already knowing the answer but wanting to work toward an explanation. Nicki didn't answer the question and said with a hint of a slur, "I'm special, Jack. Rachel told me. I'm special, and you are special. Rachel told me. We're going to be together forever."

"I know. She told me everything." The conversation seemed to calm Nicki's romantic desires.

"Did she tell you we might be soul mates?" Nicki asked.

"Yeah, and she said that even if we're not, we'd still be joined forever."

"Do you want to be my soul mate?"

Jack looked deeply into Nicki's eyes and said, "With all of my heart."

"I love you," Nicki said before issuing another series of kisses.

Jack took a breath and said, "I love you too," and they continued the make-out session.

The flow of feelings ebbed, and Nicki had an idea. Drawing herself upright, Nicki said, "Jack, I've gotten to where I can contact Rachel pretty easy. Why don't we contact her right now?"

Jack cast a look around the park. No one would be out on a damp night like this. He took some deep breaths to slow his racing heart. At this point, Nicki could've said, "Hey, let's jump in front of a car," and Jack would have agreed to it. "Sure," he said and took out his camera phone for added light.

Nick gathered herself, crossed her legs, shook out her arms, and closed her eyes. Jack was entranced. She looked so beautiful. He watched her lips move, muttering Rachel's name over and over and over. He was drawn in. Nicki's eyes opened, and she said, "Jack, while you're still in this life, let Nicki be me. Love her, and let go."

Jack's face moved closer and closer to Nicki's face. "Just go with it," he heard, and he kissed her. At the touching of their lips, Nicki's body fell limply backward. He put his hand behind her head and brushed her hair out of her face. She opened her eyes and asked wearily, "What happened?"

Jack said, "Don't you know?"

"No. The last thing I remember was buying some pot from Shelly, and she gave me a little hit." Nicki's face became scared as she sat up and looked around. "Where are we?"

Cautiously, Jack said, "We're at the park." He pulled out his phone and showed her the text invitation she had sent him.

Nicki was too panicked to be embarrassed at the memory loss. "Jack, I'm scared. I feel like I'm falling apart." Nicki's breathing was stressed, and she snatched the phone to use as a light. She was frantic. She ran the light over her arms, over her legs, over her stomach, and back to her hands. She was trembling. "Jack, what's happening?"

Jack couldn't see anything. "I think it's the drugs. Maybe you're allergic to them."

"No, no, that's not it. This is inside." She patted her hand against her chest and panted. Tears streaked down her face, and she started grabbing her arms. "I'm falling apart! Something's happening! Help me! Jack! Help me!"

Jack wanted so badly to help her, but what could he do? She obviously wasn't falling apart. It looked more like she was having some kind of emotional attack. Should he take her to the hospital? Should he take her home? Panic infected him and he froze. "What do you want me to do?" he asked.

"I don't know! Just get it off me! Just get it off me!" Nicki's energy shut down with a suddenness that threw her backward, and Jack grabbed her up in his arms.

"Nicki! Nicki! Are you okay?"

Nicki's eyes crept opened. A far cry from what they were just minutes ago, they were ugly, tired, and worn. "I want to go home. Jack, help me get home."

Jack nodded. "Sure, sure." He helped her down out of the darkness, and they made their way down the blocks to her house. Once they had arrived in front of her house, she had gained a little bit of her strength back. Jack was leading her up the driveway, but Nicki hesitated. "I can't go in that way," she said. She halfway lifted her hand and motioned to the alley. "That way. My parents don't know I'm out."

Wow, at least she remembered that, Jack thought to himself, feeling as if he'd dodged another bullet. Nicki's window was low, and she seemed well practiced at climbing in and out of it. She stuck her head out and gave him one last kiss. "Thanks, Jack" was all she said, and she closed the window and then the curtains.

Jack retraced his steps to the entrance of the dark alley. He paused before walking out into the well-lit driveway to check for anyone who might be alarmed by his unexplainable appearance from the dark alley outside a girl's bedroom. He saw the neighbor across the street pulling his trashcan out to the curb. It felt like the man was staring right at him through the dark. Maybe he had seen them walk into the alley. Maybe he was hesitating to see who had come out of the alley. Seconds seemed like hours, and finally the man retreated and closed his garage door. Jack jogged across the driveway to the street, where he slowed his pace as if he were just out for a leisurely evening stroll. He looked at the time on his phone—10:20, not late enough to need a new explanation.

❧❧❧

It was seven forty-five on Thursday evening, and Amber was debating whether or not to rat Nicki out for sneaking out. Nicki was always the reckless one, but it was Amber who paid the price of being nervous on her behalf. Amber was restless. She tried to focus on her Spanish verb conjugation, but her mind was playing out a drama with Nicki, trying to get her to come home. Amber needed someone to talk to. She couldn't talk to her parents; there would be too much guilt in her face for that.

She closed her workbook and picked up her phone. Amber tapped "What you doing?" to start a thread with Faith and hit the send button. She looked at her screen to watch it be delivered. If Faith was going to write back, she hadn't started to yet. Amber put down the phone and lay back on her bed. Her hair was still wet from her shower, so she got up, went to the bathroom, towel-dried it a second time, and brushed it out. From the bathroom she heard the chirp of a cricket coming from her room—it was a text. She swooshed her finger across the screen and saw that it was the reply from Faith. "At hospital, Matt dying."

In disbelief Amber reread the message more slowly, processing it in her mind: "At hospital, Matt dying." Amber's heart dropped, realizing that this wasn't some kind of a joke. Nicki might do something like

173

that, but never Faith. Amber tapped back, "What hospital?" Almost instantly this time, the reply came back "Memorial." Amber threw her hair into a ponytail, slipped on some warm-ups and a better T-shirt, and stopped. She was in a bind, as usual, because of Nicki. She just had to get to the hospital to be with Faith, but if she told her parents of the severity of the situation, they would want the whole family to drive up there for support—including Nicki, who was not in her room and expected Amber to cover.

"Nicki!" she muttered angrily under her breath. She plopped down on the bed and thought. Calming herself with deep breaths, she finally saw a solution. She'd ask her mom to drop her at the hospital because Matt was sick and she wanted to be with Faith. She'd say that she didn't think it was really that bad and that she'd get a ride home with Faith. This wouldn't be a total lie—she really didn't know how bad it was. Amber gave herself one last look in the bathroom mirror and went into the living room to ask her mom for a ride.

━✪━✪━

"Faith!" her mom shouted in a panic from her parents' bedroom. "Faith! Come here! Call 911!"

Faith pushed back the chair from the desk, knocking it over, her bed stopping it from hitting the ground. Moving like a deer on flight through the woods from a cougar, she turned the corners to her parents' room. She saw her mom standing over her brother, who was lying on the bed. They were both deathly pale, and this caused Faith's face to pale in fright too. Matt had been sick with what they'd thought was the flu for two days. He had felt better this morning but was planning on staying home another day to get him into the weekend, where he could rest even more.

"Mom, it will take them a while to get an ambulance here, and the hospital isn't that far away. Let's just get him to the car and go!" Her mom, Grace, was in a panic and couldn't think about what to do. Her baby boy was dying, slipping right through her maternal fingers, and she couldn't do anything about it. She was in shock.

"Go get your dad," her mom said.

"Mom, Dad's in Miami. We have to take him," Faith said firmly. "Help me get him to the car!"

Matt was about six foot two inches tall and was very muscular. His high muscle level and low body fat level made moving him almost impossible, but the adrenaline surge, and probably the help of an angel, allowed the two to move his almost dead weight to the car. Once they got to the hospital, there would be EMTs to take him from there, but it was left to them alone to get him that far. Faith could barely see from the tears in her eyes, and from the backseat, she couldn't really tell how her mom was managing to drive. Faith looked at the speedometer—sixty miles per hour. She looked at the side of her mom's face, which was pressed into concentration. Grace knew that the best thing she could do right now was to focus all her attention on a quick but safe drive.

Faith tried to look around the seat at Matt but the tight space prevented a good view. His head was limp on his shoulder and showed little control when they turned a corner. Faith reached around the headrest and tried to hold his head steady. Her fingers pressed on both sides of his face. The cool, clammy feeling told Faith that she may not see her brother alive again. She started to cry and fought back the sobs with ferocity because she didn't want to distract her mother. Their mission right now was to get him to the hospital, not to think about what may or may not be.

Grace pulled the car to a screeching halt in front of the ER. She honked the horn rapidly, and several EMTs ran out of the doors and looked at Matt. They urgently waved for a gurney and started to feel for Matt's pulse. It took three men to pull him out, load him up, and whisk him away for assessment. Grace pulled the car into the nearest parking spot and, in one motion, jammed it into park, leaped out of the door, slammed it, and ran through the ER room doors.

Faith was sitting in disbelief in the back of the car, numb with shock. Thoughts of being an only child were starting to pollute her mind. They were like flies on a pecan pie fresh from the oven. She would shoo them away, but as soon as she did, they circled all over again. She wasn't sure how long she sat there, maybe an hour, maybe a minute, but her paralysis was eventually broken when a short brunette lady with big brown eyes tapped on the window. The lady informed Faith that she was from her mom's Bible study class. Finding the door unlocked, the lady opened the door and looked with pity at Faith. The woman's strength gave Faith the strength to get out and walk in. The woman escorted Faith to the room where they had already admitted and stabilized Matt as best they could.

Grace embraced Faith as soon as she walked into the room. Feeling her mom's firm but trembling grip did not offer any encouragement. Grace returned to Matt's side, and Faith sat down in a chair near the wall. Faith's phone whistled from her pocket with the second alert of a text she had somehow missed; it was Amber. Without any thought she tapped back a reply and turned her gaze back to Matt. It whistled again, and she again tapped out a reply and turned her gaze back to Matt.

Grace was vacillating between denial and hysterics, and her friend suggested a snack.

"I'll go with you," Grace offered.

"No, you stay here. The snack shop is just right around the corner." The friend insisted to no effect. Grace stood up and accompanied her out of the room.

Alone, Faith looked at Matt's lifeless body under heavy sedation on the bed. She wondered why there were no doctors or nurses hovering but was too tangled in confusion to ask the question. The white sheets that covered him from the waist down seemed to be only a few shades removed from his pale complexion. He had an IV in his arm dripping one bag of clear liquid and another bag of brown liquid. There was a heartbeat monitor giving the bad news that his heart was much weaker than normal. An oxygen tube was secured under his nose, spraying in the life that was escaping from somewhere else; it was like trying to inflate a basketball with a hole in it. Faith stared at the heart monitor, its beeps of life both scaring her and comforting her. She hugged her knees into her chest and rested her forehead on them.

She retreated into the safety of her own thoughts, which very quickly betrayed her. Grasping her by the wrist and covering her mouth like a child being abducted from a fair, they pulled her into a windowless van and drove her to a bad and lonely place. Faith was at her end. If Matt died, she would die with him; they were connected at the heart. The heart monitor, which beeped so abnormally slow, beeped for two hearts. She wanted to cry but was too numb. A longer than normal beep sounded, indicating a brief flatline. She wondered again why the doctors and nurses were not here helping Matt, but again confusion held her in place. Faith could feel her life slipping away, and she wasn't going to stop it.

She rolled her head to the side and let one eye look at the monitor. Matt was sitting straight up in bed. Faith sprang to her feet, and before the monitor could register another beep, she was at Matt's side, holding his hand. His eyes were closed, but his mouth moved.

"Faith, I just want you to know that everything is going to be okay." The words delivered, Matt's body reclined. Although it was the same exact scene as thirty seconds ago, Faith now knew that everything was really going to be okay. It was as if Jesus had reached down, picked her up in His loving arms, and given her a comforting hug that only He could give.

Faith returned to her seat, pulled her knees back up, placed her forehead on them, and thanked Jesus for such an overt show of His love for her. Now she understood why the doctors and nurses were not in there at that moment. She praised God for the awesome, almighty, loving God that He was. She thanked Him for sending Jesus His Son to save us from spiritual death. She thanked Him for Matt and begged Him to heal him. She thanked Him for Amber and their growing friendship.

Grace and her friend returned to the room to see Faith lifting her head with a look of peace. Faith recounted what had just happened, and the anxiety in the room evaporated as a sense of tranquil concern took its place.

⬤—◯◯◯—⬤

The midsize sedan circled the oversize horseshoe driveway in front of Memorial Hospital and pulled to a halt. Amber's mom looked at her and said, "Tell Grace we're all thinking about them. I know Faith will be happy you're here."

Amber nodded and said, "I'll text you later when I know about what time I'll be home."

"Okay, sweetie. Bye," she replied.

Amber closed the door and made her way to the hospital doors, which swooshed open, letting a drift of cool, dry hospital air sweep away the cool, damp air around her. She paused and turned to see her mom's right blinker flash, and then the car disappeared into the rest of the traffic. *I hope she doesn't check on Nicki,* she worried to herself.

Amber found out the room number from the front desk and made her way down the series of halls. As she approached the room, Grace and her friend were coming out with a nurse.

"Mrs. Sparks, how is Matt?" Amber asked tentatively.

"I think he is going to make it. We have to go smooth out an insurance detail, but Faith is in the room. Just go on in."

Arriving at the room, Amber lightly tapped on the door as she opened it slowly. She saw Faith drawn up in a chair with her head buried in her arms. She looked at Matt and saw that he was indeed still alive, but hearing the slowness of pace of the heart monitor and seeing his deathly pale face, she knew that the situation was serious. She approached Faith, who seemed to have escaped into her own space, and knelt down beside her. She touched Faith's arm, and her face lifted up, wet with tears.

"Oh, Amber," Faith said as both girls stood up to exchange a hug.

"Is he okay? Your mom said he'll be okay," Amber said, trying to comfort as best she could. She'd never been in this kind of situation and hadn't practiced for it today. Faith pulled her face back, and Amber was confused by her expression. Faith was crying, but smiling.

"What happened?" Amber asked.

Faith recounted the whole story from the beginning at the house, to her feeling like she was about to die too, to Matt's body sitting up and Jesus speaking through it. "He said, 'Faith, I just want you to know that everything is going to be okay,'" Faith concluded the story.

Amber's heart was pounding at the account. She could feel her spirit crying out for Jesus. It wasn't just an emotional reaction—she'd known Jesus was real the other night at the yogurt shop, but she'd wanted more time to digest it.

"Faith, how do I become a Christian?"

Faith took Amber's hands, and they sat down. "God loves you and sent Jesus His Son to take our punishment as sinners on the cross. If you believe this and dedicate your life to following Him, then you are now a Christian, a Christ follower."

"I do believe that!"

"Well, just tell it to God with a prayer from your heart."

"Oh, God, I'm a sinner. I do believe that Jesus is Your Son and that He took my punishment on the cross. Oh, God, please forgive me and help me to obey You from now on. In Jesus' name I pray. Amen." Amber looked up with the same tears of joy that were still in Faith's eyes. They hugged each other. Amber said, "I don't feel any big burst of energy or angels blowing trumpets, but I can tell that something's different. It's like … well, it's like you said—everything is going to be okay. I feel that now." Faith nodded with joyful encouragement.

Grace and her friend walked back into the room having resolved the insurance issue. They noticed that both of the girls, while still appearing concerned for Matt, had added a joy to their peace.

"Mom, why don't we pray?" Faith offered. They all four joined hands over Matt and took turns praying. As they released hands, Amber's arm bumped the rolling bed tray, knocking a small metal tray and a plastic cup of water to the hard sterile floor in a crash. At the sound of the loud metallic clank, Grace, her friend, and Amber all jumped in fright. Faith didn't flinch—for the first time in her life. She knew that with the obvious assurance of God's love for her her days of being jumpy were over. "Thank You, God," she whispered as she took a paper towel and started wiping up the spilled water.

The cleanup done, they spent almost an hour talking, crying, and comforting one another. It was now approaching ten o'clock, and Grace finally had convinced Faith and Amber to go home and get some rest. Her mom's friend offered the ride and promised to be right back.

As they drove home, the lady, who they now knew as Kate Castle, tried to distract the girls from any more worry by telling them about her daughter, Jaye, who had just finished her residency and was now a doctor at the hospital.

"Literally, if it wasn't for Jesus and a friend's prayers, she wouldn't be here today," she said with a breaking voice. "I even named her after him!" The distraction worked, and before they'd fully realized it, the car turned into the neighborhood. The girls saw a kid walking down the street. Although he was hooded, they could tell it was Jack. *Nicki!* Amber thought malevolently to herself and looked at Faith, whose mind seemed to still be having lovely thoughts about the true love of her life, Jesus.

16

INVISIBLE VISION

Nicki had been AWOL the entire weekend and all day Monday. Jack had been exchanging texts with her, concerned that she was still freaked out over her emotionally shattering episode, or whatever it was, last Thursday night. She was claiming the flu (though he didn't buy it), and with the potential contagiousness, she wouldn't allow him to visit her. Today was Tuesday, and Jack was eager to see her, to talk to her, to hug and kiss her. He stood in the commons area with an eye toward the door she usually came through. He could see Caden and Bobby sitting on the floor next to the trophy case, which was packed with oversize golden monuments proclaiming to all the students that they were better than most others in the state.

Jack anxiously sent a text: "Where are you?"

A reply immediately came back: "By trophy case." Jack looked again in that direction. He didn't see Nicki, but he saw Caden tapping out a message. Jack's phone pinged like a submarine looking for the sea floor and read the text: "Where are you?"

He had accidently texted Caden instead. Slapping himself for his stupidity, Jack texted back, "Never mind." He brought up Nicki's name on the screen and tapped the same message, checking three times to make sure it was her name before hitting the send button again. There was no immediate reply. Jack stood there watching the screen, hoping to see the icon bubble up that showed she was writing back. Nothing.

After what seemed like hours but was really only about thirty seconds, he clicked the screen off. Frustration and fear injected themselves into his mind: frustration from Nicki not immediately responding to him, and fear from the idea that Nicki was distancing herself from him. He let his hands fall by his side, one of them sliding the phone into his pocket on the way down, and lifted his head to vigilantly scour the crowd for her.

His mind whirled, but time dropped into an almost artificial slow motion. The noise of several hundred kids crowded into a large common area was in a moment muted. Jack's head moved slowly to the left. A boy dressed goth was passing at a snail's pace only three feet in front of him. The boy's eyes met Jack's own. His mouth didn't move, but Jack heard him speak in an agonizing tone: "I'm drowning. Can you help me? Please, help me! Get it off of me! I'm drowning …"

Now passed a girl whose clothes and jewelry announced her parents' wealth. Her eyes were intently focused on her path, and Jack heard her agonizing plea as well: "All I wanted was love. I don't know how this happened. Please, no! No! No!"

Jack wanted to pull out of this horrifying dream, but he couldn't as a third student passed by about ten feet away. It was a short boy dressed very normal in blue athletic shorts and a school T-shirt and carrying a black backpack. His stride was even slower than the previous two, and he spoke as if he were drowsy. "Can someone save me … I'm …" His words trailed off into what sounded like a final struggle to inhale. Jack turned his head to see who was next and heard the boy's last word: "… gone."

At the sound of this final word, Jack moved his gaze, still in slow motion, back to the boy, but he really was gone. Jack's attention focused on the mass of students in front of him. They were all moving at a normal pace again, but there was still no volume to their voices. Jack's eyes silently took in each group, trio, couple, and individual that composed the mass. Then, just as someone would turn up the volume of a TV, the voices of the mass increased and increased and increased. Jack wanted to cover his ears but was still aware of any peer scrutiny that might judge him. The noise he heard wasn't the conversations of the students; it was a mass of people being maimed and killed by an attacking force. Shrieks of terror, pleas for mercy, cries of agony, and whimpers of death swarmed together and brought their united sting to Jack's ears, mind, and heart. Jack closed his eyes in excruciating pain. His back pressed against the wall, his knees buckled, and he slid down to sit. Forgetting about peer pressure, he drew his knees up, hugged them, and rested his forehead on them.

"Dude! The bell rang," Bobby said as he popped Jack on the head.

Jack looked up to see Bobby and Caden above him. His eyes were red but not teary.

"Are you okay?" asked Caden.

"Yeah, I think I had a migraine or something," Jack guessed.

Bobby extended his hand, and Jack took it to pull himself back to a standing position. "Did you hear about Tommy?" Bobby asked.

"Who's Tommy?" Jack replied.

"You know, we see him all the time in the mornings. He was that little short kid who had the black backpack and sat just down from us by the trophy case," Caden described. Jack had just seen him during his "migraine."

"Yeah, I just saw him," he said.

"You couldn't have just seen him," Bobby said. "Last night he committed suicide. He wrote out a text blaming his stepmom and apologizing to his little sister, sent it, and then hung himself. When his stepmom got the text at the store, he was already dead."

Jack froze and his bottom lip quivered. He wanted to cry, but his pride wouldn't let him. Bobby had never seen Jack talk to Tommy, and Jack didn't even recognize his name, so Bobby was curious why this news seemed to have such an impact.

Bobby asked, "Did you know him?"

Jack wiped his fingers over his lips to stop their trembling and then rubbed his dry, red eyes. "No, I didn't know him. I don't think I've ever even talked to him," Jack said with an edge of self-disappointment. "How could I help him? I didn't even know him."

At this last comment, Bobby and Caden looked at each other, puzzled. "Don't blame yourself, man. We can't help everyone," Bobby consoled.

Jack heard Bobby's comment and another voice: "Don't be weak, Jack." Jack snapped out of his reverie and led Bobby and Caden as they headed to class.

By lunchtime, there was still no word from Nicki. Jack walked into the cafeteria and looked for his older group of friends, but they weren't there. Neither Bobby nor Caden had made it there yet, so he sat alone at a table. Jack felt two hands grab his shoulder and hair brush by his ear as a kiss landed on the side of his face.

"Hey, Sunshine!" Nicki exclaimed as she slid her hand down Jack's arm to his hand where she could pull him up. Jack, still harassed by frustration and fear, stood up and turned to hug her. It was an embrace of relief for him. He could still feel love in her grasp.

"Why weren't you replying to my texts?" Jack asked.

"I didn't want to spoil the moment of finally getting to see you face-to-face!"

A bit insecure, Jack wasn't sure if he bought this line completely. Nicki read this in his face and gave him a big, reassuring kiss. It worked. Jack's skeptical expression had been restored to one of passive excitement. Nicki reached into her backpack and pulled out her protein bar for lunch.

"Is that all you're eating?" asked Jack.

"Hey, I've got to stay looking good for you, don't I?" she replied. This was the highest compliment she could have given him. Jack's pride swelled to a level he had never felt before. He hadn't recalled ever being quite this happy. He was under the influence of the intoxicant of love. And he loved love.

Jack didn't bring up last Thursday, but he did tell her, in a whisper, about how he had seen this demon character called Spaw in the *Mithras* game that looked exactly like Rachel. He went on to tell her about how he asked Rachel about it and she had said that the world didn't understand true life and tried to twist things around. They were both amazed at how real all this supernatural stuff was. They felt like they were walking through a dream. Jack looked deeply into Nicki's beautiful eyes and let himself go into the supernatural emotions that pooled there.

"Hi, Nicki!" a lower voice said, interrupting Jack's swim. Nicki and Jack looked up to see a Thorlike character standing above them. It was Stone Eriksen. He was a senior, about six foot four inches and 250 pounds and as chiseled as a boy could get. His jaw was protruded, giving him the appearance of a lion, and his hair was long and blond, which completed the imagery. Jack's Goliath-size ego instantly shrunk into a worm and squirmed into the closest hole at the presence of such a perfected physical specimen.

"Oh, hey, Stone!" Nicki replied with a twinkle of admiration, and she immediately stood up. Jack felt the hairs on the back of his neck stand up. Stone didn't retreat to allow Nicki room, and their faces were only inches apart, as if they were about to kiss. Jack stood up quickly and extended his hand so that, to shake his hand, Stone would have to give Nicki more space.

"Hi, Stone, I'm Jack." He wanted to add "Nicki's boyfriend," but to do so would be admitting fear. With a look of scorn, Stone turned to take the spaghetti-armed hand of this bothersome child. Jack felt like his hand was being gripped by a living statue, but he squeezed back firmly. Nicki saw the struggle that was transpiring between the two warriors, and it warmed her heart. It made her feel beautiful seeing that she was the coveted prize.

Seeing no threat from this boy, Stone turned his attention back to the object of his lust. "Wasn't that a great party the other night?" Stone asked Nicki.

Nicki cast a glance sideways at Jack, whose face was reddening with a feeling resembling cuckoldry. "Well, it wasn't really a 'party,' more like a spontaneous gathering," Nicki corrected.

"Well, whatever it was, thanks for your help," Stone said, holding his stare, which revealed his burn for Nicki.

"Sure, anytime!" Nicki replied with a friendly tone that revealed that there might be a burn for him too.

Stone paraded off from his small conquest, and Jack fumed from his big defeat.

Nicki turned to Jack, and before he could get a word out, she defended herself in a way that threatened him with ending the relationship. "He was having a problem with his girlfriend, and I told him how she was probably reacting to his comments. That's all! It was no big deal. They've been dating ever since, like, junior high."

Jack was not for one second convinced and took up a different angle. "I thought you were home contagious with the flu all weekend."

"It was a spur-of-the-moment thing. Jillian and Michele came by the house Saturday night and took me for some ice cream. I was feeling a little bit better. I wanted to come home or go by your house, but they went to Stone's instead. They were driving, so I had to go where they wanted. We only stayed for like an hour or so, and then they took me home."

"Were his parents there?"

"Who cares?" Nicki started down the offensive defense trail but checked herself. She changed her tone to one of extreme sweet flattery and said, "Jack, it doesn't matter. I'm yours and only yours.

You know that." She kissed him, but he didn't kiss her back. Instead he wrapped his arms around her in a hug as if to prevent her from leaving him. Nicki saw that Jack was pacified, and they sat back down and continued lunch as if nothing had happened.

⊷⊶⊷⊶

Jack watched the final tick of the clock, and the bell rang, announcing the end of the school day. He had agreed to meet Nicki at the entrance to the athletic area, where she changed into her cheerleading clothes for practice. From thirty yards away, Jack could see a head standing above the crowd. It was a blond head framed by a square jaw. It was Stone again.

Jack quickened his pace as if trying to save a lamb from the clutches of the lion that Stone was. As he drew closer, he could see Stone's rock of a hand touch Nicki's black hair—the same hair that had brushed his ear as she kissed him earlier that afternoon. Jack's face reddened to show everyone who looked at him that he was consumed with rage. Jack approached the two with suddenness, and Nicki's face dropped in embarrassing shock. From experience, she anticipated an altercation, and her heart fluttered in flattery.

"Get your hands off her!" Jack demanded, looking up into Stone's steel blue eyes.

"Excuse me?" Stone retorted to the disrespectful command.

Jack turned his head to avoid eye contact and muttered sideways, "I guess I have to spell it out for you." Then, reengaging his glare, he said in an insultingly slow but firm command, "Get your hands off her!"

189

Stone repositioned his body to face his nemesis instead of his game. Nicki looked around, and the crowd in the hallway pulled back as if to form a boxing ring. Her flattery now turned into embarrassment, and she pressed her way through into the girls' locker room area.

"You're not her boyfriend!" Stone rattled like a snake pushed into a corner giving a final warning before striking. Jack didn't heed the warning. His anger had convinced him that he could take down this lion and put down the threat once and for all. The official label of "boyfriend" didn't matter at this point; what really mattered was that the lifeline of Jack's happiness, his significance, was at risk of being severed. Without warning, trying to use the element of surprise, Jack clenched his fist, brought it up with all his might, and struck Stone under his left jaw.

Stone's head nudged slightly up. Jack pulled back his right uppercut and recoiled for his next blow of a haymaker from the right again. But before he could do this, Stone drew back his left fist and, as an archer releases a single arrow to drop a rabbit, let the blow fly directly to the mark of Jack's nose. The blow rocked Jack and pushed him staggering backward, but he managed to stay on his feet. His nemesis repositioned, Stone advanced to continue the assault but was halted in his tracks by a girl firmly pushing on his chest.

"Stop!" Faith commanded. Stone's eyes, full of fury, were instantly washed clean with Faith's command. Stone turned and marched off as the crowd made a path for his victorious withdrawal.

Jack still wasn't sure exactly what had happened, but what he did know was that his whole face was radiating with an earthquake of pain, the epicenter being his nose. Faith grasped his head and pulled his chin up. With one hand, she held it steady, and with the other, she removed the cover of his hand from his nose.

"Let's see what the damage is," she said in a doctorlike voice. "Ew!" she followed in a non-doctorlike voice. "We better get you to the nurse."

Retrieving his backpack, which had been tossed to the ground in his attack, Faith returned to her wobbly-kneed patient and supported him on the one-hundred-yard walk to the nurse's office. The nurse stuffed Jack's nose with gauze, broke a cold pack for him, and told him that he'd better get to a doctor because if his nose wasn't broken, it was very close.

"My mom's already here to pick me up. We'll give you a ride to the clinic," Faith offered.

"Thanks," Jack shamefully honked, still holding the packing in his nostrils.

The two walked silently outside and climbed into Grace's car. It wasn't the first patient they had strapped into the front seat recently. They were happy to help a good kid. Arriving at the clinic, they stayed with Jack until Jay arrived on the scene. Jack overheard Jay telling Grace how thankful he was that Matt was back to normal and that the whole church had been praying for him. Jack didn't even know he was ever sick. Grace gave Jay a thankful hug for his prayers, and Jay returned it with a thankful hug for helping Jack. There was a *phileo*, brotherly love, which passed through them as if they were related.

The nurse behind the desk called Jay and handed him a clipboard of papers to provide the same information in several different ways. It was a natural moment for Grace and Faith to say their good-byes and head for home. Jack summarized the account as best as he could to divert the guilt away from himself but not enough to where Jay would feel obligated to follow up with the principal. Another nurse opened a door from the side and called out Jack's name, indicating they were ready to examine his nose. Jay wanted to go back but had the contents of his wallet scattered in his lap, gathering insurance information for the insistent forms.

"You go on back," Jay said, motioning Jack to the patiently waiting nurse. "I'll come right after I finish this form." Jack, a bit relieved that Jay may not be there to hear the doctor's examining comments like "Wow, you really got a zinger," headed back, still occasionally restuffing the sagging gauze up his nostrils.

Jay completed the last line of the last form and paused. With a downcast stare he prayed, "Father God, You are the almighty and holy God of all things. Your ways are good, and You love us beyond understanding. Lord, I lift up Jack to You and ask Your blessing on him. Please keep him from drifting away from You and turn his eyes toward You. You are the Light. Let him see this. Give him discernment so that he can see evil for the deadly trap that it is. Give him wisdom to choose You, for You are good. Above all, oh Lord, let him know that You love him—so much that You sent Jesus to die on the cross so that he might have life in You. Thank You, God! In Jesus' name only can I pray. Amen."

His prayer complete, Jay returned the papers to the nurse behind the desk, paid the fee, and pushed through the side door into the sterile rooms of the clinic.

-ɘOɔɘ-

"At least it's not broken," Jay consoled as he and Jack walked from the shadow of the clinic into the light of the setting sun, which was angled straight into their eyes.

"Yeah. It still hurts, though."

"Well, the doctor said that we can either get this prescription filled or just give you some ibuprofen. You got a preference?"

"Ibuprofen."

"Okay, we'll stop at the little pharmacy in the strip center on the way home to get some. Do you want anything else while I'm in there?"

"No."

In a moment, Jay backed the truck into a spot across the parking lot from the store entrance. He looked at Jack and said, "I'll be right back."

Jack sat in the passenger seat and pulled down the visor to examine his nose as close as he could in the mirror. There was a guy who looked about thirty hanging out by the movie box on the sidewalk of the store. He was jittery and kept looking at his phone. He'd glance down at it then pull a drag from a cigarette. Then he'd glance down again and pull another drag. This dance was completed three times in the small moment Jack watched. Jack turned his view upward to the visor mirror. He turned his head at a slight angle to examine the swelling on his face. The skin below his right lower eyelid was starting to blacken, just like the doctor said it would. He pulled down his lower eyelid to examine the veins in his eye. They looked normal—no blood, at least.

With his vision screwed in tightly, he noticed in his periphery that the sunlight from outside was being shrouded. He presumed it was an afternoon thunderstorm; they could pop up at a moment's notice. It was so dark, though, that he had to investigate it further. He tilted his head against the passenger window, relaxed his eyes from close vision to distant vision, and looked up. His eyes widened in fear at what he saw. His first reaction was to explode out of the truck to run into the store to yell a warning to everyone inside. But instead, he froze in terror.

A large, black, gargoyle-type creature was descending and casting a dark shadow over the area. By Jack's guess it was as tall as a skyscraper with a wingspan of four football fields. The creature had the shape of a man in that it seemed to have a head, legs, arms, and a torso—but those were about the only similarities. Its two feet were clawed on the toes and the heels; hooked and barbed, their grip was intended to be until death. They were at the end of two powerfully muscular legs rippled with ferocity and extended for action. The hands had equally sharp but slightly shorter gouging claws, which allowed the fingers enough room to wrap and strangle. The arms mirrored the ferocity of the legs and moved in intimidating swiftness, weakening its victim with dread. The tail was like that of an alligator, solid and strong, and held at its tip a protruding barb like a stingray. Its skin looked like an impenetrable black chainmail of putrid hide. As it swooped down, under its colossal, dragonlike wings, which were now pulled back for maximum velocity, its presence polluted the air, leaving a contrail of sable soot high in the atmosphere.

Jack's mind considered the distance and speed and calculated the timing of impact. He knew he couldn't completely escape the collision, but at least he may have time to find refuge under a culvert that was only thirty yards away. Jack swung open the truck door and sprinted toward the culvert. His mind counted down the seconds: four, three, two, one, nothing. Seeing the area fully lit again by the late afternoon sun, he stopped himself just as he was about to make a frantic dive into his fraidy hole.

He looked up and saw that the massive monster was shrinking. It was now about eight feet tall and only as high as a kite. Astonished and relieved, Jack followed its soot-black trail, which grew fainter and fainter. After only three more seconds, it was the size of a bat at treetop level. Jack anticipated its landing spot like a boy catching a parachuting toy army man and jogged back toward the truck. In three more seconds, he could barely make out the little moth-size creature that landed on the fidgety man's shoulder. The small puffs of black dust from the creature intermingled with the man's puffs of cigarette smoke. Jack, locked in a stare at the creature, moved toward the man.

"What's your problem, boy?" The man lifted his chin, pulled back his shoulders, and slightly raised his palms.

Jack was still fixated on the creature that was now transforming into a black parasite only a couple of inches in size but still visible against the white tank top the man was wearing. "You have something on you."

The man lifted his arms and looked down his front for an insect or bird dropping. When he did, the creature crawled in fast motion under his armpit, bore a small hole, and wiggled inside. Finding nothing, he looked back up at Jack, who was still staring at him, and reached into his pocket to produce a butterfly knife with a four-inch blade. His hand flipped twice, and the blade was extended and pointing at Jack. "You wanna go one on one?" growled the man as he looked around for potential witnesses.

"No, sir!" Jack exclaimed apologetically. "I really did think that this thing I saw falling landed on you."

The man heard the innocence in Jack's voice and returned the knife to its hiding spot. Jack jumped back into the truck, his legs weak with fear and his hands trembling. He sat there just staring away from the man. He thought about pulling out his phone to preoccupy himself, but he didn't want the man to think he was calling the cops.

Another minute passed, and a silver Porsche Carrera GT announced its arrival by broadcasting a gangster rap song for the pleasure of the entire parking lot. It whipped into the empty parking space in front of the movie box, and the fidgety man motioned with his head for the car to go around to the side. The two teenage boys in the car, who looked like wealthy kids trying to dress poor, had a quick discussion and then pulled around to the side of the store. The fidgety man looked around and carelessly strutted down the sidewalk. Before making the final turn around the corner, he looked back at Jack, who was now watching the scene unfold. The man glared at him and shook his head side to side, letting Jack know that if he told anyone about this his life was in danger.

Jack immediately averted his eyes, letting the fidgety man know that he wasn't going to say anything. "Get it off me!" Jack heard the man's voice scream. He glanced back, expecting to see an attack, but he just saw the man casually step off the curb with no one else around. The man paused for a split second, turned the corner, and executed his business: selling two ounces of cocaine to the little rich drug addicts enabled by their parents.

Jay returned to the truck with a large bottle of ibuprofen and a pack of gum. He threw the pack in Jack's lap. "What took you so long?" Jack accused, now angry at the threat he'd received.

Jay furrowed his brow in disapproval of Jack's tone. "I was only in there five minutes," Jay defended. Jack put his elbow on the armrest and slunk his body down to rest his head on his hand. Jay turned the radio on to help Jack's mind get off of the fight, but with the two events of the past five minutes, the fight was not even a contender for his attention.

On the quiet ride home with Christian radio as the only noise, Jack replayed the scene of the huge beast coming down from the sky. Assessing the situation, he concluded that either his brain was bruised from the punch or he was hallucinating and crazy. Then he remembered the slow-motion episode from the morning and Tommy, the boy who had committed suicide. That was before the fight. Jack's eyes started to well up with tears. He lifted his head, turned it so Jay couldn't see his tear-filled eyes, and stared out the window. He saw an elderly couple walking a gimpy old mutt coming toward them on the sidewalk. An illumination came from the couple, and Jack doubled his attention on them.

As the truck moved closer to pass them, he examined them. They looked vibrant, and their skin had a sparkly translucence to it, which let out light from within them. Their brightness was like two spotlights. Less than twenty feet behind them was a brilliantly fit lady of around thirty years old. She was beautiful and well dressed in nice athletic wear. Jack looked at her to see if she lit up. To his surprise, her skin became as the same black, ashen soot that the huge beast left in his trail. As she jogged, he heard her scream, "No! No! Get away! Get away!"

It was like Jack was looking through a special lens. He looked for the next person. A dad, mom, and two kids were walking in the same direction as their truck. Jack focused his attention. The kids were young. One teetered on a small bike with training wheels while the other swerved along on a small bike with the training wheels removed. Both of the kids had translucently illuminated skin, but their brightness was dimly lit. The mom also had illuminated skin with brightness about like a flashlight. The dad, who was walking along but in his own iPod space, was sooty. Jack coined these terms on the fly: *glossies* and *sooties*. He heard a yelp of pain from the man as they passed.

Jay slowed the truck and came to a stop at a traffic light. Jack could look at the people without the motion of the truck now. There, a youth group was gathering in a church parking lot for some type of recreational activity. Jack turned his new vision on them and took inventory. Three adults were all glossies: one bright as a spotlight bright, the other two like high beam headlights. Next to them were two sooty kids and about ten glossies. The glossies varied in degree of brightness from nightlight to headlight.

Then Jack noticed something spectacularly horrifying. Through his new vision, he saw more of the gargoyle-type creatures with the same black, ashen skin hovering ravenously in the air around the glossies. The ones around the dimly lit glossies were whispering to them through clenched fangs and blowing soot onto them through mouths open in rage. Much of the soot didn't adhere to their skin, but some of it did, resulting in a dull coat overlaying the person. The ones around the more brightly lit glossies were much farther away and trying to cast their voice to them without drawing too much attention. They too were blowing soot, but because of the distance, their lips were puckered and their stream of soot was mostly scattered in the wind.

The voices of these freakish creatures sounded like you would expect the person's own voice to sound. For a boy, it was a boy's voice; for a girl, a girl's voice; for a man, a man's; and for a woman, a woman's. And the tone seemed to match the owners' to the point where it would be difficult for them to distinguish where theirs ended and the creatures' began. The creatures crowded the air like flies on the rotting corpse of a cow dead six days. Jack narrowed his view through the cloud of flies to one of the sooty boys. One of the gargoyles had shrunk himself to the size of a monkey and was attached to his back with its claws. As one of the glossy adults approached the kid and gave him a welcoming hug, the gargoyle turned his face as if the light burned him. Once the hug was complete and the glossy moved away, the gargoyle started biting at the boy's neck, causing puffs of ash to fill the air around them.

The light turned green, and the truck accelerated forward. The gargoyles vanished from view. Jack looked at his dad to see what he looked like. He was glossy. Jack squinted from the brightness. *Okay, spotlight-bright,* he said in his mind. Jack thought about his own skin. He looked down and examined his arms—they looked normal. He pulled down the visor mirror again to examine his face—still normal. Jay was watching Jack's head turn and look at all the people as if searching for someone in a crowd. He saw him squint when Jack looked at him.

"You okay?" he asked with more than an edge of concern.

Jack flipped the mirror back up and tried to cover, "Uh, yeah, I was just seeing if I knew anyone, and then I got a splitting headache."

"Humph, that would make sense," Jay answered, sifting through his observations for clues to Jack's peculiar behavior. He'd been acting very strange over the past month, and Jay was increasing his observation, scrutiny, and prayer.

17

FLASH FLOOD

Over seventy-two hours had passed since Jack had caught Stone's stone fist with his nose. As the swelling decreased, Nicki's interaction with Jack also decreased. It seemed that badges of jealousy didn't match Nicki's popular fashion sense. Jack understood this and respected the distance, accepting it as a type of punishment for his insane attack. He'd much have preferred for her to love him no matter what, but somewhere in his own heart, he considered himself lucky to have her acceptance, so he didn't push it. This hand being dealt and Caden's parents off for an extended weekend at Las Vegas, where worldly people go to do worldly things and not talk about them to each other later, he invited Jack and Bobby over for a night. On tap were hours and hours of *Mithras*, spy movies, a few beers, and all the talk about girls a boy could take.

Jack had introduced Caden to his dad one day when they happened to see Caden and his mom shopping at the local sporting goods store. Caden's mom was socially polished and came across as the most heartwarming person you could ever meet. Whether Jay bought it completely was unclear, but at least he could put a face and an adult name with Caden. Between this, Bobby's good credibility, the lengthening leash of trust, and the small twist of truth about Caden's parents' whereabouts, Jack secured permission to spend the night.

At the sound of the doorbell, Caden pulled down his hockey mask and went sliding in his socks across the hardwood floor to answer the door. He pressed his masked face against the frosted glass to ensure his guests could see it and then pulled the door back and launched at his victims with a pretend knife in hand. The two would-be victims quickly turned the tables on this Jason, one grabbing his knife hand and twisting it behind his back and the other waylaying him with Bondlike karate chops to the back of the neck.

The playful act was broken at the sound of a car pulling into the driveway. It was a nine-year-old Honda Civic with a white plastic pyramid on top that read "Pizza Tut." Both the car and the hardworking community college driver seemed out of place and uncomfortable for this delivery. Pizzas in hand, the driver kicked the door on the car to a close. Not to be conquered so easily, the door swung defiantly back open. The driver, with a smirk of determination and embarrassment, now seeing he had an audience, rebalanced himself on the drive and with the force of a black belt delivered a kick that echoed through the neighborhood. The door laughed at such a serious attempt, recoiled itself from the doorjamb, and delivered its own blow, sending the driver hopping back and nearly tossing the pizzas.

In recognition of his defeat, the driver took a walk of shame up across the plush grass to the three tragic actors who had watched this comedy play out.

"Ted, when are you going to get rid of that thing?" Caden asked, having formulated a good relationship with the driver over the once-, twice-, and sometimes thrice-a-week deliveries for the past couple of years.

Ted smirked again at the thought of his antagonist and said, "As soon as you sell me your old Lamborghini Aventador in the garage."

At this revelation, Jack and Bobby looked at each other with raised eyebrows.

Bobby mouthed, "Lamborghini."

"Wow," Jack mouthed back.

The driver, Ted, handed the pizzas to Caden who handed them to Bobby. "Thirty-five even," Ted said. Caden reached into his pocket and pulled out a fifty-dollar bill.

Ted (in his usual politeness) opened his change pouch, but Caden (in his usual politeness) halted him and said, "Dude, keep it."

"Thanks," replied Ted with an appreciative nod. "See you later." This curtain closed, the boys entered the house theater for their next performances.

Pizza gone, sun down, and the first 007 movie over, Jack's phone pinged, alerting him that a message had been launched his way. He pulled out his phone and announced, "It's Nicki." He read the text: "What are you doing?"

He tapped back, "At Caden's for the night," and hit send.

His phone instantly pinged again with "☹ I'm bored."

"She says she's bored," Jack said.

"Invite her over," Caden offered.

Jack was relieved that Nicki's boredom may have given him a get-out-of-jail card sooner rather than later for how he had embarrassed her in his scuffle with Stone, so he took Caden up on the offer and texted back, "Come on over."

His phone pinged. "☺ Fun, on my way." Jack updated the boys.

Headlights flashed across the front windows of the house as a car pulled into the driveway. Each of the boys watched, expecting to hear the closing of a car door and then see the headlights retrace the windows as Nicki's ride continued with its evening plans. Instead, there was the silencing of an engine, the closing of four car doors, and the appearance of four girls through the frosted glass. Caden and Bobby looked at Jack, who looked at Caden, hoping that Nicki was not about to overstep her permissive boundaries.

"Uh, she didn't mention any friends," Jack apologetically uttered.

Caden jumped up. "Sweet! I'll get it."

Jack looked at Bobby. "I guess that means it's okay."

Curiosity itching, Jack and Bobby made their way to the lengthy entryway to see which friends Nicki had brought. Caden, opening and then holding the door open to personally greet each one of them with a warm smile, endeared himself to them by saying, "Come on in. Make yourselves at home." The girls made their way in with an air of cordiality and marveled openly at the extravagant décor—dropping the air of cordiality and honoring Caden's invitation as soon as they confirmed Nicki's claim that his parents really were out of town.

The group passed into the living room, but Nicki and Jack lagged behind in the entryway. She took both of Jack's hands and held them in her own. Then she leaned in and gave him a kiss on the cheek. Jack received the kiss coolly. Nicki released his hands, put her hands on either side of his face, and gave him a lengthy, passionate kiss that told him everything was back on track. Jack smiled and gave her a nice firm hug, indicating to her that he was glad. She took his hand, and they walked into the living room to join the others. There was no more swelling on Jack's nose.

Caden, being the good host, offered the girls a drink. "We have almost any soft drink you can think of, water, bubbling water … wine, beer, liquor … coffee, tea, milk?"

The girls—Ginger, Kristi, and Emmy—all giggled. "You got a scotch on the rocks?" joked Ginger.

"How about a vodka martini?" Kristi added.

"I'll take mine shaken, not stirred!" finished Emmy.

The group laughed at the shared banter, and an atmosphere of festivity was uncorked.

"For real, though, Caden, do you have any Crown?" Ginger asked.

Eager to please, Caden answered, "Sure! Straight up?"

Ginger smiled. "No! With coke, please."

Caden went to work behind the closest bar. "Emmy, what about you? What'll it be?" he asked.

"You have any vodka and cranberry juice?" Emmy asked.

"Sure do!" Caden replied, lifting a clear bottle with a black label from the assortment of liquors.

"I'll come mix it. It's not that I don't trust you … I just know what I like!" Emmy put an obvious emphasis on this last line, which made both Caden and Bobby want to follow her around for the rest of the night.

Caden slid over in the bar area to let Emmy create her art. "Kristi, last but not least," said Caden.

Kristi turned her eyes up and pushed a few strands of hair behind her ear as if considering her final answer on a game show. "I'll just take a beer," she said.

Caden replied with a smile, "What continent?" Kristi looked confused. Caden read her expression and elaborated, "We've got beers from around the world. What kind do you want?"

A smile crossed Kristi's face as she realized the plethora of experimental options. "How about Australia? I've always liked kangaroos!" she happily replied.

"Good choice, mate!" Caden said in his best Down Under accent.

"Hey, Caden! What about me?" a voice rung out with some discord.

Caden looked over and saw Nicki with her palms facing up and her eyebrows raised as if she wasn't used to being forgotten.

"Oh, last but not least, for real this time!" Caden replied.

"I'll take a margarita!" she said.

"Ah, something from south of the border! I'll need to get some more ice for that one," Caden said as he reached down into an ice bend and started scooping ice into a machine next to the wall for that particular drink.

"Oh, cool, you're going to make margaritas!" exclaimed Ginger. "Make me one too."

A knock on the door sounded lightly through the buzz of the room and was immediately followed by the door chime, indicating that people were coming in. It was three more from the cheerleading team accompanied by two more from the baseball team and four more from the football team. Caden, still hard at work as the bartender, continued taking orders and setting out drinks for anyone and everyone. It wasn't long until sixteen turned into twenty-four turned into the thirty-two and finalized at forty. Somehow, the little three-boy, relatively quiet evening had mutated into an all-out high school party.

Upon the arrival of Sam, Jordan, Moose, and Jerome, Jack and Bobby led them upstairs to the media room, where they started an online game of *Mithras*. Since the game accommodated only four, Jack played the role of coach. Then Moose relented his position to refill his drink, and Jack took command, leading the team to levels and challenges they had only read about online, each accomplishment being celebrated with high fives all around. Even Bobby and the other bystanders were caught up in the bonding celebration.

Downstairs, without the distraction of a video game, the mood had taken on an even more inebriated frenzy with other types of games. Some games involved quarters, some involved ping-pong balls, some involved gestures, and some involved just words—but they all involved excessive intoxication. Caden had abandoned his post at the bar, which was now a free-for-all, and moved to the post as keeper of the music. The crowd yelled out requests from TrashMouth to Eminem to Katy Perry, and Caden tapped them up and poured them out. Having a natural preference for the rebellious anger of TrashMouth, Caden frequently heard those votes the soonest, even though they weren't always the loudest. The atmospheric conditions of the downstairs were perfect to nurture the rebel buried in each of the kids, who only lacked a cause to dig it up.

A small faction, led by Nicki, who tired of the natural events downstairs but were still under alcoholic influence, ascended to a higher plateau and moved upstairs for more supernatural events. Of the ten followers who had made the pilgrimage, four opted for the demonic warfare of *Mithras* and joined the original team, who had been battling for over two hours. The other six, composed of two boys and four girls, engaged in a short conversation about the spirit world and then slid their seats from the cushions of the three-quarter circle couch to that of the spotless, plush, snow-colored carpet, where Nicki was already seated.

A Ouija board was sitting on a contemporary, low, black coffee table, and none of the seven had any recollection of how it may have arrived. This lack of recollection added to the haunting nerves growing like mold within their hearts. The six followers joined hands around the table, and the two next to Nicki placed their hands lightly on her as she placed her hands lightly on the planchette. The specific question at hand was whether Ginger's most recent boyfriend was cheating on her at college.

Nicki, not being a supernatural rookie, took the lead and called forth any spirit that was in the area. She didn't want to bother Rachel with any of these lesser spirits, but she did want to impress them with her superior person. All the kids grew silent, and Nicki's hands moved the heart-shaped wooden instrument as if another's hands were moving them. The pointed tip went deliberately toward the word *no.* Nicki lifted her hands from the indicator and exhaled as if she had just accomplished quite a feat. The others dropped their jaws in reverence, and Ginger smiled enthusiastically. "I knew he really loved me!" she exclaimed with renewed confidence.

Jack had just led his team from the fifth circle of hell, which was based on Dante's portrayal in the *Inferno,* which had proved to be an especially difficult and time-consuming task. This circle was a swamplike region where the wrathful were engaged in eternal battles at the water's surface. Although of human spirit, they vehemently grabbed and clawed at the flying demon team's feet and submersed them in the murky water, where other humans would choke and detain them. Finally breaking out of this wicked lair, the team jumped to their feet and exchanged the now customary high fives.

Jack sat back down in his chair and then immediately sprang to his feet. A loud commotion had erupted in the upstairs den just outside of the media room. Voices shrieked and screamed at the top of their lungs as if a roaring lion had been dropped into their room and with the doors locked was maiming anyone who still had a heartbeat.

"Get them off of me! Help! It's in me!" one voice shouted.

Another cried, "Oh! Save me! Save me!"

And still another yelled, "Let me go! Please, let me go! Please!"

Jack darted out of the door, his face pale and panicked. The other boys just watched without saying a word, because his step had been too quick for a reactionary comment.

Jack didn't know how he would help when he saw what was attacking the others; he just knew he had to do something. Pulling himself to an abrupt halt at the doorway, his heart in his throat, he saw seven kids on the floor seated around a table with a TV-tray-size board on it. Fourteen eyes hit him at once, all asking the question, "What's wrong?"

Jack exhaled in relief that there was no psycho with a knife or roaring lion.

Nicki looked up with a confused expression and said, "Hey, what's up?"

Jack just smiled, his face changing from a panicked pale to an embarrassed red, and said, "Oh, nothing, just wanting to see what y'all were doing."

Ginger said, "We're talking to the spirits! They said that David isn't cheating on me after all."

Jack wasn't sure what this meant but said, "Cool," and with a nod indicating that he had gotten what he came for, he retreated into the small hall, shook his head, and had a conversation with himself.

What the heck was all that screaming? What is happening to me? I must be going crazy. At this last self-comment, Jack's blood flushed from his face again, returning it to a panicked paleness. *Holy cow, I really am going crazy. Should I tell my dad? I need to tell someone. Holy cow, holy cow, holy cow! No! This can't be happening!*

Jack cautiously approached the corner of the wall again and sheepishly edged his head around to spy on the seven. His face, already pale, completely emptied of blood—as did his heart and legs—at the sight. There were seven sooties in a circle holding hands. Standing in the middle of the small black table was a large, black gargoyle whose torso extended through the ceiling. Behind each sooty was a similar but human-size gargoyle. These gargoyles were kneeling, and each had one of its hands clawed into the back of its person's neck, forcing his or her head into a bowing position, its other clawed hand pointing toward the larger gargoyle. Through their extended hands, they appeared to be receiving some type of power that was visibly circulating through the joined hands of the group. The power pulsed through all their beings, and their soot composition vibrated slightly, shaking off a fine black dust that covered the ground.

The gargoyle behind Nicki felt Jack's gaze and spun its head completely backward on its body. It locked eyes with Jack. Jack was paralyzed like a mouse before a viper. Jack watched as the gargoyle shot from his kneeling position up through the ceiling, leaving a blast of soot behind. Jack moved his eyes back down to Nicki, only to find what looked like the same gargoyle in the same position but with its head staring at the feet of the larger gargoyle.

"Jack! Where are you? I need you!" a voice called.

It was Rachel. Jack responded in his mind, "How do I get to you?"

With all the noise, Jack needed to get outside for some fresh air. He descended the decadent staircase closest to him to go downstairs. His descent gave him a higher view of the still twenty-plus people below. His vision changed as he looked at them, and he sat down on the staircase so as not to fall in his trance. They were mostly all sooties, with the exception of about eight of them who were dimly translucent. The black gargoyles were flitting around in the air like a swarm of bees moving from flower to flower, collecting every bit of nectar possible in an oversize patch of blooming flowers. *Flitting* was an accurate word for their moves because there was a hint of exhilaration in the air. The gargoyles were enjoying their work, although their faces seemed to show otherwise. Their faces were deeply and permanently etched with a scorn of rebellion and cruelty and when not in a gnashed position were formed into an eternal scream, which echoed across time to all who hear, "Woe, woe, woe to me!"

"Jack! Where are you? I need you!" Rachel desperately called again.

Jack arose to complete his descent and was met by two intoxicated boys who were coming out of the small orchestral performance room. They had been deep in a debate about whether or not homosexuality was a sin and needed a tiebreaking vote.

"Hey, Jack," one boy said, stopping his exit. At his pause, three girls and another boy followed from the room. The boy continued, "Jack, you're a Christian, right?"

A girl said, "Doesn't your dad work at that church on the highway?"

All their eyes were fixed on Jack as if he was some type of theological expert. He liked the admiration but wasn't sure exactly where this conversation was going. The boy continued, "Alan says that God hates homosexuals." Jack noticed a collective frown on this statement—except for Alan, the staggering boy who raised his beer at the comment. "But *we*—we say that homosexuals are born that way and that there is no way God would send them to hell!"

Jack noticed a collective nod of approval. "So," the boy continued, "are you a Christian?"

Jack felt cornered by the group's approval. They dangled acceptance and popularity in front of him, but he was too scared to grab it. This fear exposed his cowardice to himself, and he became rebelliously angered.

"No, I'm not," he admitted.

"But your dad works at that church, right?" the girl insisted.

"No, he just goes there a lot," Jack dodged.

"So he's a Christian, but you're not?" the girl persisted.

"That's right. I am not a Christian. Sorry," Jack said, preserving his neutral rating from the group. As soon as the bit of air that passed through Jack's mouth pronouncing his apology, a boy who was playing some type of farm animal drinking game in the other room stood up on his chair and crowed like a rooster across the room. All the kids around him laughed and sprayed their drinks across the already soaked table. Jack's stomach turned to nausea, and his eyes welled up with tears, although he couldn't understand why.

Slamming the door behind him, Jack walked outside and hopped up to take a seat on the tailgate of the $80,000-dollar four-wheel drive pickup that had never seen a spot of mud in its 253-day life, parked with two wheels on the street and the other two on the carpet of grass. Jack started a mental conversation with Rachel. "Rachel, where are you?"

"Right here, Jack. What did you see?"

"I saw demons." Jack shivered as the words passed his lips, and he realized that was indeed what he had been seeing.

"That's right, Jack. Stay away from them. They'll drag you underwater and smother you there."

The imagery of the fifth circle of hell he had just played in *Mithras* came before Jack's mind. "But how?"

"Keep your mind's eye fixed on me and I'll guide you. I can't do it for you, sweetheart. You have to be strong." Rachel's encouragement made Jack feel as though he'd been weak, which insulted his pride.

"I know."

"Jack, you have to do it. You have—" Nicki's voice broke off like they had lost their cell phone connection.

"Jack!" a voice called from the dimly lit street lined with cars. Jack looked up and saw two girls on bikes pulling to a stop by the truck. It was Amber and Faith.

Very surprised and somewhat ashamed, Jack said, "Hey! What are y'all doing here?"

"We were bored and saw that Nicki posted on Twitter that there was a party at Caden's, so we thought we'd just ride by to see who was here. You know—just curious," Amber explained.

"How did you know where he lived?"

"She posted the address."

"Are you serious?" Jack was bothered that Nicki had taken such a liberty. Amber and Faith picked up on his intonation and were silent. Jack looked up, his eyes having been lowered with distaste, and saw that both Amber and Faith were glossies. Amber was dimly lit, but Faith was pretty bright. Without thinking, Jack asked Amber, "When did you become a Christian?"

Amber reacted with curious surprise. "The other night. How did you know?"

She looked at Faith, whose face was just as surprised and curious as her own. Faith shrugged her shoulders. This was confirmation that his occasional vision was real. Not only could he see demons, but he could also see who was a Christian and who was not. Tears welled up in his eyes again, and again he didn't exactly know why. Ashamed by them, Jack jumped off of the tailgate and invited the girls inside.

Faith looked at Amber for her response. "Nah, I prefer the outside," Amber said. "It's more my kind of crowd." Faith gave a small nod of agreement and silently exhaled in relief.

Jack insisted, "Come on. Everyone knows you, and it's not that bad in there. Besides, you can hang with me!" Jack pointed his thumb toward himself and smiled.

"Sorry, I like it out here better, and we were really just passing by," Amber politely refused. The girls, still straddling their bikes, took their seats, pushed off, and started pedaling. "Stay out of trouble!" Amber said over her shoulder.

"Yeah, take care!" added Faith, praying in her mind for God to help Jack look at Him instead of the junk of the world.

"Sure, sure!" Jack replied. He paused at the door, took a deep breath, and rejoined the party.

At two in the morning, Jordan's voice came over the speakers. "Okay, listen up! You don't have to go home, but you can't stay here!"

Seeing that Caden was passed out on the couch and there were only about a dozen people still around, Jordan had figured it was the responsible thing to do. Jack took the prompt, escorted the last group of his new friends to the door and locked it behind them. He surveyed Caden's house, which was a literal disaster area. Beer cans and plastic cups were everywhere, spilled drinks coated the finely polished wood floor, all the precisely placed furniture was imprecisely rearranged into a tizzy, and the stench of fermented liquors suffocated the air. It was as if the entire peacock house, once so beautiful and proud, was wrung and plucked in a matter of six quick hours. And adding insult to injury, each one of the perpetrators strutted out with a delighted smile, vowing to return one day for more. The house groaned in miserable anticipation.

Jack finished the shutdown procedure, turning off lights and games and neon signs that for some reason were arrayed around the bar and kitchen area. Exhausted, he collapsed into a soft leather recliner in the now dark living room, which was only dimly lit by the margarita machine he had failed to turn off. His eyes blurred from social exhaustion alone—Jack never did make good on his promise to the group to have a beer. He stared at the drink machine, which swirled its frozen lime green drink in a melodic rhythm—*mmm, mmm, mmm*. Jack's gave into its hypnotic song and fell asleep.

—◦◦◦◦—

"Jack, you have to try harder!" Jack heard the demand before he even opened his eyes. "You're not going to make it," Rachel chided, "if you don't open your mind more."

"What do you mean, Rachel? Nicki and I are back like before, and we had a great party tonight."

"How much did you drink?"

"None. I was too busy with friends."

Rachel shook her head and grimaced in concern. "Jack, you're totally missing the path. Don't you remember our old days at all? The sensual parties of Bacchus that lasted for days? Jack, you were the host. You were the one who people rallied around. They didn't do this because you were narrow-minded and weak, but because you led the way, helping everyone to open up and strengthen their spirits."

Rachel's lashing cloaked in love jabbed Jack, and a grimace fell across his face—only it was one of pain instead of concern. He stowed his emotions and closed them up in silence. He could tell by Rachel's eyes that she was sorry for the harsh words, and she proved this when she continued, "Jack, I just want to help." She cupped one of his hands in both of hers like a treasured gift. She lifted it to her lips, and in an act of humiliation, she kissed it and looked into his eyes with care. Jack accepted her apology, if that's what it was, and reaffirmed his vow to do anything he could to know her more.

Overcoming his hurting pride and realizing that he really did need her help, he asked, "Okay, what do I need to do?"

"Understand yourself and how to let yourself go. The more you go with the flow of life, the more of life will flow into you. Float with the music, the nectar, the candy, the pleasure—everything that life has to offer. Just go with it."

"Nectar? Candy? What do you mean?"

"Jack, alcohol and drugs, despite what you've been brainwashed to believe, were created for the very purpose of spiritual enlightenment. Sure, some abuse them, but in the end, they just move more quickly to their true place in life, which fulfills their being. It's all good," Rachel said with a pleading expression.

Jack nodded. "This is scary," he admitted before he had time to stop his words.

"You can do it. You've done it before. Just go with it."

Jack pulled his hand from Rachel's, put both his arms around her, and hugged her firmly. "I can't do this without you, you know?" he said with tenderness, his heart melting.

Just like when Nicki had given him the compassionate embrace, Spaw gasped for air from where he sat perched in a treetop, hidden from view. Anything resembling the strength of the enemy, even as counterfeit as this was, made him choke with disgust.

Rachel peered back into his eyes. "I'm here for you."

Spaw had to leave; Jack's softhearted vulnerability was pricking him hard.

The hollow-feeling image that Jack was embracing and confessing to vanished right before his eyes. The air was empty and silent, with only the humming of what sounded like an electrical motor. Jack stood there alone. He called to her hoping she would return. "Rachel? Rachel?" She had gone.

Unsure of how to go home without the drink that she usually gave him, Jack decided to explore the lush woods around him. He walked forward twenty paces and bumped into some type of invisible wall. It gave his fingertips a mild electrical shock when he touched it, but he could feel that he could penetrate it. He pushed his hand through it and watched it disappear as if into another world. Curious and thinking that this might help him get home, he pushed his face into the wall. The shock was uncomfortable but bearable, so he pressed his entire head through so that he could see without the electrical blur. It was dark and the air was thick. The only light was from a few dim rays emitted from where he stood. It was like he was in an endless cavern and his tiny candle was the only thing piercing the darkness.

His eyes strained to capture the details of an almost imperceptible movement in the distance. Something about one hundred yards away seemed to be moving toward him. It was a small, black speck that even from this distance impressed the image of a wasp into his mind. He stretched his neck out farther to extend his vision. There was a second black wasp that was passing the first. Now a third was coming close behind—now a fifth, a sixth, a bunch. Jack stopped counting and let his eyes take in the fast-approaching mass. They were now fifty yards away and closing in fast.

In fear, he started to retreat, pulling his head back, but it was stuck. His quick breathing turned into hyperventilation, and he lifted his hands and feet and pushed them against the wall in an attempt to retract his head. His feet slipped through the wall and off a ledge, and he fell to his bottom. He tried to use his hands, but the wall seemed to still be intangible to them. He never removed his stare from the flying army that was bearing down on him.

As they approached, he could see that they were about the size of vultures. Their bodies were indeed like wasps, and their tails seemed to have stingers, but their heads were like mosquitos with sharp probes extended forward. The swarm fell on him as one, and their force knocked Jack six feet backward. None of the swarm penetrated the wall, and Jack lay back on the ground with a concussion. The pain was so intense that Jack blacked out completely.

"Jack ... Jack ... Jack ... I think I'm ..."

Bobby shook Jack's arm and tried to arouse him from his sleep. Jack was sweating through his light fabric T-shirt, and drool drained from his open mouth, which was tilted down toward his shoulder. Jack's eyes unconsciously opened, and he stared into the oversize recliner his head was sunken into. Collecting the light of the day, his eyes closed tightly as he winced in migrainelike pain. Bobby glanced over at Caden, who was still passed out on the couch, and sprinted through the living room around to the kitchen sink, where he announced his presence to all with dry heaves brought on from the beer he had consumed less than twelve hours before.

Caden wearily turned himself over on the couch and laughingly exclaimed, "Dude! That's sick!"

Jack opened his eyes halfway and started to laugh. Bobby lifted his head and rinsed his mouth out with water.

"Better?" Caden asked.

Bobby looked at him through reddened eyes and replied, "Yeah."

Caden sat up, holding his head, and turned to Jack. "Dude, you look horrible! How much did you drink?"

"Oh, I don't know. I lost count," Jack lied.

"Let's eat some breakfast," Caden suggested. "Food is good for hangovers." At the imagined sight of breakfast, Bobby convulsed into a few more dry heaves in the sink. Caden and Jack looked at each other and laughed through their own pain.

Caden moved around to the kitchen, pulled a blender out from beneath the counter, and said, "Well, if we can't eat anything, maybe some protein shakes will be just as good."

Bobby and Jack made their way to the modern, raised dining table, which was still covered with the residue of spilt beer smeared around by the clump of paper towels still drenched and sitting on an elegant stool. Each boy was in pain but for different reasons: Bobby from margaritas, Caden from beer and fifty-year-old scotch whisky, and Jack from a dream of an attack of large black insects. Caden produced a bottle of ibuprofen to help in the relief effort along with the shakes. Caden and Bobby rubbed their foreheads, recalled what they could of the night, and vowed in their mind to do less next time. Jack rubbed his forehead, recalled what he could of the night, and vowed in his mind to do more.

"Man, you were ninja last night on *Mithras*, Jack," praised Bobby. "Sam, Jordan, and Jerome were following you around like a hero."

Jack smiled at the thought of his older friends and the admiration it brought from Bobby.

Caden piled on, "Yeah, and you and Nicki standing there making out right in the middle of everyone … *bam!*" Jack smiled proudly but tried to play it down. Caden continued, "Nicki's just hot! I didn't know y'all were that heavy!" Jack couldn't play it down anymore, and a wide grin covered his face.

Bobby reached over and punched him in the shoulder. "Snap out of it! Just because she looks like a Bond girl, that doesn't mean that you're James Bond!" Bobby kidded.

Jack's pride swelled to epic proportions. Wishing he could let the praise continue but realizing that he couldn't show that he enjoyed it quite that much, he turned the conversation toward the suffocated house. "Wow! Look at this place." Bobby and Caden surveyed the condition. "When are your parents coming home?"

Caden had a look that showed he could care less about the house. "They won't be home until Monday. I'll pay to have someone come clean it," he said.

"Huh, must be nice," Bobby said.

Caden smirked. "It is!" They all laughed.

Jack's phone vibrated in his pocket. Fearful it was his dad, he pulled it out in a rush. It was a Pepper Alert—a special tweet from one of the guys from TrashMouth to their raging-hot fans they affectionately referred to as Peppers. "Hey, TrashMouth is doing an impromptu concert this Thursday at Flicka's!" Jack announced.

"Sweet!" Bobby and Caden said together. Jack's mind started working on how he could leverage this to please Rachel and heat things up with Nicki at the same time.

Caden pointed the remote at the oversize flat screen in the oversize living room and clicked it to life. The voice of an announcer of a college football game blared over the surround sound speakers. The boys grabbed their protein shakes and migrated to the couch to watch the game. Caden picked up the phone and ordered "the regular" from Pizza Tut. He finished the order with "Have Ted bring it, please."

18

FLATTERED TO DO MORE

While she never could get excited about the return to learning that came with Monday mornings, on Sunday night, Nicki was ready to get back to the next day's chapter of the social drama for which she lived. Dressed in her pajamas, she returned to the bathroom to finish drying her damp hair before bed. She wiped the steam that still covered the mirror, opening up a circle for *that girl* to peer through. She paused, and they locked eyes as so many times before.

"What do you want?" Nicki asked.

"To not be you!" the girl scathingly replied.

"Why not? People say I'm pretty," Nicki defended.

"But what do you say?"

"I think I am …"

"No, what do you *really* say?"

Nicki anticipated the girl's words, so they didn't sting so much this time. "I'm fat, my nose is too big, my arms are too hairy, and I don't know why anyone likes me?"

The girl smiled. "Now you're seeing what I see!"

Nicki's eyes filled with tears, and she let out a sob.

"So what are you going to do about it?"

Nicki stared at her wrists and the small scar that was there from last year. Her eyes moved to the pair of professionally sharp scissors in the drawer next to her. Her phone's vibration and suggestive sounds moaned from her room, indicating a text from Jack had arrived.

Flicking the bathroom lights off, she ran away from the girl in the mirror to see what he had to say. Jack had forwarded the tweet he had forgotten to send her the previous day: "Pepper Alert: Impromptu concert at Houston Flicka's this Thursday! Be there or die." A second text followed: "Let's get a group!"

Happy for the interruption, Nicki tapped back, "Sweet! I'll get a group and let you know."

Jack sent one more, "K, love you."

Nicki's heart felt happy to be loved by someone, and she tapped back, "Love you too."

Nicki lay on her bed and made up her mind to finish some homework she had due tomorrow in government. After about thirty minutes of attempting to concentrate, she turned onto her back and let her mind wander. An image of Stone floated in her imagination along with a twinge of guilt. Ignoring the guilt and choosing the pleasure, she followed Stone. She dreamed about what life would be like dating someone so big, strong, handsome, and popular. She smiled as she mused about how envious other girls would be of her. She pictured her life after high school, Stone in the NFL and her going to all the games in a Texans jersey with "Eriksen" on the back, letting everyone know that she was the pride of his life. Nicki's mind fought to continue the fantasy, but her body escorted her into sleep.

-⊖⊖⊖⊖-

"Nicki!" Rachel cheered as she gave a hop of glee and wrapped her in the excited hug of high school girlfriends. Nicki was flattered by the warm welcome and immediately returned the embrace. "Nicki," Rachel's tone immediately became graver, as if she had an update of a dreadful event, "I'm worried about Jack ... and you too."

"What do you mean?" Nicki asked, wondering how the excited, flattering greeting had flown away so quickly.

"Well, you are a naturally special spirit. You know that." Nicki's feeling of flattery returned. "But Jack is not going to make it to the higher clander unless he tries harder."

Nicki had to force her thoughts away from her own special self to be concerned for Jack. "How can I help?"

Rachel smiled at her offer, as though Nicki had lived up to her expectation. "I need you to encourage him—maybe even lead him into some things that will expand his mind. Unless his mind is opened more, he won't be able to handle all of the truth he needs to be joined with us. I know the things we talk about at all of our meetings may seem unreal when you get back to your earthen life, but the day will come when your time is finished there and you'll be locked into your eternal choice forever."

This last statement helped Nicki to understand the gravity of the situation, and her cheeks relaxed, letting the half smile drop from her face. Her eyes showed that she was in deep thought about what she could have done differently and what she would do next time.

"I know just what to do," Nicki remarked. "We're going to a concert this week, and I'm getting a group of people to go with us. I'll make sure we have a good warm-up party before it starts."

Rachel smiled approvingly and added, "And maybe have a private 'warm-down' session afterward. And … maybe even …" Rachel raised her eyebrows and gave a calculating smile accompanied by a wink and a nod of the head. Nicki understood the silent message and smiled with feigned modesty. Then the frail mask of modesty cracked and fell, revealing a smile that delighted in the idea.

"Thanks, Nicki! I knew I could count on you!" Rachel's face glowed as if Nicki had just reunited her and her lost puppy. She squeezed Nicki with another cheery hug and kissed her on the cheek. Nicki's heart melted and her devotion hardened.

Spaw was eager to end the session. Nicki was a good enough instrument to use against Jack, but that was about all she was good for. There was no challenge in her destruction; she had already bathed so deeply in the currents of the world that lesser demons could easily finish her off.

Rachel looked intently into Nicki's eyes to terminate their meeting. Nicki, not yet prepared to release the bubbly feelings that so pleasantly percolated through her spirit, pulled back and turned away. Rachel slowly and firmly pressed her hand against Nicki's cheek and, like a lover trying to convince the one he wounded of his steadfast love, guided Nicki's face around to her own. Nicki relented and matched

Rachel's stare, letting it draw her in as usual. Nicki felt her spirit plunge headlong into those refreshing pools of bliss.

She closed her eyes, inhaled deeply, and let herself dissolve into her feelings, sinking deeper and deeper into the life-giving liquid. She lifted her arms above her head to glide with her hair, waving in the downward drift, and stretched her toes in a point to hasten her descent. She wanted more sensation, a deeper drink. The more deeply she drank, the more deeply she thirsted. If this was what life in the Ohm was like, she wanted it now and forever. She felt her entire spirit become one fantastic smile that radiated a joy she had never known before.

Her joy was broken too soon when she felt her toes, then her feet, then her legs, and finally her whole body break from the gentle caress of the liquid pool and into hot, burning air. She continued to fall, but now she was being pulled by gravity through a fiery atmosphere, like an asteroid plunging to earth. Her toes, still pointing down, were cutting the way, and fire shot up all around them, engulfing her body in a bright white cone of flames.

Her mind was still in shock at such a violent and abrupt change. She was only convinced of the new reality when her eyes, such credible scouts, reported back sights of her skin being charred by the heat and peeled back by the force of falling. Nicki opened her mouth to scream, somehow thinking that it might soothe the pain, but instead she let out exhalations of pleasure, as if her experience were reversed. Reeling in pain, Nicki retracted her arms and legs, pulling herself into a ball. She clenched her muscles so tightly she felt the pain move inside, and the pain outside disappeared.

Nicki's iPad alarm sung an enchanting song of a goddess within that needed to somehow be released from its owner's body, a song that had won many awards and had indeed changed many girls' lives, all for the worse. Exhausted and sweating, Nicki opened her crying eyes and moved to swipe the alarm off. She buried her head in the soft foam pillow in denial that it was Monday morning—again.

19

SEEING TRUTH, SEEING LIES

When Nicki and Jack talked about their individual experiences with Rachel, neither one of them provided the complete picture. Their discussion was more centered around the bright promise of what life they could earn than around what life currently was—a pattern eerily similar to those promises made by sin in general. Sin is the large fine chocolate Easter bunny that when bitten proves itself hollow and of a cheap, waxy type of chocolate. It is the mirage of a pool of life-giving water to the traveler dying of thirst that proves too good to be true. So Nicki and Jack chose to praise their chocolate and their water but did not mention the disappointment and unquenched thirst as they worked for it.

Jack rounded the corner of magnificently architected suburban houses to see the magnificently architected suburban elementary school, number twenty-three in the award-winning district. He could see two cars parked in the teachers' parking lot close to the playground and basketball court. He recognized the spotless four-wheel drive pickup truck that he'd perched on the other night in front of Caden's house. This, as he discovered that night, was Sam's.

The other car in the lot, which he also recognized from Caden's party, was the equally spotless, white, four-door foreign sedan of Ginger, who had brought Nicki.

With some degree of embarrassment from having to rely on his feet for transportation, Jack approached the already laughing and joking group. He was in that awkward range of being close enough to recognize them and to be recognized, but not close enough to greet them. He therefore walked with his head bent down, casting sideways glances and avoiding eye contact, which might lead someone to say something to him that he couldn't yet understand.

Finally drawing up within twenty yards, he raised his eyes. The group was in a loose circle, and Moose was entertaining them with his impression of pop singer Miley Cyrus, opening his mouth like a cottonmouth moccasin giving a prestrike warning and sticking his tongue out as far as he could down and diagonally to the left. A burst of laughter encouraged him to continue the mimicry, which he did by sticking his pointer fingers up like two little goat-size spikes on his head and then cocking it sideways. A second burst of laughter coaxed him to finalize the cheap imitation with a bend of the waist, a twerk of the bottom, an expression of having swallowed nasty cough syrup, and an equally horrible rasping of, "We can't stop! And we won't stop!" At this, the girls provided a background chant of "It's our party—we can do what we want!" and the group roared with laughter, some to the point of tears. Sam jumped down from the truck bed to give Moose a high five as he stopped being Miley Moose and returned to just being Moose.

Jack, emerging from the awkward zone, joined the circle and catching the end of the performance joined in the laughter. Moose grabbed him and gave a welcoming Miley face so close that Jack could smell the iced cappuccino Moose had downed after school. The group embraced Jack without hesitation and Jack felt at home with friends.

With Jack's arrival, the final welcome was given, and as the sun said its final good-byes, the crew said their own to the cheap imitation music of Moose and set out toward the true music of TrashMouth. Nicki pulled Jack to the backseat of Ginger's sedan, forcing another one of the girls to ride with Sam, a move that the girl welcomed. Although advertisements claim that the backseat could seat three adults comfortably, Jack wondered how waiflike three adults would have to be to validate this assertion. On his right was Nicki, and on his left was one of the girls whom he had denied being a Christian to. The music was turned up so loud that it made the lack of conversation with this girl much less awkward.

Jack leaned into Nicki, and Nicki took his right hand and held it, their fingers interwoven. Jack put his face into Nicki's hair in an attempt to whisper into her ear. "Did you talk to Rachel today?" he asked as if Rachel was one of Nicki's everyday friends.

She pulled back her face to look him in the eyes and shook her head. Then she put her face into Jack's ear and whispered back, "No. I only go meet with her about once a week. But I meditate to her every day." Jack nodded and drew up his lips in a pleasant smile, indicating he'd heard her and that he supported her.

There was a pause between the songs, and naturally, the five passengers attempted to take the moment to talk. Nicki looked across Jack to the girl on the other side.

"So, Dana, how are things going with the dance team?"

Dana inhaled and opened her mouth to tell of their preparations for regional competition when an older but very popular TrashMouth song rose up and dominated all other sounds. In an instant, all five were watching each other toss their heads forward and backward and listening to each other sing as best they could. The driving cadence and grungy pitch of Blood's overwhelming voice made each of them believe their own voices to be not quite as bad as they thought, so they all sang out at the top of their lungs.

"Banshee! Banshee! She wears purple and scarlet sitting on the beast. Banshee! Banshee! She's got a cup of desolation to serve at the feast. Banshee! Banshee! She stays drunk on the blood of the holy and pure. Banshee! Banshee! She's my banshee lover; she's my idol for sure. Banshee! Banshee!" Jack, feeling completely free to play himself, started jamming on the air guitar as the hard-hitting guitar solo pounded out over the speakers, which were being tested to their limits. Ginger thumped the steering wheel like a bass drum. The other girls preferred the invisible background guitars and were looking around with enjoyment and giggles amazed at their own liberation in the music.

Much to his annoyance, an eyelash or some other tiny object landed in Jack's eye. He swiped at the culprit and immediately returned to his guitar so as to not miss a chord. His eye stung again, demanding another rub. Jack put down his guitar and rubbed both of his eyes for good measure. When he opened them again, they felt as if someone had taken two fists of charcoal dust and rubbed them directly between his eyelids and eyeballs. He involuntarily hunched forward and threw both his hands over them to protect them from any more dirt. He rubbed them stiffly and tried them again. All better. He sat back up to a thick cloud of black soot filling their mobile temple of worship.

He looked to his right at Nicki. She was a sooty. She tossed her head forward and back, her hands still mimicking the pulsating guitar, ash flying off of her as if she were an outdoor carpet beat out after a dust storm. She paused, and seeing Jack's face motionless and close, she moved in to kiss him. As her rotten black lips approached, Jack saw a clawed black finger where her tongue should've been. In the blink of an eye, Jack cringed and then heard Rachel's voice: "Go with it!" He did. He pressed his lips to Nicki's and felt a burning like he had just pressed them to a hot frying pan. He reached around Nicki's head and pulled her face more firmly into his. He released his embrace and opened his eyes. Nicki had a wide smile across her beautiful face. Jack tasted his mouth; it tasted like cotton candy. He smiled and, with swollen pride, felt like a man.

Ginger pulled the car into the spot right next to Sam's truck. The surface lot was thirty-year-old asphalt and had more than a few potholes showing its neglect. The other group was assembled at the tailgate to wait for the team to be whole again. Since the club was on the outskirts of downtown in an area that served predators ranging from crazed homeless men to gangbangers, even the boys were on alert.

Nicki pulled Jack back for another amazing kiss, which put them about ten paces behind the group. This done, Nicki took Jack's hand, and they followed the herd toward the club. There was a homeless man sitting on the ground next to a bench, and the larger group ahead walked by him without notice. His clothes were ragged like the rest of his person. He had shaggy, unkempt hair and was pointing an object at Jack and Nicki. Jack, thinking it was a gun, slowed his step and pulled back slightly on Nicki's hand.

Nicki looked around at Jack. "What's wrong?"

Her instincts sensed Jack's mood. Jack motioned with his head toward the scruffy man. Nicki glanced at him and replied, "What? A sleeping homeless man?"

A bit embarrassed by Nicki's courage to pass him, Jack continued at Nicki's pace. The man stared intently at Jack, continuing to point something at him, but Jack's pride wouldn't let him react again. They drew within a few steps of the man, whose bright blue eyes seemed strangely illuminated by the dim streetlight and were intensely focused on Jack. Jack looked at the object in his hand. It was a small black book, ragged like its owner. A stern and clear voice came from the man. "I am the Lord your God, who brought you out of the land of Egypt, out of the house of slavery. You shall have no other gods before me!" Jack's heart raced with fear. His throat became choked with a mucus that had that cotton candy taste, and he involuntarily spit it toward the ground preacher. Jack saw the mucus land on the man's face, but the old man didn't flinch. Mucus clinging to his unshaven cheek, the man repeated his words in a voice that was like steel wrapped in velvet. "I am the Lord your God, who brought you out of the land of Egypt, out of the house of slavery. You shall have no other gods before me!"

At the sight of Jack's spit landing on the worn blanket of the sleeping homeless man, Nicki let loose some expletives and laughed a muffled laugh so as not to wake the sleeping giant. She pulled Jack quickly ahead, and he joined her laughter. Nicki was in control of Jack's emotions, whether she realized it or not. When she smiled, he smiled. When she frowned, he frowned. When she laughed, even at things most would not find funny, he laughed.

Within a hurried ten steps, they were again part of the group. Nicki reported what Jack had done, and the group laughed at Jack's bold act. Outside Jack was smiling with them and accepting their acceptance of him. Inside, Jack's mind tried to make sense of what the man had said. It was as if Jack was sung a certain ditty when he was an infant and, hearing it as a young man, couldn't quite recall the tune or the words. Jack thought, *I believe in God. I believe in Jesus. I also believe in the freedom He gave us to have fun and enjoy life. Egypt! What's Egypt have to do with anything? I'm not in slavery! That's stupid.* Jack's nose itched, and he tried to lift his hand to scratch it,

233

but Nicki was holding it so securely he couldn't pull it up. *Slavery!* Jack's mind pointed out.

"Don't let her go," Rachel's voice said. "She'll help you. Go with it."

━◌◑◌◌━

"Who wants a drink?" Jerome asked the group. Ten hands lifted to shoulder height indicated they were all thirsty. "Okay. I'm gonna need some help," replied Jerome.

The obvious three helpers who could possibly pass for being twenty-one years old—Sam, Jordan, and Moose—fell in line, and they trekked toward the bar. Jack looked around. He had never been in this club. In fact, the only other time he'd been in a club was the last TrashMouth concert, which wasn't all that long ago. Jack was amazed at how lucky he was to have a band of this magnitude play twice in Houston within such a short time.

Looking around, Jack realized that the Peppers, TrashMouth's most loyal fans, looked exactly the same—it was déjà vu all over again. In fact, he thought he actually recognized some of the people from the first time. One girl of average height and weight wore camouflage pants and a wife beater and had a buzz cut. There was nothing particularly memorable about that—what stuck to Jack's memory was when she turned her face toward him.

She had the name "Blood" written across her forehead underlined by a row of black eyebrow piercings. Her eyes were dark and empty, as if meth had injected its devilish toxins and sucked out her spirit. Just below these holes, where an athlete might wear eye black to minimize the sunlight's glare, two words were permanently inked. Beneath her right eye was the word *Life*, and beneath her left was *Death*. Seeing Jack reading her face, she drew near to him and closed the skin over her two holes to reveal the writing on her eyelids. The right eyelid read "My." The left eyelid read "Is." Jack read it together: "My life is death."

As she'd done the last time Jack had seen her, the girl continued her display by frowning for an instant and then opening her mouth and sticking out her tongue with a hiss. Jack smelled the stench of her breath and wondered if she ever brushed her teeth. The next person Jack imagined that he recognized was a hairless person, either a boy who looked like a girl or a girl who looked like a boy. This person was slight in build and seemed to have taken great lengths to maintain a waxy, pale complexion. The person had no hair on his or her head— no eyebrows or even eyelashes. The person wore a black long-sleeve, button-down shirt over black skinny jeans, which were in stark contrast to the pasty bare feet that stuck out at the bottoms. His or her eyes were sunken, hollow, and dark. Much like the buzz-cut girl's eyes, if these were the windows to the soul, this house had been abused and abandoned years ago. This person didn't seem to notice anyone as he or she floated through the crowd. This person seemed like some type of ghostly apparition moving stealthily through the bodies around him or her. Jack swept the crowd with his gaze and recognized the feeling in the air. Just like the last time, there was that same eager thirst for a deep drink of something. It was an empty assembly of empty souls begging to be filled with significance.

"Beer is here!" announced Jordan as the group snatched brown bottles of fun for themselves.

"Let's move out!" Sam commanded as they tightened their ranks and moved in to become one with the mob of people surrounding the stage. Being a larger small group, they were only able to get to the middle of the herd, which was about a hundred feet from the stage. Settling in, they turned their eyes outside the group and their conversation toward what they had seen. There were almost as many weirdos here as in a bar in Austin, which gave their pridefully normal group a lot of preconcert judgmental entertainment.

A large clock held in the grip of an enormous golden dragon struck nine o'clock. This chiming, which sounded like the banging of an ancient Chinese gong, set the rhythm for the same group chant as last time. "Blood! Blood! Blood!" Eight times the group chanted with the dragon and then carried it on with a more frenzied pace thereafter. A thunderous boom shook the building, and a plume of smoke billowed out from behind the drum pit, filling the entire stage area and pouring over the front rows of worshippers.

The group of normal kids looked around in fear, thinking that a bomb had gone off. Nicki grabbed Jack's hand on the left and Ginger's hand on the right. The lights were shot out, and in the darkness, there were spontaneous shrieks of terror. Nicki's grip on Jack's hand tightened to the point of pain. The disturbed chant of the worshippers started up again: "Blood! Blood! Blood!" Jack's heart pounded, and he tried to recall if this had happened last time to assure himself that they were all safe. Adrenaline pumped through his veins, and he clenched the fist of the hand not held by Nicki, preparing to fight his way out of the crowd should there be a panicked evacuation. Another clap of thunder burst forth, and a cylinder of light displayed an oversize statue on the stage of a powerful angel wielding a large sword.

The worshipping crowd gasped at such a religious symbol, and several people wailed in sorrow. After providing enough time—about twenty seconds—for the dramatic effect to make its full, glorious impression, the booming rhythm of a bass and snare drum filled the arena with a militaristic air. Blood, the lead singer, marched on the stage wielding a medieval sword of his own. He was wearing armor of black leather and spikes and turned to face his followers.

He kneeled down as if being knighted by them. They chanted back their approval: "Blood! Blood! Blood!"

Blood stood, turned to face the angel warrior with sword raised, and charged. The angel seemed to come to life and swung his sword at Blood. Blood blocked with his own sword and then struck the angel across the midsection, which was just above his own head, with a mighty slash. As the blade cut through the angel, a guitar screeched. A red mist shot forth over the first rows of the crowd that had recently been anointed with smoke. The angel crumpled into a heap, burst into a consuming flame, and then was seen no more.

Blood dropped his sword by the drum pit, turned back toward the fanatic crowd, which was now roaring with the satisfaction of vengeance, and lifted his hand above his head in the sign of a goat in tribute to Satan. Guitars built on the initial slashing screech, and the music erupted and flowed like a river of molten lava, filling the worshippers with hot praise. Jack's spirit buoyed up with the rest on the current. Along with the music, he could feel other elements in the stream of euphoria as well. Passing before his mind were some he recognized—drugs, alcohol, and sex—and some he didn't recognize but impressed him as being equal in intoxication. Jack sipped at the stream and drew everything in—good, bad, and ugly.

"You shall have no other gods before me!" a voice whispered. Jack opened his eyes, and with a face of disgust, he took a drink of beer to rinse out his mouth. His mind argued, *I'm not worshipping anything—I'm just listening to music!* His beer was warm and bitter, but he pressed it to his lips, turned the bottom up, and drained it. It gave him a sensation of recklessness. He slammed the bottle on the floor, shattering it into hundreds of tiny sharp shards. He grabbed Nicki's arm, and she turned her attention to him. He kissed her again, and she kissed him back. Deeper and deeper they drank of this element until they both felt that they either had to stop drinking or leave for a more appropriate venue. Each still needing the approval of the group, they exchanged this brand of intoxication for that of the music.

No longer satisfied with the high of the music, Jack looked around for another element. The buzz-cut girl, whom Jack thought of as a friend now, was a few people away. She was smoking a small cigarette pinched in her small fingers and smashing her head with the beat. Jack stared at her, waiting for her to pause for a drag. His plan was to make eye contact with her and then make a gestured request to share her cigarette. A puff of smoke blew into Jack's eyes, and he rubbed them. He opened his eyes to see the girl's skeleton covered with a thin bag of putrid flesh. The only thing that had not changed about her was her eyes, still dark and empty.

Something was indeed sucking the life out of her, only it wasn't meth. A skeleton robed and hooded in black that looked like the grim reaper hovered above her horizontally with both of his hands holding her head. He was inhaling her much like she was doing to the contents of her small cigarette. Feeling Jack's stare, the reaper stopped his drag and turned his mouth toward Jack. Jack's eyes widened, but he stood his ground. The reaper inhaled, and Jack felt an intoxicant push into his veins. He had never tried meth, but he knew without a doubt that this was its demonic backing.

Jack jerked his stare away and closed his eyes. He looked up, and the reaper had returned to his business with the buzz-cut girl. Jack looked around; everything else seemed to be as normal as it should've been. He remembered the hairless boy/girl, and his eyes combed the crowd with limited sight. He dropped his gaze to the ground and noticed a pale film covering the floor. It reminded him of the boy/girl, and he stooped down to examine it. Slowly extending his fingers with cautious curiosity, he gently felt the film that everyone was trampling underfoot.

Upon contact with his finger, the film morphed into a figure arising from the floor, and the boy/girl appeared so close to Jack that they were almost in an embrace. The person whispered abusive things in Jack's ear: "The only thing you deserve is to be punished! You're pathetic! You freak! You're nothing!" Jack, with his head bowed, listening to the repeated assaults, saw that four black rats had moved close to the boy/girl's feet, one at each heel and one at each set of toes. He could see that they were the ones speaking, each with one phrase, and that when they did, the boy/girl's mouth whispered its message. The rats sank their teeth into the boy/girl's bare feet and pulled away to their corners, stretching the boy/girl to be trampled once more.

Jack had had enough, and his stomach was turning—whether from the repulsion of the things he had just witnessed or from the beer, he didn't really know. But then again, he didn't really care. He turned to dip his cup into the music again and, opening his throat, poured the scalding lager into his spirit. A fire was kindled there, and Jack began to rock at a higher level than the others. He violently pogoed and was being noticed by others nearby who were infected as well. From the stage, Blood saw the whole beautiful act of worship. A simmering pot boiled over with a furious rage in homage to TrashMouth.

Typically Blood would pause after a song to preach his gospel, which his congregation would hear echoed in the next. Seeing the worship though, the band played continuously for the next thirty minutes, getting drunk from the praise of their idolizing Peppers. Finally, stopping for a drink, Blood took the microphone and with shallow breaths pointed into the crowd and said, "You!" Everyone roared. Blood held his point and said again, "You! Bring that Pepper onstage!"

Jack was saturated with sweat and out of breath, but when the people from the crowd hoisted him above their heads and surfed him to the stage, he forgot all about his need for oxygen. This was his oxygen. As Jack was riding to the stage, Blood ran to the side and got something from a roadie. He met Jack at center stage and with a shrieking voice yelled, "This guy rocks!" The crowd went wild, taking Jack's approval from Blood as their own. Blood gave Jack a TrashMouth concert shirt and a flash drive with their most recent and yet-to-be-released music. Jack stuffed the flash drive into his pocket and lifted up the shirt for all to see. The crowd roared again at itself. Blood held Jack's hands high in the air as if he'd just won a prizefight, and the drums gave rapid-fire beats, indicating it was time for the show to go on. Blood patted Jack on the back and motioned for him to return to the crowd. Jack took two steps to the front of the stage and then dove back onto the wave that had carried him up. He rode it back to his spot and then pulled himself back to earth—although his heart was still floating at an unreachable height on the current.

Sam and Jordan pushed to Jack and enviously looked at the shirt. They gave him high fives and went back to the music. Nicki reached into Jack's pocket and looked at the flash drive, which had the TrashMouth logo on it. She slid it into her own pocket and gave Jack a sweaty but appreciative kiss. They exchanged looks of pride, each realizing that when they fanned the other's pride, their own was fanned as well. Both were of the same mind, and Rachel whispered, "Way to go! Way to go with it!" They were both eager to talk to Rachel.

Several songs passed, and the peak of the wave returned to a normal but still invigorating level. Jack caught the motion of something on the floor about ten feet away. He returned his attention to the stage, and then another motion on the floor caught his eye. He looked downward to see five snarling dogs moving through the legs of the crowd as though they were intangible. They stood about waist-high and appeared to be black chow chows, only their coats were short and eaten up with mange. Something in Jack's gut told him that these dogs were there for him. Confident that no one else could see them, he yelled in Nicki's ear, "I'm going to the bathroom." Nicki nodded.

Jack's eyes immediately went back to the dogs that were slowly but steadily approaching. *Nice doggies!* he thought as he backed and turned his way through the wall of bodies that prevented his escape, but his plea didn't faze the dogs. As he got to the outskirts of the crowd, he moved at a faster pace and eventually jogged into the safety of the bathroom. He opened a stall door and looked at the commode. It was covered in alcohol-infused vomit. Nonetheless, Jack knew he had to get on it and close the stall door, which he did. He held his breath, hoping that the dogs were just a hallucination caused by his moshing. He listened. There was another person in the bathroom singing to himself a Culture Club song from the eighties. "Do you really want to hurt me? Do you really want to make me cry?"

The irony of the song and the dogs smote him. *Rachel,* he called in his mind, but there was no answer. He heard the snarls of the dogs again and dipped his head down to see the pack's paws moving toward his stall across the sticky floor. *Rachel,* he called again with the same panic. A puff of steamed breath came through the stall door and then more from the walls. The dogs' heads moved through these partitions as if they weren't even there. Their lips were curled back in burning hatred, and through their stinging teeth oozed a red drool, probably from their first victim. "Rachel!" Jack screamed out loud with such fear and panic that the Boy George wannabe scrambled out the door. "Rachel! Help!"

Jack, knowing he was about to be in a literal dogfight, was preparing to climb up and try an escape on top of the stalls when he heard Rachel's saving voice: "Go!" Immediately, the dogs scampered away, their paws sliding across the filthy tile as if a fire hose had been turned on them. Jack shivered as his body relaxed and his blood flowed back to his face and brain.

"Okay, what was that?" Jack asked.

Rachel replied, "Are you still seeing demons?"

"Yes. But I think I'm getting used to it."

Spaw was furious that the enemy was helping Jack to see demons. "That's why I sent the guard dogs," Rachel lied.

"You sent them?" Jack was amazed.

"Oh, they weren't going to hurt you! Hey, if they weren't so ferocious, they wouldn't be able to protect you."

This point made sense to Jack. "Why could I see them? And why can I see any of this supernatural stuff?"

"It's a blessing! Seeing your slow progress"—Jack winced at this jab—"I petitioned Athena, and she permitted it." Jack turned this over in his mind and sat down on the commode. Rachel continued, "It's so you can see the enemy's tricks. Some things will be painted as 'evil' and some as 'light,' but remember, the only thing that is evil is what takes you further from the Ohm and me. This makes the enemy's lies more obvious. Jack, in all my millennia, I haven't seen anyone as blessed as you."

Jack sniffed and caught the distracting reek of the vomit he'd seen earlier on a commode—but it wasn't just a commode. It was *his* commode. He bounced up and felt the back of his pants, which were moist with the vile juice. He quickly turned and gave his own heave into the seat. This done, he cleaned his face and his pants in the sink and went back to join the group. The house lights were up, and the Peppers were already filing out of the club in a zombielike progression.

Jack's group was waiting in the same spot as when he'd left, and when he approached, they all started bowing to him and hailing him as King Pepper. Jerome yelled out, "Speech! Speech!"

Jack smiled and played along. "Ladies and gentlemen, the secret of life and happiness is this: just go with it! Ride on the current of life!"

Surprisingly, they all seemed to take this secret in, swish it around in their mouths, and swallow it. "Ride the current!" Ginger exclaimed and gave Nicki a heck-yeah high five.

"YOLO!" Jordan said.

"That's right, baby! Just go with it!" Moose added.

Jerome attempted to summarize, "You only live once, so just go with the flow!"

Sam slapped Jack on the back and kept his hand there for a few paces as the group joined the zombies' line at the exit. Jack smiled at him and inwardly relished the praise of the group.

Jack and Nicki whispered their good-byes to Ginger as she very lightly tapped on the gas to move her car as quietly as possible down the street so as not to wake up Nicki's parents. Nicki's parents rarely waited up for her. Over the years, Nicki's friends and excuses had worn them down, and now they treated Nicki's behavior more like that of a cat. She'd come home at some point; she always did. Besides, neither of them was prepared to draw a hard line with her. Their own childhoods convicted them of the hypocrisy.

In the damp and stagnant postmidnight air, Jack and Nicki returned to their practice of soap opera kissing. Nicki had counted the evening a success and was recalling her last commitment to Rachel of a warm-down session.

"Come on!" Nicki said and grabbed Jack's hand, tugging him toward the door.

"What do you mean?" Jack innocently asked.

"My parents are asleep. Let's go to my room."

Jack smiled and slightly shook his head as if Nicki was crazy, and then his own inner voice chastised him, *Just go with it!* Jack was in an emotional headlock and couldn't move. Nicki opened the front door with her key, and the door chime echoed through the house. They both flinched and pulled their heads down as if this would silence it. Nicki slowly closed the door again with a grimace as the tattletale chime repeated its alert. They stood there in silence, watching the passage to her parents' room to see if they would investigate. No one came.

Nicki grabbed Jack's hand and slowly led him through the entryway toward the left turn to her hallway. *Click. Click.* A door handle turned, and its door was pushed open. Nicki's mom appeared across the way. Nicki altered their course and made for the kitchen.

"Oh, hey, Mom!" she said quietly. "This is Jack. We just got home and wanted to get a drink."

Nicki stopped there, feeling like too much information might give her away.

Nicki's mom was not amused and didn't even look at Jack. "Nicki, you said that the movie ended at ten o'clock. It's one o'clock in the morning." Her mom tried to reign in her tone to prevent her dad's hyperinvolvement. Nicki put on her mask of remorse and then turned to face Jack with a wink.

Jack was already pulling back toward the door. He pulled the door open, and the tattletale chime announced his departure. Nicki stepped out and gave him an innocent kiss on the cheek to prevent any further speculation from her mom. With a smile, she said, "I'll see you in the morning ... king!"

Jack looked over her shoulder and caught the glare of her mom still fixed on them and decided that now would not be a good time to smile. He too put on his mask of remorse and turned to walk home to face his own centurion and tattletale chime.

Jack gripped the handle of his front door, ready to be announced. He quickly swung the door open, slipped in, and closed the door behind him so that the two chimes would only sound like one, minimizing his chance of being caught. He turned the deadbolt on the door and expected any moment to hear his dad's voice with a statement exactly like that of Nicki's mom. No one said anything. He turned and looked in the living room. There was no one. He looked at his dad's door; it was closed. *Wow, I guess he does really trust me,* he thought.

A twinge of guilt hit Jack's gut for abusing a degree of trust he hadn't fully realized he had. But this twinge was quickly dispatched when the glory of his night replayed in his mind. After exchanging his sweat-soaked shirt and vomit-moistened pants for a clean T-shirt and shorts, he stretched out across his bed as far as he could and smiled. His eyes adjusted to the darkness, and the green glow of a charger dimly illuminated his room.

He looked around, thinking about how everything in there seemed so juvenile. His sports memorabilia on the shelves and a US flag, a Texas flag, and several animal hides and horns decorating the wall—all these in a matter of hours were outgrown by the new man. Jack was his own hero. His mind shifted to Rachel and her tale of himself in ancient Athens. Before, he had only wanted to believe it, but now he did believe it. He understood how he had been holding himself back from the hero that was dormant within him. Not anymore. Now, knowing his own secret, he would slowly but surely let others in on it. He would be the hero they wanted—no, needed—him to be. And such were his thoughts as he reluctantly let sleep darken his eyes.

—◇◇◇◇—

A soft nuzzling on his cheek awoke him very gently. "You are so valiant— so bold and daring," Rachel whispered. "I'm so proud of you."

Jack turned in to her kiss, and as usual, he melted into her eyes. "You are so beautiful," he replied with a deep sincerity he never could have imagined.

"That was the lover I bid farewell in Athens. You are that man."

Jack would have blushed under such praise, but he knew that Rachel was just stating the truth. "It felt so right. It felt as if the real me finally cracked through its prison wall and caught a glimpse of daylight."

"Go to the light, Jack. Mount up on the life current, and let it take you to where you deserve to be—the place that is rightfully yours." Jack's spirit was heightened, and his mind tried to put scenes to her words.

"Let me show you something," Rachel said, and she sat him upright. Moving behind him, she softly pressed his temples with her hands. In an airy singsong voice that sounded much like one he would have imagined an ancient priestess of Athena to use, Rachel began to repeat a chant. *"Iona ic shoor ta sweech, ver-tu iona dred. Iona ic noor ta swooch, ba gee zeph-ros hed."*

After Jack stopped trying to make sense of the words, which was at about the third rendition of the phrase, his mind relaxed, and an image played before his mind. It was like a film being shown from a first-person perspective. In the first scene, his view was of a crowd of several hundred citizens crowded around the lower part of a wide flight of marble stairs. He looked to his left and saw a man in typical Athenian garb holding a pan flute. He looked to his right and saw a man dressed similarly holding a lyre. Both of the men were looking at him expectantly. A voice, much like his own, uttered a few excited words in Greek as his view turned toward the man holding the pan flute, and his hands placed a crown of leaves upon his bowing head.

The view turned back to the crowd roaring in approval and then faded to black. In the second scene, his view was of his surroundings spinning rapidly and then coming to an abrupt halt as he watched a discus spin through the air from an extended arm and skip along after having made an indention on a flat field. He turned to an applauding crowd and saw Rachel beaming with delight. After another fade to black, in the third scene, his view moved from his own hands folded in prayer upward to the feet, knees, torso, and crowned head of a large statue of Athena. He looked to his left and saw a tearful Rachel comforting him in an ancient tongue. He stood up, turned, and moved toward a large archway that served as the portal to the temple.

Spaw was exhausted at the exercise. Not many demons could conjure this type of deception. He turned his face upward and beat his chest in pride.

Rachel released her touch, and the movie ended. Jack's mind whirled at the concreteness of the images. The colors, the details, the voices, the people—it all looked so ... so real.

"Why didn't you show me this before?" Jack asked.

"You wouldn't have been able to bear it. Isn't your mind turning now from seeing this *truth*?"

Jack lingered on her last, emphatically spoken word. "Yeah. I guess."

"You were a master of the current. You didn't just swim along; you cut through it like a leviathan."

"I swam too?" Jack asked without any thought.

Rachel slightly rolled her eyes and said, "I'm talking about the current of life—the passions of ancient Babylon, which spread across the world at the beginning of time." Rachel paused but knew she needed to continue so that Jack wouldn't choose the path of conversation about creation. "Just think about how much the world depends on the passions of life: sex, music, food, drink, beauty, luxurious things. The whole world would crater in a second if these things disappeared. That's because these things are what keep life floating. These things are the current that carries us to the Ohm." Her hands slowly rose up as if lifting a chalice of fine drink to the sky.

Spaw had had enough. He needed to return to the territory, lest any other demon challenge him in his depleted state.

Pulling her hands back down, Rachel produced the metallic cup, and Jack eagerly took it from her and drank. He had developed a taste for the sweet drink and the effect that it produced. His eyes closed as Rachel stroked his temples and disappeared from his sight. Jack lay there in a dark state as his mind replayed Rachel's soothing chant word for word. *"Iona ic shoor ta sweech, ver-tu iona dred. Iona ic noor ta swooch, ba gee zeph-ros hed."*

At the final pronunciation of the last syllable, everything seemed to freeze. Time froze; light froze; he froze. His fingers were numb, then his feet, then his arms, then his legs, then his stomach, then his chest, and then his neck. A sensation of dread blanketed his thoughts as he realized his mind was next. He began to miss his dad, his sisters, and Nicki. He thought about his dog, Harley. He noticed his mind slowing to a crawl as if it was going under heavy sedation. He felt null and void. He felt dead.

When his alarm chirped good morning, Jack gasped for air as if he'd had an asthmatic attack. Tears of relief flooded his bloodshot eyes, and he relished the deep breaths of life he drew in. It felt good to not be dead. Jack thought back to just over six hours ago. He had been in the club with his group. They were bowing to him and flattering him with compliments of adoration. This surge of energy, despite the horrible and short sleep, hoisted him out of bed, eager to get to school for more.

20

SURFING THE CURRENT

Typically, Jack liked to get to school at least fifteen minutes before the first bell so that he could catch up with Bobby and Caden on what had transpired since the previous day's last bell. He had a lot to fill them in on, but despite his enthusiasm, he couldn't quite overcome his lethargy from the lack of sound sleep. As he opened the door to the commons, the bell rang. He glanced toward the trophy case and saw Bobby and Caden looking at their iPhones, and he started in their direction. His step was checked, though, when he thought about Nicki. He took a sharp left and headed to meet her at her locker, knowing that she was always running late and would go straight there.

Jack was surprised when he turned the corner and saw Nicki already at her locker checking her face in a small mirror hung on the inside door. Putting the last touch on her crimson lips, she pocketed her lipstick and, seeing Jack's face, turned and put the crimson color on his left cheek with a kiss. She wiped it with her finger and then took her lipstick back out to touch it up again.

"Hey!" Jack said.

"Hey!"

"I thought you'd be late today after staying out so late."

"Late? No, I'm used to it! You look beat."

"I am. I didn't sleep very well."

"Too much partying?"

"Too much something, I guess."

Nicki closed her locker and grabbed Jack's hand. They started down the hall, and a peculiar sensation came over them. It felt like everyone was looking at them. They approached three junior girls from the drill team, who broke off their conversation and looked at them.

"Hey, Nicki!" one girl said. "I heard y'all rocked it at the concert last night!"

Nicki smiled broadly and replied, "Yeah, TrashMouth was epic!"

"When you go next time, let me know. I'd love to see them in person!" the girl said.

"Yeah, will do!" Nicki promised.

Ahead, three seniors on the football team whom Jack had heard of through Sam but had never spoken to personally were walking toward him.

"Jack! Bro! What's happening?" one of them exclaimed as they all three put their hands up for consecutive high fives.

"Good concert?" another asked.

Jack nodded. "Yeah, it was beast!"

"Next time!" the guy pointed at himself, at Jack, and then back at himself.

"Sure!" Jack replied. Jack gave Nicki a strange *Twilight Zone* look as if to ask, "Is this really happening?" Nicki smiled with enjoyment. Two girls walking shoulder to shoulder stared obviously at Jack as if Nicki didn't exist and then giggled as they passed. Jack smiled at the compliment, but Nicki stopped him with a somewhat playful look of jealousy and an elbow to the ribs. Jack laughed and moved his hand from hers to around her shoulders, pulling her closer. They felt like a royal pair, a type of popular attraction, and it felt like it should've felt—intoxicatingly delicious.

Following a few more long halls of tribute, they finally arrived at Nicki's class with exploding egos. Jack pulled Nicki close and then saw her teacher approaching the door from inside the classroom.

"That was a bit strange, don't you think?" asked Jack. "It's like people want to be like us."

Nicki grinned and said, "Yeah! Pretty cool, huh? I guess we should just get used to it!"

The teacher was now standing at the door and looking down his nose as if to ask Nicki if she planned on joining the class today. Nicki gave Jack a peck on the cheek and turned to greet her teacher—but not before she whispered in Jack's ear, "There's more where that came from! Meet me at Ginger's car for lunch."

An electric shock shot through Jack's body from the suggestion, and he inhaled deeply to shake it off. He moved his glance off of Nicki's backside to the teacher who was still standing in the doorway, eyeing him.

"Hi … uh … bye!" Jack said and turned for his own class on the other side of the building.

All he could think to himself was just how right Rachel's guidance had been. "Go with it. Go with the current of life." *Yeah, that really is the secret to being happy,* he thought. *I'm not just riding the current—I'm cutting it up!* At this, Jack bent his knees and dipped down as if he were riding a surfboard.

"Kowabunga, dude!" a small, pimply-faced boy said as he jogged by, tardy to his class.

Jack smirked, rolled his eyes, and shook his head slightly. "Shut up!"

21

PRAYER ASSAULT

Jay was a praying man. He had been watching Jack carefully over the last few weeks but still gave him his space to learn on his own—perhaps too much space. He noticed that Jack seemed to be drifting away, becoming more and more distant from the family, and wisdom told Jay that this was not a good place for any child of God to be. It was about four in the morning, and he awoke feeling an urgent need to pray for Jack. He got out of bed, went into his closet, where he usually read the Bible and prayed, knelt down, and began pouring his heart out to God.

"Father God, You alone are sovereign and reign above all things. And You love us beyond what I can imagine—so much that You sent Your only Son, Jesus, to endure the torture and anger on the cross so that I wouldn't have to. God, You have put me over these kids to help them know You, the only true meaning of life. I'm seeing Jack getting caught up in the current of the world, and he needs Your help. God, I pray that You might send Your protection for Jack, that the evil forces that are attacking him might be kicked away, and that he might see evil for what it really is and come to know You more.

You are so very good. You are our glorious King, the Defender of the weak, and our almighty God. To You alone I lift this prayer for help in the mighty name of Jesus, my Lord and my God. Amen."

After continuing in prayer for Jack, Avery, and Anna Claire and ending in a time of praise of God Himself, Jay stood up and could sense that God was at work. This done, he returned to bed and slept soundly for another hour before getting ready for church.

⊶⊙⊙⊶

During that same hour, Jack had a dream about Rachel. Although it was still very vivid, it lacked the overexaggeration of their trancelike meetings.

Jack and Rachel were sitting on a small bench perched at the end of a pier. The water was a lily-pad-covered lake of about twenty acres where they were watching about a dozen alligators moving here and there across the surface. The skies were a vivid blue without a cloud to be seen, and the sun was bearing down, adding to the heat. Jack reached down into a small blue cooler and pulled out a root beer float with two striped straws.

Having lived only in ancient Greece, Rachel hadn't ever had a treat like this, and Jack smiled widely with Rachel as the sweet cool refreshment passed her lips. Jack's smile then faded, and his eyes had their turn to widen as he saw a fourteen-foot alligator climb up out of the lake to join them on the pier. The root beer float glass dropped from his hand and shattered on the deck. The alligator was heading for Rachel, but Jack intercepted him and produced a long sword from his side. He drew it back, about to strike, and Rachel cried out, "Stop! It's a baby!"

255

Jack looked at her as she spoke and then turned back toward the alligator. It was gone, and in its place was a little toddler with jet-black curly hair and a white flowing dress that flitted in the breeze. Rachel scooped up the baby and sat back on the bench as if it were her own child—their child. Jack, feeling guilty, tossed the sword into the lake and took his seat next to Rachel to adore the child. He reclaimed his smile and turned his eyes down to look at the babe in Rachel's motherly arms.

His face grew pale as he saw a hideous, green, scaled face with reptilian eyes staring at him. The baby opened its mouth in a laugh and displayed alligator teeth accompanied by breath reeking of stagnant swamp water. Jack looked at Rachel in shock, but Rachel smiled a soothing smile back to him, as if they were the perfect family.

From the clear sky, there was a flash of lightning, followed by a clap of thunder. Jack looked at Rachel, and her face showed her fear. She looked at the baby, who was waving her algae-green, scaled hands and was now crying at the explosion of sound. Jack looked up, and a cloud of redbirds swirled directly overhead, about as high as an airplane. Their air maneuvers completed, they vaporized, and a light red rain began to sprinkle. Rachel was oblivious to the shower, but her flowing white dress became stained and drenched. She glanced from the baby to Jack, and her smile was nothing less than pure adoration of him.

Jack then saw the beautiful, smooth skin of her face erode under the raindrops. Her alabaster skin gave way to the same scaly, green complexion of the baby creature. Jack's expression showed Rachel the devastation, and she began to frantically reapply the dissolving mask. A second clap of thunder reverberated from overhead, and the percussion devastated Rachel. Her body crumpled sideways, and Jack caught her in his arms. The baby was knocked to the pier and crawled into the water, much like a turtle escapes from a log when an intruder comes near.

In desperation, Jack yelled for help. He looked up to find that the lake in front of him was now the usual river crowded with his friends. Every last one of them rushed from their floats to the pier where Rachel now lay, their faces stricken with panic and concern. Jack was relieved at their willingness to help, and he felt her mouth for breath. Like the rest of her face, her mouth had been affected by the rain. Instead of those pretty red lips that covered those perfectly white teeth, he saw a hole in the dark green, scaly leather, and in the hole were dingy, jagged teeth.

Repulsed, he looked for help to the mass of people now encircling him. At the sight of Rachel, much to his surprise, their faces contorted in outrage. "You let it get killed!" "Why didn't you do something?" A little boy lifted up the sword Jack had discarded. "Here it is!" he announced triumphantly.

The voices now changed. "You killed it! Murderer!"

In disbelief and disgust at the crowd's unsympathetic response, Jack leaned forward again to hold what he knew must still be his wife. Her skin felt like soggy leather, and her body was dense, like a saturated log. Hurt by the allegations of the mob, he wiped away the tears that blurred his vision and found that the body in his lap was that of a large alligator. Horrified, he sprang to his feet, and the Destroyer's corpse flopped onto the pier. Jack stared at the mass of people who now glared at him through the same reptilian eyes of the baby. All his friends from the river were really its children. Jack grabbed the sword from the small boy who hissed at him through alligator teeth. He swung it around in a defensive fury to guard himself from the avengers. Like frightened frogs, they plunged back into the safety of the current, cursing Jack as they went.

The blender obnoxiously destroyed the placidity of Sunday morning as it announced to the entire neighborhood that a chocolate banana protein shake was about to be ready. "You want one?" Jay asked as Jack turned the corner to join Avery and Anna Claire, already at the bar calling dibs on the one now ready.

"Sure," Jack answered.

Always looking for an excuse to talk about spiritual stuff with the kids, Jay started, "You know what? I had the strangest feeling last night. I woke up about four o'clock in the morning and prayed for y'all."

"About what?" asked Avery.

"Well, it was spiritual warfare," Jay replied. Jack propped his chin on his right hand and rolled his eyes. Jay was watching him for a reaction, and there it was. "What?" he asked, directing his attention at Jack.

"Huh?" Jack said as innocently as possible.

"You rolled your eyes."

"I did?"

"Yeah. So what do you think?"

"Well," Jack said, thinking on the fly, "I guess I'm not so sure about that kind of angel and demon stuff."

Jay saw this as a validation to his call to prayer. "You're not?" he prompted.

Jack felt as if a trap had been sprung, and he wanted back out. "Well, I don't know."

"Whether you realize it or not, we live in a spiritual battlefield that we can't see," Jay said, glancing at each of the three kids in turn. "It felt like last night you were under attack, so I prayed." He rested his gaze on Jack.

"Me?" Jack said. "I'm doing just fine."

"Don't underestimate evil, and don't underestimate the power of prayer in stopping it. This is real stuff, Jack. It's not a game."

"Thanks, but I think I can handle my own battles."

"You are your own person, Jack, and you're smart; I just hope you're wise too. Just keep an eye open. That's all I'm saying."

"What about me? I'm my own person too," remarked Anna Claire.

Jay pushed a shake in front of her and put a hot-pink straw in it. "That's a fact!"

Avery cleared her throat. "And me?"

"Yeah, that goes for you too!" Jay said with a small rub of her head. Avery smiled and pulled her formerly perfectly brushed hair away.

-ᴑᴖᴑᴖ-

At church, the family entered the worship center on the lookout for familiar faces to greet. Avery had her phone hidden in her purse to secretly get off a few texts during the music, Anna Claire had her usual pen and bulletin to do a little artwork when the preacher started his sermon, and Jay was walking with a spring that pronounced this as one of his favorite places. Jack led them to their usual area to the right side of camera two, their usual area for worship ever since the kids were young. As they started down the row of twenty seats, the people already seated began politely pulling their feet back to let them pass.

Jack's attention was strangely drawn to a man he was about to pass seated in the middle of the section. He didn't know why he was struck by him, but his eyes were riveted on the man. As he approached to move by, the man pulled his feet back, and Jack looked squarely in his face. The man's eyes turned from white to brown, his eyebrows pressed down, his lips pulled back showing his dingy teeth, his face twisted into a scowl, and a growl rumbled from deep in his chest as if he were a wolf who had been wounded and trapped and was about to defend itself to the death.

Startled, Jack leaped forward to escape the hideous man, tripping over the feet of the next person and falling to the floor of the crowded aisle. Jack quickly looked up at the man, expecting him to pounce on him and tear him to shreds right there in the church, but when he made eye contact, he saw the man was simply just a normal man who was about to extend a hand to help him up. Jack quickly stood up without help, apologized for his fall to the two men, and sat down as quickly as he could in the next open seat down the row.

Ordinarily, he would have been embarrassed and concerned for what others might think of him, but he was so freaked out that all he could do was to try to slow his heart down and gather some rational thoughts.

"Are you okay?" asked Jay.

"Yeah, I'm fine. I just tripped over my own feet. That's all," said Jack. Jay was satisfied with this answer and mistook the flustered look on

Jack's face for embarrassment. The music started, and Jack got to his feet with everyone else. He knew the songs but hardly ever actually sang them. He didn't want to do anything that others might see as dorky or weird.

While he was able to calm himself outwardly, inwardly Jack's mind was racing. *What was that all about? Am I going crazy?* he asked himself. But then he reflected on Rachel and was quickly soothed, *Wow, I guess this is what love can do for someone.* For the rest of the music, while the others in the congregation seemed to be trying their best to worship Jesus, Jack's mind was a dimension away worshipping someone else—Rachel.

The praise band took their seats, and the large screen dropped down to play the message recorded from the Saturday night service. The pastor came on, prayed, and said, "Sometimes I'm amazed at how people can claim to devote their lives to following Jesus and then turn right around and wink at sin with demons behind it—just because it's pretty or entertaining or pleasant. Ladies and gentlemen, demons are real, and they are at work to do anything they can to prevent you from worshipping the Lord of Lords and King of Kings, Jesus Christ. Turn to Mark 1:21–28, and ..."

Jack's head drooped down as if bowed in prayer, and he fell asleep.

"Help! Jack, please help me!"

Jack recognized the voice as Rachel, and he called back to her through the trees, "Where are you?"

"Here."

Jack looked on the opposite side of a giant oak tree to find Rachel sitting down, hugging her knees and trembling as if she were freezing.

"What's wrong?"

"Jack, you have to get out of here." As she spoke, her body dimmed slightly, becoming transparent.

"Rachel! What's happening to you?"

"I'm evaporating back to the Ohm. But I can't leave without you! You have to get up and leave that place!"

"You mean church?"

Rachel's transparency spiked, and for an instant, Jack could see the leaves pressed underneath her. "Okay, okay, I'll do it."

"Hurry, Jack! Hurry!"

Jack's eyes opened, and he felt as though he'd been gone for about ten minutes. He inadvertently turned his ears back to the pastor, who was still finishing the same exact sentence as when he dozed off: "… we'll see how these created beings obey the Holy One of God, Jesus of Nazareth."

As the pastor completed his sentence with "Jesus of Nazareth," a camera flash shone forth from his mouth, and a burst of hot wind blew across Jack's face. Jack quickly recalled Rachel's urgency and tried to stand up to excuse himself to the bathroom, but he couldn't move. He tried lifting his arms, but they felt like lead. He tried lifting his legs, but gravity held them down. His neck was stiff, and he couldn't turn it in any direction. He was a living statue anchored firmly in place by hardened concrete and metal. At every mention of Jesus, the same camera flash and hot wind shocked the air.

After the second mention, Jack saw five familiar dogs running down an aisle. He followed them as best he could with his eyes, which were the only things he could move. The five large, mangy mutts scurried out through a back exit with their tails appropriately tucked under their rear ends. Although Rachel had said that they were there for Jack's own good, he was glad to see them go.

For the next thirty minutes, Jack was reminded about the reality of dark forces, which, using ordinary things of the world, wanted to destroy him, and about the infinitely more powerful God, who loved him and had proved it with Jesus on the cross. At the conclusion of the service, the large screens were rolled up, and another pastor came forth to extend an invitation to anyone who wanted to receive Jesus.

With this offer, a large, hot wind blew from the round stage on which he stood. Jack's neck was loosened, and he caught a glimpse of movement to his right. The man he had tripped over and who looked so beastly was standing up against the gust. His appearance was that of the typical sooty that Jack had become used to seeing from time to time. As the man moved forward down the aisle, the hot wind blew sweeping soot from his body. The gust was strong, but it didn't push against the man's physical body, which moved steadily toward the stage, his head hanging and his hands wiping tears of both shame and joy from his eyes. The pastor stepped forward and took the man's hand. The strong gust intensified, and several small, black gargoyles were blown like dust from the crevices of his soul across the assembly and out through the back wall of the worship center. The man's countenance already showed that his burden was lighter.

22

ANGELIC INTERVENTION

The school-day tortoises of Monday through Friday had crossed the finish line and were now watching as the weekend hares of Saturday and Sunday were about to race by. Friday evening had arrived, and Jack was making his preparations, as well as preparing Jay, for another night on the suburban town. "Okay, so you do remember that I won't be back until around midnight ... ish ... right?" Jack asked in more of a statementlike tone to Jay.

"Oh, no, I guess I don't. What's the big plan tonight?"

Jack gave a look of slight exacerbation at Jay's lack of mind reading ability and drew in a breath. "It's this boy Wyatt's birthday, so his parents are having a party for him at their house."

"A birthday party? Do you need to bring a present?" Jay remarked with a bit of sarcastic humor that Jack didn't find amusing.

"Anyway, Nicki and I are going to ride with Jerome and Ginger"—Jay put a strange look on his face to signal that he didn't know Jerome and Ginger—"so we'll be at the party until they get ready to leave," Jack said, already setting up Jerome, the driver, to be the scapegoat for anything that might go wrong.

"Who are Jerome and Ginger? Obviously one of them is old enough to drive?"

"Yeah!" Jack said with a tone of obviousness. "I've told you about them a lot of times," Jack overemphasized, playing off Jay's occasional forgetfulness. Jay wasn't completely convinced, so Jack continued, "Nicki and Ginger have been friends for years." Jack waved a hand to strengthen his point. "And Jerome and I have been hanging out a lot at school. He's a really nice guy. Trust me, you'd think so too. I'll tell them to come in for a while next time," Jack said, hoping that he could make the same "next time" offer again.

"Sure, that'd be great. Just make sure that you have your cell phone so I can buzz you. I'll probably touch base with you just to see how things are going." Jay floated this in part as a condition and in part as a threat to keep Jack as honest as possible without infringing on his growing space.

"Sure, that's fine!" Jack said, accepting the threat and conditioning and calling Jay's bluff a bit.

A *tap, tap, tap* hit the door. Jack's expression changed from one of careful negotiation to one of excitement.

"Wow, people actually knock on doors still instead of texting from the car," Jay observed.

Jack hurried to the door, but Jay followed him anyway. "Hey!" Jack said to Nicki, looking over her shoulder to the bright orange jeep waiting in the street.

"Hey!" replied Nicki. She looked over his shoulder at Jay's inquisitive face.

"Hi, Nicki!" Jay said. "How've you been?"

Nicki started to step around Jack, but Jack shifted to block her path. "Oh, just fine!" she managed to reply.

"Big party tonight?" Jay continued, Jack now reddening under the gills.

"Yes, sir. It's Wyatt's birthday," she exclaimed.

"Good, good." Jay nodded. "Well, y'all have fun!"

Jay knew any conversation beyond this would be like throwing a rock at a wasps' nest from close range. Jack looked around with an internal sense of relief but an external display of slight aggravation.

"Bye, Dad."

"Bye!" said Jay.

Jay turned and locked the door behind him. There was that strange sensation again—something wasn't good. He felt like a deer that couldn't exactly see or smell the hunter in the blind but took off in a sprint, sensing that something just wasn't safe. So Jay postponed for the moment seeing what the girls were up to and went straight to his closet, hit his knees, and prayed, "Father God, You are an awesome God, and I come to You in the name of Jesus, Your Son, to ask You to protect Jack tonight. Lord, please keep watch out over him, Nicki,

Jerome, Ginger, and all the rest of their friends. Protect them from any incident or accident. Help everything that happens tonight to be somehow used so that they know You more. I give You all the glory my little life can offer and ask this in Jesus' name. Amen."

-⚭⚭⚭-

Without thinking Jack tugged at the seat belt in the two-year-old jeep, but it just wouldn't come out. Realizing the problem, he abandoned his effort instead of asking Jerome if there was some kind of trick to getting the thing to extend. This was his first time riding with Jerome, and he didn't want it to seem like it was quite the new, exciting, big deal that it was to him. He looked around. The others had their seat belts on. He looked at Jerome, who was exchanging glances between the road and the radio. Jack waited until his eyes were back on the road and made another tug on the belt. Nope, it was still stuck. He gave it up for good this time.

As soon as the jeep turned the corner exiting the neighborhood, Jerome floored it. The off-road tires made a deep hum as he quickened its pace under the revving of the V8 engine. In a matter of seconds, Jerome moved into fourth gear, each pump of the clutch announced by a crescendo of the straining horses under the hood. Jack felt his weight pressed back against the seat, and he reached forward to grip the passenger's handle above the glove box in front of him. Nicki and Ginger laughed at the g-force, which literally moved them from forward leaning to a backward leaning position. Jerome heard their laughter and smiled. He cast a sideways look at Jack to check his response. Jack shared in the blast, but he didn't want to show his kidlike thrill; nonetheless, his face noticeably brightened, telling Jerome that the sudden acceleration had had the same impression on everyone.

"What do you want to listen to?" Jerome tried to ask over the roar of the wind. The girls were so hunkered down in the back trying to protect their well-crafted hair from the wind that they didn't even hear the question, much less respond. Jerome looked at Jack as if the question was directed to him alone.

"What?" Jack had seen Jerome's mouth forming words but didn't understand any of them.

"What do you want to listen to?" Jerome motioned to the radio, poked it, and then pointed down, giving Jack permission to find a station on the radio or opt for the iPod. The jeep swerved to the right to avoid a car that was considering darting from near the median to a strip center entryway but soon realized that the orange jeep was coming much faster than expected. Jerome slightly bumped the horn to warn them not to cross until he was through. All the passengers shifted their weight back to the left after having it involuntarily shifted to the right with the sudden movement. Without a seat belt, Jack's shift back was apparent, and Jerome smiled at him. Jack gave an upward nod and grinned. Nicki tapped Jack's shoulder, and he twisted his head backward so that she could yell into his ear, "He usually has good music on his iPod!"

"Huh?"

"He usually has good music on his iPod!"

Jack pulled back to look Nicki in the eyes. He shook his head and turned one palm up to indicate that there was no way he could hear what she was saying. Nicki waved him close back and pulled his ear right next to her lips. She yelled, "The iPod!" Jack pulled back and gave another upward nod accompanied by a wink. Situating himself forward again, he picked up the iPod and hit play. Although the roar of the wind was loud, it was nothing compared to the booming tunes that gushed forth from the eight speakers. This jeep was meant for an outdoor experience, and its speakers were meant for an outdoor concert.

Jerome gave the brakes a few pumps and brought the jeep to stop behind a lane of eight cars at a congested intersection. The tunes billowed out, polluting the air with bass beats that rattled the windows of the other cars. Several drivers who had been enjoying the cool air of the fresh, darkening evening with their windows down now rolled their windows up to lower the annoyingly high volume.

Jerome picked up his phone and tapped out a text. Send. A car honked from behind. Jerome looked up to see a thirty-yard runway. He stomped on the clutch, shifted straight into second gear, revved the engine, and then relaxed his clutch foot for liftoff. The orange jeep obeyed militarily and immediately sped through the cluster of cars ahead of it. Jerome, who enjoyed the power of the jeep and his own power to excite his passengers, felt his smartphone buzz on his lap. He reached down for it and picked it up in his left hand. The motor screaming it was time for a shift, he stretched his right hand down and moved the stick into third gear, guiding the steering wheel with the back of his left hand, which still held the phone. He was only traveling fifteen miles per hour over the speed limit, about five less than usual. And speeding tickets? Who cared? Those were annoyances that came with being a parent—or so his parents' actions taught him.

Nicki leaned into Ginger and yelled, "I wish you would've driven!" Ginger nodded and shrugged. In any case, Jerome had never wrecked before, and he was notorious for his fast and furious driving agility. Jack's grip tightened on the handle in front put there for situations like this. Jerome got a kick when his passengers did this.

Now in fourth gear and back to cruising speed, Jerome switched his phone to his freed-up right hand. His eyes vacillated between the phone and the road—three seconds on the phone followed one second on the road and a jerking adjustment of the wheel. This was the pattern that continued until he had completed reading a small string of texts. Jerome's eyes lifted to the road for a moment and then back to the phone with a new pattern as he tapped out a response—five seconds of attempted tapping and backspacing on the phone, two seconds on the road; five seconds, two seconds; five seconds, two seconds.

Jerome had just completed his fifth second of the tapping when he heard Nicki scream from the backseat. His head flashed instinctively backward, where he saw Nicki's mouth gaping open and her eyes stretched wide and staring ahead in terror. Jerome's world slammed into slow motion as his eyes shifted back to the road. An oncoming Lexus SUV was attempting to cross an intersection in front of them and, as most drivers were prone to do, underestimated the velocity of the orange jeep. Letting his iPhone fall wherever it would, Jerome seized the wheel with both hands, pulled the jeep to the right, and slammed on the brakes. The jeep veered to the right under his commanding instructions and avoided a direct hit. The good soldier, however hard it tried, couldn't overcome the excessive speed, which overwhelmed its high center of gravity and sent it tumbling, instead of rumbling, down the road.

The slow motion that Jerome and his passengers had been thrown into immediately threw them back out with the violence of the somersaulting jeep. Each of them entered the surreal moment as if being tumble-dried at a Laundromat—except for Jack. Jack was the sock that never made it to the dryer. On the first move of the orange jeep's bottom to usurp its top, Jack was catapulted like a pilot who had called for Mayday and pulled the ejection handle.

Upon this release, his slow-motion movements continued at an even slower pace as he flew through the air. Instead of the safety of the empty sky, Jack saw that the space was filled with an audience of black, sooty gargoyles gaily watching him with smiles and points. One gargoyle in particular stood out to him—its eyes had an element of familiarity, reminding him of Rachel.

Having had enough of the taunting, Jack's attention turned back to his trajectory. He looked up and saw the trunk of an oak tree, about eighteen inches in diameter. His face, followed by his entire body, met the sturdy tree, which sent his body flailing to the ground, mangled and lifeless. But somehow this *should have been* reality was avoided, and Jack continued onward through the tree. His body landed limp on the sprinkler-system-softened ground, but his conscious mind plunged headlong into the muddy earth, piercing it like a misguided arrow angled into the ground. In his now diminishing awareness it seemed as if he was waist-deep in the earth and his upper body was constricted. His legs rested limp on the grass and were useless toward any effort of extracting himself. Silence engulfed Jack's world and his awareness was reduced to only that of his breath, of which he had none. He was suffocating under the earthen blanket and was more helpless than someone in a coma.

Frustrated, he attempted to draw air into his lungs, but to no avail. His mind trembled and then writhed in intense agony as he felt the cold touch of death seize his chest. He wanted death to have mercy on him and finish its job, but it only squeezed and released, squeezed and released. Several moments of torturous teasing resigned Jack to accept that this was now and forevermore his station. His mind stopped its struggle and fell numb yet keenly aware of his suffocation without death. It wept profusely under impending eternal bitterness.

"It was a miracle!" a lady who witnessed the whole accident said to an officer who was taking notes to help him complete the mountain of paperwork back at the precinct. "The jeep started flipping"—she pointed and waved her hand in a rolling motion—"and that boy," she said, pointing to the boy lying on the soft grass in the median, surrounded by paramedics, "was being thrown straight into that tree." The officer paused and examined the tin can of a jeep, its resting position, the tree, and the landing strip of the boy. The lady continued, "It had to be a miracle! He was flying through the air, and then it was like angels just swept his body sideways around the tree to that patch of grass." Tears came to the lady's eyes as she listened to her own report. She lifted her shaking hands to her face to wipe away the tears of fright and joy. She smiled, laughed, and shed more tears. "Oh, thank You, God, for saving that boy's life."

"Ma'am," the officer said, interrupting her praise, "what about the others?"

The lady moved her gaze to the orange jeep resting on its side. A team of firefighters and more paramedics had already pulled two kids from the jeep and were loading a third on a stretcher for transport to Memorial Hospital.

Her face became grave, and she said, "Screams."

"Ma'am?" the officer said, examining her stare.

"All I heard were the screams of teenage kids. It was horrible. Oh, I hope they're okay."

The officer jotted down some notes as she became lost in replaying the horrifying scene. "Then what?" he asked.

The lady said, "I pulled my car into that parking lot"—she pointed across the three lanes between them and the lot—"and I ran over to the jeep to see if I could help. You know, in case there was a fire or something. Then, I dialed 911 and started telling the operator what had happened and where we were." Her mind noticeably drifted again.

The officer, seeing this, comforted her. "Take your time, ma'am."

"I don't know if there's anything worse than the screams of kids." The officer nodded empathetically. "You know, officer, so many kids are loved. I wonder why they can't see it?" She looked at the officer, searching for an answer.

"I guess they just may not recognize what real love is sometimes," he offered.

The lady nodded as the profoundness of his answer sank in. "Will they be okay?" she asked.

The officer nodded and said, "I've seen worse. I think they'll be just fine."

An expression of relief washed over her face, and she shook her head. "It's a miracle. A miracle!"

The officer and his younger counterpart had all but wrapped up the gathering of the eyewitness statements and were comparing notes.

"Well, Joe, looks like another miracle situation!"

Joe nodded and replied, "Yep! It's been about half a year since the last one out on the highway."

"Which one was that?"

"When that flatbed bumped that little Honda Accord from the side and pushed it into the concrete median. They were both doing about seventy. The car started to flip, but the witnesses said that it was like a giant hand reached down and kept it flat until it skidded to a halt."

"Hmmm." The younger officer nodded thoughtfully.

"Makes you think about going to church, doesn't it?"

"Yeah. We've been meaning to go for a while now."

"Well, no time like this Sunday!"

"Yeah … maybe so."

The startup of the ambulance sirens was so sudden and loud that all the witnesses were startled. One of the four sped ahead of the others, which were moving at pace more in line with the speed limit. The light was on in the back, and people strained their eyes to see if CPR or some other maneuver was being done, trying to discover how bad the unconscious boy's injuries were.

"Memorial ER, this is station fifty-nine, unit seven. We have four inbound transports." After a pause of static and a click, a voice on the radio answered back, "Copy that, fifty-nine seven. What's that status?"

"It was a car wreck. One, potentially critical teenage male thrown from the vehicle and unconscious. Two, noncritical teenage male, conscious. Three and four, two noncritical teenage females, both conscious."

"Copy that, fifty-nine seven. Staff is ready to receive. On call is Dr. Jaye Castle."

The driver instinctively nodded, showing that he was pleased to be leaving this kid in such capable hands. He knew that she was one of the best. "Thanks. Out."

The driver put down the radio and focused on the safety of the drive. He tapped his brakes and paused before running through the intersection of steady, nonyielding traffic. Over the past few years, he had grown more used to the nonyielding types and to giving them plenty of time to clear the intersection. It seemed that most drivers nowadays thought that they should be the one more driver that squeezed through. If they only knew just how important time was in these situations. But then again, they probably didn't really care—until, of course, it was their kid in the back. The driver shook his head when a lady in an SUV squealed to a halt not two feet from his passenger side bumper and gave him an indignant gesture.

⊸⊙⊙⊙⊶

Jay had finished his prayer and joined Avery and Anna Claire in the living room. He made them put away all electronics and had lit the candles for an electricity-free night. They were just entering the debate of what game to play first when the home phone rang.

"I'll get it!" Avery popped up from the table and headed for the phone.

Jay looked at Anna Claire. "So much for a complete electrical outage."

Through the candlelight, Jay and Anna Claire watched Avery's expression for a clue revealing who it might be, but Avery's face didn't offer one. "Yes, sir. Just a second," Avery said. "Dad, it's some man for you."

275

Avery's gut told her that this wasn't a time for kidding, and she handed the phone to her dad. Jay, noticing her lack of animation, had a perplexed look on his face as he took the phone.

"Hello ... yes, this is he." The girls watched with heightened curiosity.

Anna Claire, searching Avery's face and still finding no clue, mouthed silently, "Who is it?"

Avery shrugged. "I don't know."

Jay's voice crinkled. "Is he okay?" Silence. "Yes, sir ... yes, sir ... okay ... thank you." Jay beeped the phone off and flicked on the lights.

The girls looked at their dad as if expecting an immediate answer. Jay mechanically moved toward his room. "Dad!" Avery called, interrupting his thoughts.

Jay stopped and looked at them, tears welling up in his eyes and his mouth locking up tight to prevent a bad report. "It's Jack."

These little words were the ones they were dreading to hear, the ones their guts had told them to expect but found impossible to prepare them for. "It's Jack"—two syllables that were like two bullets, one for each of their hearts. "It's Jack"—one breath of vibration that shook the strength from their small knees and expelled it from their small eyes in tears.

"It's Jack ... he's been in an accident," Jay continued, moving on to the part of hope. "He's okay, but he's in the hospital." The girls both sobbed, and Jay instantly moved over to pull them together in one family hug. "He's okay," he said, his words consoling himself as much as them. "I just need to go down there to see what's going on."

"Can we come too?" they asked in a simultaneous plea.

"Sure. You may want to get your iPads, because we may be there for a while." The girls leaned over the table and each blew out a candle. Wiping their tears, they went to gather their stuff for the trip. Jay resumed the mechanical collection of his wallet, cell phone, and keys. Within a couple of minutes, they were all in the truck, which was doing its best to stay within the posted speed limit while making the most haste it could on the way to the hospital. They spoke only a few words to each other, but the silent words of prayer sounded like three televangelists competing for an audience on the same stage.

⋲⋗⋐⋗⋐⋗⋐⋗⋑

"Jack ... Jack ..." Jay touched his arm. The nurse had cautioned to let him rest, but he and the girls needed to see some sign of awareness. Jay knew of two situations where friends had lost adult children to a permanent comalike state after a car accident. One was an early childhood neighbor who was in a car wreck. The other was a church friend whose daughter was hit by a car. His heart and prayers went out for both of these situations and he had seen how God had worked in them, but he didn't want to have to endure so severe a trial. "Jack ... Jack ..." he repeated, applying more pressure to his arm.

Despite the heavy sedation, Jack's eyes slowly and drowsily opened halfway and then closed again. Anna Claire put her hand on Jack's arm next to her dad's. "Jack ... Jack ... it's Anna Claire."

Avery leaned in too, adding, "Jack ... it's Avery ... open your eyes."

Jack's eyelids lifted with a struggle and only managed to get about three-fourths of the way open. His eyes rolled sideways toward the disturbance, and then his lids fluttered closed again. Jay breathed a small relief, seeing that there was indeed brain responsiveness. He patted Anna Claire's extended hand on Jack's arm and said, "He seems to be okay. Let's let him rest." Seeing their puzzled looks, Jay explained, "He heard us, and he responded. That's a great sign. They're giving him a painkiller, so I think that's about all we're going to get from him for now."

The girls looked back at Jack, examining him more closely for evidence. His face was pale, especially under the fluorescent hospital lights, and had some scratches and swelling, but it looked far better than they had expected from someone who had been launched just over forty feet from a tumbling jeep. Jay lifted up the covers to see what else might be bandaged. The girls ducked their heads to see as well.

"Good thing he wore clean underwear," Jay said, trying to lighten the air.

The girls answered, "Humph, yeah."

No other bandages were visible apart from some medical tape on his left ribcage. At the lack of casts and wrappings, Avery turned to Jay with a look of slight confusion, as if she were missing part of the picture. Jay interpreted her look and answered, "Looks pretty good from the outside." Jay thought about voicing his real concern being on what was happening inside but, knowing this would add to the anxiety, kept it to himself. Avery was consoled by the remark, not taking the liberty to deduce the next logical sentence, and moved to take the more comfortable-looking guest chair in the room. Anna Claire, seeing that it was okay to take a seat, followed suit, taking the next most comfortable-looking guest chair. Jay kept his position on the unpadded one pulled close to the bed. He kept a light touch on Jack's arm, and with his wrist lying on the bed and his head lying on his arm, he prayed.

23

A TORNADIC PRAYER

Spaw and his servants had a riotous laugh seeing Jack fly through the air like a ragdoll thrown from the hand of an angry toddler. The comedic act over, Spaw kept a keen eye out for anything unusual. He knew that when things became unusual, Christians did unusual things—things that usually frustrated and foiled his leveraging the situation for his own personal gain and glory.

Spaw heard three whooshes in the air above him. Three demons had rushed by. He instinctively turned his attention to the direction from which they'd come and spread out his wings, ready to take to the air for battle, assuming it was an invading force. Twenty other demons speedily followed the first. Spaw pushed his great wings down and instantly shot up fifty feet. His eyesight sharpened as he peered to the east. His riddle was solved when he saw the remnants of a large flock of small redbirds twisting into a tornado-shaped cloud. The thousands of birds continued to circle tighter and tighter until they had completed the full tornado shape and burst into flames.

A tornado of fire that stood ten stories high was twisting through the air and moving faster than most demons could fly. It was as if it were in fast motion while its victims were in slow. Spaw's inclination was to fight back—but how? Spaw shot back down to the lower area and summoned all his servants to him. He commanded them to form a sphere around him with shields held up so as to make an enormous ball of armor. Spaw took his position, cowering at the sphere's core. He heard a crash of thunder from the outer layer and then felt an excruciating pain across his scalp. A bolt of red lightning had penetrated the protective formation as if it wasn't there and struck Spaw in the head.

For a moment, Spaw was dumbfounded with amnesia, his eyes closing instinctively with his grimace of pain. When he opened them, he was in a new world. He pushed his way out through the bodies of beings amassed around him and surfaced in the air. Drawing his sword, he attacked the body of demons that had exploded from the balled formation. Glancing off to the west, Spaw could make out a small, red cloud of birds flying away from him. This frightful image brought him back to his senses, and he cursed and struck at every demon still within his sight.

Contemplating the situation, Spaw recognized the power of prayer. He knew some strength had been injured within him—he could feel it, though he didn't know exactly what it was.

Angered at the thought and blaming it on Jay, Spaw summoned Anxiety to distract Jay from more assaults. Anxiety was a wiry demon whose head color was constantly changing. His eyes flitted anxiously around as if he were the target of everyone's violent attack. He appeared in a bowing state, casting agitated glances up from either paranoia or irreverence.

"Long live Spaw in power!" he exclaimed as his gaze jerked to the right and then centered up to Spaw. Spaw considered striking him for his lack of graciousness but refrained, as this was a matter of urgency.

"You know the one. Now go!" Spaw commanded.

Anxiety nodded his head as if going toward a full bow but, casting a microglance at Spaw, took three sprinter-paced steps as if to avoid a slash from a sword and then burst into warp-speed flight, leaving a wake of floating black dust.

The more Spaw thought about the audacity of the tornadic attack, the more infuriated he became. He turned his mind to Nicki and summoned another servant called Rage. In Spaw's thousands of years of watching human dysfunction, he was confident that her dad would be ripe for the using. Rage arose from beneath Spaw's feet like waves of heat rising from an overcrowded Texas highway on a suffocating summer day.

"Your grace," Rage uttered in a low, stale tone with seemingly artificial politeness. He was a hefty, crimson demon whose face looked like a balloon that longed to explode and be released from the excessive pressure within. His lips were constantly pressed, holding back the torrent of words that might bring on his destruction at any second.

"Rage, my ally," Spaw flattered, knowing that Rage would find a point of contention with anything and everything, "I need your hand."

The crimson face deepened to black, and behind his narrowed lips, he was grinding his serpentlike teeth to nubs. He bowed his head and spit a fragment of tooth on the ground. His eyes maintained an untrusting and crazed stare at Spaw. "Your wish is my command, my liege. Just name it," Rage gutturally replied.

Spaw could see the vapors of fury mounting in him and delighted in this game. He paused to watch the boiling pot. Rage's lip curled up in a snarl and then was forced back into its firmly pressed position. Spaw noticed the movement and took and held a breath as if about to speak. He released it without word. Rage's eyes widened and his nostrils flared. His wings drew back, and his clawed hands clenched tightly. Spaw's entertainment was disturbed when another demon, Bile, approached in a sniveling crawl. Bile was of a sick, pale, greenish tint with the remnants of red hairs spiking from a bald head now covered by a small skullcap of metal. His arms and legs were visibly thin, and at their tips were claws that were unkempt and fractured from neglect. Bile hunched up into a ball, bowing beside the conversation he was interrupting.

"All hail the mighty Spaw," Bile whimpered in puny tone.

Spaw glanced down at Bile and then back at Rage. Rage's crazy eyes were filled to the brim with the fire of fury, and he drew back his lips to show his fanged teeth. Spaw knew what was going to happen next, and it pleased him. Rage, with a look of insanity that threw all reverence for Spaw to the side, opened his mouth as wide as his upper torso and, much like a python grips a small, fuzzy mouse, grasped Bile by the head. As Rage locked his grip, Bile squealed with panic. Rage's chest heaved as he exhaled, inhaled, and then clenched his jaws together more firmly. *Crack! Crack! Crack!* The hardness of Bile's head crumbled under Rage's power.

Bile's wings, which were flitting with agony, fell limp across his back. Rage, still entranced in temporary insanity, completed the bite until his upper fangs met his lower fangs, confirming the destruction and leaving the head hanging on by only the sinewy neck muscles. Rage gulped, taking Bile's head further into his mouth on a swallow. Spaw, taking in the obliteration, drew back his own wings and opened his own mouth and claws. He drew back his huge clawed hand and swiped it across the hunched back of Rage, leaving four gashes its full width. Rage coughed up Bile's head from his mouth and then arose in a vengeance to face Spaw.

Spaw drew up to his full height and breadth and showed himself to be ten times more formidable. Rage lunged at his throat, but Spaw caught him by his own. Rage struggled and uttered paragraphs of curses. Spaw pulled back his lips as if to imitate a smile and shook his head.

"I could have Bile for dessert and you for the main course!" Spaw warned.

Rage heard the threat and gave up his futile attack. In a defiant manner, he pulled Spaw's grip from his throat and snapped to an attentive stance.

Spaw continued, "Like I was saying, it is John Tingle." Rage brightened himself into an explosion of fumes and disappeared. Spaw looked at the remains of Bile, which were starting to twist again. He gripped the demon around the chest with his clawed hands and held him in front of his face like a piece of meat. Spaw shook his head and muttered, "Irreverent trash." Putting Bile's head into his mouth, he closed down on the demon's neck to completely separate it and ensure that no life would ever return to him in this world. He then consumed the rest of the pitiful wretch as other demons approached but maintained a large distance from Spaw's reach.

❧❦❧

Nicki, Ginger, and Jerome were seated in the emergency room waiting area. Their emotions cycled from embarrassment to guilt to shame to concern to sadness and back to embarrassment. Jerome thought about his dad telling him a story of when he was in high school. Four teenagers were drinking and driving. Their car wrecked, and one of the girls died. The other three struggled with that trauma for years, and the driver, unable to escape his guilt, committed suicide in college. Now Jerome had a better appreciation of the account.

"I should've known better. I've seen hundreds of kids get into wrecks from texting. I should've known better," Jerome punished himself.

"Accidents happen, Jerome," Nicki told him. "You didn't mean for that to happen."

"Yeah, but it did happen," Ginger, less forgiving, scolded. Jerome didn't get angry; he accepted the disciplining remark.

"I know! I should've known better!" Jerome replied and shook his head, which was lying in his palms. "Man, if Jack died ..." Jerome said, continuing his vocalization therapy. A tear welled up in his eyes and dropped to the floor.

"But he didn't die! He's going to be okay. You heard the doctors," Nicki countered.

Ginger corrected her, "The doctors said that he looked okay from the outside but they still had to check for internal damage."

Nicki turned her dejected gaze to the ground.

"I don't know what to do," Jerome said.

"How about praying?" Ginger offered with an element of sarcasm. Nicki shook her head. This wasn't a time for sarcasm. Jerome got up and paced the sterile white hall with his head hung low.

"Sir! Sir!" a woman's raised voice emphatically pleaded.

"John! John! You get back here right now!" a second woman's voice loudly commanded. "You can't do any good like this!"

Nicki, Ginger, and Jerome all looked up at the red-faced typhoon heading their way down the hall from the hospital information desk. It was Nicki's dad. Nicki's face brightened at the sight of her parents. She was naturally happy to see them and wanted to give and get a big hug from them. But her brightness immediately turned pale when she saw the rage in her dad's eyes.

"What the heck were you thinking, Nicki?" her dad demanded without even asking if she was okay.

"Dad, please ..." Nicki begged, in tears—some from hurt, some from embarrassment, some from the anger of rejection.

"No, ma'am! You did something stupid, and I want to know what you were thinking!"

Nicki's mom said, "John, she was in an accident. It wasn't her fault!"

"Nothing is ever her fault!"

"Dad, please ..."

Nicki's dad grabbed her by the arm and jerked her from her seat. Nicki cast a glance of embarrassment at Ginger and Jerome, who both ignored the disturbance and moved down the hall to give them space for their dysfunction. John pulled Nicki sideways with his left arm, and drawing back his right arm, he spanked her across the bottom like a disobedient child. Nicki began to cry in earnest, not at all from the physical pain—the spanking didn't even faze her—but from the slap of angry disappointment. Her mom pressed in between the two bodies but was unable to break John's hateful glare scalding Nicki's heart.

"I've had enough of your junk! You treat your mom and I like you are the parent, and I've had enough!" he announced, his volume now attracting the attention of the security guards, whose glares had a slight calming effect. "This is not good! You are not good! All you do is cause us trouble! You're worthless!" These last words echoed through the hallway for everyone to take in, sift, taste, and vomit back out of their ears. Nicki's mom sobbed at the scene.

Nicki sobbed and fell to her dad's feet. John cast his punishing glare down heavily on her head. "Get up! Get up!" John commanded as if he had just captured an enemy who had been in pursuit of his life. "Go to the car! This is going to cost me a fortune! Get out of my sight!" he scathingly added.

Nicki's mom grabbed her arms from the back and helped her to stand. Nicki buried her sobbing face in her hands and moved slowly toward the door, trying to give her dad a chance to repent. She wanted him to come to her, to hug her, to say that he loved her and that everything was going to be all right. But he didn't. His rage-filled eyes burned her back all the way out the door and into the parking lot. She buried herself in the smallest corner of the backseat and wept profusely until she could get to the safety of her own room, where she froze her crushed heart to numb the agony.

Spaw had just finished consuming Bile when he heard a sudden approach and the words "Long live Spaw in power!"

Spaw bristled for an attack and saw the fidgety servant Anxiety. He sensed failure in his short and poor timing. "Speak," Spaw commanded. He had very little time for Anxiety.

"I did as you commanded, great one, but his brightness kept me too far for any type of strong attack." Spaw's brow furrowed in anger, and Anxiety's gaze lowered to show his fear. "Seeing this, I released three arrows, but they were extinguished in his shield of faith, and he doubled his strength of prayer. There was nothing else for me to do. He was so bright," Anxiety finished with a tone of amazement.

"You did *what?*" Spaw screamed, shaking the air for miles. Anxiety, already nervous, started to throw himself down in humility but stopped and started to take flight—and then stopped again and started to throw himself down. He was so distraught he didn't know what to do. His mind landed on flight, so he took three quick steps away from Spaw and drew back his wings for a quick propulsion.

Spaw quickly drew in a breath and then exhaled a burst of flames that charred Anxiety's wings, causing his momentum to send him tumbling forward in roll. Anxiety, a torched, disfigured body of soot writhing in agony, uttered his plea for his life: "My lord … he was too bright!"

Anxiety looked at Spaw to support his appeal, but seeing Spaw curl his lips back and hearing a hiss from those fiery lungs, he changed his attitude to one of defiance. "You, little worm, wouldn't have been a match for him either!" Anxiety proclaimed, pulling his courage to continue the insult. "You, little worm, couldn't defeat a praying man, and you—"

Spaw whipped his tail around with its scorpionlike stinger and plunged it through Anxiety's neck. "Silence!" Spaw commanded.

And there was silence.

24

PRAYER-INDUCED DREAM

Avery and Anna Claire came into Jack's room at the hospital and pulled the shades open slightly to let in a few beams of sunshine. A ray cast itself across Jack's forehead, and the girls could see his eyes moving back and forth behind his lids in REM.

"Look, Anna Claire, he's dreaming," Avery said.

Anna Claire watched as his eyes twitched and his pulse seemed to quicken. "I think we should pray for him to have good dreams," she suggested.

Avery nodded. "Good idea." The two carefully touched Jack's side and arm and held hands. After a minute or so, each having interceded to Jesus for Jack, they took their places in the seats they had claimed last night and discussed what Jack would want to talk about first when he awoke.

Jack's dream began as usual, at the same river and with the same cast of characters floating alongside him.

As his friends floated downstream, he lifted off of his tube and started floating upward toward heaven. Higher and higher in the sky he moved, eager to see paradise. He moved through a cloud, which dimmed the dream's light. Then the cloud became denser and denser until it felt, looked, and smelled like swamp mud—black, sticky, with a stench of rotten eggs. It felt as if he were a stake that someone was plunging deep into the mucky mix of earth and water. He began to suffocate under the mire. He could make out other creatures moving about him. They were hideous and vile, reeking of evil.

As he continued his ascent, forced to gasp for breaths at the risk of vomiting from the smell, he caught the whiff of something sweet. He took in a deep breath but only filled his lungs with the nasty pollutants of evil. But there it was again—an aroma like incense. As it passed, he heard the utterances of small sweet voices; it was Avery and Anna Claire. The sweet cloud covered his mouth and nose and gave him freer breath. Jack inhaled deeply again and took in the beautiful bouquet.

The sludge began to loosen, and Jack could feel himself moving faster as if he were a bubble about to finally make it to the surface of a tar pit. Emerging upward, he found his feet were on a solid ground of rock. He looked around to see that he was literally front and center of a group of sixty others stretched in a formation of three rows of twenty. The crowd was a mix of boys and girls like himself, all dressed in ragged, soot-covered robes.

Jack looked down at his own garment to see that it was just as filthy as the rest. *How is this possible?* he asked himself. *I go to church, like, every Sunday. And I even go to church events during the week. And I've been baptized.* His astonishment peaked, and he had to verbalize his question. He looked at the boy next to him and started his appeal, but when he opened his mouth, a gurgling sound replaced his words, and black tar overflowed from his mouth onto his feet. With the horror of seeing his vomit covering such a pure white floor, he closed his mouth tightly and wiped the remnant on his chin with the sleeve of his robe, leaving his chin blackened.

A trumpet blasted, and all eyes turned to the staircase before the ragged assembly. A man appeared with a dazzling appearance. The only human word to attempt to describe Him was beautiful. His eyes were like a flame of fire, and on His head was a crown. His robe was white but had a stain of blood on the side. It was Jesus, King of Kings and Lord of Lords! Jack froze under this phenomenal recognition.

Jesus said, "If anyone is ashamed of me and my words in this adulterous and sinful generation, the Son of Man will be ashamed of them when he comes in his Father's glory with the holy angels." At this, an angelic being joined Jesus on the platform with a scroll. He unrolled it and began reading names. One by one, people approached the front step when their names were called. Jesus' eyes scanned the crowd. The sensation of deep sacrificial love was heightened when His gaze met Jack's. Jack eagerly waited to hear his own name. With each call, he just knew the next words would be "Jack, my good and faithful servant," but they weren't. Twenty-seven names were called, and twenty-seven people now stood facing the front step before Jesus and the angel. In the twinkling of an eye, their robes flashed a brilliant white, which matched their now glowing faces.

The angel descended the steps and escorted the group down a hallway of seven arches. Jack's face broke out in a feverish sweat as he pulled up the memory of when he had denied being a follower of Jesus at the party. The sound of his own words made him ashamed. He swallowed hard, and his throat choked on the syrupy black tar that refilled his mouth. He recognized the words by their bitter taste on his tongue. All the ones now left behind looked around in a fret. Some fell to their knees, some shook their fists, and some just froze like statues in disbelief.

Jack fell on his face and sobbed bitterly. He felt himself sinking back into the muddy realm, dejected and rejected. He struggled to cling to the solid rock around him, but it was like quicksand, pulling him back into the suffocating mire where he understood he was to be engulfed for eternity. But then, wasn't this the exact choice he had made? To follow the current of life? To "go with it"? To chase acceptance from people instead of Jesus? To pursue Rachel and the Ohm? To reject the grace of God in Christ to hew out his own life path? By choosing these other things, he had rejected Jesus. He had rejected the grace of a holy God, which had been bought at so dear a price and offered to him for free. Free! Why hadn't he chosen grace? He didn't know. The muddy realm was bad enough, but this unanswerable question of why would be his constant torment for now on. Hopeless, Jack gnashed his teeth and wailed.

-oOOo-

Avery and Anna Claire watched for several minutes as Jack began to sweat and grind his teeth. His fidgets and expressions worried them.

"Maybe we should wake him up," Avery said. Anna Claire just stood there, not knowing what to do. Avery turned to her with a scared face. "Should we wake him up?" she asked. Anna Claire was becoming too frightened to respond. Avery grabbed Jack's arm and pushed it back and forth. "Jack ... Jack ... wake up! Jack!" Jack's eyes became still, and his face wrinkled in horror and then relaxed. "Jack! Wake up!" Avery persisted. Jack's eyes fluttered open slowly as if he were still under the influence of the sedative. He turned and saw Avery and Anna Claire staring closely at him with concern riddling their faces. A grin lifted his face, which removed the girls' burdened frowns and replaced them with lightened smiles. They were relieved Jack was awake, and he was relieved that his nightmare had been just that—a nightmare.

25

ENTER MITHRAS

Immediately following the great expulsion whereby the Dragon and his rebel angels were evicted from heaven, he, the Dragon, perverted that heavenly label of "angel" to a new pitiful label of "demon." Relishing in the newfound power to twist God's creation, his appetite evolved from a heated bubble to a cosmic volcanic eruption. In imitation of the Almighty, he established for himself an unholy trinity by appointing the Beast and the False Prophet to craft his usurpation of power. The Beast would eventually become flesh by inhabiting an existing human to be the Dragon in flesh for political subjugation. The False Prophet would similarly crawl into humanity to provide signs and wonders to deceive people and secure all worship for the Dragon in religious conquest.

Ranking just below the unholy trinity were Gog and Magog, who were given the appointment of commanders over the dark military forces to execute the various wicked strategies on creation. Below them, the demonic governmental subhierarchies were to be determined by strength, ferocity, and intelligence. This contest took shape in a series of battles that were collectively known as the kingdom wars. These battles were viewed with great pleasure by the Dragon, as they perfected the force and vengeance which he supposedly needed to conquer the Almighty and secure all worship for himself. Mistrustful alliances were made at the threat of excruciating pain, and the wars were beyond description in brutality and darkness, without mercy for the weak or broken. It was a time of initiation when that treacherous lot who were previously good were plunged into the darkness of evil for the first time. It was a time when God, in His sovereign omnipotence and mercy, let evil be evil. And so it was.

Mithras had proved himself extraordinary in every demented way and was a favorite among Gog's generals. Of Mithras's greatest acclaim was his flawless implementation of a strategic and cooperative effort with Baal, a general of Magog, which the Dragon himself devised. The Pinnacle Victory, as it is called, took place when the Word, Jesus, became a man in an attempt to save man. With the unholy trinity and Gog and Magog, relentlessly attacking Jesus at every point, Mithras used his control of the Roman army and Baal his influence over Jewish leaders to execute the physical murder of Jesus. Not only were they successful at killing Jesus, but they actually were also able to accomplish it by the most torturous means possible: crucifixion. The Father's extraction of His Son's body signified nothing, as this was clearly a pinnacle victory, which demonstrated His weakness and retreat, and was still heralded by the Dragon himself as a precursor of the final victory yet to come.

The conquest of Jesus now finished, the Dragon and his forces turned their attention directly toward man, the creature God loved so much even in its despicable state. Over the past two thousand years, Mithras had continued to exercise his governmental authority to destroy the spirits of men in preparation for the final victory yet to come. In some ways, his objective was difficult; the forces of Light were still breathing, and he continually had to protect his position of authority from other demons who coveted his high position. In other ways, his objective was simple; all he had to do was to prevent man from worshipping the Almighty in the slain Jesus. It didn't matter if a man looked one-thousandth of a degree or 180 degrees away as long as it wasn't directly at Jesus. So any distraction, big or small, was sufficient, and this was made especially easy, as the Dragon had already injected evil directly into man's nature. No, man left to his own devices was easy—it was those who listened to that still, small voice of the enemy that were difficult.

Mithras was a ruthless general and had to be in such a ruthless army, so when he heard a tale of a tornado of fire in the western quadrant, he went to the scene as quickly as he could to extinguish the cause. Upon his arrival, he found Spaw consorting with his cohort of the four most powerful servants in that quadrant. Mithras presented himself directly in the middle of their circle in a flash.

"Is there a problem, Spaw?" Mithras demanded.

The cohorts prostrated themselves low, and Spaw bowed his head briefly; he didn't want to show any sign of fault or weakness. Spaw knew this might be coming and had already planned an answer.

"There is no problem that requires your attention, great Mithras."

"Then what of the report about a tornado of fire? Was that a lie? If it was, there is more than one servant that will deserve punishment."

"There was indeed a tornado of fire, but it was due to a particular servant who is no longer in my service."

"That's not an appropriate answer! Try again!"

"I sent a servant, Anxiety, to attack a little praying man. Finding that the man was too bright, he foolishly decided to shoot some arrows at him, which were perceived and extinguished. The prayers that followed resulted in a tornado, causing the loss of twenty servants and this wound." Spaw pointed to his forehead.

The brief report, a mixture of lies and truth, was convincing enough—Spaw admitted to being wounded, which made Mithras rise up in a feeling of superiority and lecture the huddle. "As you all know, it was *I* who slew the cosmic bull, *I* who punished his legions across the heavens, *I* who am second only to Gog himself, and *I* who controlled and gained the worship of the entire Roman army in Mithraism! It was *I* who gave them their strategies, their weapons, their determination, their fury, their victories. It was *I* who used them in the Pinnacle Victory. Your lenient Athena of old, Spaw, may have had her devout Greeks, but she was consumed by me and my legions thereafter. *I* had the largest and most loyal empire that ever existed in history. Wodan had a flash with his Nazis, and Baal is still having success with his radical terrorists, but they both show too much of their face, which causes normal peasants to become abnormally difficult, like Dietrich Bonhoeffer, Corrie ten Boom, and the even stronger underground cells in the eastern quadrant today. No, Spaw, *I* am too great to tolerate weakness! If I ever hear of any tornadoes of fire or even a flicker of fire in my hemisphere, you will pay with your existence!"

Spaw was beaten down by these words and lowered his head during the discourse. Mithras expected him to be beaten down more, so he drew his sword and swung it through the air at Spaw's head. Spaw ducked and fell down to his knees, allowing the sword to swoosh above him. Mithras completed the swing and brought it back across the air, leveled again at Spaw's head. Spaw fell prostrate, joining the others who still cowered low, and the sword again swooshed above him. Mithras glowered at Spaw and stepped forward to put his foot on his neck. Mithras transferred his massive weight to press punishingly down. *Crack!* Spaw's mouth opened in pain, but he knew that any resistance would be as futile as Anxiety's had been against him. *Crack!* Spaw's lower jaw was being displaced. He cut his eyes upward to defy Mithras's glare.

Upon eye contact, Mithras continued his lecture. "You've seen my creation of technology evolve over the past decades and how it is being used to demolish human spirits. It is an addictive distraction more prevalent than drugs. My most recent assault is an ingenious video game called *Mithras*. It is a powerful weapon and is producing millions of direct worshippers and even cult followings for the Dragon and me. Spaw, I even included your seductive image of Rachel in the game. So you will understand it when I reemphasize that I cannot allow any weakness in my regime! Forget the little praying man! Turn all of your efforts on my new tactic! If you don't, you will pay with your life!"

Mithras lifted Spaw with one of his clawed feet and dangled him in the air. He brought his scorpionlike tail around and drew it across Spaw's neck, which still pulsated with pain. His eyes looked lustfully at Spaw, imagining the taste of such a powerful subject. For an instant, Spaw doubted he'd survive this entrapment and clenched his jaws in preparation of his consumption. Mithras drew his tail back and pierced Spaw's neck, injecting a painful toxin. Laughing, he released Spaw and watched as he writhed to and fro in a ball of venomous fire. Had Mithras not stayed to watch, Spaw's cohorts may have finished the job and battled for his seat, but they feared Mithras too much to make such a move in his presence.

"Spaw, what say you?"

"Mighty Mithras, slayer of the cosmic bull, should I fail you again, I will be prepared to die."

Mithras smiled, seeing that Spaw understood the situation completely, and then his smile vanished into a cold and serious glare. Then he vanished as quickly as he had come.

Spaw's subjects peered up at him from below. He raised his tail and in less than a second had pierced each one of them on their bowed backs. Writhing in fiery pain as he himself had done just moments before, he knew this powerful reminder was needed to prevent any ideas of a coup d'état.

26

THE CRAZY TRUTH

The smell of a turkey potpie roused Jack from his daylong nap, and he opened his eyes to see his dad sitting next to him on his bed.

"You hungry?" Jay asked in a quiet tone so as to not completely shatter the serenity.

"Famished," Jack replied and hoisted himself gingerly up. In an elderly fashion, he slowly rotated his legs over the bed's edge, letting his feet drop slowly to the ground. Jay pulled the TV tray closer to him and held the cup of milk, knowing that the flimsy platform seemed to delight over spilled milk. Hadn't anyone told it that that type of action made people cry? The stiffness in Jack's joints and the soreness in his muscles reminded him that even lifesaving blessings could still hurt.

"I guess it's better to be hurting and alive than painless and dead," Jack offered as an attempt at humor. Jay smiled a little, but the reminder that Jack had been thrown from a speeding vehicle still froze him to his core. He offered a *Thank You, Lord!* prayer in his mind for what seemed to be the thousandth time in the past twenty four hours.

In his moments of deeper reflection, Jay was overwhelmed with the grace of God in so miraculously saving Jack's life. What had Jay done to deserve this? What had Jack done to deserve this? What had any of them done to deserve anything from God? The answer: they had done nothing! After all, that was the fantastic thing about God's grace. It could not be earned. No one could earn it. It could not be won. No one could win it. It could not be bought. No one could buy it. It was only through love for Jesus that Jay or anyone could receive such a magnificent gift as a personal relationship with the almighty Creator. God was that good of a God! Jay knew this, and he praised Jesus for it. On some days this praise was more heartfelt than on others; today's was perhaps the most heartfelt ever.

Jack could tell that something in him was different. In his recollection of himself, he could now see a youthful arrogance that had tarnished his image. He wondered if it had been as obvious to others as it now seemed to him.

"Dad ... thank you," Jack offered in a quiet voice.

Jay didn't have to ask what for; he didn't have to wonder if it was for bringing the food; he knew that it was just for being a loving dad. He placed the milk on a nearby desk and then carefully put his arms around Jack in a fatherly hug. "My pleasure, Jack."

The special moment of affection ushered in another special moment of transparency, and Jack said, "Dad, I need to tell you something."

Ugh! Jay's stomach went queasy. Although he had always handled the tough issues with the tender strength of steel wrapped in velvet—that was, in the strength of Jesus—their introduction always produced a queasy feeling in his gut and a slight tremble in his knees. He shot a quick prayer heavenward: *Jesus, help me to listen and have Your wisdom.*

"Yeah?" Jay responded.

"I've been seeing and hearing strange things over the past few weeks."

Jay had an attentive and thoughtful look. "Like what?"

"I see dead people," Jack said, quoting a movie and smiling a bit to let Jay know that that wasn't it. Jay chuckled and Jack continued in a serious tone, "No … I think I've been seeing and hearing demons." Jay's look turned from a slight smile to one of deep concern, but he let Jack continue. "Well, not like really talking to me." Jay was a bit relieved. "More like I see them hovering around people and attacking people." Jack paused to let this sink in and to test Jay's reaction.

Jay's expression moved back to one of deep thought, and he gave a slight nod of his head, indicating his attempt to understand without judging. Jack was relieved to see that his dad didn't think he was loony. "Why do you think that they are demons?"

"Well, they look like what I'd expect demons to look like, but that could just be based on my own preconceived notion—I don't know. They look like gargoyles that are made of filthy black soot. They have clawed hands and feet that they sink into people. They also have these alligatorlike tails with stingers on the ends." Jack slowed down as he saw his dad trying to keep up in his imagination. "Another reason is that the people they get closest to, even inside, seem to be nonbelievers."

"How can you tell if someone is not a Christian?"

301

"Well, when I see someone who I know, or think, is a believer, their skin is translucent, kind of glossy, and they have some kind of light that lights them up from the inside. Some are dim, others are light, and some are real bright. The others—most people—are covered in a black soot, like the demons. It's kind of like ash from a fireplace or graphite powder."

Jay's mind instantly went to a verse of the Bible where people who thought they were in Christ were surprised to find that in the end they really weren't, because they had deceived themselves. Feeling like a student just before he or she finds out a grade on a big exam (multiplied times a hundred), Jay asked, "Which one am I?"

Jack started to laugh heartily until he was checked by his aches. "Don't worry. You're a glossy!"

"A glossy?"

"Yeah, I've seen so many that I call them sooties and glossies."

Jay smiled in relief. His smile affirmed to Jack that Jay definitely didn't think he was crazy.

"So that's how you can tell?"

"Yeah. See there were these two girls I was talking to. Well, you know Faith, from church. She's definitely a Christian. But her friend Amber—she's Nicki's sister—I'm pretty sure never was. So when I saw that Amber had a light in her, without thinking, I asked her when she became a Christian. They both looked like they had seen a ghost and asked me how I knew. I guess she had just received Jesus in the past few days or so. Anyway, I moved on to another topic so that they wouldn't think I was some kind of freak."

Jay continued nodding and thinking. His mind was flipping through Scripture to find some type of explanation, but he found none.

"So do you think I'm going crazy?"

"No. I'm not sure what to think, but I don't think you're going crazy."

Jack started to tell him about Rachel, but for some reason a feeling of shame stopped him cold. Jay hugged Jack again and prayed for discernment and wisdom for him before letting go.

"Dad, so what do you know about demons?"

"Well, it looks like a lot less than you do." Jack was again comforted by his father's confidence. Jay continued, "I know that they are real, but I don't think most people understand just how real they are. Now, I don't think that there is a demon behind every bush, but they are agents of Satan who want to destroy us by getting our eyes off of Jesus." Jay looked into Jack's eyes to see if this was shaping up to be another religious lecture or if Jack was tracking and wanted more. Jack nodded to give the green light, and Jay continued, "We—that is, humans—are naturally evil, thanks to Satan, but we can't tell where our evil ends and the influence of the demonic forces begin. So while we can't pretend like demons can't influence us, we can't blame every evil or bad thing on them either. Really, this is a moot point, because no matter what the source of evil, we, as Christians, are to fight against it and keep our eyes fixed on Jesus."

"So how do they influence people or get into them?"

"Well, I suppose there are a couple of ways. You see, there is a type of 'world system' that works to distract people from God. Think of it this way—if you took away the evil twists of sex, money, drugs, alcohol, and vulgar media, what would happen?"

Jack started to work this through in his mind and found it to be a much bigger and deeper contemplation than he initially thought. "Wow, yeah. The whole global economy would grind to a halt."

"Yeah. It's not that this stuff is necessarily bad. God invented sex and music, right? But Satan has corrupted them and made them instruments through which his demons can move people away from the one true god. It's kind of like a massive cosmic current stirred by demons that sweeps people away to an eventual fatal waterfall. And the whole time people are floating to their deaths, they're having the time of their lives. Sin feels good, right?"

Jack nodded, and his face showed the resonation of the point.

"Another way, I guess, is when people invite the demons straight into their spirits—like when people mess with the occult or false religions."

Jack's face dropped a bit because the beautiful face of Rachel burst into his mind accompanied by the idea of abandoning her which gripped his heart. Jay saw the change in expression and probed.

"Have you done anything like that?"

"No," Jack lied, "but I know this girl at school who has."

"What'd she do?"

"Well, she says that she channels and talks to dead people."

Jay shook his head in sympathy for this girl, only a kid, falling into such a powerful trap. "People think that they're talking to dead people, but it's really just demons who are acting like dead people. When people die, they either go immediately to heaven or immediately to hell. There is no in-between, especially one where they could communicate with the living."

"So *if* this girl is really doing this, what should I tell her?"

"Well, you could tell her to ask the dead person if she can talk to Jesus. I'd like to hear what her spirits would say to that. The demons flee at His name!"

"Wouldn't they just say that He never existed or something?"

"There is too much historical evidence to make that claim. Christianity is the only religion that is based on a whole lot of real evidence. No other religion even comes close, but most people don't dig deep enough to see for themselves."

"Humph, well, I'll mention that to her the next time I see her."

"And the most powerful thing you could do for her is to pray. Prayer is the most effective weapon we have in spiritual warfare. It's like a nuclear bomb God has given you to use at will."

"Humph, well, I'll mention that to her the next time I see her," Jack repeated. With the thought of Rachel pulling at his heart, his interest in the conversation wavered and fell to the ground like a windless kite.

Jay received the prompt, stood up, rubbed Jack gently on the back, and left him with his food and thoughts. "Let me know if you need anything."

"Sure. Thanks," Jack replied.

Jack's mind was crashing with the consideration that Rachel might be a demon in disguise. He knew what his dad would think. But then again, his dad was so deep into Christianity that he probably couldn't see her objectively. Jack reasoned with himself, *Well, if she is who I know she is then she shouldn't have a problem with Jesus. Maybe she even knows where He is in the Ohm. That would be cool!*

27

A FRIEND IN NEED

It was only the third quarter, and the Texans were watching as their twenty-point lead at the half evaporated right before their facemasks. How many déjà vu games could happen in one horrid season? Now used to being let down hard by his favorite team, Jack sat in the rocking chair, sifting through the unpopped kernels at the bottom of the bowl for the few remaining bits of popcorn. There was a knock at the door, which served as a starter pistol for Avery and Anna Claire's race to see who it was.

Avery got there first and opened it. Anna Claire stuck her head around and saw who it was. As fast as she ran to the door, she now ran away from the door toward Jack. He looked at her as she barreled up to him. "Who is it?" he asked.

Slightly out of breath, or at least acting to be, Anna Claire reported, "It's that girl from the math club! The pretty one. She came by your room at the hospital, but you were still asleep. I forgot to tell you."

"Uh, well, thanks a lot!" Jack played.

Anna Claire, unsure if his tone was real or phony, puckered her lips and turned to go back to the door. Avery was already escorting Faith into the house. Jack glanced down at what he was wearing to make sure he was as decent as a banged-up person should be. It wasn't his most flattering pair of athletic shorts and two-year-old Texans shirt, but it would do.

"Hey, Jack! I knew you were probably in isolation, so I thought I'd come make sure you were following doctor's orders." Faith held up a gallon tub of Blue Bell Krazy Kookie Dough ice cream and a DVD of *Napoleon Dynamite*, both being among his favorites.

"Oh! Sure, come on in. I was just about to turn this"—Jack gestured flippantly to the screen—"off. I hate being a Texans fan." Faith glanced at the TV to see the quarterback throw his second pick-six of the day. Jack snatched the remote and muted the announcer, whose pitch was becoming more animated with each five-yard mark the cornerback passed as he raced toward the end zone: "He's to the thirty-five, thirty, twenty-five …"

Excited to have Sunday afternoon company, Avery grabbed the DVD and slid it into the player. Anna Claire stood there examining Faith from head to toe and trying to think of something to say to show everyone that the two of them went way back.

"So how is math club going?" Anna Claire asked.

Faith's eyebrows shot up as if to say to herself, *Busted!* She smiled with not a small degree of red embarrassment on her face. "Oh, I should've told you at the hospital. That was just a joke my friend was playing. We're not really in the math club." Faith looked at Jack, and he laughed. Anna Claire furrowed her brow and looked at Jack to see if he was laughing with her or at her. She decided that he was laughing with her, so she laughed too.

"I'll take that!" Anna Claire said, snatching the ice cream and running off to the kitchen.

Avery saw the ice cream escaping in untrustworthy hands and called out, "Anna Claire! I'll do that!" Avery scurried after her to ensure they all got equal portions.

"Have a seat." Jack motioned Faith to the couch and held his seat in the rocking chair.

"I hope you don't mind me coming over unannounced."

"No, not at all." Jack waved his hand to add sincerity to his answer.

"I thought that Nicki might be here, but Amber said that she was at home sleeping."

"Yeah, she stayed out pretty late last night, and I'm pretty sure she was hammered. She sent me a text at like two thirty in the morning that made absolutely no sense at all." Jack smiled embarrassingly at the thought of his girlfriend being so carefree while he was recovering from a near-fatal accident. He continued, "It bothers me that after being in such a bad wreck, although she wasn't really hurt, she'd hit the party scene again so soon."

As he heard his last words, he wondered why he had provided that extra detail. There was just something about Faith that invited complete transparency. She was safe, trustworthy, filled with integrity. Even the most socially unaware could pick up on that within the first two seconds of meeting her. Faith nodded in a counselorlike way and said, "Humph." Just her one syllable spoke volumes. Faith would never say it out loud—he thought she lacked the courage—but Jack read in her an intuitive warning that he was giving his heart to a carnivore for safekeeping. Nicki didn't care about him; she just cared about satisfying her own hunger.

Avery and Anna Claire reentered the room, and junk food was served. They distributed four bowls of equally measured ice cream, two giant bowls of popcorn, and four bottles of Dr Pepper. The waitresses becoming guests, the girls seated themselves in the two spaces designated by the cushion lines on either side of Faith, who took the center one. Although the girls had seen Faith from a distance at church, they had never really met her. Having now done that, they liked her from the start —Anna Claire in the front yard washing the dog, Avery the night she came by the hospital with such a deep look of concern in her eyes that Avery almost mistook it for love.

The next two hours consisted of simultaneously quoting almost every line in the movie, spoiling their dinner appetites, sharing a few tosses of popcorn and a few drink-spewing jokes, and just enjoying the pure fun of each other's company. Faith's ringtone went off—"And now I'm like baby, baby, baby, ooh!" She scrambled to mute it as three sets of eyes looked at her and laughed. "What? A girl can't like a little vintage Bieber?" she said, joining in the laughter.

After the laughter tapered off, Faith stood up. "I'd better get going. That was my parents. I'm sure they're wanting me to start heading that way for dinner."

Anna Claire responded by grabbing her hand. "You can't leave yet! Why don't you just eat with us?"

Faith's heart was warmed, but she pleaded her case. "I'm sorry. I promise I'll come back another time."

"Great! Next Sunday! We'll make this a new tradition. Sunday afternoon movie night!" Anna Claire jumped to lock her into her commitment.

"You can't have an afternoon movie night!" Avery corrected.

"Sure you can!" Anna Claire retorted.

"Okay!" Jack mediated. "Well, thanks for coming over, Faith. This was great." He stood up to join her as she was already moving toward the door. Avery and Anna Claire continued their debate as they resumed their waitstaff roles and started the cleanup. Faith got to the door, opened it, and stepped out onto the porch. Jack moved out and closed the door behind him. Faith hadn't planned on saying anything about Nicki—it wasn't her style—but the words just rolled off her tongue.

"Jack, I've known Nicki for a long time, and I've known you for a long time, at least at church." Faith had a microexpression of confusion at this claim. Had she really known Jack for that long? She guessed she had. Did she really know Jack that well? She guessed she did. She was surprised at how she could know him without formally knowing him, but she did. She continued, "Well, be careful. Nicki's pretty wild, and she's into some pretty weird stuff." Faith paused to assess Jack's reaction. He was listening but not showing any indication of approval or disapproval, so she continued, "I mean, you obviously know about the alcohol, but Amber said that she's been doing some drugs."

Hearing her words, Faith stopped dead in her tracks. She didn't want to come across as stabbing Nicki in the back. "Jack, I'm sharing this with you as a friend, not to hurt Nicki. I like Nicki and want good things for her."

Coming from anyone else, Jack would've been skeptical at the motive, but Faith's sincerity was overwhelming. "Faith, I won't tell her. I promise."

Faith sighed in relief at Jack's promise of confidentiality. This assurance gave her the safety to make her last point. "Okay, just one more thing. She's been messing around with spirits and stuff."

Jack acted surprised because he knew he was equally guilty. "Really? Like what?" he asked.

Faith read his response, sensing a chink of insincerity, but continued, "She's been contacting some spirit named Rachel that supposedly died in ancient Greece. But those spirits can't exist; when people die they go immediately to heaven or hell. It's really a demon that's just playing her." Faith felt really strange and awkward saying these words, but a peace within her affirmed her boldness.

Jack drifted off into a daze. There was that word again—*demon*—and used in association with Rachel. Jack felt a smoldering anger in the pit of his stomach, but his appreciation and respect for Faith wouldn't let it bubble up while she was still here.

"Wow, that's pretty wild. I'll have to think about that," Jack remarked, looking into Faith's eyes for any sign that she might know about his involvement and was just politely dancing around it.

"What do you mean?" asked Faith, edged with skittishness.

"Well, she's never mentioned anything to me. So I'll have to think if I've ever seen any signs of it."

Faith felt uneasy now. She felt as if something in the conversation had changed, and she wanted out. "Humph. Just promise me that you won't rat me out to Nicki," Faith implored. "You know, I really do care about her."

Jack again saw her overwhelming sincerity. "I promise. I wouldn't do that to you."

Faith saw his reciprocal sincerity. "Thanks! You're a good friend." She turned to leave.

Jack nodded and lifted his hand to wave. "Yeah. See ya."

He likewise turned and went back into the house. Closing the door behind him, he found himself a bit awestruck at such a good person. The sense passing, he went into his room and turned on his Xbox. "All hail Mithras!"

28

A CHILL IN THE AIR

Throughout the night and the next morning, the powerful warning of Faith provoked so much fear and heart pain that Jack convinced himself that his only means of protection was to draw back from Nicki. It was with these thoughts fresh on his mind that Nicki found him.

Walking up to him with a bounce, she exclaimed, "How's my miraculous superman?" a reference to his flight from the jeep.

Jack faked a smile and said, "Still pretty sore."

She went to throw her arms around him, but with a wince and raised arms to prevent the infliction of pain, he fended her off.

Nicki felt the rejection, and her smile turned upside down. Dismissing it, for she had never really been rejected and couldn't imagine that it would start with someone so "normal," she began recounting her weekend after Friday's mishap. "Jerome's jeep was totaled, so we all crammed into Ginger's car for the party Saturday night. It wasn't as good as the one at Caden's, but it still rocked."

Jack lifted his head with another fake smile, and she continued, "Oh my gosh!" Nicki stopped and turned her face toward Jack. "Remember how I told you that Stone and his girlfriend were having problems?"

Jack's heart sank, which affirmed his decision to pull it back from Nicki's hand. "Yeah," he said with tone indicating that he could care less.

"Well, she showed up at the party with two of her country friends, all dressed up in their boots and painted-on jeans and stuff, and she started talking smack to Vanessa, who was, like, hanging all over Stone. She actually said, 'You made me redneck crazy!' and then she slugged her. Well, Vanessa, being all into cardio kickboxing, throws a roundhouse kick and hit the Miranda look-alike in the face."

Jack, still trying not to seem interested because it involved Stone, whom he hated, had his interest piqued at how this fight would turn out, so he nodded to tell Nicki to continue the play-by-play. "Well, I guess a country girl can survive because big country grabbed Vanessa's hair and wrestled her to the ground like a steer. Then it turned into just a big catfight until Stone and some of the other boys broke it up."

Jack grimaced every time he heard that name Stone. "So what happened then?" he asked, wanting to hear the finale.

Nicki concluded, "Well, Vanessa has a black eye, but I think big country ended up getting the worst of it. She cussed Stone out and then slapped him pretty hard, but he's so big it didn't even faze him.

They finally left, and then we gave Vanessa an icepack and a few shots of tequila, which made her feel better."

"Wow. I'm sorry I missed that … I guess," Jack said unconvincingly.

"Yeah, Stone was pretty embarrassed for a while, but he and Vanessa ended up together, so I guess they both got over it."

Hearing Nicki's tone of admiration for Stone again, Jack's gut spewed his disdain. "Who cares about Stone!"

Nicki stepped back, her eyes wide in judgment. "Whoa! Somebody woke up on the wrong side of the bed today!"

"No, it's just that Stone, the arguments, the parties—what does it really matter?"

"Well, it matters to you, Mr. 'I want to be popular'!"

Jack was aghast at Nicki's observation. Had he been so transparent and easy to read? His mind locked up, and he couldn't speak or react.

"Don't be so naive, Jack!" Nicki threw out this last insult and then stormed off into the safety of her classroom.

Jack's mind went to work replaying the scene over and over and over, as if it were the mirror that would disclose the tiniest blemish on his face that everyone could see except for him. Jack's body moved mechanically down the hall as his mind staggered under the reality of Nicki's blow. It wasn't five minutes more when he took his seat in class and his phone buzzed with a text. It was Nicki.

"I'm sorry. Shouldn't have said that."

Jack stared blankly at the screen. He knew that Nicki would see the message as "delivered," indicating that it had made it to his phone, and then the little rounded callout box filled with an ellipsis, indicating that Jack had read it and should be replying any moment. The seconds seemed like anguished hours. He could picture Nicki sitting there in class, her hand holding her phone under her desk, her eyes watching the teacher and flicking down to see the callout fill with his response. He was sure that she was confident in a forgiving answer like "Nbd, ly" ("No big deal, love you") or, at minimum, "Kk, talk later, ly." *How many times does Stone text her a day?* Jack wondered, reminding himself of the snowball that had started this avalanche of his emotions. The burn shaking his mind into action, Jack tapped only two times: "K" and the send button.

The phone vibrated in Nicki's lap, and she glanced down at the next opportune second. "K." She shivered from the coldness of the message and then felt herself get hot with anger. "So this is what rejection feels like. Well, forget him!" Nicki muttered below her breath and then quickly looked around with a smile in case anyone noticed. She checked the teacher, who was still sitting at her desk with her face in her computer screen, and tapped out her own brief reply: "W/e!" ("Whatever!")

Jack felt his phone again, and the buzz pattern indicated that Nicki was continuing the thread. His heart wanted to grab it, but his mind rebuked him. He slid his phone out of his pocket, and without looking down at it, he powered it off. It felt as if he had shut down the power to his life-support machine, and he could now feel his heart twisting and convulsing within, seeming to make its final gasps at life. It, death, felt horrible.

29

REVENGE

Nicki's pale hand was wet from turning on the shower, and she fumbled with the lighter before dropping it to the floor from her perch on the bathroom countertop. She stood in a bank of fog overflowing its curtained boundary on its way to a buzzing fan, which inhaled it and then exhaled it atop the house. The sinking of her self-esteem within and her strong and smiling shell without created a painful vacuum that sucked at her entire being. She had underestimated the pain of rejection, and she needed some way to escape it.

Stooping down, she reached behind the commode and retrieved the lighter, her fingers darkened by whatever else typically accumulated in such a place. As she climbed back onto the countertop, the girl in the mirror of the medicine cabinet waved at her, motioning for her to clear a circle of fog and hear an urgent secret. Nicki ignored the girl and, grasping the lighter more firmly, tugged a tiny item wrapped in cellophane from her pocket. Unraveling it, she pinched a small white cigarette and let the plastic drift softly into the sink.

Flick! Flick! There was fire, and Nicki lifted her unsteady hand to her quivering mouth, which now held her solution. Nicki inhaled her troubles and then exhaled them into the exhaust fan overhead. She looked down at the girl in the mirror, who was now slapping the glass profusely, enraged at being ignored. Nicki, her hand already steadying, replaced the joint to her puckered lips, inhaled her troubles again, and exhaled them again. She felt her racing heart slow and her pain dissolve. She glanced down at the girl again, whose slaps had turned into fists pounding for attention. A third time, Nicki inhaled and then exhaled. She staggered, almost setting her foot in the sink, but steadied herself by grasping the medicine cabinet, where her thumb cleared a small area of steam on the mirror.

Nicki's face fell pale, and she saw an angry eye straining to see through the peephole she'd just created. She could see the eye flaring in the rage of rejection, but her words were muffled. Nicki laughed, inhaled, and then stood upright with her hand next to the girl's eye to exhale into the fan. She squatted back down and traced a backward message to the girl so that she could read it properly. "! K C U S U O Y" Nicki laughed at the irony as she sucked in her last bit of troubles and blew them up. Her laughter growing louder, Nicki steadied herself to climb down from her pedestal. She then crawled into the shower, sat down, and cried. The water felt like a warm rain gently massaging her head. She closed her eyes and let herself slip into the peace of meditation.

-⊕⊖⊖⊕-

The temperature of the rain became cooler, and the hard, white tub softened, causing Nicki to raise her eyes. She was seated at the base of one of those large oaks, raindrops meandering their way down from leaf to leaf and onto her head.

319

"What's the matter, sweetie?" Rachel comforted, stepping around from the back of the tree.

Nicki intentionally let her face look pitiful and replied, "Oh, I'm okay. Just a bad day."

Rachel sat down and mimicked her downcast posture. "How is Jack? I haven't spoken to him in a long time," Rachel inquired, as she really wanted the information.

Nicki was a bit taken aback by the topic so quickly abandoning her own problems, so she tied her answer back in. "He was a jerk today. It really hurts."

Rachel slid her arm around her back and started rubbing. "What did he do?" she probed.

Nicki rested her hands on her knees to emphasize her pout and replied, "He ignored me. Well, first he got mad at me because he was having a bad day, and then he, like, just started going cold and acting distant."

Rachel's expression became more serious, and Spaw knew he had to address the matter quickly. He couldn't let his pawn, Jack, leave the game and cost him his revenge on Jay. Rachel responded with love, "Aw, you're right. Boys are such jerks sometimes. Why don't you—nah." Rachel let her truncation draw Nicki in.

"What is it?" Nicki inquired.

"Well, if you want—but only if you want, though—I can have an angel of peace breathe on you."

Nicki lifted her head, and the idea of having peace brightened her eyes. "Sure, why wouldn't I want that?"

"Well, I just don't want to show you too much of the world you're destined for, because it would dampen your life on earth."

"Who cares?" Nicki said. "It's damp enough already down there."

Rachel stood up, her light white dress dancing with the breeze, extended her large, colorful wings behind her, and closed her eyes. A rhythmic humming came from her mouth and was soon followed by a song of enchantment in an unintelligible language. In a moment, the raindrops stopped, and a single ray of light broke through the clouds and angled itself beneath the oak. A cream-colored bird drifted down the ray and alit on Rachel's extended finger. It wasn't a white dove, but it had its own tranquil beauty.

"This is an angel of peace. Can't you feel its blessing already?" Rachel said.

Nicki nodded, although she hadn't really felt anything yet. Rachel guided the ceremony. "Okay, close your eyes and take six deep breaths. I'll hold the angel close to your face, and you'll inhale its peace." Nicki relaxed into a meditative lotus blossom position and began to inhale deeply, as she had just done on her bathroom perch. Rachel held the demon, Scorn, close to Nicki's face, along with a freshly plucked flower to disguise the odor. The demon opened his beak and released a slow exhale over the flower, which Nicki pulled into her lungs. By the sixth breath, Nicki and the flower were wilted. "There. Do you feel better?" asked Rachel with a coaxing smile.

Nicki felt worse but wouldn't admit as much. She nodded and muttered, "Uh-huh." Her eyes drooped, and she slumped on her side to the ground.

Rachel flung the bird off of her hand as if it had released a dropping there. The sudden motion sent the bird tumbling across the dead leaves, where it turned black and then took on its more natural shape of a gargoyle.

"Long live mighty Spaw! Will there be anything else, my lord?" asked Scorn, his knees and head still in the leaves.

Spaw moved his eyes up as if in thought. "No. Get out," Spaw commanded.

Scorn curled his wings about him and disappeared in an implosion.

Nicki had the sensation of falling to her death through a bank of thick clouds. After a few seconds, the bank cleared, and she saw that she was approaching a large body of water at a devilish pace. Curling herself into a ball, she felt the bone-shattering pain of impact and then a deep plunge into an icy depth. She gasped to regain the wind that was knocked from her only to draw in a breath of cold water. Opening her eyes, which had been tightly sealed for landing, she found herself lying in her bathtub with the cold shower still sprinkling her. Without care for the frigidity—she was still under the artificial peace of the sedative—she slowly raised her water-wrinkled hand to turn off the rain. Wrapping herself in her towel, with her body and mind still soaking, she stumbled to her bed, fell headlong into it, and went straight to sleep for a few hours.

About three thirty in the morning, Nicki felt a labor pain and bit her lip to suppress it. She lay there in her bed panting as it subsided. Two minutes had passed, and she felt the onset of a second. With sweat beading on her brow, she bit her lip again so that the pain wouldn't find a voice and wake anyone else. It subsided again, and Nicki examined her stomach as if to see it bulging with pregnancy. One minute passed and another pain came. Nicki moaned silently, and her teeth scratched into her lip, causing it to bleed slightly. Almost instantly another one came. It was the most pain Nicki had ever felt in her rather short life.

She buried her face hard into a pillow and released her agony in a scream. Tears flooded her eyes as she felt the razor-sharp pain in her lower abdomen drop and then rise up under her ribs in a simmering burn. Her mind ran up to Jack, pointed an accusing finger in his face, and said, *You! It's your fault!* Wiping her brow on her still-wet towel, she reached over and grabbed her iPad. Tapping up a tweet, she felt Rachel's presence nodding affirmatively. Unbeknownst to Jack, it wasn't Vanessa who was the one comforting Stone after the altercation at the party—she had ducked out from embarrassment. It was Nicki who had given him the forbidden lips that had salved his loneliness, but because they each had another significant other, they agreed to keep it "their little secret."

Nicki didn't want to play that card yet but posted an announcement of things Jack had said against Stone, adding threats and belittlements of his manhood. They were all lies.

30

SAVED BIG BY A SMALL PRAYER

Meandering into the school, Jack noticed people looking at him and pointing—not in the complimentary way they had done previously, but with looks of excited pity. He hadn't checked any social media but was curious what story had broken. He made his way to the trophy case, where Bobby and Caden were alternating between talking and tapping their phones. As Jack drew up, they both looked at him, then at each other, and then back at him. Their faces had an element of confusion and shock on them. Bobby started, "Dude, did you see what Nicki posted?"

Jack shook his head wearily. "No. Why? What is it? Is it bad?" Jack couldn't imagine how bad it could be; all he'd done was allow some space between them.

"I think you'd better look at this," Caden murmured almost apologetically. Jack took his phone and narrowed his morning eyes to read. His jaw dropped and then pressed shut tightly in anger.

"These are lies! Why would she do this? She's crazy!"

"Yeah, she may be crazy, but what about Stone? He's psycho!" Bobby said as he glanced around for the man-size boy in the crowd of kids. Jack's eyes closed in exasperation as his face recalled the shot of pain from Stone's rock-hard fist launched from a sling.

"What are you going to do?" asked Caden, looking around like Bobby.

"I guess I'll go talk to her ... or him, whoever I see first."

Almost on cue, the crowd parted like the Red Sea—only it wasn't Moses walking between the waves. Stone had anger issues—issues that served him well on the gridiron but not on the playing field of life.

His deep voice reached Jack before he did. "Get over here!"

Bobby thought a microprayer to God for help. Jack moved out to meet Stone with his hands in front of him as if to repel the beast. "Look, Stone, I didn't say any of those things." Jack's denial didn't slow down his hard strides. "They were lies."

"Oh, so now you're calling Nicki a liar!" Stone built on the word and created his own chivalry, now protecting Nicki's reputation. Jack prepared to duck under a punch, but instead Stone came forth and, with the force of the hind legs of a mule, pushed Jack backward. Jack slammed into the wall, which knocked his breath out of him, and slid to the ground.

In an instant, he could see the same violent mob assembling and announcing, "Fight! Fight! Fight!"

Jack paused on the ground, buying himself some time.

"Get up!" Stone commanded, standing there waiting with raised fists. Then a small miracle happened: two large arms only slightly smaller than Stone's grabbed him in a bear hug from behind. It was Moose. Stone's head turned sideways to see who was interfering with his business. Then stepping in front of him were Sam, Jordan, and Jerome.

Jerome, still feeling guilty for the whole jeep thing, spoke first. "Uh-uh! Not on my watch, you don't!"

Stone's temper defused with the interruption. Sam spoke next. "Look, Stone, don't be stupid! You'll get kicked off the team if you fight! Especially someone so much smaller than you."

Jordan reinforced the point. "And there goes your chance of any college ball!"

Moose felt Stone's statue-hard muscles relax to a more human tension and released his lock. Stone's glare still struck fear into Jack, who didn't make any sudden movements.

Sam reasoned again, "Look, Stone, you know that most of the times things like this may or may not be true. Heck, he probably really didn't say any of it."

Stone looked sideways at him allowing for that point. Stone returned his look to Jack and warned, "Look, you little punk! If you ever come close to saying anything about me, I'll kick your tail so hard you won't be able to tuck it when you run!" With this promise, the tension in the air was gone, much to the mob's disappointment, and Stone retraced his path to the other shore.

Bobby followed up on his prayer with a, "Thank You, God!"

Jack moved up to his friends, shaking their hands and his head at the thought of what might have happened. "I can't afford to go back to the doctor for the third time. Thanks, y'all!"

They patted Jack on the back in congratulations, and Jerome offered, "If he threatens you again, you let me know. I got your back!" Jack smiled big at this security. He also smiled big at the thought that they would still be his friends even without Nicki.

"Wow! How lucky was that!" Caden exclaimed and patted Jack on the back as the others had done.

"Yeah. Did you see how quick the crowd was to see me get beat up? I was watching Stone, but all I could hear was 'Fight! Fight! Fight!'"

"You know, after we watched that other boy get beat up, I had a gnawing feeling in my gut. It was like guilt or something," Bobby said.

Caden said, "I know exactly what you're talking about. I think it is guilt. I've been feeling it whenever I play *Mithras*. It's like that game is warping my mind, and something inside me is telling me that it's bad. What did you do?"

"Well …" Bobby looked as if he felt a bit awkward. "I asked God to forgive me, and I felt like he did. It was a big relief. I'm not going to be a part of anything like that again."

"That worked?" Caden asked. "I'll have to try it next time."

Jack rolled his eyes slightly and then felt Rachel applaud his proof of loyalty to her truth. "All right, I'm going to class," Jack said, ending the conversation, and he turned to go to his locker, which he halfway expected to have been trashed by Nicki.

31

LONGING PLANTS A DARK SEED

For two days now, Jack had managed to avoid Nicki, and Nicki had managed to avoid Jack. Between the paranoia that lingered from Stone's threat, the looks and whispers in the hallways, his suspicion of more from Nicki, and the fact that it wasn't that long ago that he had been in a traumatic car wreck, Jack hadn't been sleeping well at all. He was exhausted, and the same body that begged for rest aroused him during sleep to remind him of its request with aches. Jack had given up on any decent sleep, and he lay on his bed contemplating life and wondering if or when he would ever get to see Rachel again. Just as sleep blankets us when we stop trying to pull it over us, so Jack's mind relaxed and floated up to Rachel.

•◦◦◦•

"Nicki is just a jealous peasant girl!" Jack was elated to see Rachel, and he sprang to his feet and embraced her. Rachel repeated her insult. "She's just a peasant! I can't believe that she'd treat you like that!"

"Hey, hey, calm down." Jack stroked her dark, silky hair. Rachel's eyes sparkled red at his compassion, and she hid them on his shoulder. "It's fine. As long as I have you, I couldn't care less about Nicki."

"But she was so convincing. She seemed to be a friend. Who knew she'd turn in a flash and start lying about you? She's not going to be in my clander—I'll make sure of that!"

"Hey, let's just put it behind us and focus on what is really important."

Rachel smiled and, with her eyes darkened again, looked at Jack with a longing tenderness. "I can't wait for you to be here with me. Jack, you have to hurry. I'm just so eager."

"I know," Jack comforted. "I'm doing the best I can."

Rachel looked at him and let him see that she was in deep contemplation. "You know …" She paused. "No, I couldn't ask you to do that."

Jack took the bait. "Do what? What is it?"

"Well, I think you're refined enough to join me at our close proximity in the Ohm. If that's so, you could just graduate now," Rachel suggested and then watched Jack, her face showing the same hope as when a boy finally scrapes up the courage to invite a girl out for dinner.

Jack nervously laughed it off and remarked for clarification, "You mean like kill myself?"

"I knew it'd be too much for you. I'm sorry—it was just selfish, wishful thinking." Rachel withdrew the suggestion but left it lingering in midair and then pushed it a bit more. "I guess if you have to think about it, then you're not completely ready."

"Well, wait a minute. I've come a long way."

"You have. I'm so proud of you. But forget about it."

Jack paused to think and said, "Well, if I end up going backward, like to just an average kid, then I might just do that!"

At this suggestion, even somewhat in jest, Rachel seemed to reel at the thought. "Then we could be together forever!" she said with glee, bounced into the air, and pulled Jack into a firm hug. Her eyes reddened again, and she buried them in his shoulder again. Jack felt as though his eternal bliss had already begun. He didn't want the embrace to end. In rapture, he pulled back out of the hold and then started forward to meet her lips.

He closed his eyes in expectation and found himself falling head over heels through the air. His eyes shot open in time to see that he was dropping into a large mouth of stone with large teeth that were biting and grinding. He felt his body land on the hard rock of a tongue and felt the molars crush down on his legs. He writhed in agony and tried to pull them up to his chest, but instead of them moving to him, he slid down to them. The molars came down again, crushing him across the abdomen, and he felt his organs move under the enormous pressure. His mouth opened wide in agony, but it was too much for a scream of any sort. The molars retracted and he slid down further. Again they clenched, this time on his head. Crack! Crack! Jack heard the sound of his skull being crushed and then felt a pain unlike any before. Then ... silence.

-⟨○⟩○⟨○⟩-

Jack awoke in his bed with his head engulfed in the same skull-crushing pain as when he was in the giant mouth. "Oh, Lord, help! It hurts! It hurts!" The pain started to taper off and eventually leveled off enough to where Jack could squint his way to the bathroom for some ibuprofen. As much as his heart refuted it, his gut had to admit that something just didn't make sense about his spiritual visits to Rachel. Previously he had been able to dismiss it by just being new at the whole transcendental experience, but now there was too much of a pattern evolving. He thought about Nicki and her visits to Rachel. Were they as painful as his were? A sense of pity brushed across his heart for her. He dismissed it and turned his mind back to Rachel's face. It was the most beautiful thing in his life.

32

READY! AIM!

The old truck finally fired up after a few turns, and the lights illuminated the early-morning mist hovering in the air. Old-fashioned pipe organ music played a classical hymn, and Jay tried to see if he could guess it before the elderly radio voice told its name. Although not really of that generation, he loved the old hymns. He loved the stories in and behind each one of them. He imagined the small churches they were sung in and the struggles of the people who sang them. Did they have any more or less struggles than the people of today?

He was sure they didn't. Evil was evil from the garden, and its objective remained constant. Coasting down the short driveway and then being fed a bit of gas, the truck worked its way out of the neighborhood onto the interstate along with the thousands of other cars trying to beat the Friday morning rush. Jay wasn't going to work today. His one-and-a-half-hour trip was to visit an old friend in a more normally paced town. Lenny and Jay had become friends through Lenny's son, David. David was a friend from the neighborhood and church who had been diagnosed with terminal cancer at only forty years of age. Jay visited David frequently during his final year just to talk about whatever came up. During a valley in that horrid year, David had been hospitalized. Lenny had come into town to stay with his son and Jay met him on a visit. There was an instant bond of friendship between them, and that friendship had lasted even to this day. But now, it was Lenny's turn to endure the trial of cancer, which he was doing with a boldness in Christ like his son before him. It was Jesus who had brought them all together, and it was Jesus who was their favorite topic of discussion.

Beating rush hour through Houston and then taking a more leisurely pace thereafter, Jay timed his arrival so as not to be too early. Pulling his faithful and tired truck to the curb, he approached the door of the light-brown brick house. He tapped on the door and waited, hoping that his well-intentioned visit didn't turn into an early-morning inconvenience. The door opened to show an older man with a youthful sparkle in his eyes.

"I hope I'm not too early," Jay said quietly in case anyone else might be sleeping in.

Lenny shook his head, smiling. "No, come on in!" He motioned with his hand in an oversize gesture. "How was your drive?" It was the usual type of question a man asks another man after a road trip.

"Perfect. I made good time." It was the usual type of answer a man gives another man after a road trip. After some warm-up conversation about family and the latest reports from the doctors—who actually said that he should've been gone over two years ago—the conversation turned, as it always did, to Jesus and spiritual issues. These conversations were a mix of theology, books, personal struggles and insights, and others' struggles. Both of them could discuss these things for hours, but knowing that limitations of health must be regarded, Jay quickly turned to Jack's recent disclosure of his spiritual sightings.

"Have you ever heard of such a thing?" Jay asked with an appearance of deep contemplation.

Lenny shook his head. "No. I've heard of missionaries in remote places running into demon-possessed tribes but never anyone who actually saw them."

"I definitely believe him, and I believe it has God's fingerprints all over it. I just can't figure out why. Not that I could or would need to, but it would just seem strange to let someone see this without something else going on."

"Well"—Lenny pulled at his long mustache—"the one thing you can be sure of is that there must be some pretty severe spiritual warfare going on." Jay nodded, and his mind raced, thinking about Jack in such a tremendous battle at such an early age. Lenny suggested some prayer support, and they held hands and prayed.

"That's a good start, and I'm sure you've been praying already, but I'm going to put this one on the Warrior Wire."

Jay looked puzzled. In the years of knowing Lenny, he hadn't yet heard of this. Lenny read Jay's face and explained, "The Sunday school class I teach, Senior Warriors, has a prayer chain we call the Warrior Wire." They both chuckled at the name. "Yeah, you laugh, but it's a good old-fashioned telephone prayer chain. I tell you one thing—the Devil doesn't think it's so funny! We've seen the power of God work in tremendous ways."

Jay recognized the blessing to have such an amazing team of prayer warriors to help Jack. After a couple more hours of conversation, a light lunch on TV trays, and an exchange of heartfelt good-byes, Jay picked up his keys to drive home, and Lenny picked up his phone to drive the Warriors into battle.

33

FIRE!

Spaw was prostrate in the sixth chanted repetition of his sixth and final prayer of the day to his dark lord. "Satan is great. He is my master, and I am his slave. He is my power and gives me success in battle. My worship is for him alone. Satan is great above all."

Concluding this last utterance, he lifted himself to his knees and listened. There was a whirring sound in the atmosphere around him. Instinctively, his wings stood erect, and he sprang to his feet, ready to pounce. His eyes scoured the heavens, as did his ears. He had never heard a sound such as this. The whirring was getting louder, but he couldn't exactly tell from which direction it came. His servants were starting to panic like herds of animals escaping a forest fire; only they were coming from several different directions.

Spaw narrowed his eyes to lengthen his vision and saw seven clouds of red descending from high above. The clouds began to take the shape of funnels, and Spaw realized what was about to come down. Immediately Spaw thought that he should recall his servants to the same protective formation he had used with the first tornado, but his courage failed him, and his stare became fixated on the spirals now bursting into full-flamed tornadoes. Two of his cohorts flew up to him for guidance, but finding him like a statue, they took to their wings and fled.

The seven tornadoes whirled recklessly at light speed across the territory, and many demons were again swept pell-mell to their eviction. Spaw snapped to attention and reached for the scar on his head. He now realized that the injury the lightning bolt had given him had weakened his courage. Unable to muster any protective forces, Spaw shot like a falling star across the sky, weaving in and out of the flames.

Safe outside of the storms' radii, Spaw turned his head back to see if they had died down. Seeing that they had, he brought himself to a complete stop, uninjured. Seeing the smoke billowing from such a far distance, he lifted his fists in rage and cursed the enemy. A high-pitched whirl sounded through the air, and much faster than even he could fly, a flaming spear sailed over the gulf, struck him in the chest, and exited his back just outside the base of his right wing. Spaw was thrown and twisted violently backward and again lay prostrate. He closed his eyes in agony, and in defiance of such a blow, he pulled himself to his knees and then stood, upright but hunched over. He would live to fight another day, but that may take a while.

Swallowing hard, he looked at the flaming spear that had been hurled so far. He walked over to it but was afraid to touch it. He sniffed. It was that same aroma he had smelled that day in the truck when Jay's prayer had pulled Kate Castle from his grip. Enraged, Spaw stomped on the spear. It sizzled into dust at his touch. Unable to fly just yet, Spaw started back for his abode at a jog. He knew these storms might be a good indication that he was losing Jack. And that was not something he could live with.

He saw another demon, Mercury, flying overhead, and he summoned him. Mercury realized that Spaw had been injured, but seeing that it wasn't fatal, he determined not to betray him to others who were eager to advance. Spaw gathered his strength to hide his weaknesses. His second-biggest concern was Mithras finding out and coming to fulfill his promise. Spaw grabbed Mercury by the throat to show the still potent state of his strength and asked, "Where is Mithras?"

Mercury, moving around the globe on a daily basis, gaspingly reported that Mithras was embattled with Baal over a dispute in the eastern quadrant and wouldn't be available for several days. Spaw, having what he needed and not trusting Mercury with the confidentiality of the question he had asked, took Mercury's head in his powerful jaws and chewed until he separated top from torso. This done, he swallowed the evidence that any discussion had ever taken place. The meal strengthened Spaw, and he took to his wings in a slow but steady pace.

34

THE TRUTH COMES OUT

Without the regular company of Nicki, Jack felt hollow. He wondered how he could ever really be as happy again without a girl as encouraging and pretty as Nicki to share his life with. Sunk in a moment of depression, which was aided by it being a Friday night without any popular plans, he closed his door and switched on his Xbox.

"All hail Mithras!"

"Yeah, yeah!" Jack sarcastically remarked into his headset.

"Servant Jack, I'm not sure I understood you correctly," a strange monotone voice answered his sarcasm. Jack ignored it, hoping it would go away. Then the fanatic stranger spoke again. "Servant Jack, Houston, Texas?"

"Yes," Jack replied, his face falling flush sensing a threat at the announcement of his general location.

"Servant Jack. All hail Mithras!" the stranger repeated in an intolerant tone that pushed Jack into submission.

"Uh, yeah, hail Mithras," he murmured with a twinge of nausea.

"Enter into my service!" the voice commanded with a hint of swagger, and Jack's game of service began.

Jack had continuously advanced from the level of follower to worshipper and now to servant in Mithras, and he was now able to time warp to the higher levels on his way to attack heaven itself. His first-person character circled the air above ancient Rome and spied a bonfire of heavenly activity in the Coliseum. The emperor Nero had dressed Christians in animal skins and was feeding them to a ravenous pack of wild dogs. Christian prayers were engulfing the arena in flames and angels as the competing demons swarmed like vultures for opportunistic assaults.

Somehow amid the confusion, he found that Jordan, Sam, and Jerome were online and joining the party. He didn't want it to appear as if he were stalking them, so he ignored them and hoped they would notice his call sign. They did.

"Jack, is that you?" asked Sam over the headset.

Jack's spirits were lifted, although his mind wondered why they hadn't invited him over to play.

"Hey, yeah, it's me," Jack replied.

"Cool! What's the best approach here?"

Sam's question flattered Jack. It felt good to be back in the expert role with his friends. "I can take the lead if y'all want to just spread out behind me. I'll use my flare glare to cut us a path to the arena floor."

"Good deal! We're ready!" Jordan agreed as the team swooped down through flames and glowing angelic bodies. The team finally alit on the dirt floor of the arena to beat the dogs to the massacre.

Only an hour had passed, and after several attempts, the team finally accomplished their mission and passed the level. Jack could hear the congratulatory yells over his headset, and he wished he was there.

"Do y'all want to go to the dungeons next?" asked Jack, ready for more.

"Sorry, Jack, we've got to go," Sam said. He didn't give many details as to where they had to go, so Jack filled in that it was some gathering or party that he wasn't invited to.

"Oh, that's fine!" he said without any suspicion of disappointment. He saw their online status icons disappear, and he felt lonely.

Jack didn't like being alone. He thought back several months when it hadn't seemed to bother him so much. What had changed? He wasn't sure, but he had a dull ache in his soul that needed some kind of ointment. His mind turned to Rachel and felt a desperate whimpering in his heart.

"Jack ... help ... hurry ... ooh."

Jack closed his eyes to concentrate more and paused his breathing for additional silence.

"Jack ... you have to come now ... I need you ... ooh."

Jack lay back on his bed and let his mind coast transcendentally upward for a minute. He found himself sitting down in the usual woods with the familiar hum in the distance.

"Jack ... over here," Rachel's voice called to him.

Jack swiveled his head but saw no Rachel. His eye caught a motion in some tall grass. A hand, fair and beautiful with red-tipped nails, was raised. Jack sprinted to the hand and found Rachel lying in agony at the other end of it.

"Rachel, what happened?" Jack asked as his heart sank and then quivered in his chest. Rachel struggled to open her enchanting eyes, which were now wrenched in pain.

"Our time is up. Something happened, and the Ohm has compressed our time. We only have a few minutes before I have to go back to my clander, and you ..." Rachel stopped and let a tear drop from her eyes. "You ... will be relegated to the Pergyss."

Jack's mind raced, wondering what could have happened to cause such a drastic change. The only thing he could think of was Nicki, but Rachel had said herself that they didn't really need her. Jack looked down, and through Rachel's pale white dress, he saw a spot of red on her right ribcage.

"Rachel, you're bleeding!" Jack observed and cradled her in his arms. Rachel grimaced and then let a small smile of pleasure spread across her face at his embrace.

"I'll be all right ... oh ..." she played.

Realizing that her situation was serious, Jack asked, "What can I do to help you?"

Rachel's smile uncontrollably broadened, and her eyes twinkled. Jack noticed this, and it struck him as peculiar. "Oh ... the only thing you can do now is to graduate to eternity, where we can be joined," Rachel whimpered as a last hope.

Jack clarified again, "You mean ... suicide?"

Rachel lifted her body a bit on her own strength. "Jack, that word has been given such a stigma. All you're doing is transitioning from one life to your true life. It's like taking a chariot ride—like we used to do." Rachel paused and looked into his eyes for her next play.

The words of Jay about the name of Jesus came back to Jack's mind as if he were standing beside him: "Demons flee at His name!" If Rachel didn't flinch at the name of Jesus, then Jack would join her. But if she did, then at least he would have found her out for what she was. Jack's whole body transformed into one giant agitated nerve and trembled with fear—the fear of offending her, the fear of self-murder, the fear of finding out the truth.

Rachel perceived this change and calculated her next urgent plea. Jack spoke first. "Rachel ..." Jack hesitated, and Rachel sat up completely on her own strength. "Rachel ... I was just wondering if you, by any chance, knew who ..." Jack paused again, seeing Rachel's eyes widen as if they were anticipating a tsunami.

"Oh ... Jack ... I can't live without you! I need you to hurry back and transition. There's a gun in your room. Oh ... please ..." Rachel implored him hastily.

Jack gathered his courage, knowing that he must ask the question, and he quickly spit it out, "Rachel, I need to know if you've ever seen *Jesus!*"

In the instance of a fatal shot, a silence hovers as the echoing crack dissipates. And so it was with Jack's utterance of this one name,

Jesus. Jack, on his knees, holding Rachel's previously limp and dying body, stared at her, and she stared back at him for what seemed a silent hour.

Then, just as fast as the first shot rang out and ushered in complete silence, a second shot rang out and ushered in pandemonium. A ferocious, beastlike roar blasted saliva across Jack's cheeks as it erupted from Rachel's smooth mouth. Instinctively, Jack sprang to his feet, dropping Rachel on the ground, but to his surprise she beat him to a standing adversarial position. In one lift of the arms and stretch of the wings, the shell-like facade of the beautiful Rachel was shattered. Jack found himself now face-to-face with a humongous, powerful, and now enraged creature in the gargoyle form of a demon.

Spaw flashed forward at Jack in a pounce, and in the instance before his hooked claws made contact with Jack's throat, Jack called out for help. "Jesus!"

The power of the name sent Spaw flying backward as if flung by a bomb blast. Jack looked around him for an escape but saw none. The only thing his eyes could focus on was the infuriated predatory demon whose eyes were riveted on him. Spaw started crawling back to Jack even before the push of the blast subsided. His claws were digging into the ground and flinging earth and leaves behind him.

Jack felt a confidence wash over him, and he said boldly, "In the name of Jesus, get away!"

A circle of power rippled from Jack in an even larger blast, and Spaw was sent flailing horns over heels about fifty yards away, where he thudded against a large oak tree, which splintered under the collision. While still watching Spaw gather himself for another assault, Jack saw a redbird fly past the demon's head toward him. Spaw stopped to watch the bird; he had seen this kind before, and it hadn't ended up well for him. The red bird, leaving a small stream of flame behind him, streaked over Jack's head.

He heard a voice emanate from it: "Come!" Jack turned and saw a full-length mirror standing the distance of a driveway behind him. He saw his true image standing there, where he had left it, what seemed like years ago. The redbird pierced the surface of the mirror leaving a ripple of light across its surface. Jack sprinted to follow. He could see his false image, the one that was beautifully exaggerated, become larger and larger as he closed the distance. From behind him, he could hear Spaw dashing madly and closing fast. Jack was within two more strides of the portal, and he caught the image of the fuming beast lunging through the air. Jack, still in full sprint, did a headfirst baseball slide into the lowest part of the mirror as if it were a rabbit hole.

Spaw, jetting at eye level, collided with the mirror and crashed to the ground. Still sprawled on the ground but safely on the other side of the mirror, Jack looked through his reflection to see the flaring demon insanely pounding, scratching, and biting at the glass. Still trembling with the fear that the demon might break through the shield, Jack closed his eyes and prayed, "Oh Jesus, thank You, Lord! I'm so sorry for what I've done."

⊸∞∞⊸

Jack opened his eyes to feel his face buried in a tear-soaked pillow but breathed a sigh of relief when he looked around and saw that he was safe in his bedroom, which was dimly lit by his clock. It was two thirty in the morning. Jack's pulse hadn't completely slowed to normal yet, and he took some deep breaths to try and help it. Impressed upon his mind was Ephesians 6. He grabbed his phone and tapped up his Bible app. The bright light was harsh on his eyes, and he clicked it off again. Surely this couldn't be divine guidance. The impression was so faint—it must be his imagination.

Jack lay back in his bed and closed his eyes. His curiosity now sat him back up, and he tapped up the app again, scrolling to Ephesians 6 of the English Standard Version. He read the first verse: "Children, obey your parents in the Lord, for this is right." *What? That's not very profound,* he thought, doubtful of the impression. He *knew* it was just his imagination. Then an impression came a second time to his mind: Ephesians 6:10. Jack's curiosity moved him to scroll further down, and chills burst through his body as he read, "Finally, be strong in the Lord and in the strength of his might. Put on the whole armor of God, that you may be able to stand against the schemes of the devil. For we do not wrestle against flesh and blood, but against the rulers, against the authorities, against the cosmic powers over this present darkness, against the spiritual forces of evil in the heavenly places."

In a blink, everything became clear. Jack's mind flashed back to earlier in the year when he was enthralled by a supposedly true movie involving a demonic possession and the dark power that came with it. He recalled how he had been fascinated with it—perhaps too much—and how he had playfully uttered some of the chants to scare Bobby and the girl that was with them.

His mind drifted back to the first time he'd seen the white bird in the woods that had led him through the mirror—only now, instead of seeing the beautiful novelty that had ensnared him, he smelled the rotten stench of death and saw the withering trees dropping their leaves at the bird's touch. He thought about the drink that had gradually tasted so sweet, but now he knew that it was a bitter intoxicant that had choked him. His mind raced through his entire ordeal—the violence, the music, the concerts, the dogs, the alcohol, the popularity, the lust, the gaming, the wreck—how much evil had he chosen to ignore because it felt so good? He imagined how God had protected him in ways he had never seen. He replayed the imagery of the vicious demon being flung backward and his escape aided by the little red bird. He understood that without God's grace, he would've been consigned to hell, the victim of his own intentionally rebellious crimes.

Jack wept profusely and vowed to do all he could to expose evil for what it was so that others might choose to trust Jesus with their lives and not have to go through what he did. Dancing with the Devil in the pale moonlight may sound poetically thrilling, but people had to know what happened once the music stopped. Now on his knees, Jack turned his eyes heavenward and prayed, "Here I am, Lord. Send me!"

Jack lay back in his bed with a peace about him that he could only explain as being from Jesus. He closed his eyes and, unexpectedly, very quickly drifted back to sleep, where he embarked on a dream more pleasant than his last.

⛓

Jack was floating in space, astonished by its vastness, which made him comprehend just how small he really was. A dazzling creature glided up to him—an angel. His appearance was of a large man with two white, feathered wings spread behind him. His robe was a brilliant white pulled tight at the waist by a golden belt, from which hung a mighty, flaming sword. His voice was firm and commanding with words that sounded more like divine music than human words. Nonetheless, Jack understood them perfectly.

"Fear not! For I am here from the King, Jesus!" he proclaimed proudly. Jack bowed his head and began to bend his floating body in worship, but the angel stopped him. "No! All worship belongs to the Almighty! I'm but a messenger. Do not worship me!"

Jack nodded, still mute from amazement. The angel grabbed Jack's arm, and they shot through the atmosphere, closer to earth. Jack marveled at the beauty of God's creation. Then the blue of the oceans turned to an inky black, and the masses of land appeared covered up. Jack looked at the angel for an explanation, but still gripping Jack's arm he pulled him closer to a high, cloud-level view. Jack saw that the black seas had indeed covered up the entire planet and that they were turbulent in large hurricane-size whirlpools.

The angel said, "Here is the fallen world. It is a system of being, understanding, and behaving manifested in organizations and channels social, religious, artistic, and educational, which has been perverted by Satan and is continually stirred by demons to lead men from God, the loving Creator." Jack's face fell limp, and he repressed the tears that pressed against his eyes.

The angel fluttered his wings and propelled them to an even lower cloud view. There were hundreds of thousands of bodies floating in the currents of the dark ocean. Most of them were facedown as dead men, but some still twitched like dying fish. From this level, the stink of rotting flesh burned Jack's nostrils, and his eyes tried to cleanse themselves in more tears, which were mixed with the sadness of Jack's heart, which broke at the sight. "See the fate of the current of life," the angel sang.

Jack's heart lightened when he noticed the deathly waters receding, and he looked hopefully at the angel. The angel replied with his own look, telling Jack to look again. He did, and the blackness completed its recess, leaving the people standing upright on dry ground. Their bodies and expressions were miserable. They were scantily clothed, and any skin that was not covered was festering red with infections or black with rot. They were all under a sentence of hard labor, carrying large boulders that burned their flesh, sending wafts of steam into the already rancid air. Amazingly, though, their faces were bright and shiny, with smiles that stretched from ear to ear. But on a second inspection, Jack saw that they wore masks that were held tightly in place by a series of screws across their foreheads. Jack was puzzled by this scene and glanced at his host for an explanation, which was immediately provided. "This is fallen man. He toils in slavery under the deception of fulfillment."

The angel tugged on Jack's arm, preparing him to move again. As they plunged down to the ground, Jack turned his head, awaiting contact with the ground, but there was none. He opened his eyes to see that they had moved below the ground but still maintained a transparent view. He looked at the people above the ground and saw that each one of them had an umbilical cord dropping from his or her navel. Moving his gaze deeper below, he followed the tangles of cords to see what might be at the other end. He was repulsed when he saw a gargantuan, filthy sow wallowing in a slough of her own dung. He quickly turned to his host again to understand this bizarre picture. The host, with a grim and sad look, reported, "This is the fleshly nature of man, which he attaches to sin."

By this time, Jack had sufficient familiarity with his host, and he ventured a question. "Can't we help them? Can't we take your sword and cut their cords?"

The angel didn't offer a reply but lifted Jack above ground, where they stood face-to-face with a man. "Well, hello there! What a fine day it is!" the man spoke from behind his mask.

The angel replied, "Sir, I can see that you are in torment. Would you like me to cut you loose and take you to eternal rest?"

The man became indignant, looked around with apparently nervous glances, and shouted, "Get out of here, you infidel!"

The angel persisted, "But, sir, you are exhausted and dying. You need help, and I can release you from your agony with one quick stroke." The host made one motion to retrieve and lift his flaming blade above his head; he cast his eyes on the man's cord, which he had a mind to sever. The man yelped, dropped his scalding boulder, and curled up to protect his cord. He didn't look up at the angel but lifted his voice in rage with a torrent of curses.

The angel looked at Jack and explained, "No one can make the choice for him. He must submit his own flesh for the killing."

With a tone of dejection, Jack asked, "So there's nothing I can do to help?" He recalled his previous vow to expose evil and his availing himself to be sent.

"Oh, there most definitely is!" the angel said. "Abide in the Light, Jesus, and His Light will show others the truth and set them free in Him. Jesus has conquered the world, and in Him, they are more than conquerors!"

Jack felt so proud of having such a sovereign King, he erupted in praise with a part of an old hymn, "All hail King Jesus! All hail Emanuel! King of Kings! Lord of Lords! I worship You!"

Upon lowering his hands from their lifted praise, he opened his eyes to find that he and his host were surrounded by people. Just from one chorus of praise, hundreds of people drew near and held out their hands, cupped for water. The angel looked at Jack. "See. You can help by pointing them toward Jesus, the Life!"

Jack rolled over in his bed with a smile on his face from such a pleasant dream. Pulling his legs over the bedside, he checked his body with his mind. He couldn't ever remember feeling so fresh, energetic, and joyful.

35

A SACRIFICE OF REJECTION

Seeing that the mirror wouldn't crack under his force and knowing that his white bird illusion would be of no value, Spaw watched Jack vanish into midair. He recomposed himself, undeterred in his quest, and returned to what had previously been his safe abode to begin plotting a different strategy. His cohort clustered around him, fearful of his temper, and proved to be of little assistance in seeing a way to regain direct contact with Jack. A loud abhorrent voice chanted through the air, calling all demons to prayers. Spaw's cohort immediately dropped in worship. Spaw dropped down, but his mind was too lost in his vengeance to echo the empty words.

His mind loosened in abstaining from the mind-numbing repetition of the chants, an idea came to him. Spaw called forth his cohort and all his subjects that served in the Houston area. Spaw stood on a raised stage as his legion bowed in fearful honor of him. He called forth a crouching demon called Rejection from his own cohort, who moved in a hunched crawl onto the platform. Rejection was an especially repulsive demon who could boast the destruction of millions of teenage lives by becoming their worst fear. Forcing himself on his prey, he could drive them to practically any deadly end in flight. Drugs, abuse, sensuality, cutting, starvation, homosexuality—there wasn't a single gate he didn't use.

Spaw peered down in disgust at the pathetic but useful creature who believed himself to be receiving a special mission. Rejection met his look and then immediately dropped his eyes to the ground. Spaw lifted his wings and took hold of the demon. Spaw's massive claws gripped his servant's horns, and the talons of his powerful feet plunged into hunched back. In disbelief, Rejection began to hiss in resistance, but Spaw's stinging tail silenced him with a slash of the throat. Spaw's huge wings raised him in the air as he separated head from body, ensuring death. Magically, a cauldron appeared atop a roaring fire, and Spaw hung Rejection above it, letting his blood fill it and boil. The legion of demons erupted in a unity of approving hisses.

Spaw ordered his cohort to the stage, and as each demon took a chalice, he began to serve gulps of the black tea to the others. The terrible brew had a terrible effect on its recipients, filling them with the same repulsive power as its deceased host. Spaw knew that this was a drastic move and not without risk. If his legion showed too much repulsiveness toward their peasants, he knew that the humans would turn and run directly into the arms of the enemy. Nonetheless, Spaw was desperate to drink the cold blood of his vengeance, which was evaporating fast.

Each one getting his hit, a common fury moved across them all as if repulsed at each other's image. Spaw roared to call them to order and then addressed them. "My legion!" he proclaimed.

"All hail mighty Spaw!" they replied with one voice.

Spaw arrogantly raised his arms to receive their worship. "I've made such a tremendous sacrifice because you have a tremendous objective."

36

A Sacrifice of Rejection Plays Out

Still refreshed from the weekend rest, Jack walked with an energetic step toward the entrance of the school commons. He heard an uproar from within and saw thick black smoke seeping out from the doors. He whispered a prayer as he quickly closed the distance and threw the door open. Expecting to find a crowd of students stricken with panic, he instead found a crowd of students stricken with cold, shunning eyes. He moved carefully through the forest of people who were as unmoving as trees in his path. Finally coming up on Caden and Bobby, their faces hidden in their phones, he greeted them. In turn, they looked up at him and ignored him without the slightest acknowledgement and returned to their own play. Jack slumped down against the wall and lowered his head to his drawn up knees. The commons was teeming with the noise of life, but Jack felt as if he had been pushed outside, a rejected outcast under the punishment of silence.

After what seemed like an hour, the bell rang, but Jack kept his place on the ground. He'd been knocked down and wasn't going to fight the masses only to get knocked down again. Lifting his eyes to see only a few distant stragglers, he pulled himself up and walked mindlessly to his first class. He was thirty seconds tardy, but even the teacher seemed to ignore him. He felt transparent, he felt unclean, and he felt like a throwaway.

Between periods, he would move silently through the hallways, keeping to himself and trying his best to avoid the unforgiving shoulders of others. Students he passed would either avoid eye contact, offer a despising glance, or a look of indifference; of the three options he wasn't sure which hurt the most. By fifth period, he had almost convinced himself that this was all just a bad dream. What could he have possibly done to elicit such severe rejection?

He pushed his head into his locker as if to search for something, although it was really just an attempt to temporarily escape from the hurt and hide the tears that awaited permission to flow. Inside, his mind habitually turned to Rachel for a comforting hit, but then he immediately rebuked himself and turned instead to Jesus in prayer. A strong confidence washed over him and renewed his strength.

"Hey, Jack!" he heard a voice call from behind. It was the first time in the entire day anyone had spoken to him.

Pulling his head back into the light of the hallway, he saw Faith. Good old Faith, trustworthy Faith, delightful Faith, beautiful Faith! Oh, what a great friend was Faith! Jack was so happy that, much to her amazement, he gave her a big hug as if they were long-lost siblings suddenly thrust into reunion.

"Okay! Good to see you too!" Faith said with a look of pleasant surprise on her face.

Embarrassed from a tear that disobediently fell, Jack turned his head and sentenced it to absorption on his sleeve. The bell rang out, announcing the start of sixth period.

Faith blurted, "Well, gotta go! I just saw you and thought I'd say hey ... so hey!" She spun on her heels and started down the hall.

Jack wasn't about to let what felt like his only friend in the world go that easy. He quickly closed his locker and called out, "Oh, hey, wait up!" Faith turned her head to see Jack pull up beside her.

"Hey, what class do you have?" Jack was starving for conversation.

"I have physics. Mr. Jenkins."

"I'll walk with you."

"What do you have?"

"Spanish. Miss Fish. Or, as we call her, *Senorita Pescada*."

"Isn't her class at the other end of the school?"

Jack would've ordinarily been embarrassed at going so far out of his way for a girl because it may send the wrong message, but under the circumstances, he really didn't care. "Yeah, it's no big deal."

Faith wasn't sure what to make of this. On one hand, she felt flattered, as if Jack might like her as more than a friend. On the other hand, if he was just doing a random act of kindness, she didn't want to be her own trickster who fooled herself. So she logically concluded that it was probably just the latter and walked along, enjoying the small talk.

37

AND PLAYS OUT MORE

The next day at school was a bit better. There was no soot-filled smoke seeping from the doors, and when Jack walked in, he only received a few cold stares and averted gazes. As was his habit, he made his way over to Bobby at the trophy case. Caden wasn't there yet.

"Hey, Bobby."

"Hey, Jack."

Jack was relieved to see that Bobby hadn't ignored him again. Bobby could see the small expression on Jack's face and explained, "Hey, sorry about yesterday. I was just in a real bad mood. My mom started yelling at me for eating all the cereal. And—I'm not exaggerating—she was coming unglued! Over stinking cereal! Anyway, she apologized today, so everything seems to be back to normal." Jack nodded in acceptance of the apology.

Caden walked up and greeted them, "Hey, Bobby. Hey, Jack."

They returned the greeting. Caden continued, "Hey, Jack, sorry about yesterday. I was just in a real bad mood." Bobby and Jack looked at each other and laughed.

"Dude! That's what I just said!"

They all three laughed and took up their standing positions holding up the wall, waiting for the bell opening the school for business.

-◇-◯-◇-◯-◇-

The bell for first lunch rang out, and Jack was on his way to the cafeteria when Sam, Jordan, Jerome, and Moose came walking by on their way to the parking lot.

"Hey, little buddy!" Moose said to Jack.

Jack was relieved to find that they weren't ignoring him again either.

They all paused, and Jordan put his arm around Jack's shoulders and asked, "Hey, Jack, you want to come with us to lunch?"

Jack's heart swelled; finally he was being included. He guessed that they had really started to like him as a friend, not because of his gaming skills or Nicki's popularity.

"Sure! Where are we going?" he gladly accepted. Jordan looked around at the others, and they all smiled. "Well, you see … there are these two freshman girls who are pretty wild." The group nodded and smiled at their plan, except for Jack, whose gut told him this was about to head south. Jordan continued, "We told them to meet us for an extended lunch at Moose's cousin's apartment, which is only a mile away. We're going to blow off class and let's just say that the movie we're going to watch should deliver a pretty good time!"

The group started laughing, and Jerome added, "Yeah, in fact it's called *Cindy Delivers*! Get it?"

Jack's heart sank at the title because he knew what kind of movie this was. He still wanted to be friends with four of the most popular guys in the whole school, but he knew that he couldn't be part of something so—well, so nasty. Jack's face gave the answer before he said anything. By his look, each one of the boys felt his condemnation of the act slap them squarely across their strong jaws.

"Well … I already told Faith that I'd eat with her today," Jack lied.

Jordan pulled his arm away from Jack and shook his head with an eye roll to give an insult of his own. Moose followed with his own insult. "Aw, how innocent! We shouldn't have even thought about defiling the virgin boy!"

The group laughed, and Jack felt the sting of their whip. But it wasn't over yet. Sam looked at him and smirked. "I'm disappointed, Jack! I thought you were growing into one of us. You are still just a kid!"

The boys, all shaking their heads in pity at innocent little Jack, turned to head out for their adventure. Moose, however, bent down to Jack's ear and whispered, "Listen, if you tell anyone about this, you won't just have Stone to deal with. Got it?"

Jack stared straight into space and nodded his head. The feeling of betrayal and rejection mixed with a threat of violence hurt his gut more than any punch ever could.

38

A MISSION OF BETRAYAL

Spaw was pleased with the degree of injury he was able to inflect on Jack through Rejection. But Spaw was not one to rest on his last success; he was constantly dissatisfied and planning his next attack. Seeing where Jack had turned, he knew that he must nudge him into a new direction. His newest poison of choice was Hatred. Hatred was a hydra-type beast with so many heads that it was humanly impossible to defeat. It offered a gentle head for its victims to strike down and then slithered another from behind, where it secretly chewed its venom into its victims' heels. It was easy for people to slay the type of hatred that leads to violence, but just as the victims were congratulating themselves, they chose to ignore or exclude another because of inconvenience or a lack of similarity. How broad and camouflaged was the hatred that violated the love of Christ.

Spaw's aim was to inject some of Nicki's hatred with the dart of betrayal. He perched on a branch and carefully weighed his words and maneuvers as he waited for Nicki to appear. Spaw listened to the air and set one of his cohorts to the hum of the Ohm. The demon started up, and within six notes Nicki appeared in the patch of clover below. Spaw bolted down from his roost to assume the mask of Rachel.

Nicki lay back in the clover, letting its coolness soak into her body. With her eyes closed, she rolled her head to relax her neck and let the earthy aroma bring tranquility to her lungs. Opening her eyes, she found that she wasn't alone. Rachel was lying next to her in the patch with a pleasant smile to match Nicki's. "It feels good, doesn't it?" Rachel asked as she curled up into a ball and then stretched spread-eagle over the green.

Nicki mimicked her motion. "Oh, it sure does."

Eager to get to business, Rachel sat up and pulled herself into a cross-legged position. Nicki again mimicked her to begin the conversation.

"So what's new?" Rachel asked with an eager schoolgirl look to disarm Nicki.

Nicki hesitated because she knew how highly Rachel thought of Jack, but her own feelings of scorn were too intense to avoid the matter. "Rachel, I don't care how special Jack is in the true life. He is absolutely not that in my life." Rachel looked shocked and nodded as if to agree with Nicki, who continued, "He rejected me!"

Rachel moved her hand to cover her opened mouth and inhaled in surprise, saying, "Oh, sweetie, what happened?"

Nicki gritted her teeth, feeling a kick of scorn from within her, and spit out a cussword in an attempt to better describe her opinion of Jack. Rachel almost let loose an audible laugh at seeing scorn work so well. "Wow, that bad, huh? I'm so sorry, but at least I can see what needs to be done," Rachel consoled.

"What's that?" Nicki inquired.

"True love. Isn't that what you want—what you need?"

"With all my heart, Rachel. I don't like this feeling. I want it gone. What do I need to do to get more true love?"

Rachel gave her a warm, sympathetic smile to pave the way for her words. "Well, brace yourself because you're probably not going to be able to fully understand the next step, but you'll just have to trust me."

Nicki continued to fidget from the discomfort of her scorn but looked with hope at Rachel and nodded.

"Nicki … if you want to experience true love, you need to win Jack back. He is your key to being fulfilled."

Nicki's face became downcast at this. She stood and turned away from Rachel, taking a few steps in grimaced contemplation. Spaw became indignant at her turned back, but realizing the delicacy of the matter, he bore with the insolence. Rachel stood, stepped after Nicki, and embraced her from behind. She whispered into Nicki's ear with a tone of assurance, "Nicki, I know it's painful and goes against everything you are feeling right now, but love will win in the end."

Nicki gritted her teeth and swallowed hard. Intellectually, it made sense, but her emotions were just so blistered that she knew this was going to be difficult. Rachel read her and continued imploring, "Nicki, think about it like this. You didn't get that killer body from sitting around all day and eating cupcakes. No, you worked hard. You did things that you didn't like. You starved yourself, you woke up early, you exercised—you had to earn it. Well, this is like that.

You have to fight through your hatred and get him back. Then, once this is done, only then can I show you the next step, which will take you closer to the Ohm."

Nicki loosened up at seeing that there was a bigger picture Rachel was working from and turned to submit to her plan when the scorn within her began slashing her in rage. "I can't do it! I won't do it!" Nicki pouted and rolled out of Rachel's arms.

Rachel drew up to her again for a flattering compromise. "Wow, Nicki, I underestimated your pain. Well, there is another way to accomplish the same progress in the Ohm."

The feeling of this offer already appealed to Nicki, and she met Rachel's eyes with a look indicating as much. "Oh yeah? What is it?"

"Well, it's betrayal," Rachel said with a scheming look.

At this suggestion, the fire of scorn burning inside of Nicki turned to a flame of coolness, coaxing her into the trap. Nicki smiled and replied with eager eyes, "Now I like the sound of that!"

"You still have to get back together with Jack. But the whole purpose will be so that you can betray him with one of his friends."

"Can't it be with Stone instead?"

"No. Revenge is best served cold, and the only way to chill it is through someone he loves as a friend."

Nicki's mind clicked to the extreme logic, and she shivered from the feeling of cold water being pushed through her veins. "Rachel, you are so good!"

Rachel smiled and gave her a warm hug. "Just remember—the point is to get you closer to the Ohm. Jack and his friends are just tools to help you get there quicker." Nicki returned her smile deviously; she was truly going to enjoy this task.

"Oh, I almost forgot!" exclaimed Rachel, as if she had almost neglected to give Nicki something of great value. "Because this won't be a very easy thing to do, I'm going to teach you something very important. It's the spell of enchantment."

Nicki's grin widened, and her eyes narrowed in want of this new power. "A spell! That's awesome, Rachel!"

Rachel grabbed Nicki's hands and looked her in the eyes. "Okay, here are the words to remember ..." Rachel broke out in a cold, hissing melody. "*Shhhhen-chan-tran-trasss, shhheeck sssuut yyyaq. O-po dre-noirrr. Shhhhen-chan-tran-trasss.* Repeat this six times while thinking only about Jack, and the spell will be cast."

Nicki, despite her grades indicating that she struggled with fact retention, repeated the words and mimicked the tone as if she had practiced them in her sleep. Nicki was noticeably proud of her accomplishment, and Rachel affirmed her act by pressing their foreheads affectionately together.

Nicki felt their foreheads touch and her mind continue forward into Rachel. Or had Rachel been pulled into hers? She couldn't exactly tell. Whoever's mind it was, Nicki was seized by the fear of what her departure would be like this time. They were always horrible and left her feeling shattered and undone.

Spaw dropped his mask to watch Nicki's departure. He always enjoyed these exits in which he could creatively torment his peasants. At that moment, Nicki became aware of her cold heart, which pulsed with chilled blood. She felt her heart burn with the type of freeze produced from dry ice. She exhaled with the pain and tried to inhale some warmer air to help stave it off but had no success. With every breath, her now motionless, frozen heart extended its freeze across Nicki's body until she was completely immobile. A second wave of an even deeper chill followed, and Nicki heard her brittle body begin to shatter. In pieces, Nicki's person was an ice pile on the cool patch of clover, which seemed to now sing a song agonizing over her arctic presence. In rebellion, the clover warmed itself in its own melody, causing the fractured ice to melt and pass through to the soil below.

Her body was still numb and in need of thawing, but her mind was in fluid disarray, spread in the melt. She felt crazy and disoriented. She tried to gather her wits, but that was like trying to collect a thousand raindrops as she plunged beside them headlong to the ground. Feeling herself undone in mind and absorbed in insanity, Nicki sobbed, feeling hopeless.

-◇◆◇◆-

Amber and Faith had returned from a youth event at church and were on their way to Amber's room when they heard Nicki sobbing from behind her door. Amber tapped on the door as she opened it. Nicki was sitting on her bed, her face wet with tears. Her disoriented and angry face jerked up to meet Amber's peek through the widening crack. "What?" Nicki exclaimed.

Amber's eyes widened in shock at the sudden and stern remark, as did Faith's, who stood behind her. "Uh, I just heard you crying and wanted to see if I could help," Amber offered in an apologetic tone. "That's all."

Nicki, without softening and now feeling the burn of scorn reignite in her gut, scolded, "Get out!"

Amber hesitated. If she pressed, would Nicki soften? There was obviously something very wrong, but was it really any of her business? Could she really be of any help? These were the questions that convinced Amber to just gently close the door and leave Nicki to be Nicki. It was one of those decisions that she knew one day she might have some painful hindsight over—"I should have ... I could have ..." Nonetheless, she was helpless to help right now, so she walked away.

39

THE MISSION BEGINS

Nicki had been devising a plan on how to best approach Jack for a couple of days. The plan now complete, she had taken her regular social Friday night off to initiate her mission by repeating the hideous spell to ensure success. Feeling the scorn in her gut and reeling from the devious excitement, she tapped out a brief text to Jack. "Need to talk, I'll come by tomorrow." She hit send, and with cool hands, she put in her earbuds, swiped up classic TrashMouth, and played out the various scenarios in her mind—most of them involving Jack being injured in both mind and body.

-◦◦◦◦-

It was a gorgeous Saturday morning, and Jack awoke well rested from a low-key Friday night of hanging out with Caden and Bobby. Grabbing his phone from the charger, he looked to see if any of his friends had yet given an indication of how they might pass the day. His heart jumped to his throat when he saw the text from Nicki. He swiped it open and, with butterflies in his stomach, tapped back "Kk" before he could really weigh the pros and cons of seeing her.

The speech balloon popped up, showing that she was already up. It exploded with a reply: "On my way!"

Jack looked at the time: ten o'clock. He knew that with her immediately being "On my way!" she was eager to have a face-to-face conversation. But what could it be about? Wasn't she hanging out with Stone, that big dummy? Did she want to apologize? Jack's mind played out a multitude of ways this might go, most of them involving him and Nicki kissing and making up.

A *tap, tap, tap* on the door left Avery and Anna Claire, who were still in their pajamas, scrambling toward their rooms. Jack announced to everyone within earshot that he would get it. His heart fluttered as he easily made out the compact brunette image through the frosted glass of the front door. Swallowing his nerves in a gulp, he pulled back the divider and saw Nicki's seemingly sincerely apologetic face.

"Hey," she murmured with meekness. This image and expression was a curveball for Jack. Since when had Nicki ever possessed either remorse or meekness?

"Hey," Jack replied and invited her into the house. Something else was different. She was wearing somewhat modest clothes: a pair of shorts that went down below her extended fingertips, a shirt that had a normal neckline, and only a touch of makeup. Although her attire didn't tease out the male imagination, its discretion was just as attractive. Nicki rubbed his arm when she passed by, and Jack remembered just how much he missed her touch.

"Is there somewhere we can talk?" Nicki asked in an inflection to match the humility of her appearance.

"Sure, why don't we go out back? I'm sure once the girls get dressed, they'll come back and try to find us."

Opening the back door, Jack fended off the attention-starved jumping dog, Harley, and with enough chastisement, she seemed to get the message that they weren't here to play.

"I love your dog," Nicki said and extended her hand toward the disappointed mutt. Harley kept her distance and studied Nicki with a skeptical look. She glanced at Jack and then quickly back at Nicki. Almost as if she could sense something wasn't right, she positioned herself between the two with her back pressed against Jack's leg and her insightful eyes watching Nicki from a safe distance beyond her reach.

"So what's up?" Jack started the conversation.

"Jack, I just wanted to say I'm so sorry for everything I did."

Jack nodded to receive the apology, and inside, he appreciated just how much she was taking responsibility for the malevolent acts. This was completely unlike anything he'd ever seen from her, but it felt good.

"Jack, you've been an example for me. I need to slow my life down and not be so ... well ... wild." Nicki looked down; admitting this didn't seem to be easy for her. Jack took all this flattery and authenticity in, and his pride puffed up. He was intrigued and then asked himself if this really could be a hint of true love.

"Nicki, I just wanted to slow things down. I didn't want to walk away from you." Jack could feel his emotions overriding his rationale. "I still care for you a whole lot."

Nicki smiled as if she was relieved to hear that he still loved her. Knowing the power of touch, she scooted her chair closer, leaned forward, and extended her hand above Harley's head toward Jack.

Harley was comforted by Jack's pleasantness but refused to give up her protector role in the middle. Jack leaned forward and took her hand, cradling it in both of his. In her touch, he could feel regret, and he offered forgiveness. In his touch, she could feel naïveté, and she offered deception.

Jack got to his feet and nudged Harley to the side with his foot. He pulled Nicki close to him and exchanged her hand for a hug. He inhaled and took in the aroma of her hair and perfume; another sensation he had forgotten how much he missed. He pulled back and kissed her on the cheek and then moved his kiss to her lips. She pulled back and reminded him with a pleasant smile, "Slow." Jack nodded in the reflection of his own advice and exchanged the hug for her hands. Taking their seats again, they began to catch up on the latest social news. This felt good. Nicki felt good. It all felt good. This "easy" was how it should be. The simple enjoyment of each other's presence sure felt like real love.

The pleasantness of the moment reminded Jack of the dangerous deception of Rachel. Jack's blood ran cold at the thought of willingly shattering such enjoyable serenity. He prayed in his mind, "Lord, help me to care for Nicki with the truth more than I care for how great it is to be here with her." This support requested, Jack leaned forward with a loving face. "Nicki ... I've got something I need to tell you."

Nicki wondered at his sincerity. Was it real, or was he faking it? Her cheeks dropped her smile. "What is it?"

"Well ... basically ... by God's grace ... I've found out that Rachel is, well, really a demon." Jack tensed up his emotions and face, awaiting Nicki's reaction.

Nicki perceived his position and made her play. "Oh, wow! Well, I quit contacting her as soon as you broke up with me." Nicki smiled to let her last words distract Jack from his warning. "Yeah, I could tell there was something bad about her."

"Whew! That's great! But what was it that made you stop?"

Nicki searched her actual experiences for a quick reply and surprised herself with the answer. "Well, every time I came back, it was like something was trying to kill me. I just finally had enough and figured that anything like that couldn't be as good as she was pretending to be."

"It was like that for me too!" Jack was amazed at the similarity and wondered why they hadn't shared this before. Regardless, he was elated to hear of such a great decision by Nicki. Maybe she was really turning over a new leaf.

Avery's face looked through the back door. *Aha! There they are!* she thought. With Anna Claire behind her, the detectives swung open the door and called Harley to play. "Oh, I didn't know y'all were back here!" she called to Jack and Nicki. "Go get some dog treats," she whispered to Anna Claire to further their cover. Anna Claire nodded and retreated to the pantry.

"Hey, Nicki, have you talked to Chloe lately?" Avery asked to start a conversation.

"Not today," Nicki replied with a welcoming smile. Jack's look to Avery was anything but welcoming.

Anna Claire returned waving the dog treats that finally convinced Harley to leave her post and play. "Here, girl! Here, girl!" Harley added a spring to her step to get to Anna Claire quicker before she ate the treats herself, or so Harley thought.

"Okaaay, so much for a peaceful conversation!" Jack remarked as he stood up, surrendering to the intruders.

Nicki surrendered too. "Yeah, I'd better go anyway." She didn't want to stay a moment longer than her part required. "I told Emmy I'd swing by her house for lunch."

Anna Claire, undeterred, disregarded Nicki's excuse and continued the conversation. "So you're a cheerleader?"

Nicki was flattered by the admiration in her voice and said, "Yep! Do you like cheer?"

Anna Claire shrugged her shoulders. "I've never tried it. It looks fun, but I'm not sure if I'd like yelling at all the people."

Nicki smiled at the innocence of the observation. "Well, you don't really yell *at* them. You kind of yell *for* them, hoping they'll join in encouraging the players to win the game."

Anna Claire let this tumble for a second in her mind and then offered, "Wow, I guess I never realized how important encouragement is to winning."

The profoundness of this quick remark hit Nicki between the eyes. At once, her childhood flashed before her eyes. Her parents were seated quiet and on their hands. It was she who picked up the pompoms, it was she who cheered, it was she who applauded—every type of encouragement was led and given by herself to herself. Or was it? The second life that flashed before her eyes was that her parents really were cheering for her, but not in the way she wanted. Their cheering was for character, but she wanted performance. In her recovery from this slap in the face, Nicki rolled her eyes and stepped around the small sage. Anna Claire—and Avery, who watched from a few steps away—caught the derogatory look, and both furrowed their brows, insulted. Jack, ignorant of the injury, followed her out. Harley pounced on the girls to wrestle for the last treat, which pushed the water under the bridge so they could return to their jovial selves.

After saying a short good-bye and watching Nicki walk away—even modestly dressed, she was still gorgeous—Jack returned to the backyard for some dog play. Avery asked the obvious question: "So are you and Nicki getting back together?"

Jack thought for a split second and answered, "Yeah, I think so … but not anytime soon."

Anna Claire, recalling Nicki's eye roll, said, "I like Faith better. She's prettier and nicer!"

Jack wanted to respond with a quick "Whatever!" but instead the truth of this splashed his thoughts. He nodded as it softened his mind-set. Jack glanced down at the rust-bitten wrought iron patio chair where Nicki had sat; below it was a pile of black soot attached to a trail that led into the house. *Lord Jesus, help me to help Nicki. Soften her heart so that she can see You*, Jack prayed.

Nicki had intentionally swaggered as she walked away from Jack, knowing where his eyes would be. As she moved down the street applauding herself for her Oscar-worthy performance, she felt something shift the slightest bit from within her. It felt like some tiny crystal of ice, frozen for as long as she could remember, thawed and slid. It felt like a drip of shame.

40

A LITTLE CLOSER

Jack had almost grown used to the general rejection he felt now at school. Although he still couldn't figure out how or why it seemed so widespread, at least it provided more time for his own thoughts. He glanced around for a friendly face, and finding no one, he realized that no matter how much he could console himself, the loneliness would still hurt. He saw Nicki sitting with the same group he had once thought would be his friends too, but they didn't seem to even know who he was anymore. He caught Nicki's glance in his direction and a spark of hope flickered—there was eye contact. Nicki rose from the flock and started walking toward him.

"Hey, eating alone again?" she asked.

Jack was embarrassed at the observation. "Just me, myself, and I today!"

"Well, I would say, 'Make some room,' but it seems you've got plenty."

Jack played on. "Ouch." Nicki smiled at his uplifting spirit.

"So where's Caden and Bobby these days?"

Jack shook his head and shrugged his shoulders. "I don't know."

"You know, I've done more soul-searching, and it's great not to try so hard to be popular. Now I don't feel like I have to go to every event and put on some act so that people will like me. And with that, I don't have to lie to my parents or stay out too late. It's amazing how it's all connected. But now"—Nicki smiled with a renewed sincerity—"it seems like life is easier." She thoughtfully nodded at the resonation of her own words. Jack nodded in agreement and smiled with delight at seeing his influence already showing signs of improvement within her.

"Wow, Nicki, that's great!" Jack was proud of her, and it showed in his voice and his face. "You are a great person. You're smart. You're pretty. Just keep being yourself, and you'll never regret it!"

Nicki smiled coyly and looked directly into Jack's eyes to appear as if she was taking in every word and soaking them up to boost her self-esteem. But what was taking place inside was quite the opposite. Nicki's performance continued, and her mind was at work coaxing the little insect of a boy further and further into her web. "Patience and pursuit," Nicki felt an encouraging voice say.

After a few minutes of small talk, which had a great impact on Jack's heart, Nicki excused herself by reason of needing to talk to Emmy before the bell rang. As she returned to her flock, Jack pondered the value of just one friend, something he had always taken for granted until now.

Entering the cafeteria, Faith and Amber saw Nicki leaving Jack and several empty seats next to him. They noticed a strange smile on her face that had a hint of deviousness to it. Amber looked curiously at Faith to see if she had noticed it too, and Faith's same curious look said that she had. Jack saw them coming and naturally looked around the table to make room for two, but there was already enough for eight.

"Are these seats taken?" Amber asked with a poke at the obvious.

"Uh, yeah. I'm saving them for the basketball team," Jack lightheartedly replied.

Faith paused for a second, taking it more literally than Amber, who already set her lunch down across from him. Faith laughed at herself and quickly sat down to hide her gullibility.

"So what was up with Nicki?" Amber probed to get an explanation at her curious expression.

"What do you mean?"

"Well, she had this weird look on her face when we just passed her. Some weird little smile."

Jack was convinced it was from his positive influence on her and lightly remarked, "Oh, we were just talking about some funny stuff." Wanting to save Nicki from any embarrassment with her sister, which might hinder her progress, Jack played it off and worked to change the topic. "So what are y'all doing eating lunch so early?"

Faith took the question to enter the conversation. "Well, we're going to Meeks Junior High to be student mentors."

"Wow, that's great." Jack liked the idea and could see himself doing something to pass along his wisdom one day too.

"Yeah, some of those kids have it pretty tough at home. They just need a smiling face and a good friend."

Amber nodded in agreement, and they all continued the discussion of how they could each make a difference in the kids' lives. By the time the next bell rang, telling them they should get moving to their next appointments, they were all sharing in the envisioned fulfillment that comes from helping others.

41

CLOSER ...

For just over a week, Jack had taken up a role that felt more like a life coach than a boyfriend with Nicki. He enjoyed the new kind of friendship and was eager to see it grow into a stronger and purer love than before. They exchanged texts several times a day and a nighttime thread to tie it up. Nicki shared her innermost struggles, and Jack provided a listening ear and guided her toward more wholesome decisions. The relationship seemed to be in a much better place. Jack was even thinking about putting the L word back into the mix, but he didn't want to pull such a magnificent soufflé from the oven half-baked just to watch it flop again. No, Jack wanted the real deal and was prepared to continue patiently watching, waiting, and building in hopes that it would prove to be greatly enjoyed by both of them.

As for Nicki, she continued her own patient watching, waiting, and building—only her pastry was more of a pie, with Jack's minced heart as its filling, a pie that would be served cold and only one of them would enjoy. To this end, Nicki took up her phone and tapped out a message: "Hey G, need some advice. My feelings for Jack are growing more than I ever could've imagined—so deep that I get nervous thinking about it. I need him to know how much I love him. Should I tell him now or wait for him to say it? You're the best G! XOXO!"

The message was drafted to Bobby, not Ginger, and completing it with a dastardly smile, Nicki hit send.

Bobby and Jack were in the chemistry lab heating up the wire handle of a striker used to light their Bunsen burners, which they planned to leave for Caden to grab in a few seconds. Bobby's phone blipped announcing a text, and he lifted it up from his pocket to see who it was.

"Hey, it's Nicki." The boys exchanged a confused glance, and Bobby read the contents. His face smiled wide in surprise. "Dude, you got to read this!" He handed the phone to Jack and let the words soak in.

"Oh man! She didn't mean to send this to you!" Jack exclaimed with his mouth falling open and smiling in astonishment. The phone blipped again with a second hot message:

"Bobby, how embarrassing! This was for Ginger. Pleeeeeease don't say anything to anyone about it! IOU big! N."

"What should I do?" Bobby asked and looked at Jack for help.

"Just tell her you won't, and for sure don't let her know that I read it too."

Bobby tapped a reply. "No worries! I never saw it! ;)"

Almost immediately a final comment came back: "THANK YOU!!!!"

Bobby looked at Jack. "She *loves* you!" he said with a comical look that made Jack break out in another grin.

"Yeah, yeah!"

"Well … do you *love* her too?"

Jack let his eyes drift to the ground as he considered the question. The interactions that had felt so positive and good over the past week flooded to his mind with the answer. Nodding his head and raising his eyes to meet Bobby's, he answered, "Yeah, I think I do."

"Ouch!" Caden shouted from behind them, throwing the metal-handled striker on the counter and shaking his mildly burnt hand to cool in the air. Bobby and Jack turned quickly and broke out in a gregarious laugh at the sight.

42

RACHEL HELPS NICKI FIGHT

Nicki was lying on her bed pumping the beat of club music into her head to distract her from the chill she couldn't feel anymore in her heart. After much calculation, she had determined that Caden would be the dynamite she would light to blow up Jack's world. He wasn't the most attractive boy, but he would do. He was rich, liked to party, and more importantly, was vulnerable. He seemed the most eager for attention from girls and the most appreciative when he got it. In his want, Nicki easily detected his weakness.

Making this determination final, Nicki turned her mind to Rachel and began to conjure herself up to her in meditation. Nicki felt her mind go dark as if her candle had been snuffed out, and the smoke drifted up to a higher plateau. Relit, Nicki came back to her senses at the feet of Rachel, whose heavenly face shone fair against the backdrop of her colorful wings, which cast their shadow around her.

"Peace of the Ohm in you!" Rachel exclaimed enthusiastically on seeing Nicki waft in. It was strange, but Nicki was starting to feel as though she was somehow superior to Rachel in the natural rank.

She reprimanded herself, but in her deep thoughts she fantasized that she must be anointed for a clander position closer to the Ohm.

"I've figured out who I can use to get revenge on Jack!"

Rachel shifted her enthusiasm to an eager curiosity. "Who?"

"Caden."

Rachel turned her eyes up, mulling over her answer. Her head began to nod, and a smile crossed her face, showing that Nicki's decision was perfect. Rachel read her thoughts and said, "Yeah. He definitely has a weakness in wanting attention from girls, and well … you're gorgeous. So yes, I think you made the perfect call!"

Nicki was already affirmed by the agreement, and the echoing of her own logic set flame to her spark of superiority. Nicki's eyes revealed the spark, and Rachel saw the glint. Seeing the great progress in this peasant away from the enemy, Rachel hugged Nicki and happily remarked, "Oh, look at you! You could graduate right now, and you'd be so close to the Ohm!" Nicki received the compliment with a grin and hoped she hadn't tipped her arrogant hand in her expression.

"Thanks, Rachel. I couldn't have grown any if it wasn't for you."

"It's all about the Ohm, Nicki. Just remember that—because that's all that really matters."

"Rachel," Nicki switched topics, "do you have anything to help me with Caden?"

"What do you mean? You have the spell I taught you."

"Yeah, but I mean more for me. The thought of seducing Caden isn't particularly appealing to me, and I know that I'll need a perfect performance to pull him in completely."

Rachel smiled her sinister smile, walked over to a nearby patch of pale pink flowers, and plucked one. Nicki could hear the musical tones of the flower shimmer the air as Rachel held it before her face. Nicki inhaled its fragrance, closed her eyes, and let it bathe her mind in tranquility. Rachel opened a small pouch fastened around her waist; she had planned on this moment coming to pass. She pulled out a clawed finger from the sacrificial offering of Rejection and sprinkled several drops of blood onto the flower. The drops singed the small petals like acid, and its tones turned gray.

"Breathe it in, Nicki. Deep, little peasant, deep," Spaw whispered openly as Nicki's mind drifted.

The acidic burn penetrated deeply into her lungs, and she could feel the gray spread across her skin. She opened her eyes and found her hands and arms to be the same gray shade as the flower still under her nose. In a horror she glanced sideways to see a mirror standing just beyond the patch of clover. She ran to the mirror and examined herself. Her whole body was a hideous gray. She grabbed the mirror with both hands and pulled her face close to it. Peering into her own eyes, she saw an image of Jack. She gnashed her teeth and banged her forehead against the mirror to shatter it.

Pulling back, she looked again and saw the image of Caden. Her face relaxed, and in her new attraction, she pressed her lips against it. The mirror gave way under her kiss and pulled her into the same cage, which held the other girl who always tortured her. With a newfound fury Nicki pounced on the girl with her claws and teeth. The girl in the mirror shrieked and tried to wrestle herself out of Nicki's skin-cutting grasp but was unable to. Nicki bit and scratched and beat the girl, whose resistance was diminishing under every blow. Exhausted, Nicki collapsed to the ground. Her victim disappeared with the cackling laugh of a fairy-tale witch. Nicki struggled against her depleted energy and lifted her face to the reflection of the mirror. Her jaw fell slack when she saw her scratched, bitten, and bleeding face. She looked down at the pool of her strength in the blood-soaked ground and blacked out.

Spaw laughed hilariously at the deranged violence of this tiny peasant. Her fury whipped up only to magnify her own torment; she was destined for eternal doom under his craft.

43

A SECRET OF SUCCESS

Nicki had spent all day Friday figuring out how to get close to Caden that night. She had heard that his parents would be out of town in Vegas, as they usually seemed to be, and was eager to take advantage of such impeccable timing. Rushing home from school and making excuses to her friends for bailing on their party plans, Nicki changed into her hunting clothes, which were more like her previous daily attire. Tight short shorts, a white top that revealed her secrets, and makeup that hid them—she was ready to spring her trap.

Not old enough to drive, Nicki's only transportation to Caden's neighborhood was her bike, which actually created the perfect excuse. A leisurely evening bike ride to help clear her mind from a tough week would make perfect sense to anyone who asked. As she rode down the greenbelt sidewalk, passing a lot of other people who were clearing their minds as well, Nicki's mind became clouded and confused. She was a cauldron of ideas: simmering scorn, cold revenge, decomposing rejection—but, at the same time, an inkling of thaw was hidden somewhere.

Spaw could see the turmoil on Nicki's face and hummed soothingly to her, "Ohm … Ohm … Ohm …" It worked. Nicki's expression became resolute, and she focused her mind on what she'd say when Caden answered the door. However, nearing his house, she was pleasantly surprised at luck having put Caden outside washing a sports car. Caden, especially alert to a hottie riding down his street, turned the brass nozzle to shut off the water and waited for the girl, whom he already made out as Nicki, to get within talking distance.

"Hey, Nicki!"

"Hey, Caden!"

"What brings you to my neck of the woods?"

Nicki pulled her bike up and dismounted it in Caden's personal space. Caden instinctively took two steps back as she answered.

"Oh, I was just out for a bike ride down the greenbelt and found myself here."

Caden nodded. "Oh," he said, and his eyes took in all the sights Nicki offered. Nicki watched Caden's gaze and hid her smile from the flattery.

"What are you doing tonight?" Nicki paused to let him evaluate the intent of the question and, before he replied, added, "I heard your parents were out of town again?"

Caden swallowed hard and felt his stomach tense up in nerves, but he reminded himself of who Nicki was and suppressed his racing hormones.

"Yeah. They go to Vegas a lot. I'm just washing my car. Well, it will be my car in a year."

"Wow! Really? This is your car?" Nicki dropped her bike and stepped to Caden's side as they both turned to admire the fire-engine-red Porsche 981 Boxster that awaited its monthly bath.

"Yeah, I've driven it a few times on an open track, and it can fly."

Nicki didn't want to get too bogged down in the gearhead techno talk, so she shifted the conversation. "Why are you washing it? It doesn't have a speck of dirt on it."

"Are you kidding?" Caden swiped his finger across the highly polished metal. "It's been sitting in that garage getting dusty for over four weeks now." He lifted his finger to show a small bit of fine white dust on the tip.

"Oh, well! By all means, it's filthy!" Nicki laughed with obvious sarcasm and pushed Caden's shoulder.

"Yeah, right!" Caden took the joke. "You want to help me wash it?"

"Only if I can drive it."

Caden fumbled for a response—the thought of anyone driving his high-dollar toy paralyzed his mind.

"I'm just kidding!" Nicki relented and Caden gave a sigh of relief. "Well, I'm kidding for now!"

Caden smiled and measured out the special cleansing detergent into the bucket. "You want to scrub or rinse?"

"I'll rinse. I wouldn't want my rings to accidently scratch your precious!" she joked.

Nicki took command of the hose, keeping its brass nozzle a safe distance from the car. Working together, they finished the wash job in hardly ten minutes. Seeing that the last rim was scrubbed, Nicki took the opportunity to raise the stakes, and she let a burst of water hit Caden square in the back.

"Oops! Sorry!"

Caden arched his back at the chilly water and looked around with a painful smile. "Ow!" he said, not certain if it really was an accidental spray. Then his uncertainty was confirmed when a second burst of water hit him in the shoulder.

"Oh, no, you didn't!" Caden yelped as he stood with his hand up to stop the now free-flowing stream of water drenching him. Caden charged, and Nicki backed away with the hose as her only defense. With his face down and the top of his head receiving the brunt of the assault, Caden struggled with Nicki over the weapon. Not to be easily defeated, Nicki turned the spray downward to soak his still dry legs and feet. Caden finally managed to get control of the situation and start his revenge. Nicki twisted, and he turned the direction of the spray toward her. She squealed as the cold water blasted her back. Expecting a retreat, Caden slowed the spray, but then, surprisingly, Nicki spun back around and made a charge of her own for the hose. Caden opened the nozzle to full throttle, and Nicki tackled him to the ground. She grabbed the nozzle and jammed it into the ground, and then, finding her face right next to his, she kissed him. By this point, Caden was so unconscious of anything other than this gorgeous girl that he kissed her back.

"It's freezing!" Nicki said and faked an exaggerated shiver.

"You want to come inside and dry off?"

"Sure," Nicki replied with a smile. She congratulated herself on the success. *Wow! I am good!*

"Bravo, Nicki," Rachel echoed. "Bravo!"

44

BAD TURNS GOOD

Caden jumped up ready for a fight when the TV somehow turned itself on and screamed at the top of its volume, startling him from a peaceful sleep. He scrambled to find the remote, but before he was able to mute the interruption, he heard an evangelist ask, "My friend, have you opened your free gift? Have you received Jesus as your personal Lord and Savior?" Caden switched the TV off, and the evangelist faded—but his question lingered.

Hello! Remember me? Caden's head shouted in a hangover. Knocked back to the couch, he tried to gather the pieces of what had happened last night. There was Nicki, the water fight, the drinks, kissing, more drinks, more kissing, and, well, that was the best he could do. In his recollection, his stomach surged at the idea of his betrayal of Jack. Jack was a good friend, and while they hadn't been lifelong buddies or anything, Caden valued his friendship tremendously. And now, well, now this—the girl Jack loved and who, he'd thought, loved Jack. He thought about Nicki and how attracted he was to her yesterday, but every attraction now seemed like a repulsion. Leaning forward, he covered his face with his hands. "What have I done? What have

I done? What have I done?" Tears filled his remorseful eyes, and he tried to figure out a way to retract the bullet into the rifle before it struck Jack's heart. He shifted in his seat, and the TV flicked back to life. The evangelist was still speaking. "My friend, have you sought the forgiveness that can only be found in Jesus Christ?" Caden reached next to his leg, hit the off button, and once again, the evangelist faded, but his second question lingered. Forgiveness! It was Caden's only hope to somehow destroy the treacherous missile headed for his friend.

Caden looked at his phone. It was only nine o'clock—just enough time to get to Jack before some reckless comment on the social media tentacles, which slopped juicy gossip around almost as it happened, laid a sucker on his heart.

Positioned in front of the TV with a bowl of Lucky Charms and his iPhone, Jack switched his attention between college game day and the ESPN phone app. His phone called out with a swoosh followed by an SOS vibration indicating a text from Caden awaited his attention. Jack read the text: "Are you home?" He looked at the time—9:26. There was a tap on the door. Jack pushed the TV tray, which screeched across the tile, and walked to the door. He was expecting little Lucy from across the street, but instead he saw a much taller person looking through the glass. He pulled it open, and there was Caden, out of breath and pale as if he'd seen some kind of horrible accident.

"Hey, what's up?"

Caden's eyes were downcast. "Hey, I know it's early, but ... well ... you got a second to talk?"

Assuming something had happened with his parents, Jack replied as a supportive friend, "Sure, sure! Come on in."

As he escorted Caden into the living room, he assured him of privacy from listening ears. "My dad and sisters are out on a breakfast date, so we can just talk here."

Caden was relieved they were completely alone. He wasn't sure how Jack would respond. He already made up his mind that he wouldn't fight back if Jack started punching him; he figured he had it coming.

Jack sat on the couch and leaned forward, his elbows on his knees, and Caden slumped into the rocking chair, his face etched with sorrow.

"What's wrong?" Jack asked, now starting to get butterflies at the hundreds of ways the question might be answered.

Caden closed his eyes and started, "Jack, I'm so, so sorry!" Jack could read the regret on his face, and his stomach plummeted at the apology, which already told Jack that something had been done to him, Jack. "I could make a million excuses, but the fact is there is no excuse."

Jack's stomach dropped below its rock bottom. "What, Caden? What did you do?"

"Nicki." Caden's eyes welled up with tears. "Yesterday Nicki was riding by, and we started talking, and then somehow we started kissing, and then ..."

"Okay! You can stop now!" Jack reddened and gritted his teeth. Rage filled his body, and his vision tinted in red. His fists involuntarily clenched and his nostrils flared. Caden braced himself for the attack and held both of his arms up in front of him. Jack pressed his eyes shut, squeezing tears down his cheeks. He knew Nicki was a wild horse. How could he have ever really thought that he could tame her?

But why Caden? Why now, after they had seemingly gotten closer than they ever had before? A million questions started assaulting his mind, and then the flood of rage exploded in his gut again. He could feel himself being tossed by the waves of the angry ocean. He was dashed onto the rocks, and the waves grabbed him, scraped off his hide, and then dashed him again. All he could do was pray, so he did.

Oh, Lord, this hurts. I need Your help!

Caden watched Jack struggle like a cage fighter in a death grip. Knowing he was the cause of his friend's agony, he closed his own eyes to await his judgment.

"Caden," Jack said, raising his bloodshot eyes framed by his tormented face, "forgiveness is not always easy. It's a decision and a process. Jesus has forgiven me of so much more than you could ever do to me, and because I know this, I know that one day I'll be able to think about this without much hurt at all. But for now, I just need you to bear with me … as a friend."

Caden's arms dropped to his lap, where he wrung his hands without realizing it. "Jack, I am so, so, so sorry. It was a mistake, and I don't even like Nicki."

Jack shook his head and closed his eyes again, wincing under the fresh pain. "I believe you. I just need to think about this … to pray about it. I can't forgive you …" Caden's heart shook at the last words. "But I know it's possible with Jesus."

"Jack, it may not be the right time, but one day … can you tell me what you know of Jesus?" Caden had just experienced the most powerful testimony of love he had ever seen. He could sense, not just from the forgiveness Jack was struggling to give him, that Jack and his family seemed to have something different. They weren't perfect—he knew Jack too well to believe that—but there was a peace about them that was solid. It was almost the complete opposite of what he experienced in his own family.

At this question Jack felt a serenity wash over his heart. He could tell that this moment was not his moment but was an opportunity to serve his Lord. Opening his eyes, Jack saw that Caden was a sooty, and his heart melted at the thought of Caden spending his eternity separated from Jesus in the torment of his decision.

Jack leaned forward and, with the help of the Holy Spirit, started, "Jesus is beautiful …" He explained the gospel of Jesus to Caden and then asked him if he'd like to follow Jesus by inviting Him into his own heart with a prayer. Jack watched as Caden prayed the most heartfelt prayer he had ever heard before. Then, a gleam of sparkling water burst forth from Caden's blackened figure, transforming his appearance to that translucent shimmer illuminated from a Light within that Jack had come to recognize as someone saved. After the amen, the boys stood up and embraced in a brotherly hug.

"I'm so sorry, Jack." Caden's guilt still punished him.

Jack shook his head and comforted him. "Hey, what could have been evil turned out for something much, much better!"

Caden nodded. "What about Nicki?"

Jack threw his hands up and shook his head. "What can I say? I actually feel sad for her. It must be hard to be her." Caden nodded at the truth of the observation.

"So you wanna watch the Aggie game?"

Caden chuckled. "Yeah, sure!"

45

MISSION BETRAYAL

Nicki had been watching the regular weekend chatter all day on her various social media sites. She didn't think Caden would be revealing their little secret, and she wanted to serve it to Jack herself and in person. Continuing her plot, she tapped out a message. "Hey, come over tonight, need to talk."

Jack replied almost immediately, "What time?"

Nicki thought for a second to estimate what time her parents would be leaving for the movie and tapped, "8p." She wanted to remove any obstructions to Jack receiving the full impact of what she would hit him with.

Jack glanced at his phone as he knocked on Nicki's door at eight o'clock exactly. His spirit felt the peace that surpassed understanding, but his mind kept taunting him with accusations of abnormality. He stayed fast in his prayers for help from Jesus and beat back the accusatory wolves that surrounded him. Nicki opened the door, and the first thing that struck Jack was her immodest expression accompanied by her immodest dress. His flesh immediately tacked and pushed him toward glances of lust, but he doubled his prayers to get strength from above.

"Hey, come on in," Nicki said, her voice taking on a more somber tone. Jack watched her carefully but kept his eyes fixed on Jesus. He knew that this wasn't a casual conversation, but one of spiritual warfare, and he understood his own weakness. Jack followed without a word, which Nicki thought was strange but wrote off as him just mimicking her own tone. He was such a follower, after all. Nicki took her seat on the couch and motioned Jack to sit next to her. Jack's instincts shouted a warning to him to keep some physical space between them to help him maintain a clear head. Heeding the wisdom, he sat down an arm's length away, but Nicki reduced the distance to an elbow length. Jack adjusted his seat as a nonchalant way of recapturing the distance, but he was blocked by the armrest. Hemmed in, his mind once again sent up a heavenward flare for help.

Nicki opened with some trivial dialogue, but Jack didn't hear a word. He tried to maintain eye contact with her, but in his periphery all he could see were swarms of sooty black gargoyles circling like vultures waiting for some dying creature to breathe its last breath. He wondered if they were here for himself or for her. Regardless, he prayed for them to be sent away, but the answer evidently was no—or at least not yet—because more joined the demonic flock. He moved his gaze lower, and his eye caught movement from within her stomach. Although it was flat, something moved in a circular motion beneath her black ashen skin, as if it were stirring a pot to prevent it from boiling over. He noticed a small hole just above her navel where more of the dark sediment was being expelled from within, collecting into a pile on her lap. Jack braced himself for battle and rejoined Nicki's conversation.

"So, Jack," Nicki said, face shifting from somber to shameful, "I need to tell you something."

"Sure, what is it?"

Nicki's appearance braced for the delivery of horrible news, but from within she was eagerly anticipating watching the painful explosion. "Well, I was with Caden last night." Nicki stopped there without any softening apology or remorseful plea. She watched his eyes for the explosion of the burning fuse she had just put fire to.

Jack's face reddened as it had done when Caden had first told him; he was still human, after all. All his fleshly anger seemed to be pent up in that crimson expression. Nicki's eyes gleamed with satisfaction as she saw such a tremendous pressure building. Not yet seeing it ignite completely, she squirted some gasoline on it.

"Jack, I knew it was wrong, but it felt so good. I just had to go with it."

Jack recognized remnants of his own catchphrase from not that long ago. He turned his mind again to Jesus and pleaded for His strength.

Nicki watched the battle within him and once again tried to kindle the blast. "Even when I was with Stone"—Nicki threw on an "I did tell you about that, didn't I?" look—"it wasn't as good as last night with Caden."

With this last slinging of her volatile poison, Nicki had revealed too much of the ugly face of evil. Jack saw it for what it was and turned his head upward to gather strength. Sprinkles of liquid light began to rain through the ceiling and pierce the gathering demons. The sprinkle turned into a shower and the shower into a downpour, and in a matter of seconds, the air was clear, except for the black pollution Nicki exhaled from her mouth. Jack breathed in the fresh air deeply, realized the larger work to be done here, and spoke.

"Nicki," Jack said, feeling strong enough to actually reach for her hand, which she pulled back in disgust, "I forgive you." He smiled with a pleasantness that enraged her.

"What?" she exclaimed in a disapproving shock. "You forgive me?"

Jack nodded with a warm smile. "Yeah. Look, I love you, but—"

"What?" Nicki repeated at a higher volume, getting to her feet. "Get out! Get out!"

Jack held his place and tried to continue, "Look, just hear me out—"

Nicki drew her hand back for a slap but instead pointed it toward the door. "Get out! Get out now!"

Jack stood up, explaining, "Look, Nicki, Caden told me this morning—"

Nicki grabbed Jack's arm, clawed deeply into it, and scratched it when she ripped him toward the door.

"Nicki, it's Jesus …" Jack pleaded, he wanted to tell her about Jesus just like Caden, but Nicki would not stand for it. At the mention of His name, her spirit lit up with a bonfire that was shown fully in the blaze of her red eyes. She pulled him through the open door and flung him toward the street.

Jack pleaded one more time, "Nicki! Wait! I need to tell you—" The door slammed behind him like a gunshot, and the glass window fractured under its discharge. "—about Jesus," Jack finished his sentence.

46

THIS IS CRAZY

Jack had a new perspective on church now. It wasn't just a place where he would learn nice little things about Jesus with all the other kids who really wished they could be somewhere else. It was a weekly gathering of spiritual warriors for King Jesus and those who might choose to join them. It was a place to worship Him and to become equipped to do His work and fight His battles. It was a place to continually grow in and share His love. It was a place to help Jack fulfill his purpose for existing in Christ.

With this new understanding, Jack was in an unusually pleasant mood for a Sunday afternoon. However, this didn't help his procrastination of the homework that was due next day. Earbuds in, he perused the latest Christian rock songs and pondered how to start his report on Shakespeare's *Macbeth*. There were witches, ghosts, murder, and a plethora of fleshly motives behind the characters. Maybe he could weave in his assessment from a Christian view. What would a public school teacher think about such a nonworldly perspective? The world hated Jesus, so he imagined that the modern-day public school system might raise its ire against Him too. Jack closed his eyes and shook his head.

The group Third Day sung its song "Miracle" through his earbuds. Jack felt panic grip his heart, and he immediately turned to Jesus in prayer. Now he understood the sensation his dad had tried to explain to him when he prayed for him. It was Nicki. He didn't know what was going on, but he knew that she was in severe danger, and he needed to help.

He sprang to his feet and walked briskly into the kitchen, where a bottle of old ipecac syrup was stored. Being overly safety conscious, his dad had always kept a bottle when they were little in case they somehow drank something that was poisonous. The ipecac would make them vomit in hopes that enough of the poison was expelled for them to make it to the hospital alive. Jack's heart pounded as his hands and eyes worked together to quickly sift through the assortment of medicines to find the little brown bottle, which he did.

Tucking it in his pocket, he grabbed his bike and sped off down the street as fast as he could. He prayed, "God, I don't know what's going on, but I need Your help." Jack's mind countered his prayer with its own speech. *This is ridiculous! You think you're some special agent from Jesus now. Boy, are you going to be embarrassed showing up to her house with a bottle of ipecac! Talk about becoming an outcast!*

Jack slowed his bike and brought it to a stop by a stand of mailboxes. He looked at them so that if someone wondered at his stopping, they would just think he was checking the mail. *That's right. Who am I? I'm just a—hopefully—normal kid who is just a normal Christian. Oh, brother! What am I doing?*

Jack turned his bike and offered another prayer: *Lord, I'm so sorry for acting crazy.* But that same sense of urgency washed over him again, changing his mind. *Okay, God, I'm going. I guess this is what it might mean to be a 'fool for Christ.'*

Turning his bike back toward Nicki's, he rode on but at half the speed. The impression that time was indeed of the essence swatted him again, and he sped up like a racehorse to a full gallop. *Oh, man! I'm going to look so stupid! Nicki is going to attack me again and ... oh, man!*

Jack turned the corner and headed toward the cul-de-sac, where some elementary school kids were sitting at a table, giving away lemonade for a small donation. Amber and Faith were at the stand donating to the cause. Jack rode up fast and brought his bike to a stop.

"Where's Nicki?" he gasped.

Amber replied with a pained heart, "At home. Jack, just give up on her. She's bad news."

Faith nodded her agreement.

"It's not about that. I was praying and just got this overwhelming feeling like something bad had happened." He pulled out the bottle of ipecac and showed it to them.

"What is that?" Amber asked. Faith recognized it and, knowing what it was used for, turned pale.

"Ipecac!"

"And why do you have it?"

"I'm not sure! All I know is that we need to find Nicki."

Amber looked at Faith for her thoughts, and her face told her that Jack might be onto something.

"Come on!" Amber exclaimed and started in a jog toward their house. "My parents are gone. Nicki was in there about an hour ago."

Jack dropped his bike in the yard, and the girls beat him to the door. Finding it locked, they tapped on it. Jack joined them and started ringing the doorbell over and over and over, but no one answered. He looked at Amber. "Do you have a key?" Amber shook her head, her mind now paralyzed in fear. The contagious panic had infected Faith, who was already in prayer interceding for Nicki and for a way to get to her.

"Oh wait! The spare key!" Amber remembered and started digging in the mulch behind the shrubs. She came up with a small container that resembled a very ordinary-looking rock.

"Hurry, Amber!" Jack urged, his body starting to shake with adrenaline.

Amber fumbled with the rock, removed the key, and pushed it into the door.

47

SUICIDE

After passing the night boiling in fury without even an attempt at sleep, Nicki turned to the music of TrashMouth to numb the intensity of the pain that racked her whole being. But finding even this rage too weak to mirror her own, she turned finally to Rachel.

-oooo-

With the audacity of a jilted teen, Nicki flew into the arena like a witch on a broom. She landed in a thud, and the landscape seemed to quiver beneath her feet. Finding that she was alone, she shouted a demanding call for attention. "Rachel!" She turned about and looked around impatiently and screamed again, "Rachel!"

"Why, what is it, dear?" Rachel stepped out innocently from behind an oak.

Nicki darted up to her face and spewed her angry words. "Rachel, it didn't work! I did exactly what you said, and it didn't work!" She stuck her finger in Rachel's face to show who was to blame for the failure.

Rachel smirked, grabbed the dainty white finger, and twisted it, causing its owner to bend to the ground. Feeling Rachel's strength forced a degree of humility into Nicki's insolent attitude.

"Whose fault is it?" asked Rachel with a haughty glare.

Nicki didn't relent. "I did exactly as you said, and he responded with forgiveness!" Her volume increased with every word and ended in a shriek.

Rachel flared her wings, which changed from the beautiful colors of a butterfly to the monochrome black of a bat. Her eyes exchanged their shade of emerald for that of a ruby. Nicki felt her cowardly spirit bend like her finger had just seconds ago.

"Who do you think you are, Nicki? After all I've done for you! You are the failure! You parade around as if you are so beautiful, so high and mighty, but deep down you know the truth! The truth is that you're worthless. You are a throwaway girl with pathetic morals. You're an ugly little kid who has to use her poor excuse of a body to try to beg for love. Your parents hate you, your sister despises you, and your friends only hang out with you because the boys want to use you. So, Nicki, who is the failure here?"

Rachel paused to let the density of her tirade saturate Nicki's soul. It was if she had dumped several tons of sand in one heave on her, but it would take a second for the full weight to crush the life-giving breath out of her. Nicki reeled under the observant accusations. For the first time in her life, she was fully exposed and could see her true image. She thought back to the girl in the mirror and realized that

405

she was simply telling her a truth that she refused to see for herself. Nicki's spirit was crushed once and for all.

"Your only hope, Nicki"—she disgustingly spat her name—"is to off yourself and move on! Maybe the Ohm will have mercy on you and not send you to Pergyss."

Nicki beat her face in insanity. She deserved the punishment. Rachel's suggestion seemed more like a command, and it was a command that Nicki knew was her only chance at salvaging the peace of significance.

Rachel approached, and Nicki pulled her hands tightly over her face, much like a boxer protecting himself from blows. She could feel Rachel's hot breath on her hands, and then a searing pain struck the back of her neck as if it had been stung by a giant scorpion. Nicki grabbed her burning throat, choked by the injected poison, and felt dead.

-o-o-o-o-

Nicki's neck felt broken, and she coughed up bloody phlegm onto the carpet. She curled herself up in a fetal position and sobbed without hope. Spaw stood over her and blew his disparaging lies into her mind. Again and again, as if he were kindling a flame, he belittled her and verbally abused her to ensure no sprout of hope survived. Nicki pulled herself up, shattered and undone. Her arms extended since she was blind from tears, she made her way into her parents' bathroom and rummaged through the medicine cabinet in search of hope. She found it in a bottle of prescription-strength sleeping pills that her dad had gotten several years ago when he'd had trouble adjusting to an overseas time zone where he was on a work assignment. She groped her way back to her room and closed the door. With one last look around her room, she emptied the thirteen pills into her hand and gulped them down with several swigs of bottled spring water. This evil deed done, she lay back on her bed and continued intermittent fits of sobbing, interrupted only by the peaceful waves of sweet, permanent sleep and the imagined ringing of a bell.

-◦-◦◦-◦-

Amber opened Nicki's door without a knock but still cautiously in case she was still indignant. Her heart shattered instantly as her eyes took in the horrifying image of Nicki's body sprawled lifeless on the bed.

"Jack!" Amber cried out, tears already forming.

Jack was right behind her and, seeing the empty pill bottle next to her, immediately went to work. Recalling his first aid lessons, he felt for a pulse. It was faint, but he thought he felt something; at least she was still warm. "Call 911!" Jack ordered, and Faith took out her cell phone. Putting his ear a hair's width from her mouth, he felt that there was still breath in her.

"Nicki! Wake up!" Jack shook her limp body. "Nicki! Listen to me! You have to wake up!"

Amber joined in the effort from the other side. "Nicki! Wake up! Don't go, Nicki! Don't go!"

Nicki moaned at the disturbance and slightly rolled her head sideways. At the hint of hope, Jack and Amber redoubled their efforts to get her attention. All they needed was one instant of coherence to ensure that she could swallow the ipecac. Faith finished providing the information to the emergency operator, and she ended the call and prayed.

Seeing Nicki fading in and out, Jack was getting desperate and was very aware of the seconds that were now more precious than they had ever been. Nicki buoyed up and whimpered, "Huh?"

Jack lifted her head up and poured the syrup into her mouth. Nicki involuntarily coughed and sprayed the liquid into the air. Amber trembled in fear that they had missed their chance, but Jack lifted the bottle to the light and saw that he still had half left. Nicki whimpered again, and Jack lifted the back of her head again, pointing her chin into the air. In no way was he a trained medic, but he knew he had to get this syrup into her somehow. He tilted the little brown bottle and poured the remainder of it into her mouth for a final try. He felt Nicki's body tense up for a cough, and he closed her mouth and covered it firmly with his hands. Instead of a cough, he felt a gulp, followed by another and another. He opened her mouth to see it clear and heard a slow breath flowing back and forth through it.

"How long does it take?" Amber asked, still trembling.

"About twenty to thirty minutes," Jack said in a tone that apologized that it couldn't be sooner.

"What can we do now?"

"Keep trying to wake her up. Faith and I will pray. The ambulance should be here in a few minutes."

Amber sat at Nicki's head, demanding that she wake up and reminiscing about their favorite childhood memories. Jack and Faith positioned themselves on either side of her with one hand on Nicki and one in the other's hand. Through their tears, they made their pleas for her in Jesus' name.

Fifteen minutes passed, and Nicki coughed. At this sign of progress, Amber intensified her efforts and screamed at Nicki in anger to "Get back here, Nicki!" Nicki's body convulsed, and vomit filled her mouth. Jack grabbed her revived head and turned it sideways, spilling the partially digested capsule-filled ooze onto the bed.

There was a knock at the door followed by "Hello! Paramedics are here!" Amber ran through the hall and around the corner and yelled, "We're in here!" Jack and Faith stepped back and let the paramedics move in to start their lifesaving attempts. One of them picked up the prescription bottle, read its contents, and put it in a plastic bag.

"We gave her ipecac. She just threw up about two minutes before you got here," Jack said.

The paramedic took the little empty brown bottle and put it into the plastic bag with the pill bottle. "You probably saved her life."

As they transferred her to the ambulance, Jack, Faith, and Amber joined hands in prayer to thank God for saving Nicki's life—or at least her earthly one.

48

LOVE AND THE LIGHT

Nicki stepped hesitantly down the dark, cavelike passage. Blinded by the dark, she traced her way with her hands, which felt the wet, slimy walls of she could only imagine what. She heard the humming of the Ohm beckoning her deeper. Images of Rachel, back in her radiant butterfly beauty, were dangled in front of her, giving her enough courage to take the next step. There was a shout in the distance behind her. "Don't go, Nicki! Don't go!" It was Amber. But what was Amber doing here in the afterlife?

Nicki turned her head in Amber's direction and narrowed her eyes. About a hundred yards away, Nicki could vaguely see a small candle flickering. It's amazing how it only takes a speck of light to dispose of a mass of darkness. The humming in the darkness increased its volume. *I must be getting closer*, thought Nicki, turning back to her quest.

"Don't go, Nicki! Don't go!" Amber pleaded again.

It didn't make any sense. The Ohm should've been radiant with light, and where were the others from her clander whom she'd expected to welcome her in? They would be spending eternity together, after all. A twinge of confusing fear set in, and Nicki collapsed to the mushy ground. She listened to the humming of the Ohm; it was getting nearer. Then the realization struck her: she wasn't moving toward it; it was moving toward her! Jolted by fear, Nicki sprang to her feet and started to flee toward the faint glow of the candle but quickly found that her body was tranquilized and moved in slow motion. Behind her, she could hear the humming getting louder and louder. In a life-fearing panic, she fought against her lethargic body. With the effort she was giving, she could have already sprinted a marathon, but she hardly moved at all. Panting partially from fear and partially from overexertion, she dropped to the soggy floor, threw up, and passed out.

Nicki forced her heavy eyelids open, her vision obscured with a flood of tears at the sight she took in. She was in a light-filled room, and in a circle around her were Jack, Amber, Faith, Bobby, Caden, Avery, Anna Claire, Jay, her mom, her dad, and some man with a compassionate smile whom Nicki could only describe as beautiful. She fixed her eyes on the stranger, and her heart leaped with joy, which unleashed a second flood of tears, blurring her vision even further. She blinked and wiped her eyes to take in more of the man's beauty, but he was gone. She wrote it off as a drug-induced hallucination and didn't mention it to anyone.

Seeing her eyes open, the team of intercessors dropped one another's hands and spontaneously applauded and cheered. "Hallelujah!" "Thank You, Lord!" "Oh, Nicki!" Nicki was truly overwhelmed. She had never in her life realized just how deeply she was loved. The scolding words of Rachel echoed in her mind, but seeing these loved ones gathered around her, she realized that Rachel's words were all lies.

After a series of hugs and kisses, the group made way for the doctor to examine Nicki. "She'll be fine! Just needs a little rest—that's all!" At this news, they again broke out in celebration. The doctor laughed, moved at such a heartwarming display of love, and went to tell of the event at the nurses station.

Everybody had their personal moment with Nicki to tell her how glad they were that she was okay, and they milled out of the crowded room—except for Jack, who took it all in from a chair tucked in a corner.

"Mom, Dad, would you mind if I talk to Jack alone for a minute?"

Her parents were compliant but a bit stunned at the polite, respectful tone of the request. "Sure, honey, we'll go get a snack and be right back. Do you want anything?" Nicki shook her head, and they closed the door behind them. Nicki, pressing the button to raise herself to an upright position, motioned Jack to come closer. He switched to her mom's chair right next to the bed.

"Hey," she said, "I just want to say I'm sorry."

Jack nodded and fought back the tears from recovering a friend. "Sure."

"I think you were right about Rachel. She's evil, isn't she?"

Jack nodded. "Yes. Rachel is really a demon who was trying to destroy us and lead us away from God."

Nicki thought back to how she had first contacted Rachel with her cousin doing that channeling thing. "I was so stupid. How did you figure it out?"

"Basically, I mentioned the name of Jesus to her, and she turned into this wicked beast thing." Jack shuddered at the recollection of Spaw's vicious attack.

"So just by Jesus? That's all?"

"That's all? Jesus is the Son of God. He's the almighty King above everything in existence!"

"I guess I don't really know much about Him."

"Well, it's like this. God created everything—angels, people, the universe, everything—and everything glorified Him. But one angel, now called Satan, got jealous and wanted glory for himself. He turned against God, his own Creator, and convinced a third of the angels to join him. They were kicked out of heaven but allowed to exist outside, which included this planet where we live. So to get back at God, Satan went after mankind. He deceived Adam and Eve, causing them to disobey God. That is, they sinned against God. And with this fall, sin became part of mankind's natural instinct, so every single person born from then on was born sinful." Jack paused to check in with Nicki. She nodded, and her expression of intense interest showed that for the first time in her life, something seemed to be pulling everything together in a single purpose.

He continued, "For example, no one has to teach a child to tell lies. It just comes naturally to them, right?" Nicki let out a small chuckle and grinned, thinking of how that nailed her. Jack mirrored her smile and went on, "But God still loved us, so He sent His Son, Jesus, to take on the form of a man, to live a life of perfect obedience to

413

God, but then to die a horrible death on the cross, *as if* He had lived our messed-up lives. By doing this, He allows us to believe in Him as Savior and Lord and actually trade the punishment we deserve for a life and relationship with Him that we don't deserve. In other words, He made a way for us to have His grace instead of His justice by Jesus, His only begotten Son."

Nicki's interested expression was tinged with confusion. It was as if after drinking dirty water her whole life, she sipped clean, pure water, and it shocked her system. She knew she desperately wanted—no, needed—more, but the first taste had to soak in. Jack read her expression and paused, uttering a quick prayer in his mind. *God, this is Your time. Help me to just open my mouth and get out of Your way.*

"It sounds kind of complicated." Disheartened, Nicki lowered her eyes and thought of how hard she had always had to work to be popular.

Jack shook his head with eagerness. "Oh, no! It's really easy. Sometimes my words just get in the way." She tilted her head in interest and a glimmer of hope showed on her face.

"All you need to do is to follow Him."

"How do I do that?" Nicki asked with a small shrug.

Jack raised his eyes in thought and said, "Well … understand that you are a sinner, like everyone."

"I think I have gotten that part now." Nicki said slightly smiling.

"Then turn away from living your own way, believe that Jesus is the Son of God and that He died on the cross to save you, and start living His way."

Nicki nodded. "Okay, that kind of makes sense. Do I need to go to a church or do some ceremony or something to make it official?"

Jack smiled at her warmly. "The important thing about it is that it's official between you and God. If you made that decision, then why don't you just tell Him so in a prayer?"

"I don't know any prayers."

"There aren't any special prayers to know. Just talk to Him like you're talking to me—from the heart."

"Okay," Nicki said, still with a hint of uncertainty of exactly what to say and how to say it.

"How about I'll start, and then you can finish?"

"Yeah, that'd be good."

Jack prayed a brief prayer, speaking from his heart, and Nicki saw that praying really was just like talking to a friend. Jack concluded, "Okay, God, now here's Nicki." With the announcement of her name to God, all the years of stress, anxiety, anger, and every other worldly pain swirled up in a waterspout and poured from her eyes. Her lips trembled as she recognized that the One to whom she now prayed was the stranger who had been in her room just an hour before.

"Oh, Jesus!" She paused to let the uprising of emotions calm through more tears. "Oh, Jesus, I'm so sorry ... so, so sorry for messing up my life so bad. I'm such a sinner." Jack peeked up, and with this resolute admission, the inner corners of her eyebrows lifted, and her eyelids drooped in agony. She squeezed Jack's hand firmly, and he felt the grief that he had just seen on her face. "And ... I need Your

415

help." She paused again and drew in a deeper breath. "Oh, Jesus, I *do* believe that You are God's Son and that You died on the cross so that I don't have to. Thank You, thank You, thank You! And I will follow You. Oh, God, let me follow You. Amen."

Jack looked up, wiped his own tears, and saw the same cleansing gush of liquid light change Nicki into a new creation; she was a glossy now! Jack, still holding Nicki's hand, turned his gaze up and said, "Thank You, Jesus." A little black gargoyle about the size of a cat washed to the ground and writhed pitifully like a leech put onto dry land. It shriveled up smaller and smaller until it finally vanished from sight.

"Oh yeah!" Jack remembered his explanation of Rachel and wanted to make sure that Nicki realized exactly who she was. "So basically, Rachel was trying to lead us to death in hell. Could you imagine an eternity with something so evil?"

Nicki shook her head at the fear of this idea and then at her own gullibility and desperation for ever having fallen into such an evil trap. "I can't believe I fell for it."

"Hey, don't feel bad at all! I've been going to church and hearing about Jesus my whole life, and I fell right into it too!"

Nicki let that sink in and felt consoled. "Wow, it just doesn't seem real. I mean it's hard to believe that demons are so, well, real and active and stuff."

"I know." He nodded. "I heard in other countries, like in parts of Africa, demons are a lot more obvious. I guess here in the US there is more junk for them to hide behind, like material stuff, social correctness, media, substances, and even entertainment—like

TrashMouth and *Mithras*." Jack grimaced at his memory of injecting their twisted messages into his mind.

"Right. And like Ouija boards and channeling." Nicki now grimaced at her own memory. "Well, I'm done with that stuff," she added.

"Well, you may be done with evil, but evil is not done with you. That's why we have to stay close to Jesus. There is no way they'll get anywhere close to where He is!"

Nicki smiled broadly at this thought. "I love Him more already!"

The door opened slightly. "Knock, knock," Nicki's mom called out as she and Nicki's dad came back into the room. They both looked around with curious smiles, wondering what was different. "Are you still feeling okay, sweetie?" her mom asked.

Nicki looked at Jack with the same broad smile, and Jack's face mirrored it. "Mom … Dad … I want to tell you something," she started.

Nicki's parents looked inquisitively at each other and for a split second thought she was going to announce their engagement or something, but Nicki continued before that idea completely sank in. Nicki told them about everything she had done and her consorting with Rachel, who she now knew was a demon. And she told them about how she, just now, had made Jesus the Savior and Lord of her life. They were both moved to tears and, at once, hugged Nicki and told her how much they loved her. Nicki drank in their love and, for the first time ever, felt close to them.

"Mom, Dad, I want to go to church so that I can learn more about Jesus." Her parents hugged her again and gave her complete support, saying that they'd go with her. Jack sat back again and took in the whole glorious scene and again whispered a prayer. "Thank You, God!"

"Knock, knock!" Amber said as she and Faith came back in. "The nurse said that visiting hours are over."

Faith walked up to Nicki and hugged her affectionately. "I'm glad you're here."

Tears welled up in Nicki's eyes at the love. "Yeah, me too," Nicki replied, wiping them dry.

Jack stood up to join Faith, and promising to come back tomorrow, they walked out to the hallway to find their ride home.

49

SPAW'S ANSWER

Spaw thrashed in a tormented fury at Nicki's salvation. He would surrender half of his territory if he could get in that room for even one second. But he couldn't. He was locked out by a formidable angel army, and being a former member, he comprehended their overwhelming might. One of those angelic warriors now drew to confront him, and Spaw tumbled back, his arm raised before his face to protect himself from the radiance of light.

"Don't hurt me! I'm just a humble creature tricked into a fall," Spaw whined and wrung his clawed hands nervously.

The angelic being looked scornfully at the writhing maggot and spoke with a voice of sweet praising music. "Leave! These have been saved by the King!"

Spaw obeyed the command before the last syllable could echo back. He wanted no part of the King.

Now back in his lair, he exercised his rage on any of his subjects who came within his view. He was dumbfounded and muttered unconsciously out loud, "How could this puny, weak-minded, repulsive peasant boy have ruined my plan?"

"Because you underestimate the enemy!" a voice from behind him arrogantly blurted out.

Spaw spun around wildly and blindly with his claws extended. He slashed the creature across the chest, but it didn't flinch. "Mithras! How dare you enter my territory unannounced?" Spaw cried, defying his commander, partly out of anger and partly out of fear. "I didn't underestimate the enemy! I—"

Mithras narrowed his scowl and continued as if he hadn't been interrupted. "Because you underestimate the enemy, you are sentenced to the Abyss!"

Faster than a blink and before Spaw could jump, Mithras grabbed Spaw by the arm and raised himself to an enormous size. Squeezing Spaw's head in one hand like a spiked vise and his torso in the other, he snapped the demon's body. Spaw was no more. Crawling out from beneath their rocks, Spaw's formerly elite cohorts began to fight ferociously for the abandoned position of power. Mithras slammed his wings in a downward thrust, eyed the battle from above for a moment, and then roared a promise.

"I am the mighty Mithras! I will return!"

The entire territory reported back, "All hail the mighty Mithras!" and then, seeing his departure, turned on one another like the pack of ravenous dogs they were.

50

An Excited Outcast

It took the usual two turns before the truck fired up. Jay looked next to him. Avery and Anna Claire were still elated at Nicki's recovery and the report that she had become a Christian. They were chattering about it like it was the news of the century. In the backseat, Jack and Faith had a more mellow conversation.

"So do you miss not being popular now that you're more of an outcast?" Faith asked, surprised at the boldness of her question.

Jack shook his head and smirked at his own past foolishness. "Huh! Not really. I'd rather be an outcast for Christ than the most popular fool floating down the current of life to death."

"You know … it's just so hard to really understand just how much of a spiritual battle we are in."

Jack agreed, "Yeah, and now that I've experienced the downside firsthand, I want to help others to see the truth—the truth of Jesus and the truth about the evil we're up against."

"You're right. God is so awesome. People need to know that!"

"Well, where He leads, I'll go!"

"Last month was Missions Month at the church, and I went to hear this one guy from South America speak. He said that there was this cannibalistic tribe that kept attacking the tribe he lives with, who were starting to receive Christ."

"Really? There are still places like that in the world?"

"Oh yeah. He said that the other tribe is overrun with demons, but they stay way away from him because they know he is a man of the most high God. They're scared of him. Anyway, it might be a little dangerous, but a missions group is going down there to take them shoes and build a small church building."

Jack's heart fluttered as he considered Faith's words. "Oh yeah?"

"So what are you doing next summer?"

Jack smiled.